Sydney Shag &
THE SIRENS

Kelly —

Absolutely Fabulous

Cover Illustration and Design by Emily Larrabee
Premier Lecteur de Dr. Tara Andersen
Editing by Sara Kocek and David Aretha of Yellow Bird Editors
Layout Design & eBook Conversion by Erica Smith of eBook Conversions
Website and Graphic Design Elements by Drew Hogan and Brian Finke
Author Photo by Elizabeth Wiseman

For more information and upcoming events visit:
www.cyndigryte.com

Sydney Shag &
THE SIRENS
HEAVY ON THE VODKA AND A LITTLE BIT DIRTY

a novel
CYNDI GRYTE

For

My Loving and Blameless Parents

&

The Mermaids

"A wise girl knows her limits,
a smart girl knows that she has none."

-MARILYN MONROE

First things first...
A PROLOGUE

YOU HAVE to know that two things happened. One, my high school kind-of boyfriend (I used to say "kind of" in relation to boyfriends. Come to think of it, I still do—could be a problem) got married. And two, I got a card in the mail.

The definition of mistake:

> **mis•take**
> mə'stāk/
>
> *noun*
> **to blunder in the choice of**
>
> *verb*
> **to be wrong**

Uh, that would be an understatement. Though I quite like the word *blunder*. It makes this all sound less agonizing. Kind of.

Chapter 1

MOXIE

I MEAN, it's not like I've ever been the best at answering terribly important questions, let alone the easy ones. And this one really put me on the spot. Indecision has plagued me since I was—well, since as long as I can remember. Show-and-tell used to cause an inordinate amount of stress because I had so many favorite things. An eternal optimist, even if misguided as one of my grade school teachers put it. On my report card. In cursive! (Luckily, no one reads cursive.) But I always feel things will just positively, perfectly fall into place. That is until—

"Sydney, are you going to get in or just stand there?" Claudia says, her Brazilian accent making my name sound deliciously exotic. She leans out of the monstrous truck, our car service, and reaches for me still standing on the curb outside the iconic hotel.

I've got to stop doing that.

Claudia waves her hand, impatiently. She never has a hair out of place, and even in this evening's heat it shines, balancing neatly on her shoulders.

"Allow me," the inexplicably handsome hotel doorman says taking my hand and helping me into the rather tall vehicle. "You look great tonight," he smiles, causing my cheeks to flush. I think he's noted I'm showing significantly more skin than this afternoon when we were in costume for the auto show. Technically this is a work trip, but you'd never guess. He pauses, flashes his dimple again, then shuts the door.

Bette pops her head around Claudia. "Even the doorman just hit on you!" She rolls her eyes in loving disgust.

"He was just being nice, now move over you guys," I say, amused. The girls all shift a little to their right causing Claudia to swat Bette and Bette to push Gus and Gus to lean forward.

"How does your little butt need so much room?!"

"Gus, I'm going to—" I reach over Claudia and Bette and smack one of Gus' long legs. She immediately retaliates, and we're fighting across their laps and laughing when Bette, as usual, breaks us up.

There's a tap on the window. I press it down slowly. The Driskill doorman hands me a piece of paper. "I get off at ten if you want me to show you around Austin, you know, after your work event."

"Oh thanks, so sweet." I wink, take the paper and press the window swiftly back up. "The Hitching Rail, please!" I sing to the driver, and he peels off down the road.

"Everybody. Everybody hits on this one," Bette says to our driver while jabbing a thumb my direction.

I tuck the paper into my bra, look at my friends, and bat my eyes lavished with extra, extra mascara. "I mean, how can anyone resist?" I smile so big, and ridiculously, they all laugh.

"Careful, or you'll lose that," Claudia says raising her eyebrows and pointing toward the paper in my bra. I give a playful elbow to her well-endowed chest and take her phone.

"I disagree entirely." I shove her phone into my bra as well. "With small breasts, one can securely fit a whole *lot* into their bra," I laugh. "Oh, do you need me to carry that for you?" I ask, pointing to Bette's lip gloss. Claudia cracks up and grabs her phone.

"Syd, he was hot." Bette rolls the tinted gloss over her kissable lips and hands it to Claudia who brightens hers then hands it to Abby in the front seat. Bette smacks her lips a few times then adds, "Is every guy here in Austin hot, or is it just me?"

Abby, a Texas native, giggles. "Every one of—"

"Just you." Gus interrupts, adjusting her jean shorts to reveal a bit more leg as if it were even possible.

My girlfriends, the Sirens. Or so we like to call ourselves. We met slinging drinks and breaking hearts as the bold, sassy-mouthed bartenders working at the same good ol' country bar in New York City. The only country bar worth calling country in the city. We just clicked.

Our driver brings the truck to an abrupt stop and helps as we hop, nearly having to jump, out of the beast in front of the bustling Austin hot spot. Everyone out front takes note; it's obvious we've arrived. We *are* wearing semi-matchy-matchy outfits to represent the New York City bar. Cowboy boots, short-shorts or revealing jean skirts and T-shirts branded with the bar's logo and styled to show skin. We've become professional at ripping our T-shirts just so.

Waiting outside the entrance for Abby, who is tipping the driver, Bette swats at a guy's hand reaching in her skirt's direction. "You better watch yourself," she says, then immediately looks at us inquisitively. I can feel her earlier line of questioning coming on. "So, exactly what the hell is moxie?" she asks, mouth agape.

You would think she'd be tapping her toe by the way she's looking at us, arms crossed, full lips pursed. The *definition* of moxie. She pulls at her skirt self conscious and rightly so. We talked her into wearing it, and at best it covers only three quarters of her ample backside when she tips forward. We didn't tell her that though, obviously, or she wouldn't have worn the winning number. It looks killer.

Gus, not listening, slides smoke slowly from her un-glossed lips, relishing in it a bit too much. Bette, looking up, snags the cigarette and places it back into its owner's mouth, the guy Gus stole it from. He smiles. More of a drool really, and the cigarette falls to the stone-covered ground outside the packed bar. Gus winks at him then wafts the smoke away from my crinkled nose.

With Abby back at our side, Gus nudges Bette through the saloon-style doors and saves me from two western style button-downs, who insist I take each of their business cards. (Mostly because I wouldn't take their numbers.)

Bette thinks I shouldn't wear ponytails; she says it's somehow too inviting to men. Huh? I've been wearing a ponytail since the fourth grade and I don't remember it ever being a problem then. Although that *is* when I met Blake. (Ugh, Blake and his barf-amazing wedding.)

"What's your name?" the two western shirts shout almost simultaneously.

I look over my shoulder, smiling. "Sydney Shag!"

Gus and I lock arms and slip inside as Abby and Claudia glide in behind us.

"I'm still waitin'." Bette's Brooklyn accent floods the bar as she flips her spiraled reddish-brown curls off her shoulder with deliberate sensuality.

"You should never have to wait," says a guy.

"Exactly." Bette's newly single and there's no sense not letting everyone know. Her accent only comes out for two reasons: she's either very tipsy or very upset. Tipsy has already set in as we join the crowd of the rowdy but welcoming bar, The Hitching Rail.

We're representing the New York bar for an auto show promo and drinks are on the boss tonight. We're not wasting time.

"Are you serious, Bette? You don't know what *moxie* means?" I ask while scanning the crowd. I purposefully lead my friends up to the bar near "a few good men," making it look like an aimless decision.

"No way," Gus says to Bette while pulling her unwashed, stick-straight hair into a sexy pile on top of her head.

Bette looks at Gus, raising her eyebrow into an overly sardonic arch, à la The Rock.

"I'll have one of these," Gus says, paying no mind and scooting the bartender an empty beer bottle. The bartender flinches, noting that the deep voice came from my tall friend giving him eyes, and not a bearded seventy-something with a cigar spilling from his lips. Of course, if they allowed smoking, Gus would be happy to oblige.

"What?" Bette tries again, a bit impatient now. "What's moxie? And where do those guys at the auto show get off sayin' I'm full of it?"

"Bette, you're from Brooklyn and you went to Columbia; are you serious?" I say again, tucking the business cards into my bra alongside the doorman's number. Tugging at a loose fray on my jean skirt that's tickling my upper thigh, I smile at the bartender who's popping Gus' beer. It's just that Bette doesn't often get stumped on a court case from the last century, let alone a simple definition. She's been studying nonstop for the bar exam since her breakup. She was on track to take it three months after they met and got sidetracked. A two-year sidetrack.

"Syd, what does Brooklyn have to do with it?" she demands. She yanks at her skirt and gives Gus and me a dirty look. Somehow Claudia and Abby aren't as much to blame for its *short*-comings.

"Even I know what moxie is, and this is my second language," Claudia says like a know-it-all, then winks to reveal she has no idea. "I'll have a Spicy Negroni," she states to the tattooed bartender, unintentionally harsh. Her freckles seem to twinkle at him and he smiles even though she just barked at him. The accent. No one can resist Claudia's Brazilian accent, no matter what she says. She once told a bar patron to "shove off" and he stayed all night and tipped his wallet.

"A Pink Crush Margarita," Abby smiles, always ordering pink and always ordering margs. She brags that margaritas are in her blood being one quarter Mexican and all. She looks back at us. "I know what moxie is but I don't think I could define it." Abby's round hazel eyes blur slightly as the pregame shots we took in the hotel room take hold. You would need shots too after wearing those costumes.

Promoting the bar at a large-scale auto show came with a lot of extra to-do. We were dressed in costumes all day matching the year of the car we were assigned. The Boss's family has quite a collection, and our cars ranged from the 1908 Model T to spectacles like the 1981 DeLorean from *Back to the Future*. The Boss's family is, to say it lightly, loaded and she's even wealthier now with the bar in New York doing so well. Our boss was something of a debutante back in the day or so we've been told by locals. But some of the locals got a little too friendly with Bette today and she may or may not have given a few men a piece her mind when they took their "under-the-hood" questions a bit too far.

Secretly, I loved my costume. I got to wear a pony-tail and poodle skirt all day. Tray, well-known costume designer and longtime friend, had it tailored just for me.

"Yeah right, both of you." Bette drums her fingernails on the bar. "Beer me," she says to the bartender, pointing to Gus' bottle. She tugs at her skirt again and I swat her hand away surreptitiously.

"*Moxie* is slang for courage or nerve. It's having the guts or *moxie* to do something. Like…" I turn and smile at the "few good men" next to us. Who can resist a uniform? I choose a looker with a boxer's nose and make eye contact. I walk up to his pressed full dress and kiss him dead on the lips for a solid minute. The Sirens scream with delight and the men begin to clap. I pull back and smile at him, then give him another kiss for good measure and turn back to the girls with straight-faced cool. "Moxie. I mean, the term probably *originated* in Brooklyn, Bette." One of the Boxer's friends puts his hand up slowly, shaking his head in astonishment. I slide him a high five while returning to the girls. Then I look at the bartender. "Martini, please. Heavy on the vodka and a little bit dirty." The Sirens all scream again and I finally break into a laugh.

"Well done," the bartender says, grinning from ear to ear. "That one's on me."

"Hmm, never heard of it," Bette says, deadpan. She takes a sip of her beer. "But that right there, what you just did, I'm going to have to try that." She cracks a smile, then whistles. Loud. New York-style, two-finger, hail-a-cab loud. The Sirens hoot some more, and we all laugh as the bar erupts into claps.

There's no stopping the Sirens when we're on a roll.

There are six of us in all. Bette, a Caribbean island mix (blended in Brooklyn) with book smarts to match her copious curves, is our rock. She has nearly all of our schedules (and really our whole lives) memorized. She must have an Excel spreadsheet in her brain.

Then there's August, otherwise known only as Gus. A nickname that lends itself to someone you find drinking ten men fitted with trucker hats under the bar, as she so often does. But along with her strikingly low voice comes strikingly long legs and don't let her fool you, she'll try to pass for every ethnicity based on her latest audition and swears she's from everywhere, but her beautiful Japanese-influenced eyes are a dead giveaway to what genes won out.

Abby hales from the heart of Texas, like I said, and is as "bless your heart" as the modern age will allow. She wouldn't hurt a fly unless with a fly swatter and not on a Sunday. She's nearly married with a longtime boyfriend and loves long walks on the beach. You know the drill. We're the strongest two-steppers at the bar and like me, she's technique trained but all personality on the dance floor.

If I had any more personality they'd lock me up. I'm a "Midwest gem" as Grandma Shag says. (Yes, our last name is Shag. You'll just have to deal with it; I did.) She also says I'm "full of small town sweet with a heart as big as the heartland, and overwhelming like a Fourth of July finale." I once blew a hole right through her kitchen window, which may have something to do with that last bit, but that's another story. With all that personality, Bette might have drowned me in a pitcher of beer that first night behind the bar together, but I made her too much money in tips. And as it turns out, opposites really do attract.

Then there's Claudia. Claudia's a real piece of work. A royal at birth—if they had a royal family in Brazil—famous for her family status, her fiancé, her freckles and for having a flare for the finer things (make that the finest), which she doesn't know she has.

Sirens are mythical mermaid-like seductresses, muses and women of great fortune, power and influence. Who wouldn't want to embody that? (I also like to mention the name's connection to classic movie star screen sirens. My fave.) We don't have pink jackets like the Pink Ladies in *Grease* (yet) but we do all have the Tiffany's Elsa Peretti Starfish bracelet. And, you've met them all, all but Zoey.

Zoey's abroad at the moment but if she were here, she'd be easy to spot. Usually sporting rainbow-colored, cropped hair that showcases her beautiful olive skin, she's a true yogi if I've ever seen one.

The bartender's tattoo-sleeved arm places five shots in front of us. "From the gentleman," he says, and points to the one I kissed. The Boxer raises his beer and we pick up our shot glasses.

"To a great start to an already great night," Abby squeals. We raise our shots, tap the bar with them, and knock 'em back. Together, we flip and slam the empty glasses onto the bar.

Here's where in the movies there would be that record scratch noise. You know the one…

I'm looking pretty confidant, aren't I? You might even say cocky. Except, this is where you should know that my "moxie" hasn't been as intact as of late, which is why I just gave myself a wake-up call.

Let me explain.

Chapter 2
A SPARKLING EXAMPLE OF COLOR

BUTTER CREEK: SIX MONTHS AGO, THANKSGIVING

IT WAS just a short six months ago that he told me he loved me.

"Syd, I love you. I'm *in* love with you! No one will ever love you the way that I love you, and no one will ever treat you as good as I will," Blake, my high school kind-of boyfriend, says, teeth chattering.

Butter Creek is cold by November. Like seriously cold.

Just to recap, he told me he loved me. He told me that no one would ever love me the way he loved me and no one would ever treat me the way he would. (Puke. But perfect.) And here comes the good part. When he asked how *I* felt, I just stood there.

And stood there.

It was shock. I blame it on shock.

And possibly the cold.

It could have been the cold.

☆ ☆ ☆

BUTTER CREEK: FOURTEEN DAYS AGO, SATURDAY, MAY 13

Fast-forward six months and I'm sitting at *his* wedding in our hometown, Butter Creek (the number one small town on *Forbes'* list—okay, it's not, but it should be), to some girl who looks like a character out of *Little House on the Prairie*. Not kidding.

She's like some big plant genome scientist or whatever. Something to do with seeds and saving the world. Which just reminds me how very successful I am...er, if you count bartending as saving the world one drink at a time, which I totally do.

I knew he was dating this girl, I just didn't know he was going to actually marry her. I mean, I thought he would show up in the city, stand outside my window holding a ridiculous amount of flowers (you can buy flowers on like every corner in Manhattan; if you don't bring flowers, you're an idiot), just like in the movies. My apartment is totally in the best movie neighborhood ever and has five huge windows that face the street. I chose it for this very reason—I would have the perfect view of him shouting his undying love.

"Sydney Orie Shag." He knows my whole name because we've known each other since we were ten. "I love you! I've always loved you!" A taxi passes in front of him and I run to another window to get a better view, but he's hidden by a UPS truck. When I see him again, he's shouting something, but a small band-circus is marching by and playing a slightly off-pitch version of "Louie Louie." They're bang-ing on so loudly that I don't hear him at all. (The movies ought to get these things right, because that's what would really happen.) I hear him again as the band-circus moves down the sunset-lit street… "I love you, Syd. You hear me?" (Now I do.) He climbs the fire escape like in *Pretty Woman* as I crawl out the window to meet him, but not before I hit my head on the window, because I always hit my head on that window, and kiss him as everyone cheers from outside the bar downstairs.

Duh, people, this is how it was supposed to go.

But this never happened. He's never even been to New York. I guess he was trying to tell me the whole "love" thing six months ago while I was visiting Butter. In the freezing cold. Maybe if it had been raining like in *The Notebook*, and not so cold. (And maybe if I hadn't eaten all of the mashed potatoes Grandma Shag made for Thanks-giving dinner. Potatoes with three sticks of butter can't be helpful in any situation.) But anyway, he loved *me* exactly six months before he said "I do" to Misty, aka Laura-save-the-world-with-seeds-whatever-Ingalls.

So, it was his last stab, and my last chance to marry my high school sweetheart. I blew it.

I've made quite a few mistakes in my day, but this may just take the cake. The big cake. The proverbial wedding cake.

Oh, and I caught the bouquet. (Gag.)

They say the girl who catches the bouquet is the next to get married. Nearly everyone asked for a do-over when

I caught it. Half the men in the room had asked me out in high school or college, to which I said, "I just want to be friends." (We all still are.) They're all wearing wedding bands now, and the one I really adore just put a ring on the woman who asked me if I wanted her to throw the bouquet again.

No, I certainly do not. I don't believe in do-overs! I wouldn't let Laura-ugh-she's-not-even-ugly-Ingalls throw it again. I could get married, people. But, this only got me roped into the garter tradition with her young but hairy uncle. The folding chair folded when he tried to put the garter over my knee. (I was leaning back as far as I could without being noticeable. It was noticeable.) The chair buckled and he fell on top of me. The garter tradition was a smash, literally. I danced with every single one of her cousins to make up for it and drowned my sorrows by doing shots (too many) with Blake's dad.

Grandma Shag always says that "mistakes are what make people colorful" and that I'm a "sparkling example of color." The first time she said this I had just used baking powder instead of baking *soda* in her famous sweetbread. She also told me to leave the kitchen.

When I was dropped off at home (drunk) holding the yellow (my favorite color...*my* favorite color) bouquet, Gams marched over in her glamorous apron and perfectly coiffed hair and handed me a piece of her famous sweetbread. She put her hand on my shoulder, gave me a loving look, which turned into a smirk, and said, "You are sparkling, dear, just sparkling."

As if that weren't bad enough, I swear, just swear, The Sister (Krissy: prissy, prudish, and my pain-in-the ass older sister) called me a jackass under her breath and gave me the eye-flutter roll as she went upstairs to do her makeup for the fiftieth time or put on some face-freezing cream while her mean little Chi-chihuahua bit my ankle. The same ankle I had already sprained at the reception trying to do the salsa under the influence.

Chapter 3
GOALS AND OTHER BAD IDEAS

"I VOW never to go to another wedding stag," I say aloud, staring at the dried-up yellow bouquet, when I hear One Eye Joe, my landlord, yelling "mail" at my door. He does this when I leave it too long and it starts clogging everyone else's mailboxes, making it impossible to close. Oops.

This is when the second thing that happened happens.

"Syd, you would tell me if you were getting married, right?" he says. I can hear One Eye Joe's keys jangling from his belt loop as he continues to yell questions in his deep Italian roar from outside my apartment. What? I rip open the door, forgetting that I'm wearing a short dragon kimono (I had it shortened; the poor dragon lost a significant amount of his tail) and turban (my *Sunset Boulevard*-inspired thinking cap). And forgetting that One Eye Joe always leans on the doorframe as if reliving his modeling days (before the eyeball thing), my nose is practically touching his.

"Of course I would—" I nearly choke as I almost say "One Eye Joe." "Jovan, I'm saving you the second dance." Giggling, I take my mail and close the door. He holds it open, smoothes his manicured salt and pepper hair, and lowers his sunglasses, flashing his glass eye at me. It might be a super power because I freeze, stuck in its beam.

"Because you should get married. Look at you," he says, and then flinches, actually noting my eccentric look with his good eye. (The turban is my thinking cap, and I've been doing a lot of thinking about my future today). "My offer still stands for your hand," he smiles, oozing decadent charm. I can see my reflection in the glass eye and want to straighten my turban, but it holds me cemented in its gaze, transfixed.

Super powers exist.

He does a little jig, breaking the trance, and laughs at his own joke. I shake my head, grinning widely, and push him out of the doorway.

"Bye, Jovan."

"You're right, the wife would kill me," he says as the door closes on his nose. I straighten my turban. "Maybe you should think about marrying that big guy," he continues from outside the door. He sees me with Tray a lot. (Tray Wise: friend, fashion designer, and flaming.) Tray lives across the street and we've known each other forever. "Or Elan, upstairs?" (Elan: neighbor, neurologist, and neurotic.) Then, even louder, he says, "But always remember, you're my little bimboshell."

I don't even want to get into the fact that I've corrected his English on this numerous times. He means "bombshell," I swear.

I throw the mail on my entryway table, all except one brightly colored card.

I love cards! They're so much more fun than email.

The back of the envelope says: *Little Spunky, you're getting married!*

I hate cards.

Omigod, the parents have given up on the incredible career I always said I would have and instead devised a plan for an arranged marriage. (Insert panic attack here. Where's my *Little Brown Bag?*) Can they do that? (Maybe they should do that. My career is taking a bit longer to take off than expected. Well, even to get started.) I sit on my animal print loveseat, reach underneath, and sweep up a *Little Brown Bag* in case I start to hyperventilate. I open the card. Inside it says: *According to your goals!*

I start to hyperventilate.

What goals? A folded, crinkled piece of paper falls out of the card and into my lap. Against my better judgment I continue reading...

Sydney,

Oh, I just had to send you this. (That's my super-cute mom, Minnie.) *I know you just left a few days ago—I miss you already—but isn't it the neatest! I think you wrote it when you were eleven, do you remember? I was looking for one of the Christmas Nutcrackers* (Why Minnie is looking for a Nutcracker in May, I'll never know.) *when I found this adorable list of goals in your sock drawer.* (Why Minnie is looking for a Nutcracker in my sock drawer confuses me even more…but then again, it's Minnie.) *Isn't it just as cute as a bug's ear! A stewardess, can you imagine? You practically have to be knocked out to get on all your flights.* (I do.) *But you would have been amazing.* (Ever supportive.) *I remember when you swam with the dolphins. We were so glad they turned out to be dolphins and not sharks.* (The Sister wasn't.) *And then, the time you went cliff jumping…I just about dragged you back from study abroad but your dad thought it was great.* (Anything I do that's remotely life threatening, Doc, aka Jim, my doctor dad, thinks is great.) *And isn't it just a hoot that you thought you would be married by now?* (Horrifying.) *Remember you thought being in your twenties was so old?* (Yes, more horror.) *Speaking of old… your BIRTHDAY is around the corner!* (*Psycho* knife scene music here…it isn't, but puke. Minnie always forgets I have a winter birthday. Then, when she does remember, she thinks I've doubled in age.) *It wouldn't be all that bad, you know, all your friends from high school are married. Blake's wedding was just lovely.* (Minnie's doing a serious Norman Bates on me right now.) *And we received another wedding invite from the Jeffreys. Their youngest daughter is getting married!*

Wasn't she a freshman when you were a senior? (Tessa Jeffrey was like sexually active when she was twelve and thought every one of those boys was going to marry her. Doesn't count.) *Looking forward to seeing you in July, we just bought our tickets. New York City, here we come!*

I am not going to do anything over ten cents. (That's Doc. You can tell because he has completely illegible handwriting. Translation: I'm not going to do anything over ten cents. I've studied his script and forged it several times at a very successful rate, a talent of mine. There's a career idea. I could be a graphologist! Or a thief.)

Your Dad has already checked out New York City on a Dime at the library. (You can also tell it's Doc because he's only willing to spend a whopping ten cents on the trip. And still uses the library.)

Love and hugs,

Mom

and

DAD (looks like you'll be throwing yourself down Old Beard Mountain hahaaaaa) (Translation: looks like you'll be throwing yourself down Old Beard Mountain, sinister laughter.)

What's this about Old Beard Mountain?

I'd rather you throw yourself down Old Mustache Mountain (Old Beard, Minnie) *than have a career you didn't like or marry some twerp. Love you mucho lotta!* (Minnie's version of Spanish. Unfortunately, mine is just as bad.)

I look at the folded, crinkled piece of paper sitting on my knee. I turn it over and it's stamped with a skull and crossbones. (This means it's secret, Minnie. I went through a very big pirate phase from age nine to eleven.) Goals? I probably shouldn't read this after the upsetting reminder about my age, career, and wedding plans, but resisting curiosity was never my strongest suit. So, I open...

GOALS!!!!!!!!!!!!!!!!!!!!

(I still love exclamation points, so I completely understand why I needed like fifty here.)

Become a Stewardess.

(Fail. What was I thinking? Planes are complete death traps. This goal was obviously made before I realized I could drop out of the sky to a fiery death. Not according to all of the reports and nauseatingly uplifting statistics. But they're all a lie; I just know it.)

Jump out of a plane!!

(Fail. Who was I at age eleven? I get nauseous just thinking about it. And then there's that whole plane, fiery death thing again.)

Sing on a famous stage.

(Accomplished! Finally, something to feel good about. I was a big hit at our state fair. Our state fair, is a great state fair and it's totally famous. On another note, who knew I was one of those girls that put hearts on top of her i's when I was eleven. Omigod.)

Swim with dolphins!

(Accomplished, albeit by mistake. I fell over the side of a boat on a tour off the coast of Florida. I swear The Sister pushed me but she denies it to this day. Typical.)

Jump off the White Cliffs of DOVER!!!

(Accomplished. Okay, it wasn't exactly those cliffs. When I was eleven, I didn't know you would die if you did that. I don't think I knew I could die at all! That explains a lot. But I did jump off a proper cliff—an old castle built into a cliff to be exact, and it was on an adventure weekend in Europe. Flinging my body from high elevations, as long as it isn't from a plane, is oddly fine.)

Travel around the world!!!!

(Accomplish-ing. My travel list is pretty impressive, even if I do have to have a drink—or twelve—to get on my flights.)

Have a million dollars in my secret savings account from award-winning stewardessing.

(Epic fail. Clearly, this goal thing is a disaster. Granted, my secret savings account was a small pirate chest. I got a lot of skull and crossbone gifts for my birthday—it was pirate themed, of course—but I'm pretty sure it still has more money in it than I have in any savings account. Okay, I don't even have a savings account. I stash all my cash in the closet. And stewardessing? Is that even a word? But, the point is, I thought I would be this incredible career woman by now. I feel lightheaded.)

Marry a prince, like Cinderella!!!

(Omigod. My obsession with Walt Disney surfaces.)

Do all of these by the time you're old and gray in your twenties or throw yourself down Old Beard Mountain.

(And there it is. No career plan to speak of and I've just caught a bouquet highlighting the fact that I don't even have a boyfriend. Doc was right, I might as well chuck myself down Old Beard Mountain.)

Sydney O Shag

(I was obviously practicing my famous signature. I.e., totally copying Doc's. It still looks like Doc's to this day. So far, thief is my best career choice.)

———————————

So, they aren't planning an arranged marriage. (They should be if I'm going to meet that last goal.) But, I thought I would be a stewardess (er, flight attendant) with a monumental career, a husband, and a million dollars. Oh, and be able to jump out of a plane.

I breathe hard into the *Little Brown Bag*.

Someone better glue my windows shut because this is a pretty foolproof recipe for a jump.

I can't breathe. I'll probably succumb to paralyzing hyperventilation on my way out, after I hit my head on the window, because I always hit my head on that window, and they'll think I was just trying to get air. My suicide won't even be a success.

Apparently, when I was eleven, being in my twenties sounded like an old, old, lady. Who gets married in their twenties?! (Er, everyone in Butter.) But, if I was so sure my whole head would be gray, which it's not, maybe I just underestimated my life-affirming time frame?

An ambulance screams outside and jolts me. No, I should have a career path well laid out by now, and frankly, if I had paid better attention, I could have a sweet and wonderful partner.

Well done, Sydney. I'm single, money has a tendency to slip out of my hands like a drink into a barfly's mouth, and I technically don't have a career. Or a plan, for that matter.

But, I have no gray hairs!

I lean timidly toward the immense floor-to-ceiling mirror looming nearby and pull the turban off my head, letting my hair cascade out. I stare at it suspiciously.

Yet.

Old Beard Mountain isn't completely life threatening. In fact, it's a hill. I mean, it's injury-inducing for sure. It's the infamous sledding hill in Butter Creek. Someone breaks something there every year; after all, there are enough trees on it to resemble a beard. But when you're eleven and you say you may as well throw yourself down it, you mean business.

Nothing like a little reminder from your past self when you're already reeling from your high school kind-of boyfriend's wedding that you're old, never going to find a prince, never going to have money, and never going to live up to your potential. (That last one I just added for good measure, as I'm the only Shag in a long line of Shags not to go to medical school. I was going to be "stewardessing." Duh.) I take another desperately deep breath into the *Little Brown Bag* and exhale.

It pops in my face.

This won't do. This won't do at all.

I'm deciding here and now to buckle down. Starting today, I'm going to learn from my mistakes, get a career— like a doctor or a genome scientist or something—find myself a prince-like husband, and oh, jump out of a plane. But first I'm going to pass out...my oxygen to carbon dioxide ratio is way off.

Shi...

Chapter 4
RULES TO LIVE BY

NEW YORK CITY: NINE DAYS AGO, THURSDAY, MAY 18

OKAY, OKAY, I'm starting today. (Not yesterday.) Drinking nearly a third of a bottle of vodka while wearing your college sweatpants (the ones with the hole in the ass) and crossing out the names of every boy you've ever kissed because they're not a potential suitor after Googling "skydiving: all the ways you can die" does not constitute a good start. Also, emailing Bloomingdale's about the unstable status of their *Little Brown Bag* was not necessarily the best idea. (Talk about unstable...) But that was yesterday. Today will be a perfect beginning to my plan.

I hereby vow to get my act together and accomplish my life goals.

So,

Rule #1
DON'T JUST STAND THERE

Chapter 5
CROP DUSTERS AND CAPTAIN AMERICA

OMIGOD, I'M just standing here.

"All righty, it'll be a 120-mile-per-hour free-fall that lasts fifty seconds. Arms out to the side…" I can almost make out what the instructor, Bitty, wants me to do, but her Southern drawl is falling under the category of foreign language. She's instructing the group on a tandem jump and apparently wants us to display the position we're supposed to take after plunging out of the "jump plane." It's a total crop duster. The plane is so small, it may as well be a rickety, old crop duster.

And Bitty isn't very bitty; she is, in fact, tall and heavily muscled. Will she even fit in that pocket-sized piece of metal? Is everyone supposed to fit in there? There are like twelve people in this room, plus Bitty! I look around and everyone else is smiling with their hands in an overhead position. I copy them, and Bitty winks at me just like Mrs. Williams, my second grade geography teacher, used to do (even when I got the answer wrong).

I peek at the plane parked just outside the hangar again. There's a good possibility it's smaller than a crop duster.

This is not good idea.

This is *definitely* not a good idea.

WebMD says this could cause me very high anxiety, and very few people have ever recovered from a skydiving accident. Probably because a human reaches terminal velocity after falling 200 to 220 meters—and some hopefuls even say 395 meters, depending on air resistance. Like if your parachute doesn't open.

"Now, let's get into these jumpsuits!" she says. Bitty's dainty voice somehow exudes calm and excitement as she demonstrates. Everyone follows her lead with enthusiasm.

Does no one else see the crop duster?

Does no one else notice this seems like flimsy material to jump out of a crop duster in?

Does no one else notice Bitty looks like Captain America in her suit? Maybe we'll be fine after all.

I step into the blue star-embroidered jumpsuit in a trance and zip it from crotch to neck. I look over at the happiest, just-married couple in the world who've been torturing me with their my-little-pumpkin-whumpkin-cuddle-bumpkin talk the whole instructional session. I want to tell them that this is the dumbest idea in the history of dumb ideas and that I should never have signed up for this, especially on a discount from Groupon. I mean, what if my suit isn't airproof or whatever it's supposed to be because it's on discount? No wonder it's flimsy. I'm just about to tell them this but the woman's having trouble getting her very large breasts into the suit and they're too busy laughing and kissing to even notice I want to ruin their day with facts.

I look into the mirrored wall to my left and note that the suit has made me flat as a board. I try fluffing my chest, but it doesn't work. And then I remember I'm supposed to jump out of a crop duster with this boob-flattening suit on. My last fashion statement on earth. I look down. And I'm wearing flats. A wave of nausea takes over my body and I sit on the edge of a large garbage can nearby.

I don't think I can do this.

I definitely can't do this.

☆ ☆ ☆

I squint into the light, blinking the room into focus. It's dark and dank, filled with iron shelves stuffed with parachute packs. I hear Bitty's soft, dainty voice talking to people in the other room but can't quite make out what she's saying.

I'm on a gurney. Omigod, I've been injured from the jump. I don't even remember the jump. That's got to be bad. Really bad.

Wait, I hear loud, familiarly loud, voices. My two emergency contacts. This is so bad.

"Where is she?" Gus' deep, authoritative voice is audible now. She can pull off bitch and crazy at a moment's notice all while still holding on to her sexy card. So *authoritative* is like a walk in the park for her. She makes for an impressive emergency contact. I immediately feel better about my injuries.

"Is she okay? 'Cause if not, I'm going to kill her." Bette's Brooklyn accent fills the room, and I'm almost positive, even without seeing her, that she just flipped her spiraled reddish-brown curls off her shoulder with an attitude. Remember, Bette's accent only comes out for two reasons: she's either very tipsy or very upset. "Where…" She pauses, I can tell for effect. "…is she?" She's very upset.

"She's in there," I hear Bitty say, still sounding Southern but a little less sweet. They push into the room, and before I know what's going on, Bette and Gus are sitting on the gurney with me.

It's bad. It's really bad. I don't think I can move my legs.

"Syd? You fell into a garbage can and hit your head?" Gus asks in her low scratch, putting her hand on my shoulder. They both chuckle.

"What? I jumped. I'm paralyzed," I wince, trying to move my legs. They clearly aren't working.

"Oh, sorry, I'm sittin' on your legs," Bette says. "What are you doing out here, Syd? New Jersey??? I had to take like four trains just to get here." Bette is born, raised, lives, and breathes Brooklyn. New Jersey may as well be Antarctica.

"I was trying to…" Wait, I'm not paralyzed?

"Jump out of a plane? Syd, you don't even like to fly. You've already had to take Valium for our flight to Austin next week, and it's not until next week!" Gus tugs on my ponytail as she always does and I tighten my ponytail as I always do after Gus musses it. I feel a very sore spot on my head. And I didn't take Valium. It was a Benedryl. Unfortunately, I fell asleep while Gus was practicing her latest monologue for an audition. That didn't go over well.

"What happened? Captain America in there says you just seemed to pass out," Bette says, her Brooklyn calming down a bit.

I *knew* she looked like Captain America.

"Her boobs were huge…" I'm not sure why I say this, but the lovey-dovey couple next to me is the one thing I can remember before apparently knocking myself out on a garbage can. Classic.

"She must be talking about Blake's new bride again," Gus says to Bette, before looking at at me sternly. "Who cares about her? You're so much hotter and way more fabulous!"

"Unless you pass out in a garbage can again, then you can forget about the fabulous part," Bette says, slowly lifting her eyebrow.

Chapter 6
DOWNWARD DOG

OKAY, SO my first attempt at accomplishing a goal didn't go so well.

Bitty gave me her brother's business card, **Bubba & Bubba Vet Clinic Goodtown, TX**. Bitty and Bubba. I have no words for this. It's too good. I can only hope their mom's name is Kitty. I almost asked as we were leaving, but Bette, somehow sensing what I was about to say, hit me in my already bruised side before I had a chance.

Bitty said that he happens to be in town and that I shouldn't hesitate to call if I felt lightheaded or had any questions. (Like if I should get a mastiff? Because I've always wanted a mastiff.) I mean, it was very nice of her, even though he's a veterinarian. Who has the money to go to the hospital just so they can tell you that you're a dumbass? And I already called Doc; he let me know that, yes, in fact, I *am* a dumbass. I would never call someone I didn't know just so they could tell me the same thing.

I imagine it's not every day someone falls into a garbage can and manages to give themselves a concussion while going over safety instructions, of all things. It's probably on YouTube already. I feel my cheeks flush. I wonder if signing the release papers before class included the use of iPhone photos and videos. Omigod, it will rack up so many hits that I'll probably get asked to be on the *Today* show. They'll probably make me wear the blue boob-flattening jumpsuit. And there I'll be, flat as a board on national TV. Marcy Moore will have a field day with this. Marcy Moore, Secretary of the Commonwealth of Butter Creek, and the first to get boobs in the fifth grade (fifth!)—not to mention the first to point out that I didn't. She'll post it on Facebook under the guise of "Sydney's famous!" but she'll really mean "Sydney's flat!" just like in fifth grade.

I barrel through the bar door panicked about the *Today* show. I can tell Bette, Gus, and Claudia are talking about me because they immediately stop laughing and one of them makes shushing noises.

"You told Claudia about my little incident, didn't you?" I look directly at Gus and Bette as if they're in trouble. I, unfortunately, trip on one of the old floorboards so my tough girl act lasts all of one second.

"Absolutely," Bette smiles, really big. "But we didn't have to tell her—we showed her!" She holds up her phone and they all crack up again.

Kill.

YouTube.

"Give me that," I say, grabbing Bette's phone. It's on instant replay. I find myself in the boob-flattening jumpsuit, noting that the blue seems to really pop on my body. Oh wait, they've highlighted me somehow so viewers know who to follow. I perch on the edge of the garbage can, go to tighten my ponytail (I remember that part), and in extraordinarily dramatic fashion my body goes limp. I crash deep into the extra-strength trash bag, hitting my head on the opposite side of the can just as my legs stick straight into the air.

Omigod.

Can anyone tell it's me?

I watch again.

It's me.

Apparently that one yoga class, where I spent the hour debating whether or not I could talk the teacher into eating a doughnut paid off. They could have emptied me out into a perfect downward dog.

It plays again; I cringe. Oh, this is so bad. The girls are laughing again too.

"Oh, and did you really think you were paralyzed because I was sitting on your legs? Seriously, do I look—"

"No!" Gus and I blurt.

Claudia shakes her head. "Bethany, you never look fat."

Don't ever call Bette *Bethany*, her full name. She's convinced it's a fat name and will go, as we call it, Brooklyn on you. And don't even think about Beth—it's even fatter. I'm not sure where she gets these fascinating ideas, but I've learned from *that* mistake. Even though Bette knows her curves are her asset, she obsesses over the number on the scale. This leads her to asking "Do I look fat?" constantly.

"Sorry, Bette," Claudia says, sheepishly pushing her bangs out of her eyes. Her highlighted chesnut hair rests neatly on top of her shoulders, and a sprinkling of perfectly placed freckles clutters her nose and cheeks. It's hard to stay mad at her for long, especially with that silky Brazilian accent. But she absolutely butchers English. Just then it sounded like *torry-betta*. Behind the bar this is golden, worth a mint.

"Where's Abby? I thought she'd be back by now," I say, changing the subject. Claudia has never quite grasped the problem with the name Bethany. At the same time, she never wants to be called Claud, so we don't want to go down this path.

Gus takes the phone from me and Googles several delightful phrases—*dumpster diving skydiver*, *trash compacted flight student*, and *garbage can girl*—to see if the video comes up. One's a match, and she watches me fall again and laughs.

"There's a slow-motion version!" she says, overly amused.

Oh, good.

"It feels like Abby's been gone forever, right?" Bette says, stepping into her weathered cowboys, our nickname for cowboy boots. "She's just going to stay in Austin and meet us at the auto show. She wanted more time with Greg and the fam." I told you, Excel spreadsheet in her brain.

I take off my lucky green leather motor jacket, toss it over a bar stool, and throw on my cowboys. I jump up next to Bette, giving her a little hip check, and she smiles reluctantly. Gus slips her long legs into her black boots and takes her position next to me, while Claudia, who's wearing some sort of tall, fringed boot—something fabulously Brazilian, we assume—steps more timidly next to us.

"Bette, you're *bella—bella como la noche*," she says.

"I am pretty, aren't I?" Bette says, flipping her spiraled reddish-brown curls off her shoulder. We all laugh. "What?"

The music hits our cue and we fly into the most recent dance choreography, wearing comfortable jean shorts, T-shirts, tanks, and tube socks—and of course, our cowboys. We'll perform this particular number on top of the bar, showing off our precision, our belt buckles, our standout tops, and sexy style when the bar's open, but when we rehearse, it's in comfort and on the open dance floor toward the back of the bar. The dance floor is the only place in the city known for line dancing, and we boast the best two-stepping around, which Abby and I teach on special occasions.

Gus and I hit the counts hard and uniformly, while laughing and taunting each other.

"How the hell do you guys pick up the moves so fast? Asombrosa," Claudia says, baffled, and a few steps behind.

"You two are going to destroy the top of the bar again. And I want to be there when it happens this time," Bette says, shaking her head and trying to follow. "Slow down—show me!"

The last time Gus and I bartended together, the top of the bar had to be refinished. Boss halfheartedly threatened to take it out of our tips until Gus said, "Check our ring." Needless to say, it was extremely high. Boss didn't bring it up again.

We spend an hour catching Bette and Claudia up on the dances, counting every move, and clog with exactitude, until they have it down pat. Then we go over the details of our work trip, the reason for this additional dance rehearsal, leaving the jukebox pounding.

The bar is sending us to an esteemed auto show in Austin where we'll pose in costume next to vehicles in a vintage car section. Some of the cars are from the owner's very own impressive family collection, not to mention the bar's logo will be plastered everywhere at the event. We'll be making appearances at local hot spots in the evenings, wearing our favorite cowboys for clogging of course, and we all assume it won't be long before the Boss opens a new location with local investors. At least that's what we've been whispering about behind the bar.

Regardless, it will be the perfect opportunity to work on that prince section of my goals. Cars and Southern men all in one place. Can't be too hard, right?

Chapter 7
THWARTED BY PABST

AUSTIN: TODAY, SATURDAY, MAY 27

"LET'S DO this," I say, taking a sip of my martini.

The Hitching Rail is undeniably one of the oldest bars in Austin, and maybe the darkest. Once a beer bar with no frilly drinks, it now features buzzworthy cocktails along with its famous saloon-style doors. It's a lot like our popular dive in New York City, but with one very killer addition: a live band. They're rolling out one popular hit after another, led by a male singer-guitarist oozing confidence and sporting a baseball cap. A purplish light illuminates the band, and the hardwood floors are covered in scuffs and divots from years of wear. The rest of the bar is lit only by spotlights that are nestled into the ceiling, peeking through age-old dust that has settled into dirt. They must have illuminated women's fashion from ankle-length dresses to jeans to Bette's mini, all according to the scratchings on the walls. The "thing" here is to carve or write your name on the wall to leave your mark, and there are several marks that are dated well back to the early 1900s.

Though it's a great atmosphere for drinking, I can't see a thing. I stumble down a small step trying to get to Gus, who's now propped on a wood railing (a hitching rail) talking to one of the men from the auto show today. I try to regain my balance and steady my drink, but it's packed in here. Still not quite upright, I trip over the foot of a guy sitting at a table, flinging the contents of my martini into the air, and landing not-so-gracefully in his lap.

"Hello to you too," he smiles, and helps me awkwardly to my feet. But the cowboy directly behind him begins to turn around, his western-style shirt soaked with my martini, and I dive into the seated man again. "Whoa, you okay?" he laughs. I've just head-butted this guy twice. Not my strongest move. (And I was doing so well earlier.)

"So sorry," I say, still hiding and feigning to straighten his Pabst T-shirt. "Really, sorry." I peek over his shoulder at the cowboy. I can't quite see all of him under his beat-up cowboy hat, but he's trying to wipe the vodka off his shirt and inexplicably smiling. Wait, the hat has a scar…omigod. I move toward him.

"No problem, join us," the guy in the Pabst T-shirt says, standing and inadvertently stopping me from leaving. "I think you've met my friend." He gestures to the Boxer, who's headed toward us with a huge grin. "And I hear that girls fallin' in your lap is good luck," he chuckles, practically lifting me into a seat. (Thwarted by Pabst!) I stand as Abby, Claudia, and Bette walk up behind me, Abby muffling laughter. "Invite your friends; we're just ordering another round," Pabst says.

"We'd love to join. And add a vodka martini to that order—seems Syd lost hers," Bette says, pushing me back into the seat. She gives me the eyebrow that says, *I've got to get myself out there again, and this may be the perfect moment, so sit yourself down.* She can say a lot with that eyebrow.

"I'll just be right back," I whisper to Bette as she sits. I stand and point to the cowboy, who doesn't seem to be there anymore. Instead, there are umpteen cowboys in his place. Where did all of these cowboy hats come from all of a sudden? I look around for the one with a scar.

"Oh no you don't," she says out of the side of her mouth pulling me hard back into my seat once again. "I need a wingman, and you're the best." (It's all that Midwest personality.)

"I'll join too," says the Boxer, playfully pushing his friend Pabst next to Bette.

"Perfect," Bette says and gives me a "you're on" smile.

A few drinks deep and incredible wingman skills later, there's still no sign of the cowboy with the scarred hat. I've been scanning the crowd, but hopefully not noticeably.

"Who do you keep looking for?" Bette says. Note to self, I need to work on my subtlety.

Chapter 8
LUCKY GREEN LEATHER MOTOR JACKET

"OKAY, OKAY. Now more importantly, what should I have you wear to my wedding?" Claudia asks, changing the subject from work to more important things—her. She sits very seriously on a bar stool, clasps her hands together, and waits for an answer. "It's right around the corner."

It's not right around the corner unless that corner is five corners away, otherwise known as five months. But according to all her wedding planners, it is. Yes, I said "all." Claudia has four wedding planners, not counting her almost mother-in-law. (Oh yeah, Claudia doesn't need to work at the bar for money; her family's loaded. She works at the bar for fun and to spend time with us.)

"It's like fifty years away, Claud," Gus says, pulling her hair into a messy knot on the top of her head. Claudia's eye twitches. Not only does Claudia think the wedding is tomorrow, she despises when Gus calls her Claud. She's very particular about the pronunciation of her name. It's pronounced KLOW-dee-a. When I met KLOW-dee-a, she corrected me at least four times in her adorable accent (though it wasn't so adorable on the fourth time). I even repeated my name slowly; SID-nee, thinking that's just what you did in Brazil. That didn't go over well. With the correct pronunciation of *Claudia*, Gus is calling her a cloud. Much too frivolous for her taste, but Gus is oblivious. I think Cloud is a cute nickname, but if Claudia calls Bette "Bethany," we could go in circles.

Claudia continues, undeterred. "I found some really short, *muy caliente, muy colorido* dresses you might like." She pulls out her phone to search for photos. "You would be completely Brazilian-parade-wedding-ready in them!" We'll be dressed like peacocks if Claudia has her say, and I can't wait.

Claudia has decided (er, or her almost mother-in-law has) that it's un-Brazilian to have "bridesmaids," so we're all being encouraged to dress bright and "Siren-ish" to stand out. (So, basically we're bridesmaids.) Claudia even floated the idea of us wearing headdresses at one point. I sincerely hope so.

I absolutely won't be going to this wedding alone. No more weddings stag. Thank goodness for Claudia's extremely wealthy, very prestigious family, not to mention the fact that she's marrying one of the most famous artists to hit the scene recently. She'll be inviting us all with a plus one no matter what our status. "No economizing," she says in her truly Claudia way. Even though she won't have to, Claudia would rather skimp on flowers, food (not booze), or even the venue than invite us without guests. "The more the merrier. More family, more friends! We want everyone to celebrate!" she told us.

If I had been invited to Blake's wedding with a plus one, I might not have taken that last shot with Blake's dad, eaten all of Grandma's famous sweetbread, and woken up to Minnie mowing a chalk outline of my passed-out body on the front lawn. (With her tinted, gargantuan goggles and yellow construction vest, she looked like a bumblebee. A busybody bumblebee ready to buzz all up in my business.)

I encourage plus ones at all weddings.

"When you said short, I didn't think you meant *that* short," Bette gulps, staring at Claudia, who's holding up her phone proudly as the old country song "Trouble" by Travis Tritt winds up. I grab a cowboy hat from one of the beer taps—I never dance to this song without a hat—and jump on the bar. I start clogging very quickly in time with the song. I always freestyle to this one, and the girls holler as I ramp up the fancy footwork.

"Your fans, Sydney." Bette points to the faces gathering in the windows that cover the entire bar front. I wave at the noses pressed up against the glass while kicking up the footwork. They wave back as I pander to their applause. The song speeds to an end, and I swing down using a pole strategically placed behind the bar, hitting the last beat on the bar mats.

Bette shoots to the heavy wood door as Gus grabs the cowboy hat from my head and puts it on low over her eyes. "Now get me a drink, sissy," she says in her best "Old West" impression. I slide across the bar, putting her into a playful headlock. We tussle as Bette answers questions and tells the crowd to wait just a few minutes when we can officially open. I wave again and then use Gus' hand to wave some more. Gus cracks me in the thigh as soon as her hand is free, and I shriek as Bette hands me a handful of men's business cards.

"Seriously, how many business cards do you get in a day?" Bette asks, rolling her eyes and smacking Gus' thigh for smacking mine. Bette likes to keep us all in line.

I look at the cards suspiciously.

"Really, little chica, one of those might be your date for my wedding," Claudia clicks, now standing behind the bar polishing rocks glasses for her and Bette's day shift that will soon be in full swing.

Business cards are for business, not dates. Why do they give me business cards?! But I look at the men standing in the window just in case, and my eyes snag on something I don't often see in the city unless it's on one of us and behind the bar: a cowboy hat. Briefly, I make eye contact with the good-looking man underneath.

"Who's everyone bringing, anyway?" Claudia asks.

"No one—I'm done with men," Bette says, quickly. This isn't true, of course, but we've been having a hard time getting her back out there after her bad breakup.

"Syd?" Claudia asks, pulling my attention back.

"Not sure yet, but I have a plan," I say with confidence. I'm not sure what that plan is yet either, but I'll definitely have a plan, er, soon. I turn back to look for the guy in the cowboy hat but he's gone.

"We've got to get out of here before we get hammered by regulars, Syd," Gus says, completely ignoring the question about dates and who we're bringing to Claudia's wedding. She's dating several men right now, and wouldn't know how to choose.

We rip off our boots, hug the girls, and slide out the back door as the front doors open.

Thinking about my nonexistent plan and all those goals, I nervously tug at a white strand of fabric hanging from my faded, ripped jean shorts. It keeps tickling my thigh as we walk.

"Syd, stop doing that," Gus says, slipping on her oversized sunglasses. "Why are you so fidgety?"

"Oh, I don't know...YouTube?" I laugh, but really I'm worried about so much more...like a career! I mean, bartending brings in big money, and definitely pays the rent, but I've got to think long-term, right? Long-term. I've never thought long-term in relation to anything...jobs, boyfriends, saving money...

"Are you kidding? It's the best video ever, and you're going to be famous. Like America's next sweetheart. Ugh, it's disgusting—it'll make for a perfect story." Gus makes a large gesture in the air. "She was discovered in a garbage can."

"Gah, make it stop." I bury my face in my hands, but when I look again she's still going, making flashing motions with her hands as if my name is in lights on a marquis. Then she swipes my name off.

"Honestly, I should have thought of that myself. But I'm not really the sweetheart type. I'm more of a Lady Macbeth, really. You've got to know your strengths. And anyway, what you should be worried about is this heat. We've got to get out of here and to a pool, STAT!" She wipes sweat from her hairline and neck, and then for effect her whole upper body. "I'm so hot. No one should be allowed to be this hot without a pool. I swear, Syd, I'm going to have a pool in a backyard someday or kill me." If Gus puts it into the universe, it'll happen. I can already picture her backyard pool parties now.

Wait, that's what I've got to do, put my goals into the universe! I mean, I did fall into a garbage can when I put that skydiving thing out there, but it can't go wrong twice. I've just got to—

"Syd, are you listening?" Gus says, then blows cool air down her shirt and moans, but it's not even that hot—it's May. "By the way, you forgot your lucky jacket. I have to go sleep; I have an audition at six tonight." Gus squeezes me into a hug and heads to her apartment, where she'll inevitably sleep through her audition.

I walk back to the bar. I'm going to need all the luck I can get.

☆ ☆ ☆

"Omigod, Syd, he was *muy, muy caliente*," Claudia says, mock fanning herself and handing a customer a beer.

"Who?"

"Syd, who was that guy?" Bette says while shooing away a regular who's following her down the bar.

"What guy?"

"That accent," Claudia says. Claudia, of all people, pointing out an accent.

"What accent?"

"Syd, he was *so* your type," Bette says, handing me my lucky jacket. It's so like her to know exactly why I came back.

"Who was my type?" Seriously.

"I don't know, but he was hard to miss in that cowboy hat. He even took it off to talk to us." Bette swoons slightly, then moves down the bar a bit to serve Derek, who's madly in love with her. A regular winks at me. "It wasn't you," Bette says, and I swear she didn't even see him do it. Eyes in the back of her head, that one.

Anyway, my interest is piqued. A cowboy hat?

"I don't know who he was either, but he said he came in to check on you," Claudia says, making a sizzle noise and fanning herself again.

"He was worried about your head. He mentioned the fall, so it could be anyone at this point! Hold on," Bette says. She grabs her phone hidden behind the Tito's Vodka bottle and walks back to me. "Syd, you're up to 127,000 views!" She smiles so hard it turns cartoonish.

"Are you serious? Come on, this is so not funny." I look at her phone. I'm going to need some of that vodka.

"I sent your YouTube sensation to the group text," she says.

"Wait, what? You sent it to all the Sirens, so basically the whole world?" I repeat, just to be sure. Nevermind some of that vodka—I'm going to need the whole bottle. I take her phone and push "play" as if pulled by some force to watch it again. Train. Wreck.

"Of course I did! Abby and Greg think it's hilarious... look!" She reaches over and moves the screen on her phone. Abby's boyfriend Greg is pretty stuffy, so picturing him laughing makes it all the worse. She points excitedly at the phone now featuring a photo. He actually has tears in his eyes. "Oh and some others, and posted it on social, so yeah, the whole world," Bette says, and chortles. It turns into a slightly more sinister laugh. Bette is on every social network there is. Awesome.

And Zoey's in *Australia* right now, so it's already overseas. Zoey— speaking of my yoga skills and why I was ever caught in a yoga class in the first place—is abroad, helping at some yogi-guru-meditation-never-catch-me-there-in-a-million-years retreat. It's spreading like an epidemic. I watch myself fall into a heap again and feel Bette's cartoon grin spreading even wider across her face. This is so not funny, it's actually funny.

"What is Boobs McGee doing over there?" I point to the lovey-dovey couple on Bette's phone screen. While everyone is coming to my rescue, Boobs is laughing so hard that she's bent over, and her breasts are all but falling out. It's contagious. Bette and I break into a ball of fits. Even I can't help laughing at the video. I give her back her phone, which she immediately hands to Derek down the bar. I threaten him with my fist, knowing he knows everyone at my gym. He laughs.

I'm totally stuffing my bra before the *Today* show.

I head for the back door again, throw on my lucky green leather motor jacket, and smile at the customers looking at our photos plastered on the barn wood walls.

"Oh, Syd," Bette says while pouring a beer on tap. I turn, holding the door open. "He said he'll find you." Then she mouths, "So hot."

Chapter 9
A VISION

MINNIE AND Doc have always said that I teeter on the edge. I don't even know what that means, but they say it a lot. And I won't even mention what The Sister thinks. She's been trying to off me since birth, so I'll forgo any thoughts and feelings from her court. But it's time I prove I'm just as good a Shag as the rest. (That didn't come out exactly as planned, but you know what I mean.)

Jumping out of the cab, I pop into the bodega by my apartment to pick up a few essential items for my plan. If I'm going to learn from my mistakes, I've got to remember them, and, like Gus, I've got to put my goals into the universe. Or in this case, put them on the wall in my bedroom.

I can't believe Bette and Claudia didn't get the guy with the cowboy hat's name. Apparently he was in a hurry and there was a rush on Pabst. Pabst! Thwarted by Pabst. Our cheapest beer.

Claudia just texted me, telling me not to worry—that I could find him because his cowboy hat had a sewn-up rip on it, making it easy to spot. Claudia. Thinking I would find a guy in New York City because his cowboy hat had a "flaw" is hilarious and after all, it's a cowboy hat in the city. But let's be honest, they would have forgotten to tell me about the cowboy if I hadn't left my jacket. The lucky streak continues!

A little luck and a vision board. Nothing can go wrong now.

I'll prove I don't live on the edge. I live smartly with all my ducks in a gaggle, or whatever that saying is. By the time the family visits on Fourth of July weekend, it's going to be perfect, just perfect. It will show them that I'm super put together and plan on big things. Really big. I mean, I haven't quite figured out all of those things yet, but just picture super big things.

I grab some gossip magazines and a *Real Simple* magazine. Life should be "real simple," so I assume I will find some great inspiration in there.

I see a pair of Christian Louboutins in one of the style mags and decide those will go on the board immediately. I love Christian Louboutins and vow to own a pair. I've even started a Christian fund.

I spot my favorite homeless guy, Godfrey, passing by the bodega window. He stops to make goofy faces and do an interpretive dance—not quite Broadway worthy, but entertaining all the same. He's a skinny, lanky, graying man with a hint of dementia—but who *doesn't* have a hint of dementia these days? He told me once he earns enough money to fly somewhere tropical every winter. And sure enough, I never see him in the winter and when he reappears he always has a deep tan. That's something to aspire to. I make a mental note to find a palm tree and put it on my board.

I wave at him like a ten-year-old and flash a huge smile. Throwing some pin-tacks onto the counter along with the magazines, I pay the sweet cashier at the mom and pop shop as Godfrey waits to hold the door for me.

"Afternoon, Godfrey!" I bubble, dropping seventy-one cents, my change from the tacks and mags, and a couple extra bucks into his cup. I'm not exactly sure that's his name, but he's never corrected me.

"It's Good Ray," he shouts after me and I wave over my shoulder. I must have misheard him.

"Yes, it *is* a good day!" I sing back. Isn't he nice? I've never noticed before but maybe he's Australian. "G'day," I yell, practicing his colloquialism.

A gorgeous couple walks by and I smile as a reflex. Again on reflex, I gasp when I see their huge-headed baby in the open stroller. Holy noggin patrol. I absolutely adore kids, but babies still give me pause. I'm really glad I didn't make any wild goals about having babies in my twenties. That would be seriously crazy for an eleven-year-old who never even babysat.

I step up to my ornate building door just a few blocks away.

"Do you happen to be Sydney Shag? Apartment 10?" an out-of-breath voice says. I turn quickly to see a man on a bike carrying a huge package.

"Yes! That would be me," I smile at the courier. "Perfect timing."

"A package from Tray Wiserbicki. Just initial here."

When he says Tray's last name I nearly snort. Tray hasn't used his real last name since college. It's just Tray Wise, famous costume designer, now.

"Thanks so much." I smile even bigger and initial SOS.

"Are you going to be able to handle that?" he asks. "It's kinda big."

"Got it. Thanks," I say.

"SOS, that's a first. You sure you don't need help? Or saving?" he smiles flirtatiously. I always include the *O* for my middle name, Orie, which was handed down to me from Grandma Shag. Together it's the International Morse code distress signal, Save Our Ship. It can't be a coincidence. Minnie often says "Save Our Sydney," but I don't really need saving...unless it's from a prince, and I'm formulating a plan for that.

He drops his card on the box. "Just in case," he winks and zips off on his bike. The package is light but extraordinarily big. I hold the box, gossip magazines, pin-tacks, and cowboys while fighting my key into the door. Jose steps out of the kitchen from the bar below my apartment just as I coax it open.

"Hello, *linda*. Want some help?"

"I'm fine," I say breezily, even though I probably *could* use some help.

"Let me at least hold the door for you," he says and smiles. Spanish. I thought for months he was calling me

Linda, when really he was calling me *linda*, which means pretty. I took French in high school. Doc says he tried to talk me into Spanish, the second most commonly spoken language in the United States, but that I kept saying something about a prince and needing to speak really sexy. Probably not my strongest moment.

"Thanks, Jose. So sweet of you." I struggle through the first door with everything.

"Are you sure you don't want me to carry it up?" he asks, holding the second door and looking worried.

"Oh, it's really light, just big. I've got it, thanks!"

"See ya, Syd," he says, waving. I trudge up the stairs awkwardly, barely able to see each step; however, I did notice a piece of mail hopelessly crammed in but still jutting out of my mailbox. Full again?! More bills and probably my rent notice. I'll get that later. Much later.

I push open the door to my cute fourth floor apartment (that is somehow five flights up), drop my things in the living room, and grab scissors from my entryway catch-all to slice open the box. A huge white cloud of tulle bursts out. A crinoline. I love crinolines. I dig through the puffy, white, fabulous mess and find the uniform on a hanger. I inspect it, then hang both on the crown molding of the French doors between the living room and bedroom. My costume for the auto show tomorrow.

Someone should have told me I would always be in costume; I could have saved a lot of money on college and just joined the circus.

So much for that BA in journalism and mass communications including a minor—much to my advisor's unadvising—in theater studies and performance arts with an emphasis in drinking.

I pull off my lucky jacket, throw it on my favorite big leather chair, and take the vision board necessities into the bedroom.

"Harold!" I croon. I feed Harold, my overly supportive orange ball of cute. Harold's a fish. His bowl is on the dresser with an impressive view of both huge windows. He does an acrobatic flip. I can tell he already likes my idea. I grab the corkboard that I purchased during a sale at the Container Store from behind the bed and sit on the floor. I knew I would need this someday. I immediately start cutting into the magazines and other items in my room.

Gossip magazines never get anyone's best angle even when they're being nice. So beautiful Meghan Markle, who's arm in arm with Harry, Prince of "Off My List of Eligible Royalty," has a big nose in this snapshot. (How did they ever manage that?) I cut around Meghan and hold up her almost perfect picture, admiring it. She's classy, and cutting edge, and it's not like she found Harry right away—she had her frogs first. She's perfect for my vision board. Good thing *People* magazine is doing a special on princesses because the classy Catherine, Her Royal Highness (or Kate, which wasn't as catchy for a queen-to-be) is on the next page. Grace Kelly, Princess of Monaco, is going on the board too alongside my favorite functioning drunks, Kathie Lee and Hoda—best career inspo ever—and the always inspiring Louisa May

Alcott, remarkable author of *Little Woman*. Miss Alcott proved she didn't need a man to take care of her even in that day and age. See, not so much pressure to get married after all! (Even though I totally think she was a lesbian.)

I pin up the stunning and towering Christian Louboutins and add a few incredible red carpet gowns to the board. I mean, a YouTube sensation needs to look good, doesn't she? (Especially since the video isn't as blurry as I originally thought.) Excited to find this doozy, I pin the phrase "go big or go home" right next to a backyard inspiration, complete with rope swing and pond. Not unlike where I grew up. That's for the future, though, obviously, for now it's city lights and big nights. Where else am I going to wear those red soles when I get them?

Grabbing some colorful scraps of paper, I write some good rules to live by that I so astutely came up with since coining the gem "don't just stand there" and pin them up as well. If you're going to have goals, you've got to have rules to ascertain them.

I will learn from my mistakes. I will learn from my mistakes. (And it's always good to have a mantra.)

Pounding a nail into the wall and placing it proudly, I step back and look at the Pinterest-board-worthy creation. It's highlighted perfectly by my gold-metallic-striped accent wall, and I feel even more inspired than I thought. Also, the big moose head hovering above it (a drunken vintage store purchase with Gus; I mean, I couldn't just leave him there, though he's a bit more menacing than expected) gives it a certain *get this done or else* feel.

I pull off my short-shorts, toss them onto the large, over-stuffed bed, and have a quick shower. With a towel hugging my bits and a Marilyn Monroe towel sweep in my hair, I grab my DVF wrap dress. Thank goodness I hung it on the closet door for easy access instead of inside the overly jammed space. What I wouldn't give for a walk-in. I toss it on the bed too and slip on a pair of thin knee-high socks.

I admire the board for just a moment, then pin the dried bouquet smack in the center of my masterpiece and stand back again for a good look. Then, ceremoniously, I unfold the crinkled skull and crossbones stamped paper and tack up my list of goals.

"There!" I proclaim. "Well, what do you think, Harold? It's looking good, right?" I mean, there are a couple spaces left for a few more inspirational images, but I'll find those later.

I kneel on the floor and crawl under the bed, digging for my thigh-high boots, yelling, "Harold, can you believe the girls didn't get the name of the guy who asked about me? It could have been my future husband!" I laugh but hit my head on the bed frame because, really, he could have been my perfect partner.

I can't see a thing under here but feel instead for the suede. I toss out a pair of gray knee-high boots, nope, sneakers, nope, slippers, nope, my favorite jeans…wait, I've been looking for these for weeks! Fabulous find. Finally, I feel the suede and pull out my sexy thigh-highs. I sit at the end of the bed and yank them on. These boots are striking and go perfectly with the short DVF wrap I've chosen for tonight. Truth be told, I had it shortened. (Okay, I have everything shortened.)

"Harold, I know I seem picky, but really, don't you think something's been missing in the guys I've dated?" Harold paces back and forth and I can see he's pondering my question while I situate my boots. I throw on the wrap dress and move over to the dresser to get right in his face. "I need someone more like a prince, right?" He wiggles his big orange tail fin in excitement. "I mean, just look at Grace Kelly and Meghan. " We look at them. "And I've always looked good in a tiara, Harold." I laugh. He seems to nod his head up and down. I give him a little extra fish food treat because I love when he agrees with me. He wiggles his handsome tail fin again. (My board is helping already!)

I finish my hair and makeup next to Harold in one of two huge standing mirrors in my little abode, thickening my eyelashes with my favorite L'Oreal Paris Voluminous Mascara. (The look of the tube might not be earth-shattering, but this stuff is magic. It's basically va-va-voom in a bottle, and at six bucks a pop, I can wear, wear, wear! And then wear some more. See, I'm already saving money!) I smile sweetly in the mirror, thicken them again, smile again (but this time as if I am flirting with a really good-looking prince or that hot mystery man with the scarred cowboy hat), thicken again, make a kiss face, wish I had pouty lips, thicken again, make a wide-eyed scared face (thinking of Old Beard Mountain-Hill), and then mess my hair perfectly.

"I'll find a prince, maybe even tonight," I say in my best Mae West impersonation while practicing a come-hither stare. "I mean, with or without the crown, I can always get one from Tray," I giggle. Harold seems to nod his head up and down in agreeance, so I pop another flake into his bowl. "Bye, Harold," I call, grabbing my fabulous pink Prada clutch. I push through the crinoline and run out the door.

Chapter 10
TROUBLE

"HOPE EVERYONE'S having a great night!" a woman's twangy voice booms over a microphone as the live music breaks. Cheers erupt in the packed bar. "It's come to our attention that we have some famous ladies in our midst." We look at one another immediately.

Gus takes the auto show guy's Bud Light and downs it. I don't think he's finished a beer since they joined us at the table. "Here we go," she says and pulls her hair from its knot. Thick and nearly black, it lands with a silent thud onto the name of our bar on the back of her T-shirt. The T-shirt we're all wearing tonight.

Famous. Our New York City bar isn't just any bar. It's the kind of place that hires the best—two-steppers and dancers who cannot only perform intricate choreography and clog, but also pour a mean drink.

"We would like to invite the girls of our new New York City partners onto the bar!" The microphone reverberates as the crowd ramps up the clapping. So it's true, Boss is planning to open a bar here in Austin.

"We'll be just a minute," I say to the Boxer and pull Bette from her new prospect, Pabst, whom she's been calling anything but his actual name, Wade.

"My skirt is definitely too short," Bette says, to no one in particular.

We pop up onto the cleared bar with the help of all the cowboys standing at the ready. It's a bachelor party! That's where all the cowboy hats came from at once. But I still don't see the one with a scar.

The baseball cap leads the band into an uproarious intro, and as we hit four solid beats with our boot heels, a fiddler appears (she's actually the bass player; Austin is dripping with musical talent), and our song rips into a crescendo.

The choreography comes easily because the moves are so ingrained with all our rehearsals, another requirement of a bar like ours. I have fun with the crowd, smiling, pointing, and winking while seamlessly turning, chasseing, bumping, and kicking. My favorite part of this job is the crowd. The people smile and go wild while we perform. As it turns out, all those times Minnie talked me into entertaining her friends—volunteering to sing at the farmer's market, read stories at the nursing home, performing in church plays (any church; we weren't even members), while The Sister got her hair done—paid off.

The song purrs to a close as the decibel level in the bar increases. The woman takes the mic again and introduces all of us to loud applause and cheers. We each give a corresponding hello from the bar top: Claudia shimmies her chest just enough, Bette flips her spiraled curls off her shoulder and smirks, I give them my signature hip bump, Gus puts her thumbs into her jean pockets and casually extends everyone a kiss, while Abby gives a little whoop.

We're handed a round of shots as we file down from the bar, and to more applause, we raise our shots, tap the bar with them, and knock 'em back. Together, we flip and slam the empty glasses onto the bar.

The bachelor party bombards us on our way back to the table as the recognizable tune of "Trouble" rumbles from the band.

"Where do you think you're going, Sydney?" the woman's twang rings out. "A little bird told me not to let you get away…" The Sirens give me up and the bachelors, all wearing western-style yoke, two-patch-pocket shirts, lift me back atop the bar.

"I'm going to need a cowboy hat," I smile, shouting over the crowd.

"Somebody get that girl a cowboy," the bandleader croons, winking at the crowd. He stalls the start of the song with the first riff while several cowboy hats are offered up. One is thrown and I catch it.

It has a scar.

Chapter 11
TRIPLE, QUADRUPLE CRAP

HE SWEEPS me into his muscled arms and tells me how *bling* I look. How what? *Bling.* What? He moves his hand along my neck and into my hair and leans in toward my lips. I close my eyes and… *bling, bling, bling.* I open one eyeball.

Pillow.

Duvet.

Headache.

Crap.

Still in my thigh-high suede boots from two hours and God-knows-how-many martinis ago, I hear the bleeping *bling* again. I stir slightly, pulling the heavy duvet over my nearly naked body, and plant my face firmly in my pillow. *Bling, bling, bling,* my phone keeps shouting. I should never have put "bling" as my ringtone.

Unaware of anything, let alone why my phone would be ringing at the crack of dawn or how I actually made it into my bed, I wait briefly as my senses return to a conscious state. I hear its muffled screams again and venture to guess it's coming from inside the pink Prada. Struggling to lift my head and peek out from under the duvet, I focus on the clutch. Then I reach for the Prada, knocking over a last-ditch-effort-not-to-be-hung-over water bottle. Obviously it was full, until I so cleverly knocked it over, because I feel ruined. The water cascades down the stack of novels by my bed.

Double crap.

Bette thinks it's a peculiar habit that I leave so many books by, and sometimes in, my bed (including at least one under my pillow) but I always remind her of the possibility of osmosis. So even when I'm not reading, I'm reading. But I suppose I wouldn't have gotten them wet if they were on a shelf.

With my right hand now dangling over the bed, I grasp my clutch and pull it toward me. I sit up, but only barely so as to not rouse myself too much, fling my other arm over the bed, and dig through the business cards, money, Mac lip gloss, and receipts. Finally I just dump them onto the century-old hardwood floor to find the latest, overly smart iPhone. I have to hit like twelve different things before I can say hello. Apparently it's smarter than me.

"Hi, honey," Gus' drunk voice purrs. "Get down here, we're going to Austin."

What? Triple, quadruple crap and kick my ass, I thought I set the alarm.

"Be down in a sec!" I scream into the dumb, smartest iPhone ever.

I throw the duvet off my nearly naked, boot-wearing body, fling my legs out of bed, and start moving. Unfortunately, my blurry, hung-over mind doesn't keep up with my body and I wipe out next to my possessions from the pink clutch.

I get a closer look at its contents now that I'm uncomfortably eye-to-floor. A $276 tab from some bar in the Bowery? I remember that Bette, Gus, and I went for an I-didn't-die-skydiving-or-expire-in-a-garbage-can drink, but what were we doing in the Bowery and, more importantly, why did I pay this tab? Grabbing the receipt for a closer look, I see more horror. Why did I leave a $100 tip on top of that? Gah. I'll get to the bottom of it later. I need to pack, and fast.

I peel off a card stuck to my cheek as I plow to my feet and look again at **Bubba & Bubba Vet Care Clinic, Goodtown, TX**. It's following me. I quickly tack the card to my vision board in case I need rescuing from a veterinarian, but really because it fills space. There it is, on my fabulous vision board, right next to Rule #2. Rule #2! Omigod, I need to pack!

I've always been a last-minute packer. In college, I almost gave Minnie a severe anxiety attack when I left for my study abroad program after only thirty minutes of packing at 4 a.m. for a 7 a.m. flight. I can do this.

"Aaah, what's the temperature in Austin?" I yell while tearing clothes out of my seriously stuffed closet. I have no idea what to pack.

"The temperature in Austin, Texas, is ninety-two degrees and sunny." Startled, I knock a shoebox of swimsuits onto my head.

"Alexa," I say, menacingly. Alexa always startles me. An ex set her up as a birthday surprise. It was a surprise all right; I thought another woman was in the room.

She ignores me. But she's already helped; now I know the temp is sky high in Austin, and she did shock me into finding my swimsuits! I grab my tiniest bikini and some skimpy clothes that will hopefully fit if I don't eat anything with carbs. I look at the bikini bottom. I'll have to forgo eating all together. I throw them into my fabulous but obnoxious heart-covered travel bag, which I at least had the forethought to dig out of my overstuffed closet yesterday afternoon.

It's a good thing I'm a professional under-pressure packer, seeing that I do this more often than not. I feel confident about what I have in my bag until I pass by the vision board again.

Rule #2
BYLBD

Bring Your Little Black Dress. I almost forgot—again! I grab one of the at least seventeen little black dresses hanging in my closet. Always have a little black dress with you at all times. It seems obvious, but I always forget my toothbrush, which also seems obvious, so seriously, write this down. Trust me, you'll need a little black dress when you least expect it. And if you forget your LBD, I promise it will be the one time you do need it and you'll end up at an impromptu high school reunion wearing a Christmas sweater with a big, red, knit ball where Rudolph's nose should be. It made quite the impression. Reference: Christmas two years ago.

I had just pulled into Butter Creek when Penny Wood (now Taylor) called, screaming how happy, happy, happy she was that I was home. That I would never believe it, but everyone, just everyone, was going to Whiskey River, a local tavern, that night and I simply could not miss it. I pulled out everything in my carry-on. Why did I need so many pairs of socks, underwear, and thermals? Butter does get cold, but I had nothing formidable to wear. I stood in my bedroom hoping for my Fairy Godmother to arrive, twirl me around, and make me look cute for the big night out. Anything to make me look smart and successful. Instead, my Fairy Mom skipped into the room, a little manic, and gushing about the new sweater she'd gotten me and how it would save the day. It wasn't new—she found it in the attic and I had worn it at least ten years earlier—but since my boobs haven't budged, it still fit. Minnie looked so excited that I couldn't turn it down. I could hear The Sister laughing all the way from the other room. The Sister, who could have intervened and let me borrow something from her two huge suitcases full of clothes.

I left the house in my Rudolph the Red-Nosed-Ball Reindeer sweater with The Sister snorting, Doc looking worried (but quickly distracted by the dogs), and Minnie all but waving a wand. I planned on telling everyone that the new style in New York City was vintage Christmas sweaters (which it is, two years later) and that Ralph Lauren was really getting into it (which he is, two years later). I would have pulled it off too if Penny and Kat Deeds (now Jones) hadn't called me out immediately, noticing I'd worn the sweater to our seventh grade Christmas concert. Leave it to your best friends (since kindergarten!), but we laughed all night and I got to see "everyone, just everyone."

So, good luck with the Fairy Godmother thing—I've been waiting for her for years. Think of your LBD as a Fairy Godmother, and she'll never let you down.

Then I remember,

Rule #3
ALWAYS HAVE YOUR PASSPORT

...and throw it in my bag.

Who knew you had to have a passport to go to Mexico? When did that start? I'll never forget my passport again after the car trunk fiasco. I bring it everywhere now, just in case. WebMD says anyone can become claustrophobic given the right circumstances.

Always have your passport even if you're going to Butter to visit the Shag family. You never know when someone will whisk you off to Paris. I mean, everyone dreams of being swept off their feet, right? Always be prepared. *Je voudrais la la la!*

I'm moving at light speed, and if you're wondering about my thigh-highs, yes, I'm still wearing them; I've decided they're perfect for a flight to Austin. Actually, I just tried to get them off, and they won't budge. Kill.

I throw on a little T-shirt dress, my lucky green jacket (of course), and black I'm-super-cool vintage Ray Ban sunglasses, which will cover the slept-on eye makeup that's giving me the always-attractive raccoon look.

"Harold, you're the best fish in the whole fish world!" I feed my favorite fish and respond to his obvious statement with, "I do look stunning, don't I? I knew you'd think so." I smile, lowering my sunglasses to get a good look at my little orange ball. His eyes bulge rather largely. "Okay, I'll keep my sunnies on." I shove them back up my nose and give him a little extra fish food treat because I already miss him. I hit the lights in the bedroom and push through the crinoline to the living room. Omigod, the crinoline—the costume!

I rip open my almost full carry-on and shove the huge white fluff and uniform into it. Shove. Shove. Almost. I sit on it, and sit and sit to make it fit.

Finally all packed, I sing goodbye to Flipper, my oddly shaped, rather abnormally large plant (I call him Flipper, Minnie calls him Philodendron) I found on Horatio and Washington Street and stumble out my apartment door. I drag the stuffed bag down the stairs, but on the third floor I discover I can just throw my bag down one flight at a time. So much easier...why haven't I thought of this before?

"Sydney?" I hear a muffled yell coming from downstairs. A broad-shouldered, wild-haired man wearing sunglasses is picking up my bag as I get to the lower stairs.

One Eye Joe.

Rent.

Shi...

"Jovan," I say, smiling brightly and wondering why his hair is so out of place, very unusual for him.

"I knew it was you—I could see a ray of light shining down the stairwell," he says, with serious syrup in his voice.

"What are you doing here so early in the morning?" I ask, pulling my T-shirt dress a little lower.

"Syd, I heard you locked yourself out again. You need to get me a key, then you can just call me whenever you need to," he smiles, jangling the keys clipped to his belt loop.

"Oh, Joe, I know, I've been meaning to do that..." I haven't. Now I remember getting home last night. I crawled through Elan's window. Brilliant.

"You know, you're causing some damage to Elan's window. I have to fix it again this morning."

"Oh gosh, really? I'm so sorry," I say, but I really need to get past him.

"No big deal, anything for you, my little bimboshell." Again, he means bombshell, I swear. Lost in translation. "So get me a key, and—" he makes *the* face, omigod, here it comes— "and get yourself a husband. Look, your husband would gladly carry your bag downstairs for you." I try to take my heart bag from him. "Don't worry 'bout it, I got it, I got it," he says, smoothing his hair unsuccessfully with his free hand and heading down the last of the stairs with my bag in the other. "When are you going to get married and settle down? Listen, you won't be young forever, and climbing through young men's windows is dangerous." One Eye Joe turns to look at me. "And those genes, Syd." He lowers his sunglasses and gives me a once-over. "Sunshine, you need to have some kids. Pass those genes on. Kids are remarkable." The glass eye doesn't work when I have my shades on, but I slip on the next step anyway, showing even more incompetence.

"Jovan, seriously, it's way too early for this." I stagger back to a balanced state, but I'm serious. I can barely focus on the stairs, let alone think about babies with vodka seeping from my pores like this.

Where Jovan is from, somewhere in Italy, they probably get married at seventeen, so I'm probably ancient. But he's right; my friends in Butter are all happily married with, like, twenty kids. It doesn't matter if none of my friends here in the city are married. Well, except Claudia and her recent engagement. She really threw a wrench in my statistics but at least she held out until thirty and that's still a few years off for the rest of us. Remember *Little Women* and Miss Alcott! (Omigod, everyone probably thinks I'm a lesbian.)

But I'm not deterred. I'm quite proud of all my accomplishments so far. I'm well-traveled, I've held really exciting jobs (some less exciting than others, like when Kat's dad talked us into detassling and roguing corn, or the time I was hired to seat people for the "wine experience" at our local vineyard and they didn't tell me I had to be dressed as a grape), and most importantly, I've lived, really lived! (Oscar nod here.) But to some, because I'm not married, I'm practically an old maid at the ripe young age of—

"Syd, you need help?" One Eye Joe asks. Apparently I'm unable to daydream and walk at the same time while hung over.

"Oh, I'm good." I smile and start moving again.

Anyway, I decided to forget my actual age after my twenty-first birthday. Grandma Shag has always suggested losing the digits, and to this day no one knows her age. So, I figure I lost enough brain cells that night to alcohol that I may as well use it to my advantage. Memory loss relating to age, name, and important things like the fact that you're not a professional figure skater (I have a winter birthday, remember) can happen when you drink tequila.

Rule #4
NEVER MIX ALCOHOL (ESPECIALLY TEQUILA)... YOU WILL DIE!

I really blame Ivy Andersen, my college roommate, not to be confused with Marcy Moore from Butter Creek (with the boobs), for telling me Jungle Juice was "no biggy." "Practically Kool-Aid," she said as I downed a whole red-plastic-frat-boy-cup of it. Kool-Aid, my Michelle

Kwan-interpreting ass. They had spiked the "Kool-Aid" with vodka. *A lot* of vodka and rum and whatever else was lying around. Then, just when I felt tipsy, Ivy decided we should do shots of tequila. Which, of course, I thought was a brilliant idea. It was a hilarious night even if for the next few years she invited friends to my birthday party with two photos: one of me trying to do a triple Lutz on Lake Laverne and the other of my passed-out legs lying just outside our bathroom door. I vowed never to mix drinks, especially with tequila, ever again.

"Okay, okay, get me a key, my little bimboshell. I don't want to have to keep fixing windows," One Eye Joe says. He opens both doors to the building for me and hands my bag to the driver.

"Thanks, Jovan, you're the best. You know I just don't want to wake you at 4 a.m.—that's kind of when I tend to lose keys and crawl through windows." I try to forget the husband and kids comments, and about my blurred vision and fuzzy head. At least I didn't have tequila last night. Did I? No, no, I would have my head in the toilet if I had.

"Oh, don't worry about that. It could be fun, maybe make the wife jealous," he laughs. His keys rattle alarmingly loudly (or it could be all the martinis pounding my skull?) as he turns to go back inside. "So, get a husband and get me a key, and no more windows. Okay, Sydney girl?"

"Okay, Jovan. I'll see what I can do," I say, walking backward, trying to get to the finish line.

"Great." He spots his hair in the ornate iron and glass door, and startled by its unshapely appearance, he nearly jumps. He slicks it perfectly into place this time and then turns back around. "Oh, and this one's on me," he says, taking out a perfect roll of one hundred dollar bills. He comes back over and pushes one into my hand. "Get to wherever you're going safe."

"Oh no, Jovan," I say, trying to push the bill back, but he's already back to the door and moving inside. "Okay, and no more damaging windows. Thanks, Jovan!"

First, it's nearly June, and I haven't quite put together rent (more like I've spent it twice over), which he never asks about. But, he does know I'm good for it; he knows where I work. (If only I loved paying rent as much as my LBDs, heels, and whole closet. And martinis.) Second, there's a huge tab on my credit card (martinis), so this will come in handy. Third, I'm wearing my lucky jacket. I shove the crisp bill into my jacket pocket. (Fourth, he's never getting a key.)

Omigod, I didn't remind Tray to feed Harold while I'm gone. I make a quick call, after hitting another thirteen buttons to "Tray Lunatic Wiserbikikiki" (that's how he's saved in my phone), as the driver heaves my bag into the trunk. I leave Tray a voicemail telling him he has fish food duty and to call me while he's in my apartment so I can scream another "bye" to my little BFF.

The driver opens the back door of the black SUV for me and there she sits, sunglasses riding low on her nose, cigarette in hand and a Bud Light between her legs. Little hiccups escape as she greets me with a wide smile and a hazy-eyed look over the top of her delicious Guccis. I crawl in beside her.

Gus has enlightened me on the importance of showing skin. I used to wear shockingly large clothes on my small frame. (It was the style in Butter. Duh. I was so cool.) I just wish I could have figured this out in my teen years. Imagine what I could have accomplished by now. Gus takes another long drag on her cigarette, then flings it out the window unfinished.

"Sorry, Syd, I know you hate cig smoke." With a couple large hand sweeps she wafts the rest of the smoke out the window. "I couldn't find my vape, and I was desperate." She can never find her vape.

"Gus, I've been wondering…" I situate myself in the seat, pull my hair into a high pony, and pull my T-shirt dress down over the tops of my boots because the air conditioning is on full blast. Gus is probably having another heat stroke. "Who do you think the guy in the cowboy—"

"I hooked up with that ridiculous, pompous finance guy last night," Gus says as the SUV jolts into forward motion. Totally ignoring or not hearing my need to know who… "I needed a beer and a smoke STAT. Breakfast of champs. What was I thinking?" Gus doesn't want an answer; she just wants me to agree that it was a horrible idea, so I do. Gus only falls for musicians, artists, or bartenders, so this is a real slip for her. Though I should probably text her mom—she'd be ecstatic.

We all tend to like bartenders, considering that's how our group of girlfriends came together. But truthfully, and don't tell Gus, she won't listen, you should never date one. Bartenders are a rowdy, late-night group of wildcats who can talk you into anything.

"I can't believe I'm up this early. Did you have something to do with booking this?" Gus takes a swig of her Bud Light, crunching the sides of the can to summon more liquid to her mouth.

"Hmm, I don't think so." I totally did. I like flying early because the planes have probably just been checked for missing parts and broken wings and all that important stuff.

Gus bartends as many nights as possible and sleeps nearly all day unless she has an audition, and even then she usually sleeps. That's the only time she uses August, her full name. She says it sounds famous. But she assures us that when she is a big stage actress and indie-movie star (indie—the only way to be true to your craft, according to Gus), fans will know who her closest friends are because they'll call her Gus. The Sirens went to her last performance (the one she booked after the Benedryl mishap) and she was quite a standout, though it could be because everyone else was a mute Greek Chorus. She likes to do experimental pieces.

When we're behind the bar together, we're like Kathleen Turner and Sandra Dee. Technically, I should give in and bartend even more often like she does. The money is unreal! (And why I can pay my rent even when I shop too much.) But, I teach fitness classes too and love it. Plus it evens out the booze-to-bootcamp lifestyle ratio.

Gus fiddles with her thin sweatpants, which are rolled down low at the waist, and pulls the bottoms of them up to her knees. We debate about how our night actually unfolded as I try, I fear in vain, to fix my eye makeup. We decide the night is relatively clear up until the Bowery, where unfortunately we both go a bit, shall I say, vague.

"What's with the $276 tab, not including the $100 tip I left on my already completely overrun credit card? Was I just buying rounds for everyone? Omigod, please tell me it was stolen." I jab my eye as the SUV hits a bump. And why is my credit card always overrun? It's not like I don't have cash from bartending stashed in the closet. I've got to get this stuff in order! She focuses on the roof of the black Range Rover, conjuring extremely important details. My mistake; she just nodded off. "Gus? Gus?" I poke her.

"What? Oh, look in your left boot," she says, coming to and taking another swig of her beer. She doesn't comment on the fact that I'm still wearing them from last night. "Damn your small feet, or I would borrow those insane boots," she adds. She said the exact same thing last night.

"I tried to get these bad boys off but they wouldn't budge. Help me pull," I say, struggling. Comfortable, yes, but I can never get them off without a battle.

Sipping her bottomless beer with one hand, she pulls with the other while I brace myself ungracefully against the SUV door. I notice the driver peer into the rearview mirror. Not the most flattering of positions, I realize. He muffles a laugh. Most don't know what to do with the Sirens but we tend to get away with murder, hence the Bud Light in a moving vehicle and all around bad passenger behavior. My boot flies off and, scandalously, a wad of cash rains down into the SUV, including my credit card. The driver is most impressed, as am I.

"You should save that trick for a trip to Vegas," he laughs.

"There," Gus says, "is your money."

Phew!

"Makin' it rain." I draw out "rain" as if I'm drunk in a Vegas Strip Club. Actually, I think I *am* still drunk. Gus hiccups. We could be in Vegas right now.

The Sirens have always shared tabs, which explains the receipt and the cash. If we're going to blow money, then we vow to do it together with a drink in hand. But I'm elated. Jovan will need rent soon, and if I'd blown that much on drinks for one night, I might as well hurl my body out of this moving vehicle and jump off the Triboro Bridge that we're now gliding over. A wave of panic sweeps over my body even with the cash and I focus on my current aspirational mantra: *I am smart, and money will come. I am smart, and money will come.*

I forgot my toothbrush.

Chapter 12
THIGH HIGHS AND FLYING THE FRIENDLY SKIES

NEW YORK CITY: YESTERDAY, FRIDAY MAY 26

ONCE IN the airport, ultra-organized Bette, who's dragging what looks like the largest piece of luggage known to woman, meets us at the kiosks. Her bag may just be the size of one of my closets. She's been ecstatic and anxious about our little vacation from the city for over a month. And, always organized, she probably packed two weeks ago. She's like Minnie's long lost child.

Bette swings her "Neverfull" Louis Vuitton, which is always full, with such authority that as soon as she steps to the checked luggage counter, she's taken care of with light speed. And she's been talking nonstop in her childhood Brooklyn accent since spotting us and doesn't miss a beat even to intimidate the clerk with that eyebrow of hers.

"...and you know what else? I decided to make macaroni and cheese last night; I'm going to kill you guys for making me drink so much. I almost ate the whole box! It's a good thing I passed out. Then, I couldn't find my favorite dress this morning. Omigod, Gus, if you stole that from me, I'm going to kill you." (Gus did.) "And I'm also going to kill whoever decided that shots were a good idea." That was me. I remember now, and it was vodka. "I need to buy hair product. OMG, the cats were a nightmare this morning, I couldn't find Dezzie—he was...." She continues her rant but both Gus and I have tuned out and are only catching bits and pieces because we know this will go on for at least ten minutes, if not more, not to mention her accent is getting thicker and thicker. Remember, Bette's accent only comes out for two reasons: she's either very tipsy or very upset. She's still very tipsy.

When Bette takes a deep breath, sighs, and pauses, we both say "no" simultaneously. She was about to ask if she looks fat again. We didn't have to actually hear her say it; we just knew it was coming after the usual deep sigh and pause in her grand monologue. She pulls at her deep maroon, cotton maxi dress and, straightening the unseen wrinkles, replies, "Thanks. I am pretty, aren't I? And did you guys even hear what I said? OMG, I almost ate a whole box of macaroni!"

"What kind was it?" Gus asks.

"Some organic whatever-whatever kind," she says, waving the question off with her hand. "You're missing the point. Sydney, help."

"Don't look at me—I had French fries from the bar downstairs." My memory is coming back. Jose and the guys downstairs lovingly provide me with fries when I come home extra late. With the kitchen door so close to my building door, it's hard to resist fries when you've had too much to drink. Well, they're hard to resist anytime. (Everything in moderation, right?)

Gus stops Bette and me and looks at us both very seriously.

"Never ever eat organic mac and cheese. You'll want to kill the person who came up with this crap. Give me fake orange cheese powder or give me death," she says, as if it were "a word from our sponsor," then prods us to continue walking. And it's back to our regularly scheduled broadcasting.

"So, no one cares I almost ate the whole box?" Bette says, as if on cue. She looks like she might blow a gasket.

Gus and I look at each other, then to her and say, "Nope."

"Sydney, we work out together!" Bette shrills.

"I'll make you run this weekend," I reply, nonchalantly.

"I always eat the whole box. *Not* organic," Gus adds.

"Gawwwwwwwd," Bette says, using her whole range of vocal cord ability, by the sound of it an impossible three octaves. She haughtily pulls her hair into a clip that was attached to her "Neverfull" handle as if in protest. Bette always has an emergency hair clip; she never leaves the house without one.

We don't see Claudia anywhere and hope she's waiting for us at the gate as we shuffle up the escalator. I step off last, but the toe of my boot catches the rakes, a phobia of mine, and I trip forward, flinging my ticket and the pink Prada clutch onto the shiny airport floor along with my body. I laugh, embarrassed but relieved. If I'd been wearing shoes with laces, the laces could have gotten caught and it would have eaten my whole leg.

WebMD says phobias often begin in childhood. Maybe I fell into the rakes when I was a kid. The Sister probably pushed me. Or maybe I saw some weird horror flick with a treacherous escalator death scene. Nah, the Sister probably pushed me.

"Sydney, stop falling," Gus says by rote in her husky voice without even turning around. Gus knows at this point I'm on the ground, but it's such a usual occurrence she concerns herself with looking ahead and finding the shortest line for security check.

Bette picks up my things and turns to help me up, but a crisp suit beats her to it. Dropping his things to help me unruffle myself, he holds my elbow and looks at me with genuine concern.

"Are you okay?" he asks. "That was quite the tumble."

"Jeez, I'm fine," I say, pulling down my T-shirt dress that hiked to an indecent level during the escalator death scene. "Thanks so much. Body intact, ego on the floor," I laugh.

"Those escalators are tricky, right?" he chuckles.

"Already? See?" Bette sputters to Gus. "How is this possible in the airport? And how is it possible that she has no idea?" She shakes her head at me in a *you are unbelievable but I love you* sort of way, just as the suit hands me his card.

"No idea of what?" I *want* to say to Bette, but the suit is talking and I don't quite get it out.

"Well, give me a call sometime. I'm a lawyer, and you could probably use one." He laughs with more gusto this time and flashes a charming grin. Then, gripping his brief-case, he dashes off to a security line at another section of gates, turning back once to smile. Bette opens her Louis, jogs the card from my hand, and places it neatly into a pocket.

"I might be using that one if I pass the bar in July. And in case you didn't notice, which you didn't, he was hitting on you," she states.

"What?" Hold on. I look toward the suit. Really? Bette shakes her head and pulls me into the shorter line Gus has settled on.

"Syd, they don't have the balls to ask you out, so they hand you their card," she says, impatiently.

"Well, they should just ask me out." I hand my license to the TSA agent and smile really big so I look exactly like my photo.

"I'll ask you out," he smiles. Bette takes my license, shoves it into my clutch, and pushes me to the x-rays. She lifts her Rock eyebrow at him and hands over her license. She looks exactly like her photo.

I've got to start paying more attention if I'm going to meet the one. I raise my arms and the x-ray scans me. I wonder if they can see all the alcohol I drank last night. I also need to pay more attention because some of my previ-ous relationships weren't marriage or even, come to think of it, boyfriend material.

Todd Miller. He's one of the most recent and the one who gifted me Alexa. Great at presents, terrible at everything else. Nick Weatherby. Truthfully, he was blindingly good-looking but didn't know the difference between *your* and *you're*...I had to break that off, obviously. Scott Dolan. He's been on the list a couple times since college. I don't remember what the lure was there, but everyone has a crisis in their early twenties, right? Then there was a Skylar Starr, notable only for his name. I should've taken that name, though—Sydney Starr—perfect! (Now that I think about it, Skylar was probably gay.) And what about Kile Moface; I definitely should *not* have married him for that name. I mean, could you imagine wedding announcements for Shag-Moface...Syd Moface? Jump off a cliff now.

Omigod, and I almost forgot, Andy. Freakin' Andy What's-his-name. I *should* have lost my virginity to Blake, but no, no, it was Andy What's-his-name.

Rule #5
NEVER SLEEP WITH SOMEONE ON THE FIRST DATE

Pretty obvious but imperative, because I don't even remember Andy's last name. Andy...and then I go blank. That's kind of how it went too. Big mistake. Peer pressure is a dreadful thing. And how am I expected to remember his last name on a first date? I was so convinced I had turned into a slut after sleeping with him (yes, a bit dramatic) that I snuck out of the frat house without saying goodbye, without saying thank you for the movie and pizza (it was an epic date, obviously), and without my denim mini dress. He was sleeping on it. Then, to top it off, I ran into Mrs. Cobilt's whole third grade class in *his* T-shirt and my heels. They were on their way to see the children's theater performance I was starring in and running late for. Talk about walk of shame.

If I knew then what I know now, I would have slept with a slew of men in my college years and told them all it was my first time. You know, to get the hang of it and really blow their minds. Just not on the first date. (Then maybe I would have my denim mini dress.) No one tells you that, though, now do they?

We wait as Gus gets frisked quite briskly and her carry-on is searched. It must be the Lady Macbeth in her; she gets chosen every time we fly.

But who am I kidding? I could never pull off virgin more than once. I'm a terrible liar. Not to be confused with telling tall tales, which I can totally do. Very well, in fact. But I'm a terrible liar. Even a white lie makes me feel ill. Like the time in sixth grade I told the room monitor, Butter Boobs, Marcy Moore, that I finished my spelling homework and I really hadn't. That night I made myself sick with guilt. No really, I actually got a fever of 102 and vowed to finish my whole spelling book by the end of the week.

That's why I made:

Rule #6
NEVER LIE

Then I revised it...

Rule #6
NEVER LIE (WHEN YOU CAN TELL SOME OF THE TRUTH)

The guilt of the spelling book incident is so burned into my memory that I absolutely had to add Rule #6. That, and when I came clean and told Marcy Moore I had lied to her at the impromptu high school reunion two years ago while wearing my Rudolph the Red-Nosed-ball-sweater, the vein in her neck nearly blew her always-buttoned top button off her always-ruffled blouse. I could tell she thought I would never amount to much, being a liar and all. (Or it could have been the sweater.)

But I'll show her. I haven't lied since. Like when I told Doc my credit card was fine. I meant that the actual card looked fine—no scratches or anything!—however, the limit is nearly broken. *I am smart and money will come. I am smart and money will come...*

I use my credit card for several quasi-needed items in the airport bookstore as Bette waits in line to buy hair product. Gus finds the worst-best food to snack on and replaces her menacing-looking toothpaste, which TSA confiscated. A brazen suit steps in front of Bette just as she goes to pay, throws cash onto the counter for his cup of caffeine, and blazes out of the store.

"Rude," Bette says aloud, though he's already too far away to hear.

City guys. Enchanted by their own money but rarely enchanting at all. They make me want to sneak out in the middle of the night (because that's when these things happen), move to Italy, and score an Italian lover. Or France. Then I could say, "*Bonjour! Je m'appelle Sydney, et je voudrais allez a la salle de bain*," which is my only full and coherent sentence in French. Of course, I can quote almost every line in *Gigi*, which we watched at least once a week in our French class (in English, of course).

Just as we thought, Claudia is waiting for us near the gate wearing a pair of jeans and a thin wrap sweater, which she's nearly busting out of. I hate traveling in jeans because I can never get comfortable, but then again, I don't think thigh-high boots are ideal either.

"Claudia!" I call out with a wave.

"Hey, Claud," Gus says. And there it is again, cloud. Claudia brushes her bangs out of her eyes and flares her freckled nostrils just enough to be noticeable. With more sun in Austin, Claudia's angel kiss freckling will multiply and she'll be covered in little beauty marks.

"Where have you all been?" she asks, munching on an apple and tapping her foot indignantly. She breaks into a smile and hugs us all. Claudia doesn't eat anything or drink anything in the morning without her piece of fruit first. It's imperative for her to start her day right. Looking at us, clearly, we did not.

"Girls, hurry, we're boarding and it's a really full flight!" She nudges us into the boarding line.

☆ ☆ ☆

My phone blings just as I'm trying to scan my boarding pass.

Olivia: Syd darling, I swear to God this is you. Is it?

"Sorry, one sec," I say to the gate agent. I try to swipe my iPhone screen back to my ticket, accidently clicking the attachment.

"That's okay, take your time," the cheery agent says. She snoops over my phone as I try relentlessly to click away from the Youtube video featuring me in a garbage can. "Ooh, that one's hilarious!"

"Haha," I gulp. My phone blings again.

Olivia: Syd! I know you're reading this.

I look around instinctively. She doesn't. But you never know, it's Olivia. (Olivia: Impressive entrepeneur, always in the know and incredibly impatient.) A picture appears— Olivia with a naked butt behind her. Oh, and, indelibly indecent.

"It's my favorite video too," Bette says, leaning over my shoulder and wagging her thumb, giving me away.

I press everything on the screen to get back to my boarding pass. Smartphones!

Finally, I scan my ticket and laugh weakly at the agent, then dash into the jetway.

Me: (smack face emoji)

*Olivia: I knew it. It was being passed around the boardroom!
PS this is Jacques, he came straight over after my meeting.*

His penis pops onto my screen.
I trip.

Chapter 13
FIRST CLASS-y

FULL IS right. I try to squeeze past the seventy-something woman I've already smacked into on the jetway while looking at a penis. She didn't approve of the penis and she doesn't approve of me trying to sneak by her now. She's flagging down a flight attendant in the middle of first class, her white hair in complete contrast to the severe orange blush she's wearing. It must be the brightest orange on the color wheel, akin to the traffic cones Hunter Boone (neighborhood cohort) and I used to rearrange as kids.

Genius, I know—moving traffic paraphernalia can cause accidents. I'm appalled by my own behavior, kind of; I mean, we were kids and they were only for parking. But one time Officer Lorell (aka Lurch) had to reset *twenty-two* cones. To say he was mad would be an understatement. But not as mad as when another one of our slightly more offensive covert ops put him at odds with Sheriff Smitty.

I get a little elbow to the rib and I'm nearly positive it was on purpose. She just doesn't want me to get by. I perch my bag on another seat and wait patiently for her to move a few inches. Not only is she wearing traffic cone orange, she's also sporting every tacky, yet notably expensive, piece of jewelry that will fit on her body. I take a second look at her wedding rings. Bling-bada-bling. The engagement ring has a diamond so big I can only compare it to the candy ring pops we wore at Claudia's second bachelorette party. (Oh yes, second. Claudia's first bachelorette party was a traditional American style. The second was a Cha de Lingerie party, very Brazilian, and apparently there is a third scheduled that will be all about food. These wedding planners are no joke.) Distracted, I take a moment to picture the ring pop diamond on my finger. I mean, seriously. You would too.

The older woman finally moves slightly, giving me room, but I accidently bump her with my bag while trying to wriggle by and she purses her wrinkled little lips and glares at me.

"Oops, sorry," I say apologetically and then notice her Prada luggage hanging out of the overhead bin. Prada? I look down at my obnoxious heart-covered bag. A possible eyesore but sturdy, and it totally fits in the overhead bin, so there. I finish squeezing past as she huffs and rolls her eyes. But it seems "Mrs. Rich" didn't want to check her bag for the extra cash along with the rest of us "lower class" passengers. I smile to myself. Though, the seat next to her is still open and I would totally take it.

Finally out of the range of Mrs. Rich's glare (in fact, I think she's taken issue with Gus now), I find my seat. It's an aisle, thankfully. Claudia and I sit next to one another with Bette by the window and Gus on the other side of me across the aisle. I like the aisle seat because I can keep my eye on the flight attendants to see if they're panicking for any undetectable reason.

We struggle to get comfortable and settle in for the four hour and thirteen minute flight to Austin—land of beer, boots, bats, and in this case, cars. Waiting for Claudia to organize herself, it occurs to me that I've forgotten to pack underwear as well as my toothbrush. And why do I always forget my toothbrush? Revise what I said about being a professional under-pressure packer. Let's say I'm a semi-professional under-pressure packer.

I pull out my still slightly wet book (from the water bottle incident), take a quick call from Tray to say "bye" to Harold again, and settle in.

Claudia is the calmest flyer in the world and, as we take off, I death-grip the armrest while she flips through the latest gossip magazine. She's actually featured in Brazilian gossip magazines from time to time, even more so now that she's engaged to the highest-grossing young Argentinian artist, Pascal—who she lovingly calls Pax or Paxy or Polla, something sweet in Spanish, I presume. Claudia's first language is Portuguese but she speaks Spanish more often because Pascal has never been fluent. Claudia speaks five languages. (She's never even seen *Gigi*!) We all saw her in *Caras* but I couldn't understand a thing. She was either in the best or worst dressed section; I couldn't even figure it out by the fashion, but they certainly highlighted her chest. Claudia's really the only Siren that's well endowed and could easily grace a busty magazine. She's even had a few offers according to Pascal.

As the pilot changes to a westward path, I begin to perspire and imagine twisted metal, suitcases floating in water, and disarticulated feet (wearing New Balance) washing up in British Columbia. And, to make matters worse, I have to go to the bathroom.

I look across the aisle where Gus is completely knocked out on natural anti-anxiety meds with her mouth wide open, chip crumbs in her lap, and deep in sleep. What are natural anti-anxiety medications anyway? I need to check WebMD about this. Whatever they are, I need some.

Tray pops to mind, and I wonder how he's doing with his recent issues. Unfortunately, I had no idea he was dabbling with drugs until we were having a college get-together in the neighborhood. He showed up at our favorite bar tanked, skittish, and chewing his jaw. Logan, one of our steadfast friends who grew up with Tray, was particularly worried that night. According to Logan, it's happening more and more often. And he would know; he knows him better than anyone. They've been inseparable since high school and came out together at the end of our freshman year of college.

Tray and I've been friends for years. He grew up on a pig farm a town over from Butter, the same town as Logan (though I didn't meet Logan until college). Tray tells me, only now, that he thought Logan would inevitably fall in love with me and that the jealousy would put him over the edge. That and the pigs. He was right; Logan did fall for me. (How could he not? I did Judy Garland impressions on a regular basis.) He was in love with me right up until they officially came out. I always knew they were gay, of course. Once in a while I would pry but inevitably waited patiently for the announcement, which was just as fabulous as when they decided to be Barbra Streisand and The Divine Miss M for Halloween.

But hitting it big as a costume designer in New York City brings no small amount of stress. I think the pigs were less judgmental. Tray's parents are concerned it's his way of dealing with the stress of working for high-pressure, high-stakes producers. I know it's his dream, but they may be right in wanting to get him out of the surroundings for a while.

I feel a huge jolt and check the aisle for flight attendants. They haven't gotten up yet. I need vodka. Why aren't they serving yet?

We're going down.

We're definitely going down.

Another massive bounce and I reach for Gus' pocket. I've got to get to those anti-anxiety meds. But Gus flips the other way and closes her mouth. So close.

"Little chica, it's just a tiny air pocket, less than what you'd feel on an *autobús*," Claudia smiles. She pats my hand, which is gripping our shared armrest, and then flips another page in her gossip magazine like we aren't plummeting to our death.

I scan the aisle again and notice that Mrs. Rich has a seatmate after all. Does he look like the guy...? I can't quite see. I look over at Bette, who looks even more comfortable than Gus, while Claudia lays into a celebrity.

"Look at her massive thighs," she says, cringing. I lean over her shoulder. She's looking at a gorgeous film action star who happens to be very muscled. Claudia hasn't worked out a day in her life unless you count meditation. She says working out makes her fat. Um, what?

I check the flight attendants again as Mrs. Rich's seatmate looks to the side. I can just make out what looks like a hat line in his dirty blond hair. He looks familiar... If I could just get out of my...We hit another pocket of air, and I tighten my safety belt and check all the emergency exits.

Apparently the female action star reminds Claudia of her sister-in-law, which launches her into an in-depth discussion (tirade) of the seating chart for her wedding. "...and his mother can't sit next to my sister-in-law, who can't sit next to her brother-in-law's new wife, who...ooh!" Claudia has absentmindedly turned the page of her gossip magazine and interrupts herself. She stops abruptly on the page just as the announcement is made that it's now safe to move about the cabin. "Syd, where are you going? You have to see her co-star, Gavin McKn—"

"Gotta go." I really have to use the lavatory. I fumble out of my seat and would run if I didn't know an undercover air marshal would tackle me. Thank goodness it reads "Empty" as I nearly rip the door off.

My mouth drops.

"Oops, sorry!" I blurt as Mrs. Rich screams while seated on the plane's toilet. I've opened the door as wide as it goes; leave it to me. Her horrendous bright traffic cone orange cheeks turn burnt sienna right before my eyes. Poor thing must be blushing. I fumble with the door, which now feels stuck. Why won't this door close? Come on. Finally, the door rack slides up against the proper side and the little sign goes from "Empty" to "Occupied" with a fierce click.

I turn and check the other lavatory. Of course it's "Occupied" now and I have nowhere to hide. Mrs. Rich comes out. She purses her wrinkled little lips at me again, squints her eyes, and glares. Well, I didn't mean to. She sticks up her chin defiantly and fluffs her white hair into place, flashing the blood diamond right in my eyeball. Now I want to pummel her, but she barely comes up to my clavicle. Instead, I stand pressed up against the other lavatory with a dumb *I'm sorry* look. She glares again, as if knowing my sinister thought, and a chill runs down my spine.

The lavatory opens behind me and I get closed in the fold not once, but twice, as the occupant inside pushes and pushes to get out. Unbelievable. My shoulder crunches before I can get out of the way. Mrs. Rich, who clearly enjoyed that, gives me an eye roll eerily similar to The Sister's, then turns, making a "hmpf" noise as she shuffles down the aisle. I duck into the bathroom (finally) and assess the damage to my arm.

I'll live.

I turn my attention to the task at hand—hovering a few inches above the toilet. I never sit on a public toilet. It's a habit I've held since grade school. I went through a brief germaphobe stage but only because I was copying Penny, who was (and still is); but still, I never touch a public toilet, ever.

"This is your Captain (garble) (something)…(something)…turbulence…(something)(garble)(something)… seats." What? I feel like I'm listening to the teachers from *Peanuts*. What did he say? Gah, did he say back to your seats? We're going down.

Of course my bladder becomes shy because I'm thinking about twisted metal and flames again, and my quads are burning because I'm holding the squat position over the toilet. The plane jumps and I hit my head on the side-wall. Ow. I grab toilet paper; the plane hits another doozy and I tip forward, still in my squat, knocking the top of my forehead on the lavatory door. If the plane doesn't go down, there's a good chance I'll be found unconscious in the lavatory with my pants down.

I stumble back toward my seat as the turbulence worsens, noting Mrs. Rich is gabbing to her seatmate, no doubt telling him how horrible I am. If I could just get a good look, I think he *is* familiar. Maneuvering in the aisle, I try to get a better angle as the plane takes another jump. I fall into my seat and partially onto Claudia.

"What took you so long? And what happened to your hair?" she asks, her freckles bunching into a small pile on her nose. She goes back to the magazine, *her* hair resting calmly on top of her shoulders while I wonder if we're going to make it. I pull my seatbelt as tight as it goes, then rub my head and arm injuries. I lean out into the aisle in a death-defying attempt to see who Mrs. Rich is talking to. But I can only see one of his cowboy boots jutting into the aisle. They're hard to miss with their unique stitching. Claudia interrupts my sleuthing and shoves the gossip magazine in my face. She wonders if I think such-and-such's red carpet dress looks fabulous because it reminds her of her wedding gown. I'm bounced back into the upright position and made to examine several different looks. The plane is violently bouncing everywhere and Claudia doesn't even notice. I try to not scream, *We're going down, we're going down!* But we are.

Rule #7
NEVER SHOW PANIC (IT'S A SIGN OF WEAKNESS)

This crucial nugget of wisdom comes straight from Doc's mouth and can be used in nearly every situation dealing with fear.

"Sydney, don't look so panicked—it's just twelve feet. People will think you're a pansy," Doc said. I was dangling precariously from a tree limb at age eight because my overalls (yes, overalls) got caught after he dared me to climb it. I was stuck there for at least two hours trying to untangle myself. (He says it was only a few minutes.) But Doc was right. Everyone in the neighborhood who had gathered to see if I was going to die thought I was a badass after that.

Fortunately, panicking on the inside is fine. So I keep screaming in my head, seventeen minutes into the turbulence and counting. I know because I'm watching the seconds tick by on Claudia's slender, gold heirloom wristwatch, which she wears with our Elsa Peretti Starfish bracelet. To make myself feel better, I try to remember every time I've lived through a death ride and spot all three flight attendants. Oddly, they don't look panicked. Mrs. Red Scarf is handing out water, Ms. Beady Eyes is staring down a man thinking about getting something out of the overhead bin, and Mr. Laissez Faire looks down-right bored, so I try to calm myself.

I'm tempted to inquire about the choppiness (and ask who's sitting next to Mrs. Rich), but I never, ever ask flight attendants anything, especially not about turbulence. Well, not since the Flight of The Hawaii.

An innocent vacation with a then-boyfriend turned into an absolute flying nightmare...for me. During the infamous Flight of The Hawaii, I started to get airsick from the jumps up and down, so I hobbled to the lavatory. While waiting patiently to throw up, I asked one of the flight attendants, who were all mysteriously men (which should have given me a clue right there that something was amiss), if it was normal for the turbulence to be bad on this route. Dick (we will call him Dick; I'm nearly positive it was on his flight tag) answered, "No," and then, almost gleefully, added, "Good luck with that." I'm not kidding. He seriously said that. I wanted to barf on his lap.

Whatever happened to the days of the beautiful *stew-ardess* with perfect hair and flawless makeup who feels genuine concern if you have an upset stomach and gets you a ginger ale, telling you everything's going to be okay? (It's no wonder I wanted to be a *stewardess*.)

I have never forgotten that day. Dick and my almost death. Dick's cold words and high-waisted pants are seared into my memory.

Mrs. Red Scarf leans in. "Would you like some water?"

"Do you happen to have ginger ale?" I ask.

"Sure, that'll just be twenty dollars," she says. She didn't actually say twenty, but she may as well have.

"Water's fine," I smile. As she turns, I notice her hair is matted in the back.

After losing my gut, unfortunately not on Dick's lap (only because I'm too polite), I struggled back to my seat. That's where I proceeded to have what is, to this day, *I believe*, my first mini stroke/heart attack. The turbulence was intense and when I sat down, a searing pain began shooting down my left arm at an alarming rate. I was fighting this acute pain while trying to get my boyfriend's attention, but he was glued to his mini movie screen.

If I'd had the strength, I would have yelled, "Is there a doctor on board?" And then a strapping young Dr. Hotness (who wasn't glued to his mini screen) would have come to my rescue. But my diminishing strength only allowed me to wince to the boyfriend,

"I'm dying..."

"Yes, I know, Sydney, shhhh," he replied, never looking over, mind you. Then he offered his hand for me to hold, all the while laughing at the movie. So I flopped my head on his shoulder and waited for death to come. (Spoiler alert: I didn't die.)

Now I sip my water, wishing it were ginger ale. I try never to get that panicked, as I don't want to have two mini stroke-heart attacks in my twenties. I'm pretty sure that wouldn't be good. That's why Rule #7 is so valuable. And you can forget any future trips to Hawaii; I would rather have a colonoscopy.

I check on my friends; they're all asleep. I try one more attempt to see who Mrs. Rich's seatmate is, but I'll have to wait until we deplane. Her matching set of travel pillows is blocking my view. I lay my head on Claudia's shoulder, whose head is on Bette's shoulder, and close my eyes just in time for Gus to wake up in a panic because we're all asleep and no one understands that we're about to die.

Chapter 14
WAIT, WAIT...

IT'S A miracle we aren't dead. We half carry each other, half dance back to the hotel just after 3 a.m. After The Hitching Rail, we bar hopped to several other locations where everyone bought us numerous rounds of shots, and then to top it off, we convinced a little dive to stay open late. I've never seen a bar close if we're asking for one last round or when Gus is finishing a beer. And Gus is *always* finishing a beer.

"I kinda like that guy...Dave...Dan...wait, wait, Derek. Yeah, Derek. Maybe meeting someone new was a good idea afderallll," Bette giggles. Note: she said "wait" twice.

"Did you say, Derek?" Abby asks.

She smiles dreamily. "Ya, Derek. I reeally like him."

"The guy tonight was Wade. Derek's the guy you've had a crush on forever in New York," I say, baiting her.

"Ya, Derek, he's sooo cute. I've always had a crush on him," she says, closing her eyes as if picturing him.

"Ooooooh!" Abby squeals. All of us giggle. Bette's eyes open wide.

"Wade! I meant Wade!" she declares loudly.

"We all knew you were crushin' on Derek," Abby shouts, pointing and wagging her finger at her.

"Wade! Wade was cute," Bette says again, with a hiccup.

"Good, because I invited them to the auto show tomorrow. Ryan's going to get them in for free," Gus says. (Ryan's the guy she's been stealing Bud Lights from and hanging out with all night.) Then to me, she adds quietly, "If she's ever going to go out with Derek, she's going to have to break the ice."

"Wait, wait." Bette laughs. "That's the best ideaaa everrrr," she says, and hiccups several times in a row.

And there it is again, the double "wait." An undeniable sign of inebriation.

"Syd, you still have that cowboy hat?" Bette slurs.

"Yes," I say, holding up the hat. "And I swear that's the guy, you guys," I say, but not making much sense.

"It is, Syd, it is. That's the guy," Bette says, and hiccups again.

"Right? From New York!" I knew it. He's here.

"Derek. That's the guy." She smiles again, then, "Wait, wait..."

Okay, regardless of the fact that Bette's too drunk to remember, or even knows who I'm talking about, I'm almost positive the same guy standing outside our bar in NYC was on the plane with us and in the Austin bar tonight. Or am I seeing things?

"Gimme that," Bette says, putting her arm around me and taking the scarred hat. She puts it atop her head and it immediately falls over her eyes. "You know what I could use right now? Some maaacaroni and cheese. I would looove some macaroni. Wait, wait…"

Gus and I coral her into the hotel with Claudia all but sleepwalking behind us as Abby dances into an Uber with Greg.

Chapter 15
CRINOLINE, CARS, AND IT CAN'T BE

WE GET what feels like ten minutes of sleep before the sun is up and we're running around the overly spacious suite getting primped for the auto show again. The Driskill hotel is stately with beds dressed in gold fabrics, overstuffed pillows, and two huge windows overlooking the downtown. I push open the heavy drapes in an especially soft complimentary robe to give us more light and Bette moans. "Whyyyy?" She rolls from the bed to the floor with a thud.

From the other room, and I presume from the Texas-size "mini" bar, I hear the familiar sound of a drink being shaken. It *was* just sitting there waiting for us to have enough drinks last night to forget that an airplane-size bottle of booze costs ten dollars and a small snack costs eight. Doc would have a coronary. When I was nine, I accidently ate the cashews at a fancy hotel on a family vacation thinking they were free. Doc threatened to move us to the Motel 6 down the road.

Now sitting on the floor with Bette, I hold up my new underwear. They aren't exactly what I envisioned; they might just be better.

"I feel like you should have gotten us all a pair of those," she says, her eyes blinking awake.

"Right?" I laugh and hold them up. "We could have been the 'Cowboys Only' club." I had to buy what I could find on Sixth Street, or what locals call Dirty Sixth, and what I found was a pretty racy set of G-strings with "Cowboys Only" written on their front.

"Cowboys Only, huh?" Bette says, putting on the cowboy hat from last night. "I may have been drunk but *this* I remember!"

"Does my hair look right?" Gus says, walking in from the other room with a drink and pulling a goofy face. Her 1970s-style hairdo brings smiles all around. "Hair of the dog anyone?"

"Nooo! I'm dying, nothing can save me now. And it looks like Dezzie is on your head," Bette laughs, looking up at her. Dezzie is an unusually fluffy cat.

"It's sexy and you know it. I was going for the feathered look," Gus says, making another comedic face adjusting her overly-sprayed hair. Then she catches a glimpse in the mirror. "Oh, I think Bette's dry shampoo really amped it up a notch." Her normally straight, thick hair *does* look much larger than yesterday.

Bette places the cowboy hat on my head and remarks, "Who is he?"

"That's what I'd like to know!" I respond. Her eyes lock on something else, and she pulls it from my bag.

"Really, Syd?!" She holds up my bra spilling several business cards, scraps of paper, and napkins, with men's numbers on them, onto the floor.

"What? The napkins give me great cleavage," I giggle. Bette shakes her head laughing and snaps the bra at me just as I snag it.

"You guys," Claudia says, walking out of the bathroom. "Look at my jeans. They're even tighter today! They're like two sizes too small and my stomach isn't my best area." Claudia stands in front of us in her outfit of low-rise bell-bottoms, a half-shirt with a peace sign, and a brown leather long vest with fringe, which covers all possible mishaps. We all stare at her blankly. She looks great.

"Um…I would, like, wear that in normal life," Gus says, taking a sip of her cocktail, a self-proclaimed hangover remedy that notoriously includes Tabasco.

"You get to wear that and I have to look like I should be put in a recycling bin?" Bette exclaims unsympathetically as she pulls on her silver-metallic jumpsuit and holds up her skirt that can only be described as an upside-down metal funnel. "I'm the female Tin Man."

"Seriously, look at me," Claudia whines.

"Hmm, not sure you understand how we feel," I say and stand up now in my granny-panty bloomers, bra, saddle shoes, and cowboy hat. I turn giving them my signature hip bump and booty shake, which elicits laughter from all of them. Bette lets out a snort as I make a show of stepping into my overly huge crinoline. "Oh this is my favorite part," I respond. It is. Best crinoline ever.

Claudia stops laughing and waves her hands to get us to pay attention. "Syd, that's the hat. That's the guy's hat from New York! "

Everyone stops and looks at me.

I *knew* it.

☆ ☆ ☆

"How am I ever going to find him?" I ask, pushing my crinoline this way and that as we pile into our ride to the auto show looking a lot like Sandy from *Grease*. The costumes match the year of the car we're modeling, so truthfully, they're quite clever. Tray never gets a costume wrong. And next to Boss's beautiful red and white 1957 Ford Fairlane Convertible 500, my costume looks perfect.

"Well, he did say he'd find you," Bette says, trying to get comfortable. Bette's modeling the DeLorean from the movie *Back to the Future* and her metallic fashion is supposed to invoke time travel, a futuristic woman looking like something between a robot and Jane Jetson. But right now, it's invoking anger. She lets out a loud "humpf!"

Claudia's dressed like a hippie in her tight bellbottoms and leather strap adorning her forehead. She's next to a blue 1966 Volkswagen Beetle. And Gus has been showing off a white 1969 Modified Pontiac Trans Am, also Boss' car, and is in a psychedelic dress, white knee-high boots, and a hairstyle that's barely fitting in the car service.

The four of us arrive at the entrance to the outdoor auto show. Shiny cars fill the enormous space, and we gush at how on even the second day it's a gorgeous sight. We spot Abby in our "Cars of the Ages" section. Her curly, caramel hair is calmed into two cute braids sitting on either shoulder, and she looks downright innocent in a long, floral dress, bringing to mind *Little House on the Prairie*. (Little-house-on-the-get-out-of-my-head-Misty and Blake!) She's modeling the 1908 Ford Model T. Boss' Model T.

"Sirens, I've been lookin' for y'all everywhere!" Abby yells while running up to us. We group hug. She takes a good look at our outfits, which are just a little rougher than yesterday. "We're going to need a drink, immediately." Obviously a prairie outfit cannot make you innocent.

"You're speaking my language," Gus says. "Plus, there's this." She points to her larger-than-life hair.

"I didn't know it was you for a minute," Abby giggles, fluffing Gus' hair. "I've never seen you wear it anything but straight."

"I told you guys, I'm really good at getting into character," Gus replies, smugly. I immediately picture her in a 1970s-themed movie with several car chases. The hair could work.

Abby pulls us behind the Model T, where her luggage is tucked away for our late flight. "Greg's upset with me again," she divulges, while heaving out a bottle of Ketel One.

"Whoa, that bad?" I giggle.

"Friggin' fantastic," Bette brightens, taking the bottle and twisting off the top. "Maybe a hair of the dog *is* what I need." She peeks around and takes a swig. We all follow suit.

"So, what's with the novio?" Claudia asks, referring to Greg. I might just learn Spanish yet!

Abby sighs. "He's just always upset, no matter what I do. Last night it was because we stayed out late."

"What?!" Gus fires back.

"He was out too! He picked you up," I respond. It sounds too much like a double standard to me.

"Ridiculous," Bette states, putting up her hand. "Greg is not helping my headache." After everyone's had a drink, she takes another big swig and tucks the bottle back into Abby's bag.

"What do I do?" Abby folds one of her braids through her fingers nervously.

"Hello, ladies!" We all jump and turn toward the voice. It's Jeff Mint, the coordinator of the auto show and a good friend of our boss. "We open to the public in fifteen minutes, and one of the biggest philanthropists in town is visiting! She's lives between New York and Austin and we're lucky enough to have her here this weekend. A portion of our earnings go to charity, and she's promised to match it!" He claps for emphasis.

"This has been our most popular section." He points to me. "Especially you, Sydney, the kids love you. So, keep it up—it's very important she has a good time. You can't miss her. Mrs. Billingsworth wears more jewels than the Queen. And the rock on that ring finger!" He lets out a soft whistle of amazement. "Have fun! I'll be around if you need me," he bellows, then takes off, summoned by a group of girls in racecar jumpsuits. He shuffles them toward the Ferraris.

"We're way prettier," Gus says as she comically fluffs her hair and stares at their magnificent tight suits.

"I'm standing in front of a Volkswagen Bug and they get Ferraris?" Claudia says, watching them trail after Mint.

"Yah, but I have a deep affinity for looking like a Campbell's Soup can without the label," Bette says sarcastically and snorts.

"Actually, I love the movie *Grease*. I still choose our section. And apparently, we're the most popular," I say, tossing my car info card onto the ground so I can bend waaay over to pick it up, flashing all of them my bloomers. Catching on and to add to the spectacle, Bette does the robot with her arms making squeaking noises to match.

"Jackasses," Gus says, then laughs. She pulls my ponytail as I right myself and Bette stops me before I get hold of her hair.

"Get to your cars—look," Claudia points. She rushes to her VW as security opens the roped-off entrance. "Abby, we'll figure Greg out later, promise!" She yells over her shoulder.

We scurry to our vehicles and I quickly read over my car info card one more time:

This 1957 Ford Fairlane 500 has an increased power Thunderbird V8 engine, a Fairlane 500 Skyliner power retractable hardtop, sleek low tail fins, black and charcoal velour upholstery with red piping on the seats and rear package tray. The top speed is 120 mph and it goes from 0 to 60 in 10.2 seconds. The safety features, which Ford began in 1956, includes the dished steering wheel, padded dash, breakaway rearview mirror, and crash-proof door locks.

I fluff my crinoline one last time just as a flood of human beings rushes into our section. I can't help but look around for the cowboy even though I'm not even that clear on what he looks like (other than handsome) without his hat.

I've said, *It's a 1957 Fairlane 500 with a Skyliner power retractable hardtop* three million times and *No, I'm not really Sandy* with a chuckle two million. And the crinoline is a hit. I'll have to thank Tray when we get back. While twirling for another photo, I see Abby waving her hands.

"They're here," she mouths between smiling lips.

"Who's here?" I mouth back, lifting my arms. And then I remember, the philanthropist. I look for an entourage but don't see what Abby's noticed. Gus waves at me as if to point them out as well but I'm still clueless while searching the crowd.

"Hey, Sydney," a good-looking guy says from the rear of the convertible, snagging my attention. He's familiar—

"Sandy, can we get a photo with the kids?" a woman sporting Longhorn orange interrupts, addressing my character. Her three kids charge me.

"Of course!" I smile as they pummel my legs and stomach. While she snaps photos I spot the entourage approaching the Fairlane.

"It's me, from last night." The guy waves again from nearly beside me now as I pose for several more photos with the kids. I see Gus from the corner of my eye, pointing again with enthusiasm.

The two little girls run back to their mom while the young boy, undoubtedly a future Longhorn linebacker by his size, stays, insisting on one more photo op by himself.

"This is my favorite car of all time," I hear the older woman say to her entourage of several photographers and what looks like reporters. She turns and points at the Fairlane Convertable. My body goes stiff. Omigod, it can't be.

"Sydney, Gus said I should come straight over to say hi," the good-looking guy says with a gracious smile. He puts out his hand and I reach for it, barely noticing, my eyes focused on the older woman.

"I'm first!" the future linebacker shouts and pushes him just as I grip his hand in greeting. The hefty shove jolts us both backward, toppling us over the low-riding convertible and into the backseat.

"Let's get a quick photo," I hear the older woman say as I scramble to right myself. Everything feels wrong. My head is in his armpit, which is nearly in the floor of the car, and my award-winning crinoline seems to be everywhere but in its place. We struggle to recover somehow, making it worse. I pop my head up just in time for her to look back.

The scowl is deafening.

I smile.

This cannot be happening.

Mrs. Rich.

"The least I could do was take y'all to a late dinner before your flight," Ryan says, then apologizes again for yanking me into the Fairlane. "Order whatever you guys want— this is my favorite bistro!"

"He owns it," Gus interjects, her dark hair now in a more natural state. A messy knot.

"That's only one of the reasons I love it." He smiles and looks at his phone, which has dinged. "Sydney, it looks like our beloved philanthropist ended up having a fantastic time talking to reporters about being caught with her late husband in the back seat of a Fairlane. It's going to be a wonderful story, celebrating him as well."

"He paid the reporters," Gus adds, grinning.

"Did you?" I ask, thinking he must have.

"No," he laughs. "But I do know the family and knew as much to have the reporters ask her about why exactly the Fairlane was her favorite. The photo's not bad either!" He snorts, showing us the photo that's just arrived on his phone. Once again my legs are sticking straight into the air, but they're alongside his and thankfully you can't see our faces. (Though if you could, maybe that cowboy would be able to find me.) In the foreground is Mrs. Rich, or whatever her real name is. Mrs. Billings? Something like that.

"You're already trying to get another girl into the back seat of a car," Gus laughs, looking at the photo. She winks at Ryan and he takes her hand, smiling.

"You two are cozy," I say, raising my eyebrows at the hand holding, which Gus rarely does.

"And so are they," Claudia says, gesturing to Bette and Wade, who went to get us special drinks but instead are making out at the bar.

"Where's Abby?" Gus asks, ready to order.

"Still outside talking to Greg," I point. We all look out the window. They look to be having a heavy conversation.

☆ ☆ ☆

Gus hands me one of her natural anti-anxiety meds just before boarding and I sleep through the entire flight. Except for one harrowing moment, where we almost don't make it. Takeoff.

But we're swiftly in the air, and a beautiful flight attendant with perfectly coiffed hair offers me a free ginger ale.

Of course she didn't; I was sleeping. That was a dream.

Chapter 16
TRULY TRAY

I SLEEPWALK into my apartment. No time to sleep, though; I've got to pay rent. And I actually opened my mailbox and brought up the mail. Bills and more bills, that I swear are supposed to be paperless. Automatic payment is great until you see what you've been ignoring as they cha-ching onto your credit card.

Harold's all but doing flips as I feed him a big pinch of fish flakes. I ask him how well Tray took care of him while we were in Austin. He inhales the floating food in two gulps, then swims into and around his ceramic stiletto at full speed. (A ceramic stiletto looked way cooler than ceramic coral.) I'm increasingly skeptical about whether Tray fed him yesterday. He was definitely here on Saturday because I talked to him, but yesterday, I have a feeling, was a no-go.

"Tray!" I scream into the phone, ready to lay into him for not feeding my favorite fish. (Then, of course, I'll tell him that my costume was fabulous in a much more civil tone.)

"Sydney, omigod, you'll never believe—you've been gone for a year, I swear! Aaaaaaah!" he wails. I walk to the window, knowing he's waiting. Then I look across the street and wave like an idiot. He's already standing in his window and, pushing the billowy curtains aside, he immediately does several body building poses while simultaneously adjusting his headphones. I respond with a booty dance, then remember the reason I called.

"You forgot—" But he doesn't give me a chance to speak.

"I've booked a huge new show! Huge," he screams while flexing his left bicep. "It's going to be one of the biggest Broadway hits ever." Then he starts going on and on about how amazing he is.

Listening to his self-proclaimed fabulousness for the umpteenth time, I walk back to Harold and put a small pinch of fish flakes in his bowl, upset my little friend had to fast yesterday. Finally, sensing a pause in Tray's monologue, I scream, "You didn't feed Harold!"

"Who?"

"Harold!"

"Huh?"

Even worse.

"MY FISH!" I retort.

"Oh yeah, he's a bit hefty."

What?!

"So, omigod, can you believe it? Aaaaaaah! I'm coming over. Oh, and I took that big empty box from your costume to the recycling bin; aren't I the bestest friend ever?" He hangs up; I think Harold just rolled his eyes. I give him another fish flake. Hefty? Ridiculous. He wiggles his tail fin and makes a loop around his stiletto, so I give him one more flake. Okay, two.

Tray always gives me a countdown to when he'll arrive at my apartment, whether it be phone calls or texts, and today is no different.

Tray:

I'll be on my way soon hunny.

I am brushing my teeth and then leaving.

I have to send one more email and just make a quick phone call.

I'm horny.

I really need a haircut.

My hair is NOT working.

I deserve a really hot date. Right?

Syd are you there?

I deserve the perfect man right?

OMG, I look orange. My self-tanner turned me orange!

These boys make me craaaaazy.

Heading downstairs, I swear.

It's so hot. I'm so hot too…haha…

No seriously. I am, right?

I've been thinking about getting lipo.

I don't hear from him for a while and figure he's still doing his hair. I'm a tired mess from the early morning flight and our even bigger night out last night. I pull my old Louis Vuitton Speedy, a gift from an ex, out of the closet and shove a big wad of cash into it. (The secret stash in the closet. My pirate money!) I've got to get this into my checking account and pay down the credit card, but there's no time at the moment, so I zip and throw it back in. I run around my apartment picking up odds and ends and straightening the book stacks by the bed. The pages have bubbled and aren't lining up due to the water bottle incident. Shelves. I need shelves.

I take the cowboy hat out of my bag. Running my finger along the scar and looking closer, I see it's actually extremely skilled stitching sealing what seems to have been a gash in the hat. Only now do I feel a bit bad I didn't turn it into the bar as soon as I realized I couldn't find the owner. But we were sure we'd find him. Bette made it her personal mission to find my mysterious cowboy. But she was completely distracted by Wade, whom she kept calling Derek. I don't think he minded much while sucking face at the bar. And Gus was little help as Ryan had all her attention and actually, they really hit it off. Apparently she already thinks we should plan another trip to Texas, which Abby is all for after leaving on a not so perfect note with Greg.

So, instead of returning the hat, I brought it all the way back to New York. Or, really, I stole it. I stole someone's cowboy hat. I've only ever stolen one time in my whole life, and I got busted of course. (Well, not counting the little offense that sent Butter's own Officer Lurch into a spin. But I never got caught for that.)

Busted in Butter at the local Kum & Go. I was only nine, but I still showed signs of good rule following. First, I followed Rule #7: Never show panic:

I calmly told Officer Lurch that the zombies were coming...

Then I very evenly displayed a good ol' Rule #6: Never lie (when you can tell some of the truth):

...and that if I didn't get supplies (Swedish Fish) immediately to my family, who were already in the back-yard bunker, they would die. And of course, I stressed that Doc had forgotten to give me money in the panic.

1. Lie: Doc would never panic, nor would he ever give me money for candy, which was why I was stealing.
2. Lie: Zombies were not coming. (...or were they?! It's only a matter of time.)
3. Some of the Truth: We had a bunker, kind of. Doc encouraged Hunter Boone and I to build a bunker on the back property earlier that summer when we convinced him that Zombies were an immi-nent threat. He filmed us digging a hole for three days. (Best video ever featuring several great bits of Zombie knowledge from know-it-all nine-year-olds.) All hogwash, of course. We hadn't convinced

Doc of a Zombie Apocalypse. He had us digging the start of a man-made (kid-made, more like it) pond that Minnie always wanted. They finished it that fall, just in time for me to fall through the ice that winter.

4. Lie: The family wasn't in the bunker hole (now pond), though I secretly wished The Sister was. They were actually volunteering at the local food bank. I was taking a break (to steal) and The Sister was at Ben Franklin flirting with the best-looking boy in the tenth grade. (Gabe Gardner. Gross.)

Only one time. Lurch let me off, but I know it was hard for him and, considering what we would soon be plotting, he should've thrown me in the slammer.

And now, the scarred hat makes two incidents of stealing.

I rest the hat on a pin near the black feather boa on my vision board. I might find him someday and I'm putting it out there. The feather boa is to inspire me to be a light, free spirit, and that being a bit of a broad is never bad. (I think I proved that the first night in Austin. And every broad should have a boa, duh.) Then I hide my travel bag in the closet. Er, stuff it in the closet and shut...stuff it again and shut the door. All clean!

I get another text from Tray.

Honey, I'm going to buzz in two seconds.

OMG a hot guy just checked me out!

Then my phone blings. I answer but he doesn't hear me because he is singing a song from *Legally Blonde*, the musical.

"*Omigod, omigod, you guys!*" he sings, then yells, "Sydney, that guy was H. O. T., HOT! Aaaaaaah!" He hangs up and my buzzer rings six times in staccatoed succession. No one else does that; it's Tray. I buzz him in and open my door. I hear him five flights down singing again and I start in with him. The neighbors must love us.

"*Omigod, omigod, you guys!*" we sing. Then he gabs on the phone to what seems like a costume shop at the top of his lungs while trudging up the stairs. I guess I can understand why the woman who lives below me gives me the side eye.

He pushes in, still on the phone, gives me the hand signal that means Chatty Cathy is on the line, steps in front of the mirror, and starts pulling down the navy blue cargo shorts he's wearing. I'm not shocked, as you may believe me to be, since it's part of his normal routine. Every time he comes over he pulls down whatever pants he's sporting and fixes his tucked-in shirt or looks at his stomach, seeing if he's lost or gained a pound or two. Or he just wants to check out his new favorite pair of Calvin Klein underwear in the extremely tall, extremely wide full-length mirror in the living room. I had it custom made to fit floor-to-ceiling. I imagine Tray thinks I had it made for him. He finally yanks the phone from his head.

"How did you forget to feed Harold yesterday?" I scold.

"Who?" he asks, perplexed, admiring his Calvins and then pulling up his shorts. Omigod. I give up. Next time I go away I'm going to do what Claudia's fiancé does. He doesn't trust anybody to take care of his babies, the two (very fancy) Himalayan cats, which, mind you, were hers before they were engaged. He makes the cat sitter hold the current day's newspaper in front of the fur balls, snap a photo, and send it to him daily. Genius. I plan to implement this immediately.

Tray makes a screeching noise. "Weeyooow, yesterday was amazing! Can you believe it?" He hugs me hard, then says, "So, do you think I need lipo? I swear I need lipo. Did you see all that extra weight? Nothing I do helps." He moves into the open kitchen, rips open the fridge, and pulls out a chunk of Manchego cheese and martini olives. "I mean seriously, seeeeeriously."

"The new show sounds incredible!" I say, ignoring the lipo part.

He starts slicing the cheese on the kitchen bar and popping pieces into his mouth. "Do you have any crackers? You never have any food...aaaaaah!"

I don't. I eat out way too much. It's astonishing there was even cheese in there. Usually it's just the martini olives. I open one of my cupboards and find a bag of Kettle Chips. I haven't even offered them to him and he winces, "Are you trying to make me fat?" So I toss them back in among the martini glasses, wine glasses, teacups (only for Prohibition-style drinking), and keys. Omigod, there's my emergency set of keys! I steal a piece of cheese and plop into my comfy old leather chair. I pull my knees up to my chest and watch as he struts in front of me.

Tray is a tall, handsome man who, despite his (phony) protestation, looks like an attractive mix of Rock Hudson and Elvis. At the moment it's not as prominent because he's rocking a stunning ombréd turquoise faux hawk. (His hairdresser is a big deal too.) He grew up only a town over from me. As a pig-farmer-in-training he was afraid of the pigs "with all that snorting and dirty mud" and tried to avoid them like the plague. While his brothers got right in the swing of feeding and corralling them, Tray became a regular at his grandma's quilting circle. And on weekends, instead of fishing with his dad and brothers, he chose to go antiquing with his mom. If that wasn't enough to "out" him, in high school, instead of talking enthusiastically about taking over the farm with his brothers, he was enthusiastically designing and sewing a dress for his prom date.

"I know. I look fabulous today, don't I?" he says, sweeping some of the turquoise out of his eyes. "Did you notice my new shorts? Fabulous, right?" he does a model swivel and adds, "H & M on sale. See, Syd, you should learn to shop only during sales." This from the guy that buys top-of-the-line fashion fabrics, luscious silks, odd pieces of rare metals, historic scraps, and really anything it takes to produce his masterpieces. But he always gives me a little savings lesson for the day. He knows shopping is my Achilles heel. He sashays into my bedroom, presumably to find props, and I hear a squeal.

"Did you bring a cowboy home from Texas?" He walks back into the room wearing the scarred hat and trying to impersonate a cowboy, which plays more like Nathan Lane's character in *The Birdcage*. "This isn't one of yours; you're holding out on me, now spill it." He leans with rugged cool on one of the Toledo stools at the bar. It swivels, and he yelps. Not so rugged. We both laugh as he tries to regain his manhood.

I give him a quick rundown of the remarkably short details. And as I talk, I hear how absurd it sounds. A guy I see outside the bar just happens to be on the same flight as me, and then just happens to be in the same bar.

"Oh, this is good, this is really good, this is destiny!" He lights up. I've accidentally activated his crystal ball. "This is like the time I met that silver-haired hunk and we kept running into each other at all the gay bars!" (This is nothing like that time. Tray was stalking him.) "This is the one, Syd. I can feel it!"

Just like the time he "felt" I should date my co-star in our college production of *Funny Girl* (gay), just like the time he "felt" I should be with the guy from the gym (meathead), and just like the time he "felt" sure I should be with the bartender at Liberty Meat (only the gayest bar in the city). Maybe it's better we didn't find my mystery cowboy if Tray can "feel it."

In the midst of self-loathing, eating chips, and checking the fridge again, he asks me to help him today and, of course, I will. The bills I've just seen are making me nauseous, and it'll be the perfect distraction. And, of course, he "needs me terribly."

Speaking of need, I'm going to need some caffeine immediately. Tray puts away the one bite of cheese that's left (really just the rind), throws away the empty bag of chips, and offers to make the run to Starbucks while I get ready.

I keep singing the mind-droning (but adorable!) *Legally Blonde* song while I freshen up. I still can't get the song out of my head!

"Alexa, play getting ready music," I say.

"I thought you'd never ask," she responds. I look at her. A bit cheeky.

Is Alexa supposed to be able to say that? Tray obviously taught her new skills.

I pull out my new moisturizing, make-me-a-young-and-beautiful-goal-achiever cream. I'm sure they said exactly that in the commercial.

Rule #8
ALWAYS WEAR SUNSCREEN

Luckily this moisturizing miracle cream includes SPF. I've always worn sunscreen after our family trip to Grand Cayman. I turned a hideous shade of lobster the first day and couldn't even put on a life vest. Always a strong swimmer, I wasn't worried, until I swear The Sister, wearing hers, tried to drown me in the ocean. She said she thought

I was a sea turtle and was trying to "turtle surf." That's not even a thing. Minnie and Doc somehow thought that was an adequate reason for keeping me, the "sea turtle," underwater with her feet. We weren't even in the sea.

I've never forgotten sunscreen since then, and it's even more important now what with the whole reminder that I thought I would be old and gray in my twenties. WebMD says getting too much sun damages the skin, which leads to wrinkling and premature aging. So, you can never start too young!

I smear my face—a little extra can't hurt after a weekend of late nights and all that Austin sun—then rummage through my closet.

Me: Olivia, do you know a Broadway producing team that goes by "Times 2"? I'm helping Tray. Any insight? What do I wear?

Olivia: Of course I know them, darling. They're only one of the most prolific producing teams on Broadway. They're my age and have been together-together since college. Before it was even cool to muff dive (tongue emoji). This will make or break your boy. We're talking star status. But they're known to fire people just days before curtain. Be on point, they're sticklers for budget.

Me: Jeez, no pressure.

Olivia: Don't worry they'll love you! Wear the dress I gave you from high street. Watch out for the skinny one.

Me: What about the skinny one?

Olivia: You'll see

Me: Okay, wish us luck! See you Thursday!

Olivia: Luck has nothing to do with it. Speaking of Thursday, do you think I could pull this off?

A photo of Olivia wearing a miniscule piece of leather over her ample breasts posing with three models in beautiful, architectural lingerie pops on the screen. The fashion show Olivia's invited me to on Thursday will apparently feature a fantastic new female lingerie designer.

Me: Yassss! Haaa!

Olivia: Perfecly padded. (wink face emoji)

Olivia has the most delicious sense of self, which she lovingly describes as "perfectly padded," always while patting her pocketbook and laughing.

London fashion is always wonderfully feminine without being overtly sexy. Great choice, Olivia. It's cool enough for the warm weather but stylish enough to meet producers. I brush on a little extra blush so I look awake (don't worry, not like Mrs. Rich and her traffic cone orange) and run downstairs, where Tray's waiting. He's holding our drinks and screaming at an invisible person. I take a large gulp of Christmas Morning (that's what I call my soy Chai) and savor the delicious, happy flavor while he finishes talking to whoever's in his headphones. He screams something about getting the money in a brash tone, then hangs up, ripping the headphones from his ears.

"You okay?" I ask.

"I'm fine. People are crazy," he answers vaguely.

"Do you need some money?"

"Syd, it's fine. I don't need anything," he says curtly, and I drop it. He's never used that tone of voice before.

We cross the familiar street to Tray's apartment, saying hello to nearly everyone along the way, and pop into his building. Stepping into his airy loft apartment, I notice his latest costumes in different levels of build and extreme disarray. I've never seen his work so disorganized. He's always put together. Looking to the left, his beautiful marble kitchen island is a mess, overflowing with empty liquor bottles. I peer sideways at Tray, trying to decipher what's happening, but there's no time for questions. We only have one short hour until producers arrive.

Dresses are arranged on racks and catalogued by the time the two female producers arrive. The first steps into the loft carrying a delicate black briefcase, of about the same age as Olivia, like she mentioned, and wearing a sour, pinched expression. She's followed by a warmer, rounder-looking woman, also in her fifties, with short curls and carrying none other than a red Hermès Birkin Bag. We greet them and, without wasting time, show them a few pieces they've requested for their new production's Broadway premiere. Within moments, the pinched-face woman relaxes, apparently impressed (grudgingly) by the materials and workmanship.

Then we show them what Tray dreamed up and apparently sewed with several of his best seamstresses on Saturday afternoon until three in the morning. (No wonder Harold went without food; Tray was in a manic state of design.)

"I never saw it this way," says the sourpuss, with no real reveal as to what she actually thinks. In our quick fury getting things ready and then rushing into the presentation, I've already forgotten their names.

"I never saw it this way either, but we *should* have!" raves the other, spinning a curl with her finger several times quickly. "Thrilling, just thrilling!" she says, and I almost expect bubbles to float out of her ears and her body to lift slightly off the mosaic flooring. She touches the gowns and revels in the fabrics while the puss squeezes her lips tightly and I assume her ass cheeks as well.

"Ich." A sneeze-snort sound wrenches from her throat. "How much is this going to cost?" the puss says, lifting her chin as if trying to be taller than Tray.

"Incredible, how much is this going to *make* us?" bubbles the other, holding up a gorgeous corset with impeccable boning. Tray taught me to cinch and stuff (my bra) in college with a corset similar to this one. Cinching and stuffing, another trick I wish I had known in high school. Marcy Moore would have been so mad.

"If you'd like me to finish in this direction, we'll only be over the original estimate by..." Tray combs his hand through his faux hawk twice, summoning a number he can't find, then looks at me for help. I grab the product list and time sheet notes from his workbench.

"By..." I do a few additions in my head. "...roughly, $6,097.56." I try to make it sound like six dollars instead of six thousand. The allure of math may have eluded me, but the ability to speak in numbers never has. (Especially my uncanny ability to add up a shopping spree. To the penny!)

"Ich," the puss sneeze-snorts again.

"Incredible," the other bubbles, gazing at another costume. I can't tell if she heard the number or didn't care. She touches the male lead's dreamy suede coat and swoons.

"The structural embellishments on each costume will be tailored to the personality of the character," Tray explains, holding up two exquisite dresses fit for two very different characters. "See how the lines on this one are striking and very angular, whereas this one is rounded, soft, and, well, more comforting?" The sour puss puts her hands on her tiny hips and inspects them. Tiny isn't the word—they're all but invisible. This woman has not eaten in years; I need a magnifying glass just to see her ass, which is, again, most likely clenched.

"Ich," Puss bleats.

"Incredible," bellows Bubbles.

Puss reaches for the angular gown Tray is still holding. Bubbles reaches for the soft gown with supple fabric. I'd say Tray's vision is proving good. Their attraction to the very different looks is uncanny, one for the villainous character's gown, and the other for the bright ingénue's gown.

"Hmm...yes, I do think this will be incredible," the puss says, holding the magnificent piece up to her body and looking in the mirror near the racks. I half expect her to start enchanting, "Mirror, mirror on the wall, who is the fairest of them all?" and cackle. I actually get the shivers.

Tray is unbelievably kind to the bony terror and accommodates several more questions while Bubbles looks at fabrics with me.

"I'm just so thrilled, I can't say it enough. He's such a talent," she gushes.

"I know, they'll be magnificent on stage." I smile at her.

"Say, you look familiar," she says, hugging silk taffeta and looking at me closely. I give her a blank stare. She spins a curl between her fingers. "That's it, you're the doll that fell into the garbage!"

Omigod.

"I've got to get you in front of a camera. I know some people," she says, and shoves a business card into my hand from her red Hermès. "Now, I'll need your number." Somehow, Tray is already squeezing our shoulders and giving her my number before I have time to process.

"We've got to get to the theater," Puss says with a bored look. They say their goodbyes and Bubbles gives us several air kisses as she closes the wide framed door. We wait to hear their footsteps fade away and look at each other.

"Ich," Tray mimics the puss's sneeze-snort, and we laugh.

How we didn't open the window and let her blow out on a light breeze, I don't know, but we're both ecstatic about the go-ahead. Tray sings, "Omigod You Guys" and omigod you guys, this song is going to be stuck in my head all day. But I join in anyway, adding two-part harmony.

"But omigod you guys, I'm tired," he says. "It's just hit me. I've got to get sleep," Tray yawns, coming down from his work high. He hugs me. "She's going to call you, ya know, and she knows a lot of people. Answer the phone," he says, wagging his finger at me. Then he drags his body toward his bed, hidden behind a large Thai changing screen that was gifted to him after the close of a production of *The King and I*.

"See ya later, Liza," I say, and push the wide door open. I didn't get to talk to him about all the empty booze bottles, but now's not the time. I wait for his response to our old Liza Minnelli/Elizabeth Taylor reference and turn to wave, but he's hidden by the screen. I smell a peculiar burning scent with a sweet hint to it that I don't recognize.

He doesn't respond with his usual, "As always, Elizabeth."

Chapter 17
ROAD TO NOWHERE

"NAMASTE, NAMASTE, Syd!" Zoey screams through FaceTime.

"Zoey, hi, hi, hi!" I scream back while looking into my closet, fresh from the shower.

"Everyone loves it. You're a YouTube sensation! If they had dumped you out of that garbage can, we swear you'd be in a perfect downward dog. I can tell you haven't been meditating, but you look stellar!"

The video again. Gah.

Zoey bartends with us, but she's currently in Australia showing off her yoga teaching skills as part of her parents' movement. Her parents are astrologists slash yogi slash environmental activists and often talk about how exploding stars affect the earth's temperature and our bodies. Right now they're leading a retreat, or what they call the "Body Alight" movement, in Byran Bay. I would totally be more into it if I didn't immediately want to eat French fries when anyone mentions yoga.

"So, are you doing yoga?" she asks.

French fries. "Yoga?" I say, playing dumb. Zoey dyes her short hair pink, purple, and sometimes rainbow, depending on her mood. She says it helps when she's aligned from head to toe. She's rocking the rainbow now, and all the colors are striking against her olive skin. If her hair were really like a mood ring, I think it would have gone gray just now.

"Okay, okay, at least you did downward dog in the garbage," she laughs, quickly changing the color of her hair back to rainbow.

"Omigod, so the video. One of Tray's new producers saw it and I just went to the bodega and everyone high fived me, including my neighborhood homeless guy. I mean, how has he seen it?" I say, taking the Marilyn Monroe towel sweep off my wet hair.

"Oh, everyone has an iPhone, Syd. I'm sure Apple did some seriously rabid outreach worth millions in tax write-offs," she says, smoothing a blue section of hair behind her ear. I can see several people in a circle behind her playing what I presume are native instruments because they weren't options in sixth grade when Butter band was big. I immediately decide I was jipped when I focus on something that looks like an elephant's trunk. I would have chosen that for sure.

"Zoey, you called at the perfect time. I'm trying to decide what to wear." I swing the phone around so she can see my open closet.

"Syd, I want to live in your closet," she giggles. "I want to wear it all! Oh, what was that? Are you doing art?" I pivot the phone back to my vision board.

"Yes, no, well, kind of." Omigod, now I'm saying "kind of" in relation to my goals. I immediately correct myself. "Actually, I made a vision board."

"Stop, stop it. That is the best idea ever!" Zoey squeals.

"That's what I thought too!" I scream.

"Syd, this is huge. I seriously believe in putting all your aspirations into the world. That's how everything works, you know." Zoey, excited, leans into the phone's camera so I can only see her nose. Her small piercing, fit with a green emerald, twinkles. "The ancestors call them vision boards and encourage people to make them when their lives aren't focused." Yes, that sounds about right. And "ancestors" is what Zoey calls her parents. "Have you focused on your intention?" she asks, but doesn't wait for an answer. She leans in even more, her nostrils now covering the screen. She's really into this. "You should look at the board several times a day to help focus that intention!" She scratches her nose in excitement, then realizes she's only showing nose. She leans back from the camera so I can see her whole face again. "Would you listen to me?" she laughs. "I've been here so long I'm starting to talk like them, but anyway, I'm so happy you're doing this!"

"I'll look at the board more now and focus. Good idea," I say, making a mental note.

"And put a yoga class on that board! Okay, okay, back to the closet," she says, making circular motions with her pointer finger that's covered in henna. Digging through the closet ends up sparking so much conversation about dresses, shoes, the new girl she's seeing, traveling, et cetera, et cetera, that I lay on the bed catching up about absolutely everything and nothing at all, forgetting that I'm supposed to be somewhere.

Thank God Zoey had a star alignment emergency, something about blah, blah, blah being in retrograde and they needed to do a blah, blah, blah immediately, because it reminds me I need to get to the fashion show ASAP.

I lean into the closet and grab a cream off the shoulder number shoved between several "We ♥ Our Customers" wire hangers. (Joan Crawford would be so upset.) The dress is demure and an absolutely perfect number for tonight, especially since I have no clue what's in the back half of the closet and it was right in front.

Tonight is the fashion show produced by my always-fun bigwig British friend, Olivia, who frequents my fitness classes. She comes to nearly all of them even though she usually ends up sitting in the back texting and taking selfies of her imaginary sweat.

Olivia is a miracle worker. Where there's no money she finds it, and where there's no glitz she pours it on. She's one of the most powerful women I've ever met. Power follows her like bees to honey. And there are some rather big names on the invite list so I need to look stunning.

I roll my hair up in the curlers I've been using since high school (I might need new curling equipment) and glam up my normal makeup with a hint of smokey eye, trying to keep it somewhat light. I find it hard to do a smokey eye without looking like a heroin addict but I think I got it right this time. Standing in front of the custom mirror between the two living room windows with just my undergarments and heels, I add and add and add my mascara and dance with Alexa, who's still playing getting ready music. I wonder if anyone across the street at the same window level can see me. Well, duh, Tray, but he's only interested in men—and himself, of course. I giggle out loud at the thought but look at his window to be sure I'm not caught in my skivvies. His blinds are still closed since we met with the producers at the beginning of the week. And anyway, who looks into other people's windows?

A tour bus on the street below rolls by and I hear again how my neighborhood has played central roles in the writings of Jack Kerouac, Allen Ginsberg, William S. Burroughs, Truman Capote, and Maya Angelou. The beatniks loved my neighborhood and, apparently, so does the tour guide. He happily shares that he's stumbled out of Greenwich Village bars numerous times. I just love my neighborhood! I would wave, but I'm indecent. I turn around, bend over, and pick up the beautiful dress laying on the love seat. I hear the tourists on the bus cheer and holler. They must love my neighborhood too!

I put on the cream, just above the knee, stunner and pull off the tag. Horrible, I know. Only Donna Karan knows how long this dress has been hiding in my closet. (Thank goodness it's timeless!) I throw on my nude platform heels and some gold bangles and grab my cream Miu

Miu clutch from the same closet. Wait, should I take the vintage Louis Vuitton Speedy from my ex? I rush into the bedroom, reach deep into the other closet, past my travel bag, and hold it up. I stare at it next to my dress. I always wondered if the Louis was a knockoff. I toss it back into the closet. Plus, I'm using it as my secret stash and I don't have time to find a new hiding spot. Apparently everyone knows to look in the sock drawer. (No wonder Minnie found my goals!) I give Harold some fish flakes and an air kiss and head downstairs. With the Miu Miu under my arm and bangles clinking, I walk out onto the block.

The guys at the kitchen door all say hellos as the bartender points at my ensemble and mouths "nice" from the window, fashionably displaying a new hair color. (She's always so complimentary!) I mouth "fab" while fluffing my hair so she knows what I mean and she brightens. Minnie and Doc are always saying I should live in a small town or, at the very least, the Midwest. I mean, maybe they're right, but this seems just as small town to me.

I wave at the owner of my fave wine bar, who glides by on his bike, and say hi to a neighbor walking her dog. My block really *does* have a neighborhoodly feel. One Eye Joe catches me as I round the corner onto the avenue and I give him a hug. He holds it just a little bit too long.

"Sydney, sunshine, look at you all dressed up. You're gorgeous," he smiles, running his hand through his salt and pepper hair. One Eye Joe is quite the charmer, but his hugs always seem to linger. On the upside, he never mentions it when my rent is late, which it is now. It's sitting on my kitchen bar.

"Hi...Jovan! How are you?" I blush, almost calling him One Eye Joe. I don't ever call Jovan "One Eye Joe" to his face. Well, actually, I did once.

We were sitting at the wine bar (it's everyone's favorite in the neighborhood) and it slipped out. He paused just long enough for me to think he was upset, then let out a roar of laughter, which was actually quite startlingly high pitched. He thought it was hilarious and took off his dark glasses he's never without. (This was the first time I was rendered immobile by the eyeball super power.) He showed me his scar and glass eye but would only say "ehh, you know, I got into a thing," in his rich Italian accent while spinning his Cartier pinky ring. I bet he lost it in a knife fight or to a lead pipe. Or I bet it happened when he was bumpin' off some thug. Or when he spent time in jail for "extortion" back in the day. But he won't give up that information. Believe me, I've tried.

One Eye Joe opens the door to the taxi for me. "Have a wonderful evening, sunshine."

"Thanks, Jovan! Rent is sitting on my kitchen bar. I'll get it to you tomorrow," I say and wave out the window.

"I could just go get it if I had a—" Jovan says, as the taxi zooms off.

If he just had a key? Are you kidding me?

"Forty-second Street between Park and Lex," I sing to the driver. I tell the driver how I'm always running late and that we'll need to go as fast as possible. Lucky for me he's been a driving for over thirty years and knows all the tricks. He also knows a lot about New York and seems to have the most wonderful family. He tells me all about his adorable daughter, who's taking dance lessons at the Joffrey, and his son, who wants to be a firefighter.

Five blocks away from the glitzy 42nd Street Cipriani, I look in my cream Miu Miu for my credit card. The only thing I see is powder, mascara, dazzleglass lip gloss, and my phone. This is a joke, right? I dig through the clutch in a frenzy. I must have some money in here somewhere. And my keys. I don't have my keys. I let out a tiny frazzled yelp. The driver gives me a quizzical look through the rearview mirror and I laugh nervously as I find a crumpled twenty dollar bill.

I know I shoved a few hundred dollars in here, didn't I? I always put pirate money in my favorite clutches. Even with rent sitting at the apartment there should be some left. I go over the last couple days. Where did I spend all that money? Kill. I tell the taxi driver to stop because the meter's creeping closer to my new limit.

"But miss, we aren't there yet," he says.

"It's okay, I'll walk," I smile, but he continues driving. "Please stop, or I won't be able to tip. I only have a twenty," I say, pushing my hair from my eyes. Even my hair feels stressed. I go on to tell the driver how I must have spent hundreds on, on…what? And that I have an issue with throwing money away. (Why I'm telling this man my financial woes, I don't know, but I feel like I know his whole family. I bet his daughter at the Joffrey wouldn't twirl away hundreds of dollars and his son the firefighter wouldn't burn through it like I must have.)

He stops at a red light and turns to look at me.

"Miss, from now on, you must save twenty percent of what you bring home. You must put it away and not touch it. You will invest this money and grow this money and you will live the American dream," he says, earnestly.

"I…" I start to say that of course I know this, and that I had a pirate chest full of money when I was eleven, and even have a Louis Vuitton full of it now, but he interrupts me (thankfully) because clearly he knows that I might understand this, but I don't do this.

"Miss, you must save this money starting tomorrow. You do this and I promise you will grow an empire."

"Thank you," I say, bewildered. Yes, I need to start saving. It's one of my goals! One of the world's richest men is a cabby-turned-fertilizer-king, Tamir Sapir, America's "billionaire cabbie." Something tells me I should listen to this cab driver. I hand him the twenty and go to open the door.

"You aren't getting anywhere in those heels, and you'll definitely be late. We're going to get you to that party." He winks in a fatherly way, turns off the meter, and hits the gas.

The crisis is postponed for the moment, but I don't have my credit card, and now I really have no cash. I'm going to go to the bank tomorrow, open an account, and start saving twenty percent.

But for now, I'll have to wing it. I'm not worried about the keys. I tend to forget my keys more often than not and will just have to climb through Elan's window. Don't tell

One Eye Joe. Elan is a resident in neurosurgery; maybe we should have a talk about my memory.

Cipriani is a huge, glamorous New York City staple. I'm ushered through a giant arched entrance by Olivia's staff and led to the bar. The majestic marble, the sparkling chandeliers, the sky-scraping ceilings, the really lovely martini I've just been handed, the gold bank teller windows, the bountiful hors d'oeuvres and array of drinks... it's remarkable. As I mingle with business associates of Olivia's, I'm given word she's making last-minute preparations backstage. That's just when I hear her distinct voice.

"Sydney! I'm so glad you're here," she says, blazing a path to me. She grabs my shoulders and pulls me into a hug as I slosh most of my martini onto the floor. Then she whispers in my ear, "You've no idea the mess that's happening back there right now. If they pull this off it's going to be a miracle, an absolute miracle." Then she pulls back from our one-sided hug and booms, "Now someone get me a drink, for God's sake! I've been standing here forever. What am I, twenty?" That's Olivia's favorite line, *what am I, twenty*, and it slips from her very posh British accent to a more Cockney accent when she says it. She loves to reminisce about when she couldn't afford anything frivolous, let alone a drink, in her twenties. She gives me three air kisses (three!), smiles, and snaps, waving martinis over.

Olivia was once married to a physically and mentally abusive "arse-load loser" (her description), and after years of taking his "real ripe shite" (straight from Olivia's mouth), she made a plan, a business model to be exact, and worked up the nerve to ask for a divorce. She blossomed without him and made an extraordinary amount of money in organics. Extraordinary is an understatement. She now invests in startups founded by women like her.

Olivia pushes at her jet-black hair, which is usually, like now, pulled into a French twist and waves suggestively at a man across the room. She wears red lipstick (even to the gym), which usually needs to be swept off her teeth, also like now, and I make a quick motion toward mine so she knows. She waves again, this time more of a *you're too much* wave and wipes it off. "One day I'm going to invest in a fancy red lipstick that stays off my bucking broncos!" she laughs. And I'm sure she will. "Speaking of broncos, that gentleman over there..."

Olivia vows never to marry again unless for money, which she doesn't need, and goes through men like toilet paper. She's in her early fifties, but I know thirty-somethings who can't keep up with her. She was delighted to turn fifty and wouldn't turn the clock back even if you told her you had a genie in a bottle. She often says, "Sydney, look how high my ass sits! You think I looked like this when I was your age? No bloody way." Olivia's lost twenty-five pounds coming to my classes and always sees a model in the mirror no matter what her weight.

I take a quick moment to text while Olivia removes red lipstick from her teeth.

Me: Where are you guys? It's about to start!

Claudia: Just walking in! It takes Pax forever to get ready (you know). Where are you?

Me: Go left, I'm behind the champagne tower

Bette: Didn't you get my text?! I'm covering for Abby at the bar! She said she couldn't make it, no explanation. Gus and I are getting slammed! Check on her when you get a chance (blowing a kiss emoji)

A smartly dressed waiter takes my mangled martini, hands me another that's heavy on the vodka and a little bit dirty, and hands her a glass that's extra dirty with extra olives. Olivia takes a long sip while holding onto his tray, and her exceptionally pale skin flushes pink for just a moment. She gestures for another as the rest of the wait staff quietly urges us to our seats. Receiving her second drink with extra olives at the table, Olivia double fists martinis as she sits.

"Do you suppose this is why I can't lose all of the weight?" she laughs, holding up her drinks.

Then we look at each other and both say, "Nah."

Claudia, looking a bit frazzled, slips into her seat with Pascal (Pax) on her right just as I take mine. "Syd, Olivia, we made it! Olivia, thank you for having us. Sorry for the delay," she says, smacking air kisses our direction. Pax, always shy in a crowd, nods politely, prompting Olivia to whisper loudly to the same waiter about a bottle of champagne for the table just as the lights dim.

Two men dressed like rappers, with all their bling, move out onto the stage and reveal violins. They jump at the same time and begin playing an unbelievable mix of classical and hip-hop. I'm floored that not only are they playing with incredible precision, but they're also introducing the show, dancing, blowing out their strings, and getting the whole room amped up. (I'm not sure that elephant trunk instrument could get a crowd going like this, but I didn't imagine violins doing it either.) Everyone is cheering and clapping and, just as they disappear, the models take the stage.

They strut out in all levels of dress and undress with their long, sinewy legs and geisha-inspired makeup. Spotting three pieces that are must-haves—um, if I had thousands to spend on lingerie—I point them out to Claudia, who is here specifically to shop for her honeymoon. She nods in agreement and we both smile at Olivia, who returns it with a wink. I knew Claudia would love this before her wedding, and Olivia couldn't wait for Pascal to meet some of her art-adoring friends. "Every buyer is a potential collector, after all!" she said. The models prance off and a flurry of fabric drops from the ceiling over the runway, hanging in beautiful sheaths of crimson. Extremely fit acrobats in nude body suits appear and proceed to climb and hang precariously from each drape, creating dramatic formations.

"I look like that, right?" Olivia asks quietly, leaning into me.

"Obviously," I say, and we clink glasses.

The models return to the runway and wow the packed room of over five hundred with their dynamite attire. The lights come up and Olivia isn't at the table, but on stage saying a big thank you to all the contributors. Uproarious applause fills the air, and she invites everyone to mingle, meet the up-and-coming female designer, and hit the bar.

I talk to all sorts of well-known artists (including Pax, of course), musicians, fashionistas, and celebrity this-and-thats. Everyone adds "celebrity" in front of his or her job title here. Celebrity accountant, celebrity chef, celebrity real-estate agent. One woman just told me that she's a celebrity relationship specialist. Which really just means she's crap at her job, right? I mix business cards in with my makeup but no-money Miu Miu and continue to listen to people tell me all about themselves.

Claudia pulls me from a group of people and whispers, "Olivia was right, there are a lot of art enthusiasts here."

"I noticed! How's Pax doing?"

"You know, his palms are sweating and he just went into some really cerebral explanation of his process, which no one understood, but they were enamored," Claudia laughs. "Pax has no idea that people are so drawn to him. He just sees them as obstacles until he can get back to his canvas." We both turn toward his direction. He looks pained.

"Which you're going to need to do, like now," I laugh.

She lovingly shakes her head. "How's Abby? Have you heard from her? Bette said she couldn't come tonight because she was covering for her."

"I've texted her but she hasn't responded."

"Let me know if you hear anything." She finishes her lingerie-inspired cocktail, handed out after the show, in one swig. "I'm going to get him home."

They make their way to the door while I look for Olivia.

After speaking to a few more women who helped coordinate the show, it's finally our turn to sneak out. Olivia and I leave with a group of her colleagues and hit the more relaxed but fashionable after-party scene in the Meatpacking District. Once in the quieter, lounge-style bar, I eye the crowd for any interesting characters, aka cute guys, remembering what Zoey said. My stars are totally aligned for meeting the perfect man tonight because something is in something and I won't be able to resist the pull of something. Anyway, it's something good!

After several failed attempts to locate a smart, hilarious, handsome, staggeringly wealthy astronaut in the crowd, I determine there's no one here I would be remotely interested in (maybe I'm setting the bar too high). But I've amassed several free drinks, so I down the rest of my current martini and pick up another while looking around the bar for Olivia. I scan the dense crowd and find that a thick suit is rubbing her shoulders and she looks to be in midstory huddled amongst a group of enthralled bargoers. Just behind them at the bar door, an overwhelmingly friendly-looking—some might say cocky—man all but blows into the room. It's like the crowd isn't there, and all I see is him. He pulls his newsboy cap down a bit lower and tufts of hair curl around the base, as if he's worn it for years. Yes, he's quite handsome and I feel like I know him somehow. Or it could be the vodka. Another sip should clear that up.

He's headed my direction, and as I get a closer look he really does seem awfully familiar. Who is this guy? Do I know him? What's under that hat? He makes eye contact with me and I flash him a cute, eye-batting smile. I swear I know him. I peek at Olivia, who is now sneaking into a back room with the suit. When I turn to check out the newsboy again, he's right in front of me.

"Do I know you?" he asks, with an Oscar Award-winning smile.

"I don't think so, but you do look very familiar," I respond, taking a sip from my glass.

"I do?" he says, inquisitively. "I'd offer you a drink but it looks like you're—"

"Oh right—would you like one?" I ask, pushing a shot into his hand. I know now; I'm almost certain. He works at one of my favorite casual breakfast spots, The Grey Dog. I'm almost positive. They all seem to wear those caps, and the owner, who's always so nice, certainly knows how to pick a good-looking staff.

"Are you a waiter?" I ask.

"Waiter?" he says, looking confused. He takes the shot and flashes that smile again.

"Do you work at one of my favorite breakfast spots?"

"Really?" he says a bit indignantly. He smiles, then asks, "What's your name?"

"What's yours?" I counter, with a flirtatious smirk.

He laughs and tries, oddly, to impress me with his name. "I'm Gavin McKnight," he says, as his chest puffs up.

"Gavin, do you work at The Grey Dog?" I ask again. His chest deflates but his smile gets brighter.

"I'd like your number. What is it?" he asks and takes out his phone, ready to plug in my digits.

"What?" A bit soon, am I right? "Absolutely not."

"Really?" he says, shocked.

"You think I give my number to just anyone?" I smirk. I'm not that kind of girl. But I expect a Grey Dog business card so I can think about it.

"I think you might know who I am, and I would love to take you to dinner," he says with a twinkle in his eye and that smile. (That smile!) Did he just ask me on a proper date? I think I may consider giving out my number.

I look around to see if Olivia's back. I spot her and her now disheveled hair, watching the man's efforts from across the room. She gives me a tipsy head nod and waves both hands as if pushing me into him. Okay, what the hell, he's got that smile and I love hats.

"So? Dinner?" he asks again.

"Sure," I say, flashing my own impersonation of a movie star smile, albeit not as symmetrical as his, and give him my name and number.

"Would you like my number?" he offers.

"Goodness no. What would I do with your number? I'll get it when you call for dinner," I reply. He laughs again as if I'm missing the joke. Perplexed, I give him a cute but confused look.

"You really don't know who I am?"

"Nope, but I like your cap."

"So you're going to go out with me because you like my cap?"

"I guess so. We'll see when you call," I say flirtatiously. He laughs again and starts to tell me something, but the music in the bar seems to press up another octave and I hear a garbled something or other about HBO. Why is he talking to me about HBO? I smile, laugh, then furrow my brow as if in interest. I figure that should cover any and all reactions I might have had if I heard what he said.

"Well, Sydney Shag, I'll call you tomorrow," he says loudly, gently taking my hand.

"We'll see if I answer," I grin.

"I like you," he says, laughing. He gives my hand a squeeze, then confidently walks to the back of the bar and up the stairs. Well, he's…I can't put my finger on it, but there's something about him. Maybe Zoey was right; maybe the stars *are* aligned in my favor. Taking a sip of my drink, and grabbing another, this one a champagne cocktail, perched on the bar, I walk over to Olivia, pleased with my "hard to Shag" self.

"Not too shabby, right, Olivia? I think he's one of the waiters at The Grey Dog," I say, loud enough for her to hear.

"I think you're wrong," she says, trying to press her hair back into a French twist with one hand, the other now weighed down by champagne.

"I know he didn't say, but he probably just doesn't want to mention he's a waiter. He probably does something else too. We all do."

"He's an actor," Olivia says dryly.

"Probably. They all are, right? But this one's really cute, so actor, waiter, whatever, it might be fun to go out with him."

"No, really, Sydney, he's an actor. That was Gavin McKnight. *The* Gavin McKnight, star of the new HBO series *Road to Nowhere*. And he's been in several big movies," she says.

No way. "Get out. Really?"

"No, you get out, you Midwest poke!" she chuckles. Olivia loves to call me "Midwest" and usually adds something like "poke," "hayride," or "youngin'" after it. She finishes the last swig from her champagne flute and takes the bottle of Cristal that's tucked under her arm and refills it. Only Olivia would have a bottle of Cristal tucked under her arm like it was a bottle of bodega wine. She takes the last sip of my martini and sets it down, handing me her bubbling flute. Then she takes the cocktail from my other hand, pours the rest of the no longer chilled drink into a plant nearby, fills it with Cristal, and takes a sip. "Now, back to me, darling. You'll never believe what I just did in the backroom."

Yes, I can. I can tell by the evil glint in her eye and mussed hair that she's just shagged the thick, rich gentleman now sitting on the Victorian-style couch behind us.

I sip the champagne and meet more of her associates that are CEOs, CFOs, C hairy Os, C short Os, and C stuffy Os standing around the after-party. I start to wonder how many times Olivia has refilled my champagne and decide it is time to sneak out.

I ask Olivia to spot me a twenty for a martini and she hands me a hundred dollar bill. I feel bad but it's really for my cab. Why did she have to do that? Couldn't she be normal and give me a twenty? I have to work in the morning and Olivia never lets anyone leave, so it's this way or no way. I'll pay her back at the gym.

I Irish goodbye, (sneak out, leave without saying goodbye—Olivia taught me all the best ways to extricate myself from a party in stealth mode herself), and snag a taxi while hobbling across the cobblestone. I love the old cobblestone in the Meatpacking but sometimes wonder if the Historical Society saved it just to produce videos of people stumbling, er face-planting, on them at three and four in the morning.

While zooming by familiar streets on the few blocks home, I see Tray in a dimly lit stoop with three others. But is it Tray? It's hard to miss his turquoise hair but it's so late and all that champagne. I blink a few times but we're several doors past now.

Tray, are you out? I thought you were focusing on the costumes? I'm almost home!

LIZA! Come over! I swear I just saw you!!

Tray?

No reply. Maybe it wasn't him. It *was* dark.

And now that I'm looking at my phone, there's still no reply from Abby, which is unusual.

The doors to my building are propped open with suitcases— someone probably has a seriously early flight. Been there, done that. I tiptoe up the stairs in my nude heels and climb one flight above my door. Six flights up in heels and tipsy. So talented! I knock and scream-whisper, "Elan, get up—it's Syd! I locked myself out!" I pause and listen, but there's only silence. "Elan, get up—Elan!" He must not be home. He's probably at his girlfriend's place. I search for his hide-a-key, hidden in a crack of the doorframe. Elan always has a hide-a-key. I don't for this very reason.

I bumble with the lock, finally pushing through at an alarming rate. The door hits his coat closet with a loud thud, and I feel bad for the neighbor. I close the door, which locks automatically (they all do), and put the key in my now money-filled Miu Miu. I'll replace it tomorrow. I fumble with the middle drawer in the kitchen, looking for the knife I always use to jimmy my window. My windows are never locked but they tend to stick a little. Finding the knife, I weave into his bedroom to get to the fire escape.

But as I open the window, I hear a heavy thud and scurrying movement behind me.

"Who's there? Is someone there?" I yelp, turning and holding up the knife, instinctively.

"Please don't hurt me! I know you still love him but please don't hurt me," pleads a sweet woman's voice with an Indian accent.

"What?" I stumble forward with the knife still flashed because I'm in super high heels and tipsy.

"Please…please…you can have him; just don't hurt me! I know you still love him," the voice pleads again.

"Have who? Love who?" I ask, befuddled. I can barely make out a huddled mass in the corner between the bed and the wall. "Oh, hi!" I wave the knife and she screams.

"Please, please!"

"Oh, I'm Sydney from downstairs," I say, teetering in my heels. "You must be Janet." This is just great. I've never met Elan's girlfriend, Janet, and our first greeting is going to be at the end of a long night. My hair probably looks terrible. Why is she still cowering in the corner?

"No, no, Janet! Please don't hurt me," she winces.

"Not Janet? Then who are you?" I ask in what I intend to be a calm, quiet voice, although it comes out sounding more like a wild yell because of all the champagne.

"I'm Lydia. I know you're Janet and I'm not trying to take your place, so please don't hurt me!"

She must not understand me very well, so I slow it down. "I'M-SYDNEY-FROM-DOWNSTAIRSS!" I am seriously slurring. And why am I yelling? I need to get home. "I'LL-COME-BACK-TOMORROW!" I wave goodbye with the knife and crawl through the window, closing it behind me. I hope she didn't see my backside, because I don't think that was very graceful. If she did, it isn't going to go over well as far as first impressions go, slurring and ass in face. Ugh.

I climb down the fire escape one flight to my window, stick the knife under the latch, jimmy it open, and flop inside. What a night. I'll have to tell Elan that Lydia is cute; well, what I could see of her anyway. I wonder what happened to Janet?

I really hope Lydia didn't see my ass.

Chapter 18
SOS

GOOD YOGA is always done with the rising sun, or at least that's what Zoey said before we got off the phone yesterday. By the end of our conversation, she'd talked me into a class and reserved my spot herself. (Smart move.) But I swear the sun isn't even up, and I swear I just went to bed. In fact, I did just go to bed. But my stupid smartphone is screaming at me, and my vision board is staring at me. I have exactly ten minutes to get to class. I'll never make it.

Dashing out of bed, I curse Zoey and her big idea that I need to take yoga. In the space of two minutes, I feed Harold, who doesn't even look awake, throw on gym gear, grab my bag, notice that my rent money is missing, and run down the stairs.

The street is beautiful and quiet, almost serene, before the hustle and bustle of the city begins. It's my favorite part of the day, whether just getting home or just getting up. I run to catch a cab, but my yoga pants get caught in my shoe and I miss the curb. I stutter forward, flailing my arms, grabbing at the air. My speed picks up in a forward free fall and I hit the pavement with a hard thump, scattering the contents of my bag all over the avenue. Double ugh.

"What are you doing? Get out of the road!" the taxi driver screams out his window. I burp champagne bubbles as he screeches to a halt just inches from my body. Omigod. I get up and stand there for a moment like a deer in headlights. Not how I planned on hailing this cab. I hear a huge guffaw that takes me out of my trance and see Godfrey, my favorite homeless man giving me a thumbs-up.

"Godfrey!" I yell hello and laugh because I was caught windmilling my arms and landing flat on my face.

"It's Good Ray!" he calls back, laughing himself into a cough. He's so funny. He meant good day, I'm sure. I hope it's a "g'day" after this start.

I hold the cab that almost crushed my skull and gather my things, including my new headphones, throwing them back in the bag. I leave the coins and a few dollars that tumbled out, knowing my favorite homeless guy will be happy to have them. Though in that moment it fully hits me. Where is the rent money I left on my kitchen bar?!

Omigod, I've been robbed!

"All right, all right!" Godfrey claps, yelling after me.

I wave at him with a bloody hand. Omigod, I have a bloody hand! What else?! Not only are my pants ripped from the bottom of the outside seam to just past the knee on my left leg, but my hand is also a mess. Mental note: champagne has a detrimental effect on my body.

We peel out toward the gym as I hold my hand in an upward rescue position. I laugh a bit hysterically and the driver actually decides to ask if I'm okay. But the harder I giggle—how stupid I must have looked! Omigod, it hurts!—the more difficult it becomes to respond. We pull up to the gym, just eight blocks away, and I zoom into the entrance, wondering how I'm going to explain this look. The private gym, located in one of the most exclusive buildings in the city, is on the top floor. After pushing the elevator button several times for good measure, I wait, hunched over, trying to put my pants back together.

I stand up just as the elevator opens and look into the face of one of the many good-looking men who frequent this location. I teach here three days a week, and trust me when I say it doesn't get better looking or more athletic than the specimens in this gym. He says hello while standing what feels like two inches from my face. I think he eyes my neck, jaw, and lips, but one can't be sure when so close. I feel like I'm under a microscope. With an awkward hello, I attempt to slide sexily into the elevator—well, as sexy as one can with a bloody hand, ripped pants, and disheveled hair.

Fail. The doors close on my whole body, not just once, but three times in quick succession. He's still watching. I look bedraggled, bloodied, and now like a total nincompoop. Tugging my body through and into the small space, I sigh with relief as the doors close—on my bag. Come on!

My star alignment thingy is obviously over today.

I ride up the elevator as close as possible to the doors with a small portion of my bag tucked between them and with three sets of eyes staring at me in their perfectly matching, probably ironed, yoga gear.

It's quiet, very quiet in here.

They just keep staring.

Finally, I step out onto the gym floor and look in my bag to find a squished pair of headphones. They survived the concrete but couldn't withstand the elevator.

"Damn! Were you in a bar fight, Syd? Looks like you could have used backup," Mark laughs. "Why didn't you call me?" Mark lives here; he's a trainer and reminds me of everyone who orders a Jägerbomb at the bar.

"Mark, you have no idea. Where's yoga? I'm totally late," I say, flashing a cute smile to make up for the state I'm in.

"I miss all the good stuff. I think there's a yoga class in room four."

"Thanks, I don't want to be too late," I say, noticing him eyeing my pants. Oh yeah, what do I do about those?

"I don't think it starts for a few, Syd. You're fine." He looks serious, but he must be joking.

"You're kidding, right? I'm early?" I ask, exhaling for the first time all morning.

I dump my destroyed headphones in the trash and then stand over the bathroom sink, washing and using alcohol swabs on my road rash. It's going to be a really good day; the cab didn't hit me, which seems like a miracle now. It can only get better.

"Well, looks like Zoey was right," I hear someone say.

"What?"

"Zoey was right."

"Bette!" I scream, but seriously consider I might be hearing voices until I look in the mirror and see her standing behind me, flipping curls off her shoulder.

"Zoey said you'd need some support, but…" She trails off, her eyebrow rising slowly to its peak as she notices the blood and ripped pants.

"Don't ask; I'm so glad you're here!" I hug her and, of course, relay that I was almost killed by a cab and what a terrible way to go that would have been. It was so thoughtful of Zoey to tell her to meet me here and so sweet of Bette to come…and to such an early class. I can't believe it. But, actually I can. The Sirens are that good.

I lead Bette out of the women's locker room while mentioning that my rent money seems to have disappeared last night.

"Just cancel the check," Bette says, nonchalantly. I make a pained face. "Cash?! Oh Syd. Well, it's got to be in your apartment somewhere. Just look, knowing you it's probably in the fridge or cupboard or who knows," she laughs. "You know you stash things in odd places. Check the freezer." She's right I do. Okay, so maybe I wasn't robbed.

We move out onto the weight floor, where Derek, who happens to belong to this location, goes to high five my bad hand. I flinch.

"Hey, Syd," he says, then, "Bette." Only he almost chokes on her name. Is it me, or is he sweating even more now? "What happened to your hand, Syd?" he asks, concerned.

"Just the latest disaster. Nothing to worry about," Bette laughs, giving him the high five, which awkwardly turns into a hand hold, a hand shake, then an even more awkward release. These two are painful.

"Syd, how'd you manage that when you're so coordinated in here and at the bar?" he asks.

"It's a mystery." I smile, then trip over a forty-five pound plate someone's left on the floor. "Or not." Pull yourself together, Syd!

"Are you going to yoga?" Bette asks him.

"No, lifting weights. It's chest-tricep day," he says, trying to correct his posture to look more inflated. Seriously, these two need to date already. "But have a great class, you guys. Syd, we all thought your downward dog on YouTube was killer," he smiles, looking at Bette. Of course she'd showed him the video. I feel like these two already have several inside jokes and they're not even together. Derek high fives my healthy hand and then heads to the bench press.

"Your BF. Immediately," I say to Bette, and walk into class before she can protest and before I can do any more damage to my reputation.

I lay out my yoga mat and pretend to be wearing awesome matchy-matchy yoga gear like the rest of the team in here. They look like a team. I must have missed the phone tree about the color purple. Even Bette's wearing purple. She could have called.

We get into "easy pose," but it's not easy. I try not to laugh at my inadequacies in breathing "technique," and when I finally get myself "centered," I hear my phone screaming "bling" from inside my gym bag. I'm a menace! Bette opens one eye, having told me to put the thing on silent. She barely lifts her Rock eyebrow and I'm up, pressing mute. I swear I put it on mute. You might think this was human error but I swear my phone plots against me.

And so it goes all hour long.

High Lunge: I get stuck in my ripped yoga pants.

Warrior I Pose: My hand bleeds down my arm. Bette looks grossed out.

Happy Baby Pose: My hip joints are super, super unhappy.

Headstand: I rock this pose. Bette is impressed.

Downward Dog: I do this better than anyone in class, obviously—I'm garbage can trained. Bette points this out and invites everyone to watch the video after class. Brilliant.

Lion Pose: Bette and I "lion" right at each other and it takes everything we have not to squeal with laughter.

After class, Bette and I call Abby to see why she missed her shift. It's not like her to cancel anything at the last-minute, let alone work.

"Abs, what happened to you last night?" Bette yells into the phone, which is on speaker in the women's locker room. Looking in the mirror, she simultaneously puts dry shampoo in her hair and hands me the bottle.

"Thank you so much for covering for me, Bette," Abby says, graciously.

"Hi, Abs, I'm here too!" I bubble. "You okay?" I've never mastered dry shampoo, but squeeze a plume of the white powder into my hair anyway.

"Yes, yes," she giggles. We hear a low whisper and she lets out a muffled squeal. That seems a bit odd. The whisper sounded like a guy, but she lives with one of her girlfriends. Bette and I look at each other in confusion.

"You never answered my text last night!" I remind her.

"Oh, I'm so sorry. I got busy."

"So, you're not sick?" Bette asks.

"No, no, I'm really good," she says, sounding almost giddy, which confuses us more. "I just needed to do something last night. I'm so glad you were able to cover for me, Bette!"

"What did you have to do?" Bette pries. We look at each other again with question. A man laughs in the background and both of our eyes go wide.

"I have to go—I'll see you later!" She hangs up.

"Okay, is it me or was that weird?" Bette asks.

"That was weird. Is Greg in town?"

"Not that I know, and she would tell us. Right?"

"Could be her roomate's boyfriend," I suggest.

Looking at her phone's clock, Bette gasps. "Crap, I have to run. Cramming session at the library with some study partners." She quickly fixes more dry shampoo into her spiraled curls and grabs her bag. "I guess it could be, and Abby's the perfect girlfriend. It's not like she would have some rando over."

"Exactly," I say, but somehow not quite sold. "I'll walk you out."

Bette stops me. "Before I forget, go to the bank. You need to start putting that money somewhere safe. You can't just misplace thousands of dollars in cash, Syd." She looks at my hair and fluffs some excess dry shampoo out just before we leave the locker room, then reiterates, "Go to the bank."

Bette heads to the library to study for the bar exam, reminding me it's less than two months away. She promises to make me hit more yoga classes if I promise to make her go running more often, and it's a deal.

While waiting to instruct my own class, I order a smoothie at the gym café and check my texts:

Tray: Syd, I need help. You there? Elizabeth? I need you.

When did I get this? I quickly check the time, which indicates nearly an hour ago.

Me: Tray, you okay? Is it the designs? I'm sure they're gorgeous! I'm at the gym, call me. I'll be home later, come over!

Then I listen to my voicemails:

Hi little Spunky, it's your Mom! Call me! We'll be there in just one short month and we're so excited! We're on the cell phone. Okay, love you. Jim, you need to turn here, here…we should probably call Krissy and tell her we're almost there. No Jim, turn here…I said here…I gave enough warning…(I hear dialing)… oh, the phone doesn't work…Jim it's not calling out…why doesn't this darn thing dial out…oh gosh…Jim, another bad phone…oh

Sydney Shag, this is Gavin McKnight. I'll try you again later tonight. Have a great day. Cheers, babe.

Gavin called! My stars *are* aligned. (Even if yoga wasn't.)

I teach a rousing total body conditioning class with some seriously intense participants, and I can tell yoga has helped. Yoga might actually be good for me. And before running to the next gym, I do something unthinkable... unspeakable...

Unbelievable that I haven't done it earlier. I pop into the bank.

"So, you would like to open a savings account, and you already have a checking account with us, that's terrific! Let me get your information," the woman says, overly delighted. She shows me to a seat at her overly clean desk. I grab several Jolly Ranchers from the overly ornate dish by her computer and shove them into my mouth while answering her questions.

"So, that's your real name? Those are really your initials?" she asks. Like I could make that up.

"Yes, SOS, like Save Our Ship," I reiterate.

"Fascinating. And you've never opened a savings account? Or used your checking account?" I find a butterscotch mixed amongst the Jolly Ranchers and unwrap that as well. I'm starting to panic.

"Fascinating," she says, to another seemingly easy to understand answer. I'm not sure why. I just told her that, yes, it was a cab driver that told me to save twenty percent and that, yes, the money will come from my pirate stash. I pop the butterscotch into my mouth and chomp the hard candies a bit too loudly. It's like a library in here.

"Now, how much would you like to deposit today to get started?" she smiles, tapping her last computer key with such enthusiasm, her perfectly painted pink fingernail bounces off of it as if she were hitting the last note in a piano concerto.

"What?" I respond with a full mouth.

"We have to make a deposit now," she explains without bothering to keep her voice down. I swear everyone's looking at me.

"A deposit?" I say, accidently spitting out a piece of chewed Jolly Rancher, which skips several times across her desk in what seems like slow motion, landing on her overly clean keyboard.

☆ ☆ ☆

I run to the next gym, which is a much more relaxed environment with less competitive clientele than the last. And definitely more relaxed than the bank. I don't think Perfectly Pink Nails was impressed with my first deposit of a whopping $123.00. Then having to pull out $100.00 to pay Olivia back for last night was a real nose scruncher for her. But my account is set up, and I can bring my Louis Vuitton Speedy in later when I don't have to lug all that cash into a gym first. I bounce into a packed room of women ready for an aerobic dance class.

"I'm here, I made it," Olivia blurts, running into class with her hair still in somewhat of a French twist, wearing smudged red lipstick and what looks to be men's workout clothes. Olivia also looks like she's had quite the morning.

"Olivia!" I bubble. I can't wait to tell her Gavin called.

I make it through the day and several more classes with my pants safety-pinned together. Everyone got a kick out of the "new style." And Olivia and I got to talk about my new savings account and my plan to invest. She said it was about time and gave me some incredible starter tips. "I'll be your financial advisor," she said, deciding very quickly. "I've found that not enough women invest. They save but they don't invest, and it's my favorite thing to do, so you're in luck!" I am. This is a big score getting advice from her. "I just love growing perfectly padded pockets!" she clapped.

I trudge into my apartment late in the evening and find that I've left my curlers plugged in since last night! After unplugging them, I take a moment to look in all the likely and unlikely places for the missing cash. It's got to be here somewhere. How did I misplace that much money? Olivia is not going to like this start. But I'm lucky and it's been a great day because the cab didn't hit me, I started a savings account, and I didn't burn the building down. Good grief.

I put my voicemail on speaker and pour a drink. (It wasn't in the freezer.)

Sydney, sweetie, this is Holly. (Holly?) *It was wonderful to meet you the other day. I'm setting up a meeting with my friends at the Today Show. We've got to get you on. I'm aiming for the end of the month. We'll hit Studio 1A together! Right. Call me. You have my card. Also, I need to get hold of Tray; will you tell him to call? He hasn't gotten back. Toodles.*

Oh, Holly, the producer. The *Today* show?

Omigod, I *did* put that into the universe; I basically predicted it. I carry my phone into the bedroom and look at the vision board. Kathie Lee and Hoda are practically handing me a glass of wine.

The jumpsuit.

Someone shoot me or call Marcy Moore, same thing.

And Tray hasn't gotten back to Holly either? He's known to shut off while designing but he definitely shouldn't be ignoring the producers.

Syd, Elan here. So Lydia thought you were my ex, Janet, last night. Apparently you barged into the apartment, almost breaking down the door? She said you grabbed a knife from the kitchen and she said you were waving it around yelling something about her trying to be Janet. She said you said you were Satan from downstairs while jabbing the knife at her and then she said you said you would come for her tomorrow. Does any of this ring a bell? And what did you think of Lydia? Okay, call me.

Huh? Satan? From downstairs? Was I slurring that bad? I feed Harold, trying to remember. Well, that's unfortunate.

The phone blings, and startled, I almost drop it into Harold's bowl. What on earth could be next?

"Yep?" I answer, haphazardly.

"Hi, Sydney Shag, it's Gavin McKnight. How are you?"

"Newsboy!" I say, accidently. "I'm good," I gush.

"Haha, yes, the newsboy. How would you like to go to dinner tomorrow?"

"Depends. Where are you taking me?"

"Unbelievable. Ha! I was thinking about a little tapas spot," he laughs.

"I love tapas. What time?"

"Eight. I'll pick you up," he smiles through the phone. "Text me your address."

"Perfect, will do. Let me know when you're close and I'll come down," I beam.

"Great, see you tomorrow."

I just made a date with Gavin McKnight.

Before it settles in, my door buzzer blasts off six times in staccatoed succession. Tray!

And we have something to celebrate. I just made a date with Gavin McKnight! I shoot my hands up in the air as if scoring a goal and knock the cowboy hat from the vision board. It tumbles behind one of the French doors.

Chapter 19
THE BAR

HE REALLY is quite charming. I mean, who wouldn't want to date this guy? I stare at Gavin as he tears open mussels and plunks them into his mouth.

Plunk.

Plunk.

Except he always eats with his hands. No matter what the food. We've been on several exciting dates in the last few weeks. Hidden hot spots, cocktail parties, and his favorite restaurants, but I'm still not used to the eating. He says he learned to respect and "feel" his food on the set of his blockbuster, *Return to the Cave*. He takes a bite of frisee salad and the dressing drips down his hand.

Gavin says something about filming today, but I can't stop looking at his greasy fingers.

Plunk.

"Really, Syd, you should have come by the set! I was completely in the zone. It was intense! I was interrogating this…" Is he going to eat the shell? I mean, now he's slurping straight from it. The whole thing is in his mouth. That can't be right. "…and then I was jumping out of this building onto…" Okay, snap out of it, Syd. He's a really brilliant guy and extremely athletic. He just likes "feeling" his food. Focus.

Plunk.

"I'll have another martini," I chirp across the room to the waiter. "Heavy on the vodka and a little bit dirty!" I may have screamed.

"You're so exhilarating, Syd!" Gavin winks, then flashes a smile, as if on a photo shoot, toward a table of women across from us.

He's legitimately one of the most entertaining men I've ever gone out with. But, somehow, I'm just not sure he's my type. I mean, I think he's every girl's type. The type you have fun with, not go the distance with.

Plus, he jams nearly all his fingers into his mouth trying to wrangle scallops. (The scallops are winning.)

After dinner and a heavy make-out session—Gavin *is* a steamy kisser—I leave him hanging and grab a taxi to the bar. I push my way through an already large number of patrons and change from my trendy number from Revolve into top-of-the-bar worthy style in the bathroom. While pulling on my cowboys, I mentally go through my list of what I want in a man and remind myself of my vision board. I have goals for success and rules to help me get there, and I've got to stay focused. I never could account for the missing rent money but I've been working more shifts, teaching as many classes at the sports clubs as I can (not to mention helping Tray with his costumes) to catch up, and I've even managed to start depositing over twenty percent in my new savings account. I'm actually saving money!

I know I've gotten a little distracted by Gavin. Maybe it's a good thing he's leaving for Europe to shoot the next season of *Road to Nowhere*; after all, I'm an independent woman!

"You just made it!" Bette yells as I push up the bar board separating bartenders from patrons and step behind the bar.

"Hi Bette!" I yell, and crank the music up. The Saturday night late shift has begun. I help a couple girls onto the bar while taking a drink order and wave at Abby, who's at the other end pointing at a huge group of people pushing through the heavy front door. I *did* just make it. Here comes the crowd.

"It's Saturday night! And we've got twelve hot ladies on the bar...are you going to let them go thirsty?" I boom encouragingly. I put the microphone back into the empty Bud Light pitcher, pull the tequila from the speed rack, and start pouring twelve shots. Cocky, you say? Goodness no, just confident. I know one of the guys in the bar will pay, and it's packed. You couldn't fit another body in here if you tried. It's a big night and that means big money. Three, two, one...

A burly financier steps up and hands me two crisp one hundred dollar bills.

"I'd like to buy them all a shot," he hollers. A couple of the girls on the bar squeal thank you while shaking their hips. "I'd also love to buy you and the other bartenders a round, your choice. And," he says, pausing for a head count, "nine Jacks for the boys."

See, confidence. People love buying shots for the ladies on the bar. I'd bet on it every time. I finish pouring tequila, slip it back into the speed rack, pull more shot glasses, then flip the near-empty bottle of vodka over my hand, pouring two shots. I give Bette, who's pouring vodka sodas, a look and she tosses me her bottle. Then I finish pouring the third vodka and grab the Jack Daniel's. I sweep nine more shots out with ease, throw the money in the till, and jump on the bar. Bette takes over, handing out the shots, and pitches me the tequila bottle. I turn the burly financier around, place his head between my knees—so he's facing all his friends—and lift up the tequila. They cheer and the bar goes wild with clinking drinks and chanting. I tap the bottle against my longhorn belt buckle and wink, tip his head back, and pour a shot into his mouth, making a show of the liquor leaving a long trail from the bottle to his lips. He gulps and immediately throws his hands up into the air as if finishing a marathon. Everyone whoops with laughter.

"Make some noise!" Abby hollers into the mic and I dance with the girls to get them going. They momentarily stop in awe. Before jumping down, I pull five more ladies onto the bar. The girls love dancing with us, and we love making them look fabulous.

"I'll get up as soon as I sling some more drinks," I smile, and swing back behind the bar and finish with the burly man's transaction. I hand him his change, which he pushes back, giving me another hundred on top.

"That was awesome. I love this bar, I love you!" he says, extremely happy.

"Buy a couple more rounds like that, and I may start to love you too," I giggle.

"No really, I love you," he says again, more seriously. Bette pushes the last shot of Jack into his hand.

"Everybody loves her—get in line," she laughs, handing me a shot and lifting hers. We look for Abby, who's disappeared. What is it with her lately? We raise our shots, tap the bar with them, and knock 'em back. Together, we flip and slam the empty glasses onto the bar.

Bette and I switch spots. I hit the corner to pour four Jack and Cokes and flip five Buds and three PBRs up onto the bar. I take more cash, then hear Bette yell over AC/DC, "Syd, what's my ethnicity?"

"Pretty!" I roar back. She pushes a Heineken at the completely infatuated ball-cap-wearing man standing across from her and opens five more beers at light speed.

"Told ya," she says to him. She takes his credit card and meets me at the registers. "He bought shots for all the new ladies on the bar. This is a friggin' fantastic night!"

"Right," I exclaim, as Abby reappears quickly, lifting the bar board. She meets us at the registers.

"I swear the bathroom is going to fall through the floor! What are the girls doing in there? The floorboards are a mess, the door to the stall barely shuts as it is, and look what I did," she says, pulling her hand from behind her back. With a mortified look on her face she shows us the lock from the stall door. Bette snorts and I laugh. "You guys, it's serious, I'm so going to get fired! What am I going to do?" she pleads. Just like Bette, who always thinks she's fat (which she's not), Abby always thinks she's going to get fired (which she's not).

"A shot!" Bette bellows and hands her the shot we've been saving. "Burly over there's been waiting to do this one with you."

"You guys, seriously," she says, worried, but drops the lock into the tip jar and takes the shot from Bette's hand.

"Sell some drinks or you *will* get fired," Bette shoots back and laughs.

"But, seriously, you'll help me fix it, right?"

"Obv," we reply together, and Bette moves down the bar to serve our thirsty patrons. Abby looks at me with real concern. Somehow it doesn't seem like she's talking about the bathroom door.

Putting on a smile, Abby holds up her shot with Burly but gives it to the woman chatting him up, and everyone cheers.

A choreographed dance song comes on and we jump on the bar and clog to a good ol' country tune. We shimmy our boots and hips in time with the music, and the crowd screams. At the end of the dance, everyone cheers and asks for more, just as a line dance plays on cue. We pull some of the girls onto the bar and jump down to pass out more drinks as the jukebox blares and the dance floor fills. The front lights up; swirling red and bright white shine through the bar windows as an extremely low voice booms, "Is Sydney here?"

Bette and I try to see through the legs of the girls still on the bar and the crowd. But I recognize those lights and that voice. I jump up onto the end of the bar facing the entrance.

"Syd, there you are! Just checking on you," he shouts over the music.

"O'Reilly! Hey guys, good to see you," I whoop.

Swirling lights always mean one thing—well, that could be debated—but sure enough, it's our favorite fire-fighters. The bar is on their route and they check on us from time to time, parking the truck right out front. Our patrons always think we're being busted for overcapacity. It always ends up being great for business, though—the patrons get photos with the always-popular FDNY Engine and, thinking we've avoided disaster, they drink more after they leave.

The crowd makes a path for O'Reilly, wearing all his gear, and he picks me up, spins me around, and sets me gently back onto the bar top.

"Looks like a great night," he says, looking around. "Bette, Abby, how are you?" He leans in to hug them both. We high five the familiar firefighters as they pile up to the bar to say hello. Abby hugs one just a little too long and, if it weren't for Greg back in Texas, I think she'd have him on her arm at all times.

"Let me hear some noise for New York's bravest!" Bette yells into the mic as Abby cheers, forgetting all about the bathroom door and whatever else I swear was there. The bar hits new decibels and three people offer to buy them all drinks. One in particular gets offered several more: Heather, the first female in their crew. They all graciously decline but manage to take several rain checks.

"So happy you came by," I smile and wave as they head out. "Have a safe night!"

"Be safe," Bette waves, and heads to the end of the bar to quench everyone's newly realized thirst.

"Bye," Abby yells, paying extra special attention to the one. They give a little whoop of the siren and it's back to business. I jump back behind the bar and sure enough the drinks start flying.

"Syd, look who's here *now*," Abby whispers, and gestures for me to look behind her.

"Oh goody," I say, excited. "Hey, Bette, will you get some drinks for me over here?"

"Syd, what? I'm busy—you can't do it?" Bette says without turning around.

"Nope," I say and giggle with Abby.

"You kiddin' me?" Bette says, annoyed and slightly Brooklyn. She turns around and sees Derek at the end of the bar.

"Would you mind, Bette? Syd and I are swamped," Abby says, smiling brightly.

"You two," Bette growls, holding back a smile and blushing.

"You better say you'll go out with him this time or I'm coming over there," I scold her quietly as she passes. Abby gives her a slap on the behind, pushing her toward Derek.

The end of the night sneaks up on us with all the excitement. We even taught a new line dance that's been gaining popularity. The crowd roared and followed every step. Derek knew all the moves and looked really cute, impressing Bette. (I may or may not have told him to do some research when I saw him at the gym.) When we finally kick the last customer out (Derek!), our extra large head bouncer, Beef (if that's not his real name, no one knows it), lifts each of us over the bar, our closing ritual, and we slowly pull our cowboys off our tired feet. Dumping our tips onto the back booth, there's a loud clunk, and Abby winces. She digs through the pile of cash and pulls out the bathroom stall lock.

"Omigod, y'all, I almost forgot!" she says wide-eyed. The same panic from earlier sweeps over her face. Bette doesn't even look up; she's already deep into counting tips and grumbling about the business cards I've thrown in with them.

"Beef, can you look at the stall door in the ladies' and see what you can do?" I ask, with a *pretty please* implied as Abby hands him the lock.

"No problem. You girls break everything," he says, shaking his head and smiling as he heads toward the bathroom.

"Sorry!" Abby cries after him.

"Abby, is that it, is that all that you're upset about?" I ask, quietly. I just have a feeling.

She looks at me, "No. I think I'm in trouble—"

"Syd, seriously, these business cards? Really?" Bette says, holding up a handful, missing Abby's proclamation. "Why don't you go out with one of these guys?"

"Abby, what do you mean you're in trouble?" I ask, locking eyes with her.

"What...what did I miss?" Bette says, looking at both of us.

"Nothing. Seriously, Syd, all those business cards?" Abby asks. Her eyes dart away from mine.

A bit thrown, I inspect the cards.

"Well, for starters, this guy wants me to audition for some TV thing, this one is a financial advisor and wanted to make sure I'm investing correctly, and this one is interested in working out with me, or something. And, they were all drunk." I shrug and begin counting tips. If Abby is hiding something, so am I because I haven't mentioned that I've been going out with Gavin.

"Syd! You could date any one of them," Bette says, shaking her head.

"Not this one—this one's mine," Abby smiles and grabs one of the cards at random.

"We all know which one's yours," Bette says, referring to a certain firefighter. I whistle.

"You can tell?" Abby blushes.

"Barely," I say facetiously, and both Bette and I laugh.

"Yeah, but Greg," she says, and trails off.

"Well, Greg or no Greg we can tell the firefighter is high on your list," Bette laughs.

"Speaking of high on the list, when are you going out with Derek?" I ask, staring right at Bette.

"Ugh, now I messed up my count!" Bette says, flustered. She never messes up her count.

"See, you better go out with him," Abby shouts. "It's a sign!"

"I've got to work up to it," Bette answers.

"We're all going to have gray hair by then," I joke. Old and gray in my twenties comes to mind and I gulp.

"And you're one to talk," Bette shoots back, tossing the business cards at me, and we all laugh. "Omigod, did I tell you I *did* find a gray hair, though?" Bette says, in mock horror.

Beef fixes the door, just as he fixes everything we break in the bar, which *is* a lot, and Abby relaxes. We finish our count while giggling about all the antics we pulled tonight and looming gray hairs. Then we close out, pull down the big metal bar front, and walk with Beef to grab cabs. No food or late night (early morning) drinks tonight; we have Claudia's wedding shower in the morning, less than four and a half hours away. We remind ourselves to kill her when we get there and say good night.

Chapter 20
SHOWERS, DUCKS, AND SHAKING THINGS UP

NEW YORK CITY: TODAY, SUNDAY, JUNE 25

CLAUDIA'S WEDDING shower is at the classy Lady Mendl's Tea Salon hidden in a beautiful brownstone on Irving Place. We're all gathered around our assigned tables, adorned with florals and china, wearing sundresses and ready to celebrate. All except Gus, who's standing near the staircase in a billowy pantsuit and being reprimanded for smoking indoors. She puts out her cigarette on the waiter's tray and blows him a kiss. I assume no one but maybe Lady Mendl has ever gotten away with that.

"Thought you were quitting," Bette says, between her teeth.

"I'm trying," Gus growls.

"I'm going to stick a bunch of nicotine patches on you," I say quietly. Gus feigns strangling me and Bette breaks it up.

I broke out a pair of fabulous floral heels and a pale yellow 1950s-inspired dress from Modcloth. It's only a *small* fashion departure from a few short hours ago when we were in cowboys and belt buckles. I even pulled off an impressive pinup hairstyle to complete my retro chic look.

After so many people at the bar mentioned the views on my "famous" video again, I decided to peek this morning, and they were right. I swear, everyone's seen it; I've never seen a YouTube video of someone falling with so many views! And the comments are even better, from "She's a real Lucille Ball!" to "Is it possible she was drinking?" I would have said yes to the latter but I actually wasn't, which was probably why I ended up in the trash. And Lucille Ball is on my vision board, so that explains that. I'll take it as a compliment!

After viewing the horror flick again I found myself poring over other videos, as one does, and found several impressive hair tutorials. I always go overboard for events, so I thought it was fitting. Plus, Claudia warned us her family would be decked out and really colorful so she wanted us to "show up." And they are—it's all reds, blues, oranges, and flowering purples worthy of #ootd posts on Instagram decorating the Victorian-style living room.

Surprisingly, Bette and I arrived on time with the gang, but Abby's still missing in action.

My phone blings. Speaking of someone who goes missing in action more than anyone I know...

Tray: Honey, I have the BIGGEST surprise for you EVERRR! A thank you for all the help! I'll be over at 5! 6? What time should I come over? I'm done working with the seamstresses at 4! You're going to dieeeee

Me: Oooh!!! Come at 6!

Bette elbows me, and I put my phone down just in time.

"Welcome, everyone! I'm so happy you all could make it, and looking so beautiful," Claudia says, absolutely elegant in a white tea-length dress and diamond necklace. Her hair, newly trimmed and highlighted, rests neatly on her shoulders as usual. "Please, find your seats at the tables and I'll introduce my family to those of you who don't know them."

I see Abby through the window, her caramel curls looking as frazzled as her face as she tries twice to open the front door. When she steps into the foyer, I wave her over and she quickly slips into her seat. "I should have stayed up. I knew if I slept I'd be late," she whispers with a bobby pin in her mouth. She wrangles her hair back and smiles calmly at Claudia, hiding her breathlessness. "Thank God, I happened to see the little teacup engraved on the plaque outside or I would have ran right by the entrance!"

We're presented with lovely scones and bite-sized sandwiches with their crusts delicately removed and several fancy, freshly steeped teas. And while Claudia opens endless cards and presents we're served dessert, including their signature layer cake and tea cookies.

After the last gift has been fawned over, the Sirens congregate nearby, waiting for Claudia to say goodbye to all her guests. She hands me a basket full of cards and asks me to hold them while she hugs everyone. I perch myself at her shoulder and smile as each guest compliments her, wishes her well, and comments on the festive wedding to come. Finally, her family, the last of the guests, step over for hugs.

"Hi, Natalie, so nice to finally meet you," I say cheerfully to Claudia's sister.

"Yes, it's Natalia," she says, giving me a hug.

"Oh sorry. Natalia?" I parrot. Poorly, I assume, because she makes a funny face.

"Na-TAHL-ya," she says again.

"Natalia," I smile. "Again, so great to…"

"Na-TAHL-ya," Claudia pipes in even though I swear I just got it right. Well, at least KLOW-dee-a and Na-TAHL-ya have something in common.

"Great to meet you, Natalie!" Gus smiles, and I brace myself.

"Na-TAHL-ya!" the sisters say loudly and simultaneously.

Her enormous family heads back to her apartment, taking all the gifts, to rest before a Broadway show as the Sirens wave them off. We look at each other, and without saying anything, head to the nearest brunch spot while gabbing about all the wonderful presents Claudia received. Just a few short orders later, the table is being jammed full of pancakes, eggs, hash browns, home fries, crepes, bacon, sausage, and over-the-top Bloody Marys. Turns out, all of us were still starving. The Sirens know how to eat.

"I would like to point out that a very nice, kind, certain someone came into the bar last night for the umpteenth time," I say coyly, looking at Bette and sipping my drink nonchalantly.

"Yes, and this certain someone is always soooo sweet to Bette," Abby adds, asking the waiter for fresh squeezed grapefruit and ginger juice before he leaves.

"I told you to go out with him! You've known him for years and he's always been a saint," Gus nearly shouts. "Tell me she said yes this time. Bette, I swear, if you didn't," she scolds Bette in an extra-low, extra-raspy voice.

"You guys, what are you talking about?" Bette feigns ignorance.

"We're talking about what you have been denying for months and let slip in Austin," I say, eyebrows raised. Bette's cheeks flush slightly.

"Do you really think I should go out with Derek?" she asks. "Abso-frigin-lutely," "yes," "hells yes," and "please" reverberate around the table.

"Um...duh," Gus says. "And I gave him your number."

"What...when?" Bette says, as both excitement and horror fill her face.

"Right...now," Gus says, pushing "Send" on her phone. "Beef will send this to his friend Pete—you know, the one with the mustache." She makes the universal symbol for handlebar mustache. "And Pete, who's also Derek's friend, will send it to him. Done." She sets down her phone and picks up a sausage link.

"It's time to move on, Bette. You're ready for something healthy and real," Claudia says gently, knowing that a wedding shower has brought up many memories for Bette. Bette and her ex had always talked about getting married. She's been keeping those feelings very quiet and to herself so as to not overshadow Claudia's big day.

"Well, we'll see if he asks," she says in a matter-of-fact tone.

"Oh, he'll ask," Gus says.

"We'll see." Bette points her fork at Gus, making small stab motions. Bette's phone dings. She looks at it and drops the fork.

"Uh-huh," Gus says, and waves her sausage at the phone. "Done."

"And he asks every time he sees you!" Abby shouts.

"Okay, okay. And just when are you getting engaged, know-it-all?" Bette says, turning attention to Abby. Abby pauses, looks down, and plays with the hem of her floral sundress.

"Oh, I don't know. Do you think he's going to ask soon?" she says, biting her bottom lip.

"He's definitely going to pop the question," says Claudia.

"And if he doesn't, there's always a certain firefighter who's willing," I laugh. Everyone taunts her. Abby tosses a strawberry at me, which I catch, mock shine, then eat. She throws another, a bit aggressively. I get the same feeling I had last night. Am I missing something? I look at her inquisitively, which no one seems to notice and she seems to ignore.

"Maybe this holiday season. Maybe not, though." She straightens. "We have to get through the summer, and he wants to save more money, and then there's the fact that I don't live near him. It's driving him crazy. But I love it here. Not to mention, y'all. I just can't move yet." We all agree as the waiter checks on us, bringing more drinks and napkins.

"You could always ask him," Claudia says, reaching for the salt.

Abby's eyes widen. "What?"

"Well, no sense waiting around for him. You could always, you know, get the ball rolling," she says again, furiously salting her eggs. She looks up, setting the shaker down. "I asked Pascal." She casually takes a bite of her eggs. "I need some spice for these."

"What?" Bette says for all of us.

"Is there anything stronger than salt?" Claudia asks. Gus hands her Tabasco, staring.

"What?" Claudia says, noticing that everyone's looking at her.

"You asked him?" Bette says.

"Of course. Pax wouldn't have even thought of it. He was busy painting and lost in his art. I came into his studio, said we should get married and…" She pauses, leaning in. "…and we ruined one of his masterpieces…but it's my favorite work of art." We all clap, smile, and laugh, except Bette.

"I thought he asked when we were all with you at the apartment," Bette says, confused.

"Oh, that was just him announcing it and giving me a silly ring," she says, smiling.

"Your ring is amazing," Bette says, a bit stung.

"Yes, yeah, of course, because I was the one who picked it out," she smiles.

"Well done!" I beam, holding up my glass. Everyone cheers and clinks drinks, though Bette still looks a bit upset that she didn't know about any of it. (Her Excel spreadsheet does not like gaps.)

"Speaking of not knowing the whole story, Syd," Claudia says, turning the spotlight on me, "who's this mystery man you've been sneaking around with?" I slowly put a silver dollar in my mouth, stalling.

"What are you talking about?" Bette says, ready to pounce. Her spreadsheet is glitching on the screen. Everyone looks up from their food. Uh-oh. I take a large sip of Bloody Mary, trying to shove the dry dollar down.

Claudia leans in with an accusatory grin.

"You were seen at the Soho House by one of Pax's friends, Emilio, the one who's in love with all the Sirens. He was mighty disappointed. Do you want to tell us, or do you want me to?"

"I don't know what you're talking about," I smile, taking another heavy drink of my Bloody Mary.

"Sydney, I swear," Bette starts.

"You do so," Claudia bleats.

"Syd, you better not be holding out," Gus says, dropping a bacon strip into her lap. She picks it up, takes a bite and while chewing says, "Spill it! And pass the napkins."

"He's a certain HBO…" Claudia prods.

"Okay, I've been having a little fling with Gavin McKnight," I say, cramming hash browns into my mouth.

"Who?" everyone asks, almost together.

"Gavin McKnight," Claudia all but shouts. Everyone stops eating and drinking and looks at me. I smile with a comical mouthful of hash browns and an *oops forgot to tell you* face.

"Stop it, right now. No way," Bette says.

"Score," Gus says, laughing and trying to take a drink, her lips looking for the straw.

"Gavin McKnight," Claudia says again for dramatic effect.

"Of all people to call me out, Claudia, you're marrying a famous artist that *you* asked!" I try to change the subject.

"Yes, but we're all bored with that," she snickers. We aren't, but apparently for the moment we are—

"Give us something, Syd," Bette says impatiently. Abby's mouth is still open and she hasn't said a word.

"I'm going to a movie premiere tonight," I say, signaling to the waiter that I'm going to need another drink. Everyone gawks at me.

"How long has this been going on and you didn't tell us?" Bette says. I feel like I'm a defendant on the stand. I mean, she's nearly a lawyer.

"Not long." I look up, trying to remember exactly.

"I love him," Abby says, finally breaking her stare and silence. She takes a large gulp of her fresh-squeezed juice and leans in. "What's he like?"

"Tell us right now," Bette says, sternly. This is exactly why I haven't told them. So many questions!

But she's going to make a great prosecutor, because all of a sudden I say, "He's always exciting and has an incredible sense of humor despite all the tough roles he plays. He's so charming—it's insane. He's a fantastic lover," I smile, with a twinkle in my eye. Everyone gives a little whistle. "But I'm not sure he's..." I pause trying to think how to explain this. "...I'm not sure he's very long-term, I guess because he's kind of *everyone's* type—"

"Ach," Bette cuts me off. "Why are you looking for some country boy when you can snag big fish like that?" I guess I've said it more than once that I want a good, down-to-earth guy, and then there was that mystery cowboy I still think about. "You do this all the time, Syd. Who's this guy you've been looking for?" Bette is entertained and disgusted all at the same time.

"Oh, I don't know. No one seems right," I say, pressing a falling pin curl back into place.

"Bah, then you should have married your high school sweetheart," she says while perfectly placing butter and jam on her toast. She's just taunting me now; she knows I consider Blake the one that got away.

"Gross," Gus grumbles under her breath between bites. She had a bad relationship in high school. "Seriously, gross." Well, a couple.

"Hey, I want to marry my high school sweetheart, Gus," Abby says, then takes in a quick breath.

"Yep, big mistake, Syd. You just stood there, you had your chance," Bette says. That's it, game on.

"Oh yeah, Beth, well maybe you should put your big girl panties on and text Derek back...right now!" I say with a "mic drop" implied. Everyone cheers and Bette gasps because I called her the dreaded Beth. She picks up her phone slowly, making a show of it, and slowly texts him back. If we weren't the loudest booth before, we are now.

We giggle, clink drinks, eat, and talk more about work, weddings, and sex. Then, of course, we make a group call to Zoey, screaming how much we miss her and how much we hope she makes it to Claudia's wedding. Zoey divulges that she's met someone and hints she may bring her to the big event. (The one she told me about on FaceTime!) We light up with excitement and bombard her with twenty questions, which she can barely field.

It takes us a very long time to clear out of the diner, but we tip our waiter soaringly over the normal twenty percent so he won't mind that we've taken up his booth.

☆ ☆ ☆

A text pops up onto my phone.

Boss: Come in Friday afternoon...need to talk to you

I show Bette and Abby, who are walking in the same direction.

"Oh no! Boss found out about the stall door and is going to kill you. But it was me!" Abby shouts.

"Abby, calm down, that's not it," I say, even though I have no idea. "And anyway, Beef fixed it."

"Well, I did throw that pitcher of water in that short bald guy's face," Bette suggests.

"That was classic. And he bought like a million shots after that," I say, racking my brain for what Boss could want, but I text back immediately.

Me: Will do!

"Well, if Boss wants you to cover a shift and you're busy, I'll take it. I'm still trying to pay off student loans!" Bette says, making gagging noises.

"You'll be a lawyer soon, Bette. You won't have to worry about those loans," Abby says, smiling.

"The exam is next month, isn't it?" I say.

"Yes, and I'm losing my mind. I just want to get it over with already," she sighs. "And then I probably won't get results back until after Claudia's wedding. It's going to be torture."

"You'll pass, easy." I put my arm around Bette and Abby does the same.

We hug in Union Square, then Bette heads down into the subway. I stop Abby as she heads toward her apartment.

"Abs, am I missing something? Are you okay?"

"I'm fine—why?" she says. But I can tell she's not.

"Abby, you've been acting weird and you weren't drinking last night. Normally, I wouldn't think much of it but you snuck off to the bathroom several times as well. Tell me what's going on."

A tear breaks loose and rolls down her cheek. "Syd, I haven't gotten my period."

"Oh, Abs." I take a breath. "Okay, well how long has it been?"

"Three days!" she shouts, her body visibly shaking as if I've opened the floodgates.

"Abby, three days isn't that long. I mean, I've had times where—"

"I'm always right on time!" Abby's head drops into her hands.

"Okay, sorry. Well, what are you so worried about? It wouldn't be the best timing, but we know Greg is going to be supportive whatever you want. You two are practically married. Have you talked to him?"

She starts, then stops. Then starts again. "It might not be Greg's."

Stunned, I pause, looking for words. As far as I knew, Greg was the only man Abby had ever slept with. They lost their virginity together. "Then who?" I ask, simultaneously realizing. "The firefighter."

"I'm a horrible, horrible person," she says, the tears now racing down her cheeks. "What am I going to do?"

I hug her. "That's why you missed that shift," I say almost to myself, remembering the man in the background when Bette and I called her from the gym. "You've been seeing him?"

"Yes, and it's been amazing," she smiles, weakly.

"Why haven't you talked to us?" I pull back and look at her, though quickly realizing it took me forever to mention Gavin.

"I was going to today, but then we started talking about engagements and I got all confused. I love Greg." She wipes her eyes. "What was I thinking? The guilt is killing me, and now this! What am I going to do?" she asks again.

Absorbing as quickly as I can, I say, "Well, first you're only three days late, so we wait a while longer and then we get a pregnancy test. We get all the facts, then we go from there. One step at a time." I smile.

"What do I tell Greg? It's so awful." She rubs the tiny starfish on her Tiffany's bracelet, the one we all wear, as if it were a worry stone.

"Tell Greg whatever you want right now. But you definitely need to take some time to think. Do you still love him?"

"Yes, but I'm so confused. I've just never thought there was anyone else until I met Ducky."

"Uh, hold on, his name is Ducky? Oh, Abby, we have bigger problems than cheating, pregnancy, and the even the world ending," I giggle, hoping to lighten the mood.

"Shut up," she laughs, wiping tears from her eyes.

It worked.

☆ ☆ ☆

Five hours and a short nap later, I step into a sparkling vintage dress.

"It was designed for *Gentlemen Prefer Blondes* and rumor has it Marilyn Monroe tried it on," Tray says, adjusting the neckline. "Of course, I had the ladies take it in or you would never have *filled* it out." I smack Tray playfully.

"It's the best surprise ever. I love it!" We both clap.

"He's going to fall all over himself," Logan says, handing Tray my makeup bag. "Get photos!" He snaps a selfie of all of us, then sits on my bed.

"She doesn't need to—they'll be splashed all over Page Six," Tray smiles. "Sorry *I* almost ended up on Page Six recently for my, er, indescretions," he says, referring to the bad habits that seem to keep plaguing him.

"No more partying. This is your chance to let all of Broadway know you've arrived," I say while putting on dazzling earings that I purchased well before I was watching my spending, thank goodness.

"No more partying, no more drugs, no more anything," Logan says.

"Oh stop, I'm fine," Tray says, then shoots Logan a bossy look. "Tonight is all about Sydney."

Tray finishes my makeup, and after giving myself at least five inches with my heels, I feel downright red carpet ready. I've taken out the pinup curls, which have made a soft vintage wave, and when I look in the mirror, I feel like a true silver screen siren of old Hollywood. I've decided not to over-analyze tonight. I'm going to have an incredible time; after all, it's a premiere. And there's no arguing Gavin is a fun guy, if not a forever guy.

I peek at my vision board and smile at the red carpet gowns and the screen sirens I've pinned. More and more, this board is proving to work. I notice the veterinarian's business card. Maybe the girls are right; maybe I should pay more attention to business cards. I'll make a point to do something about that, but right now, I have a premiere to attend.

Gavin, wearing my favorite newsboy cap, squeezes me into a big hug and leads me into the Ace Hotel, where I order one of my favorite martinis in the city. Ace uses my favorite olives, Cerignolas. And because of that and the fantastic scene, I can't get enough of this place!

It's buzzing in here, and Gavin is deliciously charming. We laugh, tell stories, enjoy the smooth cocktails, and jump into Ace's photo booth to take some black and white snapshots before heading to the premiere. He leads me through the suits and dresses and down the red carpet for what seems like an endless barrage of photos, and then into the theater—all with his hand on the small of my back.

It's unusually appealing to see him on screen. I don't know how to describe the sensation, but I notice casual hand gestures and facial expressions that are his own and not chosen specifically for his character. (Omigod, the character is eating with his fingers!) It feels oddly intimate to know him on screen, and for the first time I allow myself to realize how exciting it's been to get to know him. But as much fun as I have with him, something's missing. I look down at our hands that are combined but still feel detached. Then I look at him and he's looking at himself. And there, I realize, is where that feeling comes from.

After truly enjoying the intriguing, artsy independent film he shot a year ago in Prague, everyone's ready to celebrate. And I'm in. That's the best part about hanging out with Gavin—celebrating. Plus, keeping everything at high speed is the easiest way to forget you're feeling some type of way. I just wish the Sirens were here. We decide on a place and head into Soho, where Gavin tries to throw out his name to slip by the extra large doorman on Mercer.

"Who?" the doorman asks.

"Gavin McKnight," he says again, shifting his camera angle.

"Who?"

"Gavin McKn—," he starts again as I peak around his shoulder.

The doorman interrupts him. "Sydney! I didn't know you were coming in tonight. Damn," he says, looking me up and down. "Come'ere!" Beef lifts me into a huge hug, much to Gavin's surprise.

Being a bartender has its perks. Beef works the door here on Mercer when his buddy needs a night off. Good timing. He ushers us right in.

"Gavin!" several women, men, and photographers croon as we walk into the party. He feigns surprise and then immediately poses, luring them with his smile, and pulls me into his arms.

Thank goodness Gavin's leaving for Europe or I may get used to going out with him. Smooth operator and all, and even if he *does* like the sound of his own name. Then I hear my name just as loud, and nearly louder.

They got my text.

The Sirens. And right on time.

Chapter 20.5
ALMOST FAMOUS

"SO, LIKE we were saying, we're doing a segment on facing your fears, and we think you'd be perfect to lead it off! When Holly told us who you were, we knew we had to get you," the executive producer says, shooting a wink at Holly, who's bubbling with energy and squeezing my arm. The producer's team nods vigorously.

Who I am?

"Isn't she just perfect?" Holly effervesces. I, on the other hand, think this is a terrible idea. Back in the blue jumpsuit, back with Captain America, and back in New Jersey jumping out of a plane. I need candy. Doesn't anyone have candy in here? Hoda would have candy. I need to find Hoda.

"Your YouTube video has been trending for five solid weeks in a row. Everyone wants to see more of you," the producer says, flipping through papers. Are there stats on

that? I'd like to see those papers. And why does everyone call it *my* video? It's someone's iPhone video that I'm
nearly positive was illegal to post. (Okay, it wasn't.)

But, on the other hand, I've been watching the *Today*
show like all my life and I'd get to hang out with the whole
team and jump out of a plane like...a roving reporter! A
roving reporter that's...*reporting live from...*

"I'm in!"

Who. The. Hell. Said. That.

"Incredible! Isn't she incredible?" Holly says, bubbling
over. "Wha wha-wha-wha-wha!" What did she just say?

"Wha-wha!" the producer responds. What? I can see
everyone animating but I don't hear what they're saying.
It's like the room has filled with water and my ears are
plugged.

"Wha-wha-wha-wha," says the dumb intern in the
room. What do you know, intern? I don't mean that. Sorry,
intern. I shake my head ever so slightly, to clear my ears.

"This is going to be such an inspiring segment," Holly
says, taking her phone from her Hermès.

"Won't it?!" the producer says, exhaling brightly. "We
won't shoot for some time, as you know, Holly. We plan
well in advance for segments of this nature. So, let's look
at some dates!" She nods for the intern to hand her the
tablet he's holding.

"Of this nature?" I want to say, but I don't. My mouth
opens but nothing comes out.

"I've got my phone ready," Holly says. "Again, I'll be
representing her, as you know. And of course we'll need to

talk about some logistics, and safety measures, et cetera, et cetera..." She keeps talking but the rest is like when you put a big, fat conch shell to your ear and all you hear is waves.

Just don't pass out, Syd. Don't pass out.

Shi...

Chapter 21
BUTTER CREEK IN THE BIG APPLE

NEW YORK CITY: TODAY, FRIDAY JUNE 30

WHILE PULLING on my tank top to meet Bette for a run this morning, I stare at my vision board and goals. Well, the excitement got the best of me, and apparently so did the board. I look at my life-affirming goals. "Jump out of a plane," it says, and with all those exclamation points, how did I think it wasn't going to happen? Puke. But it won't be for months. Oh, and I passed out. I stood up too quickly, obviously trying to flee the room, and blacked out in slow motion, crumpling like dead weight. When I came to, I was folded over the dumb intern's lap, with my face in his crotch and six new people in the room trying to help. Great. But they thought I was "just hilarious," such a "real girl." (A real *ass*.) *Skydiving is totally safe. Skydiving is totally safe.* No, it's not. I need a hypnotist; this mantra isn't going to cut it, people.

WebMD says hypnotherapy, or "suggestion therapy," may help me respond better to voluntarily being thrown from a moving vehicle some twelve thousand feet above ground level—by a stranger! I think this sounds a lot like the time The Sister suggested I try ant poison because it tasted like honey. I wonder what WebMD says about already getting myself roped into it? (I tried the ant poison.)

The family arrives tonight for their much-anticipated Fourth of July weekend visit. They rarely come to the city, and I want everything to be perfect, including my board. And I already asked Alexa like seven times what the weather is going to be like and she told me in several different ways that it's going to be fantastic. (If Alexa could tell me to shut up and stop asking, I think she might.) So everything seems to be in place. I've put all the last-minute touches on the apartment, making it clean and inviting, and though I didn't see Tray for days after the premiere, he showed up just in time to help me get ready. And just in time for me to tell him to call Holly again. I told him he needs to check in with all of us more often, and then that he needs to do some reconnaissance about what more Holly might have up her sleeve (or in that Hermès) with the whole fling-myself-from-a-plane thing. He quickly went into his 007 impersonation.

Together we stocked the wine rack with Pinot Grigio, my first defense against The Sister—Tray brought over the last bottles from his shelf because as Logan pointed out, "no more anything." Then he jumped right into fussing over the apartment and picking out possible outfits for me and Minnie to wear (we're updating her look) all while watching Netflix and keeping me up-to-date on his favorite series. He also arranged the peonies I picked up in the flower district just for the occasion. So I'm ready, but I can't shake the feeling that something's missing on my board. I study a flag that represents travel (I don't know exactly whose flag it is, but I should totally go there), and a picture of a perfect pie by the Food Network. Grandma Shag will be thrilled I'm working on my baking skills. I'll have to FaceTime her to show her the board.

Grandma and Grandpa Shag won't be coming to visit this time since they're on some cruise to the Bahamas. Gams, known for being a bit on the dramatic side (and they wonder where I get it), declared it was time for a vacation and not to the movies, which Grandpa calls a vacation, or she was leaving him. She decided grandly on a cruise and Grandpa agreed, only if it was on Norwegian Cruise Line. (Way to put your foot down, Gramps.)

I study the board some more. This morning, I added all the best sayings and positive words to the board for extra inspo. (I even put "linda" on it. One should always feel beautiful in their own skin, and Doc will think I'm finally studying Spanish!) I focus on the veterinarian's business card again. What's missing?

"What do you think, Harold, what's missing?" I ask my favorite orange fish. I sit on the bed and pull on my sneakers, feeling rather springy. Bette's going to get her ass whooped!

I feed Harold and it hits me. How could I have overlooked my sneakers and a workout goal? I'll put a photo of a pair of running shoes on my board and the word "Tri-athlon." What's more inspirational than crossing a finish line of a grueling race? The family is totally going to love the organized chaos of my rules, goals, and clever sayings to inspire me to greatness. My phone blings.

Bette: Where are you, I'm here

Me: Be down in a sec!

Bette and I've stayed on track with our yoga and run-ning, and today we've decided to run down the West Side to Battery Park, around the South Street Seaport, then up the East Side so she can jump on the train to Brooklyn. Then I'll run to the meeting at the bar and deposit my tips from the other night.

I grab my keys and cash—but the cash isn't there. Where is my money? Where is my MONEY?! I don't get it; I've been so organized! Not again. And rent is due tomorrow!

"Do I look fat?" Bette says as soon as I spring out of the door.

"No. Ridiculous," I say, immediately.

"Good, because I saw Derek last night," she says quickly and with a little yelp.

I beam. "You did? Tell me everything." Then I tighten my ponytail and we head to the West Side Highway at a nice clip. I can't bear to tell her just yet that I've somehow misplaced more money.

"Remember how I told you all that I had to work up to it? Well...I worked up to it. It helped that he called and then called again after I texted him back. He's so cute," she says. Bette tells me all about the night and how he's such a gentleman and how he dropped her at her door, all the way in Brooklyn, even when he lives on the Upper East Side. That alone is a sign he's a keeper. "Then he called when he got home, and we talked for hours," she swoons. I might have asked why she didn't just ask him upstairs, but one step at a time. This is a huge leap for her!

I tell her about my planned attempt to jump out of a plane again, and after giving her all the details, she declares, "No friggin' way." And four trains or not, she's "not missing it for the world." She also asked (begged) to start a fan page for me. I think Bette alone has caused all the hits on the YouTube video. Thanks, Bette.

"One more thing," Bette says, after we've finished our run. "Abby told me to tell you. She took a pregnancy test, like five of them actually. They were all negative, but she still hasn't gotten her period. She's convinced all five were wrong and she's freaking out."

"I would be too, but what are the odds of that?" I say.

"It happened to my mom. Intro me!" Bette smiles proudly at herself.

I gasp, "Omigod, you did *not* tell her that, did you?"

"God, no!"

"Okay, she's got to get a professional opinion. Can you help her get an appointment? I'm going to be crazy with the parents coming today and The Sister." I can't help but sing sinister music after saying "The Sister." Bette laughs. "Are you going to make it to brunch still?"

"Yes, and yes, see you later!"

"Wait, I have one more thing too." I take Bette's arm before she runs off. "I lost all of my tips from the other night." My shoulders drop.

"Syd, are you kidding?" Bette exhales loudly. "Not again. Come on, it's got to be in your apartment somewhere. That or someone is taking it. Seriously, does your landlord have keys?"

"No, no I've never given him a set. And he would never..." I trail off just as I realize who does have a set of keys.

☆ ☆ ☆

Sitting in one of the booths and still sweaty from our run, I wait for the Boss while chatting aimlessly with the attractive, pudgy-cheeked Budweiser sales rep. Finally, Boss yells from the back, "Syd. We're opening bars all over the U.S. and maybe even abroad. We want you to go."

I look around, confused. Is there another Syd in the room? Maybe she meant Budweiser over there?

"Syd!" Boss yells again.

"Yes?" I answer.

"Are you in or out?" Boss just says it like it is, no hello, no pre-emptive explanation. In fact, this comes out of nowhere. Literally.

"Wait, what?" I yell back.

"You're going to travel and bartend at the huge openings. You'll be training the new girls too. We've already got you a ticket for the first one. It's in less than two weeks! You loved Austin," Boss shouts. Smiling, I open my mouth to answer, but I'm not fast enough. "Great! It's going to be fun. Now where the hell are my kegs?"

The Bud rep looks at me nervously; I give him a thumbs-up and a serious *eep* face. He heads to the back.

I'm going to travel for the bar? I put travel on my vision board. That board is MAGIC! Minnie and Doc will be so impressed. I can't wait to tell them. They arrive late this evening and I've promised New York-style pizza for dinner, which The Sister probably won't eat so I'll order her a calzone and salad, which she also probably won't eat. She doesn't like anything if I've ordered it, made it, or chosen it. This is going to be so great!

☆ ☆ ☆

I hit my head on the window, because I always hit my head on that window, and lean out screaming hello. Rubbing my head, and waving like a wild person, I make a bit of a scene. Minnie and Doc turn and wave vigorously up at me, standing near their cab. I run downstairs to help just in time for the driver to open the trunk and reveal a pile of luggage as The Sister steps out of the cab.

"You'll never believe the traffic we hit," she says, dusting herself off. What is she dusting off? I hug Minnie and Doc, who are all smiles, but I can tell they're already in shock. City shock. Big cities have never been their thing.

"Well, that's home," I say excitedly and point to the ornate doors of my building.

"I knew you lived in a bar," Doc jokes.

"Not the bar," I say and look at Minnie for help, but she just keeps smiling. She smiles at the girl with a tattooed face and at the guy wearing a miniskirt, and at the cute couple decked out in red, white, and blue paint. City shock. "The doors *next* to the bar, Doc!" I laugh.

The Sister peels her carry-on, lodged between several matching luggage pieces, from the trunk and heads to the door, passing Minnie. They're twinning in sweater sets. I never did understand sweater sets.

"You guys packed a ton for only a few days," I say to Minnie and Doc.

"Those are Krissy's," Doc replies. "*This* is ours." He proudly holds up a small duffel bag already in his hand and his *New York City on a Dime* book. "Pack light, plan big!"

"Your father has been planning for weeks. We're minimalists now, apparently," Minnie says, breaking her trance. "I don't know if I have anything I can go out in!" Minnie's been extra worried about what to wear in the "big city" and now I know why...they *shared* a duffel bag. But I've never seen Minnie wear anything other than sweater sets and holiday sweaters. Sweater sets for dressy occasions and, of course, sweater sets for when you shouldn't be too fancy. Oh, and what she wears mowing the lawn (whoa). So Tray and I dug through my closet and found her some fabulous choices. As for Doc, minimalism isn't new for him. His wardrobe has consisted of the same flat front pants, a habit from the military, and a basic T-shirt or short sleeve button-down, depending on the situation, for years. That and running gear.

I start pulling suitcase after suitcase out of the trunk and inside with Doc while The Sister texts.

"I can't wait for Anny to get here tomorrow," she says, heading up the stairs as Doc and I follow with her luggage. "He just texted me that another one of his good friends from medical school is coming to the conference this weekend. I get to meet them all! Oh, do you need help with that?" she says, continuing up the stairs, not waiting for an answer. Anny, her nickname for Andrew. (I can't imagine a more neutered version of his name.) When Andrew gets in tomorrow, she'll stay with him at his posh hotel and be introduced as his bride-to-be. She's known for packing heavy, or "prepared" as she likes to say, but she must have brought her whole wardrobe for the occasion! These suitcases must weigh three hundred pounds.

Always supportive, Minnie and Doc brighten as they walk into the apartment and bubble about how much they love it as I give them the quick tour. Doc says it's "really amusing" referencing the gold metallic striped wall featuring my menacing moose and "art" board, aka vision board. (At least he thought it was artistic.) The Sister continues to text but says my animal print loveseat in the living area is "so very kitschy." She actually asked me where I got it, then said, "not that I would want one." But how nice! (It was a hand-me-down from Tray, who got it while working on a production of *Mama Mia*.) Minnie says the apartment

is so "chic" and adores how I've styled everything "just so."
She even said it looks organized. (If she opens the closet
doors, I'm outed!) Minnie and I do our *Grey Gardens*, Little Edie and Big Edie dance interpretation to celebrate as
Doc laughs and The Sister looks mortified.

Once I explain the different items, my vision board is
a hit with the parents, though Doc is a little overzealous
about the triathlon. He's online right now trying to sign us
up for the "Butter Beast." Held during the infamous Butter Olympics, it's known for injuries, which become town
war stories, which makes it the best small town triathlon
around. (Highlighting all town historical sights, like where
Bridget Bardot's body double posed for a photo with our
state fair-winning giant pumpkin in 1956, is more important than distance. They don't even measure.) The Butter
Olympics happens once a year and, thank goodness, it's
already taken place this year so I have until next summer
to prepare, but I'm going to heave.

The Sister didn't really take to the board and gave me
the eye flutter-roll. She texted Andrew through my entire
explanation, then had the gall to ask me if Flipper, my
oddly shaped, rather abnormally large plant, was poison
ivy. Flipper doesn't look anything like poison ivy. Minnie
tried to tell her that Flipper was actually Philodendron
but she wasn't convinced. But she definitely likes the large
standing mirrors as much as Tray; even though she won't
say so, I can totally tell by the way she's posing in the
one in the living room. She keeps adjusting her cashmere

sweater set and single-strand pearl necklace while posing side to side. And she looks really pleased about her new shorter bob.

"Your hair looks really nice like that, Sis," I say happily.

"I know, right." She fluffs it in the mirror and then looks back at me, letting out a little snort. "What are you doing with yours?"

What does she mean, what am I doing with mine? My hair is cute. I mean, I spent a lot of time getting ready for their arrival. I'm wearing my favorite skinny jeans, a Journey T-shirt, and little black blazer. Not to mention my hair is in a perfect ponytail. I *am* going to heave.

Luckily she looks back in the mirror, distracted by the way her beautiful but sensible engagement ring is shining in it. She insists she told Andrew to buy something practical. A total lie. She would wear The Heart of the Ocean on her finger if Rose hadn't thrown it back into the ocean to rest with the *Titanic*.

"I can't wait to show Anny my new haircut," she says. "Do you have any hairspray?"

"In the bedroom," I answer, distracted, now trying to fluff my hair.

She walks into the other room, and I'm treated to a blissful moment of silence before she shouts, "Where?"

"Top drawer of the dresser," I say, moving into the room to show her. My face and hair are blown back by a shower stream of aerosol hairspray.

"Found it."

Oh good.

A heavy sheen of hairspray covers my cheeks, lips, nose, and eyelids.

"Your fish is fat," she says, and leaves the room.

I open my eyes just in time to see Harold dart into his stiletto. I look in the mirror. I wish I could too. Now my hair isn't cute; it's sticky. I wipe the hairspray from my face, which I thought I would never have to do again after age twelve when her ultra-high, ultra-sprayed snooty bun phase ended. I fluff the hairspray out of my hair and walk back into the living room.

"Who wants some wine?" I ask with a smile. "I've got Pinot Grigio." I didn't know I'd have to pull this out of my hat so soon, but I'm determined not to let The Sister get to me.

"Thank God," she says.

I pour everyone a drink—one for The Sister, one for me, and one for Minnie and Doc to share. Minnie's a lightweight, so pacing is a plus. Doc sets it on my coffee table, two different sized tree stumps perched by a life size gold piglet sculpture by Harry Allen. He mentions it's a bit of country amidst the city. Just what I was going for! Though he did say we could have made the stumps ourselves and didn't want to know how much they cost.

Minnie opens the fridge and immediately decides we should go grocery shopping. And by grocery shopping, she means we should go to Magnolia Bakery as soon as possible. Minnie's sweet tooth is world-renowned, and though a tiny lady, she can put back dessert like a champ. The

Sister is back in the mirror looking happy and, overall, I'm feeling great. What could go wrong now? They love it here!

We get ready to turn in for the night after a lot of pizza, a jaunt around the neighborhood, and late-night Magnolia cupcakes with Tray. I was tempted to ask him if he happened to borrow any money being the only person with spare keys, but it just didn't feel right. He would ask, wouldn't he? I must have misplaced it. And anyway, it would just worry Minnie and Doc. Ugh, and that would set The Sister up to point out how irresponsible I am. Not happening.

☆ ☆ ☆

"So, Tray *wants* his hair that blue color?" The Sister mentions while looking in the mirror, staring at and fluffing hers, which hasn't moved an inch.

"Yes, isn't it gorgeous?!" I say, ignoring the inflection.

"I really like it," Minnie smiles, always positive and already taking a bite of the Magnolia cupcake she was saving for tomorrow.

"You really liked talking to the taxi driver from the airport too. No one talks to them, Mom, and you were telling him everything, like our whole life story," The Sister says while turning from the mirror. (First of all, I talk to them all the time and have a savings account because of one of them, and secondly, he probably already knows our life story because I've probably already told him.)

"Well, I *did* tell him about your big graduation coming up, Krissy. That was neat. Does Syd know all the details?" Minnie asks. The Sister is graduating from medical school next summer and will be deciding where to do her residency. Andrew *is* a doctor and was invited to a big specialty conference here on Sunday. But remember, I'm going to be super successful too. Barf.

While closing the French doors, Doc peeks in on The Sister and I in the living room arranged for bed (after having to move Flipper the Philodendron as close to the corner as possible because The Sister is deathly allergic to poison ivy). "Glad to be here," he says with a smile. "And Syd, this is a good-looking cowboy hat that was behind the door. I'm just going to hang it up." I watch as he places the hat back on my vision board and then closes the doors. I'd almost forgotten about that hat.

I've made it through the first day. It's a miracle.

"Almost scoring in the john—sweeeeet!" a guys voice carries up and through the windows from outside the bar down below.

I've *almost* made it through the first day.

Sounding like he's in the apartment with us, he continues, loudly telling his buddies that he's just stuck his tongue down some girl's throat in the bathroom and that he's just a few drinks away from getting "in there." Really? Come on! Why is the street so loud? Is it always that loud with the windows open? I mean, I guess I'm used to all the noise, but omigod.

"She's kinda fat, man," one says. "Do you really want 'em to come with us? Let's just go."

"Dude, it was *good*. Yeah, she's kinda thick, but I wouldn't mind hittin' that later." The Sister sits straight up and gasps. I look around instinctively for a potted plant. I'd like to drop it on their heads. I eye Flipper, but we're talking *unusually* large—Flipper would flatten them. (Not a terrible idea.)

Minnie and Doc don't hear this, do they? They don't understand "hittin' that," do they? I can feel my cheeks flush.

"This city is terrible!" The Sister exclaims.

"No, the city's really—"

"Fat, crazy fat, man," another says.

I really need some small potted plants.

"These guys are assholes," I whisper, almost to myself. Fourth of July weekend always brings out some rowdy crowds but this is ridiculous.

I hear the bar door open as the music wafts into the air for a moment then close as girls step out chattering. One talks to her new "acquaintance." He invites her to another spot and offers to pay the tab inside.

"Okay, we'll wait," she says. The guys bumble their way back into the bar as the music floats out again and stops as the door shuts, then, "Can you believe I actually did that?" the same voice giggles.

"Elle, that was so slutty," one girl says with sarcasm in her voice, then laughs.

"I can't believe you did it!" one with a cartoonish voice says, reiterating the sentiment.

"Yep, now pay up, ladies," Elle says. "I even copped a feel."

"Shut up!" the cartoon screams.

"Are we actually going with them?" the sarcastic voice asks.

"He's kind of cute, but nah, we have more to do. And he's got a small penis," Elle laughs, and they all crack up. "Hurry, let's go," she squeals. "Taxi!" There's a bunch of drunken laughter and then a cab door slams. I think I like this Elle character.

Did The Sister just pass out or did she mean to fall back on her pillow that hard? Everyone in the building must be hearing this. It's like a radio show on high (drunken) volume reverberating around the apartment. Minnie and Doc *must* hear it. There's no way they could be asleep that fast.

"Hey, where'd they go?" the guy yells, pushing through the bar door with the music and his grumbling friends following him out. I have to muffle a laugh with a cough. You got ditched, loser. You're lucky I don't have small potted plants.

"She said you have a small penis, now shut up! People are trying to sleep," The Sister hisses loudly out the window. "Rude." Then she hits her head on the window (apparently I'm not the only one) and flops back onto her pillow.

The Sister might not like this city, but that was more New York than she'll ever know. I'm proud. And I wish I had gotten a good look at Elle—she'd fit right in with the Sirens. She's got moxie.

Chapter 22
WELCOME TO NEW YORK

THE SUN blazes in through my northeastern-facing windows and glitters off the chandelier in the bedroom, making my apartment look extra dreamy and put together. Thank you, Mother Nature, for giving me a little lift after last night's "scene." Luckily, no one's brought it up.

The parents are going to pop by a small, free gallery (highlighted in Doc's book) this morning while I take The Sister to brunch with Bette and Andrew. We're meeting them at Pastis in an hour, and I've decided to walk her through the neighborhood to get there. That way she can do a little shopping on Bleeker Street before we eat. She'll love it!

"You know, Syd, you did a really great job with your space," Minnie says, as we get ready to leave.

"Just don't look in the closets!" I want to say, but manage to suppress the urge.

The Sister gives the eye flutter-roll following Minnie's remark, but seems to be really looking forward to brunch and seeing Andrew.

"I bet you could cook in here if you get rid of some of this alcohol," Doc laughs, standing in the open kitchen and drinking out of the orange juice carton. I'm going to act like I didn't hear that.

"Jim!" Minnie yells and Doc jumps. He puts the empty carton back in the fridge.

"Let's pop another bottle of this Pinot Grigio later," The Sister says, taking one out of the iron wine rack near the fridge. Once The Sister has a couple (ahem, bottles) we're a great team, though she never remembers in the morning and goes back to being exasperated by my every move. I have a lot of bottles of Pinot Grigio.

"Yeah, any of them," I smile, so pleased she sounds positive after last night.

✩ ✩ ✩

The store windows on Bleeker are impeccable, and The Sister is loving them. I would totally buy that dress in the Intermix window and that jacket in the Marc window and thank you, Ralph Lauren, for loving off white as much I do. The Sister wants to go in for a minute and, realizing I don't want to ruin my savings streak, I step back outside and get swept off my feet into a blind, big squeeze. Startled, I yelp.

"Hey, babe, how are you?" Gavin beams.

"Oh, hi!" I chirp.

"Heading to the Gansevoort for an interview. Come! Or I'll call you when I'm back in town," he says, tucking some of my hair behind my ear.

"I'm actually headed to brunch," I smile. "But who's interviewing?"

"I don't know, some crazy ladies on the *Today* show," he says, with captivating charm. We all know who that is. I'll be jumping out of a plane with that crew in a few months. (It seems like there's enough time to back out of that, right? No, I won't back out! #Goals.)

"Well, I hope it goes well. And tell them all hi for me," I joke.

"Of course I will, you wild little thing." He kisses me. I unwillingly swoon.

"Have an incredible time in Europe," I say, regaining my composure. He's so unbelievably charming. And just as I think that, he poses in the store window and makes eyes at himself. The perfect reminder that it's time to concentrate on my new travel opportunity and on me, not men. *Travel, money, goals. Travel, money, goals.* Not quite a mantra. I've got to get a new mantra.

"Cheers, sweets!" he grins, then swats my backside. I wave as he rushes back across Bleeker to his entourage. He jumps into a black SUV, but not before bowing to passerbys, just as The Sister steps out of Ralph Lauren with a large shopping bag.

"Did you find anything you like?" I ask.

"Who were you waving at?" she says, ignoring me.

"That was Gavin. Sorry you missed him. He's on his way to the Gansevoort Hotel for an interview."

"Gavin who?"

"Gavin McKnight."

"The guy on that new show? What is it? *Road to*—"

"*Nowhere*," I finish.

"Syd, you live in a fantasy world," she says with an eye flutter-roll. I shrug; she won't believe me anyway.

When we arrive at Pastis, The Sister talks excitedly to Bette about Bleeker Street and shopping. The one thing we do have in common is shopping, though she probably pays her electricity bill first. But I think I just got some good points for taking her to some of my favorite spots.

We're still talking shop when Andrew arrives at our table to a very loud "Anny!" from The Sister. He gives everyone a welcoming hug. Andrew is the quietest, skinniest, kindest—how do I say it—geek I've ever met. He self-consciously pats at his always-pleated pants and always-disheveled hair as we dive into discussion about his job and the medical conference tomorrow.

"Oh, I think it's going to be well worth the money," he tells us. "One of the speakers tomorrow is causing quite a stir in the medical community right now, and...," he continues as Bette's eyes nearly pop out of her head. It's Andrew's accent. Andrew is from Minneapolis but may as well be from Fargo.

We order various eggs, Pastis' delicious French toast, and mimosas for the table. And Bette and I order their well-known French fries, fried to perfection, to share as she keeps bating Andrew with questions to hear his monophthong "o."

The French fries arrive first and I immediately tear in. One of the only times The Sister ever stood up for me was about French fries, so I'm sure she's excited that they're still my favorite. I've been addicted to fries since the first fast food restaurant came to Butter.

You see, we never had a fast food joint in our tiny town, and when one arrived, it was a pure delight for an overly busy kid like me. (I never met an extracurricular activity I didn't like.) I loved going for fries, but one day Minnie told me, a girl who had never gained a pound or cup size, that I was making the wrong food choices. I was eating too many fries. For the record, it was only once or twice a week! (Okay, maybe three times.) I was devastated and thought, okay, no more fries; Minnie thinks I'm going to be fat. But The Sister came to the rescue!

"Mom, that's ridiculous—she can eat all the fries she wants! What's a little fast food going to hurt?" she protested.

I was astonished, bowled over, flabbergasted, and just plain couldn't believe she was sticking up for me. The Sister, who had never even once touched French fries. (She was always on a diet.) How was this possible? She never even liked me on almost all occasions and then this, a little glimmer of hope—hope I would hold onto for years until finally it dawned on me. If your sister stands up for you about fast food it can only mean one thing: she wants you to be fat.

The food is a hit and we manage to keep boisterous conversation going over mimosas. Bette somehow inadvertently gets me roped into throwing The Sister's graduation party, but other than that everything is going incredibly well. So well, it's causing me to worry. The Sister excuses herself to the restroom in a good mood, and I remark to Bette about how oddly wonderful this all is and quietly thank her for joining.

Just as I go to clink her glass, The Sister returns, ghostly pale and stiff. Her perfectly coiffed bob even looks deflated.

"Are you feeling all right?" Bette asks.

"Krissy? You okay?" Andrew asks. Bette turns to stare at him, still in awe. I decide I don't want to know and block whatever it is out for one more second, drinking a large gulp of mimosa.

"That was appalling! What kind of place is this?" She looks straight at me.

"What do you mean? This is one of the most popular places in the city. I thought you were really enjoying yourself," I say.

"Well," she scream-whispers, "I don't think it's very appropriate for there to be a huge, naked black..." She looks at Bette, then blunders on. "...man in the bathroom, now is it!" Flustered, she actually sits down and starts eating French fries, shoving one after another into her frown. I take another gulp. I see Bette's Rock eyebrow rise in curiosity. I give her a *don't you dare* look.

"Really, was he—," Bette starts and I cough loudly. The Sister's jaw drops and eyes widen. She chokes on a fry.

"I saw his ding-dong," she says in another scream-whisper, regaining her voice.

"His what?" Andrew asks, laughing.

"His pee pee," she says quietly, and then looks around at the people sitting in the tightly packed space as if she's said an unspeakable word. I see the sex talk didn't go well with The Sister either. (In fact, I never got one; maybe this is why.) I notice Bette's eyebrow again and don't even want to know what that one is for so I give her another menacing look, trying not to laugh as The Sister continues. "He was doing his makeup and said, 'Oh sorry, honey, just getting ready!' What if I had been with a child?" She's breathing very heavily now. "He was naked and putting on women's clothing!"

I'm almost in tears trying not to laugh, and so is Bette. Andrew is clearly amused but offers to take her outside for some fresh air while we finish up with the waiter.

"Sorry," I say, because I have no idea what else to offer. I get her famous eye flutter-roll in return as she grabs her Ralph Lauren bag, which gets caught between her chair and the table. She pulls again and again unsuccessfully until Andrew retrieves it for her, at which point she stomps to the door with a French fry stuck to her butt. I wince, but there's no telling her now.

Bette and I burst out laughing as soon as they're out of earshot.

"Welcome to New York!" Bette howls.

"Her first drag queen," I say, unable to control the smirk growing across my face. But remember those good points

I got for shopping? They flew right out the Pastis door.

"Fabulous. I bet she's gorgeous; they always are," Bette says. And just as she finishes saying so, an extremely tall, exquisite drag queen pushes open the restroom door with a flourish and sashays into the busy restaurant.

"Wow, I need makeup tips from her," I say, stunned.

"Me too! And best hair products ever. Dammit, I wish *we'd* gone into the bathroom," Bette sighs, pushing some stray spiral curls into her clip, which she retrieved from the handle of her "Neverfull" Louis.

"You know I'm going to pay for this for years, right?" I say, sinking into my seat.

"Well then, I better order us another round of mimosas," she says, bright-eyed.

"Seriously, Bette, this is not going to end well. She looked really pale," I lament, but a low, mischievous laugh sneaks out. I can't help it.

"Well, I think it's hilarious! And she'll get a sense of humor about it someday. Also, we're missing a very important bit: Who says 'pee pee'?!" We both laugh as she waves the waiter over. "We're going to need two Mimosas, pronto. Thank you!"

When the waiter comes back, we hold up our drinks. "Here's to many more years of the eye flutter-roll!" I hoot.

"Here's to the best friggin' story ever," Bette says, and we clink our glasses. I nearly drink the whole thing, knowing I've just lost another battle. I never even know we're at war so I always forget my armor.

"Oh, we got Abby an appointment!" Bette says, remembering to fill me in.

"Good. Has she decided to talk to Greg or..." I pause to smile because, well, his name. "Ducky?"

"She's told Greg they need a little break."

"Omigod, that's big!"

"Thank goodness, right?"

I check my phone for the time. "Oh, I've got to run!"

Bette hugs me outside. "See you tonight, pretty lady! I'm off to the library. The exam is this month! Omigod!" We both scream and part ways on the cobblestone.

I head to the Metropolitan Museum of Art to meet the parents by myself because The Sister is still cooling off with Andrew. I break the story to Minnie and Doc and they laugh almost as hard as Bette and I did.

As we weave through the museum, it comes alive. Maybe it's because I realize, more than ever, I can do anything or be anything, or maybe it's just because I'm excited to walk the corridors with Minnie and Doc. We come to my favorite section, and I decide to show off and see if I can impress them.

"Can you believe Sargent's Mademoiselle Gautreau's falling dress strap was too risqué and it was actually painted over? The new strap doesn't even match the other. Fashion nightmare," I say, and Doc laughs. I point to another. "Did you know that Mrs. Grace Elliott, painted by Gainsborough, had about four different husbands and they were all filthy rich? Four! And Jacques Louis David painted this guy, Lavoisier and his wife, who had the gall to marry his nemesis after he was beheaded. His most hated enemy! I bet she had him rolling in his grave," I smile brightly.

"Hey, that art history class paid off," Doc says with pride.

"No, I definitely slept through that," I snort. Doc talked me into taking an art history course in college. It was the most boring class I've ever taken and was my only mark below a 4.0. "But I've recently learned these," I say, gesturing to all the large, formal portraits in the room, "because they're more juicy than a gossip magazine, right, Minnie?" I laugh. If my art teacher had taught it that way I would have gotten an A++++. I briefly imagine the teacher from *A Christmas Story* writing plus signs all over the art history room.

Minnie doesn't answer. Where's Minnie?

She's easy to spot with her bright red little jacket wrapped around her shoulders; we find her falling asleep on a bench. Once we wake her, she decides to taxi home for a real catnap while we finish touring the immense museum. Doc wouldn't dream of leaving yet because, of course, we need to get our money's worth.

"Oh, Sydney," Minnie gushes when we finally walk in the door two hours later. Minnie looks like she's been slimed! She gives me a huge hug, knocking over the vase of pale raspberry peonies Tray had arranged. I squeeze her back, laughing at the green mess on her face, and pick up the flowers. She has on what must be an avocado mask, but I've never seen avocado quite that green. I notice an open bottle of wine on the kitchen bar. Minnie opened a bottle of wine? It only takes three sips and she's lit.

"You're back," The Sister says, walking into the living room while holding a glass of wine, and I almost jump. Her avocado mask is shaped like an evil jack-o'-latern. I should have known it was The Sister who'd opened the Pinot Grigio.

"I heard you had quite the shock, Krissy," Doc laughs, squeezing Minnie into a hug.

"I did! Isn't this city just awful?" she shrieks, which lifts the mask into an even more sinister expression. "But when Anny and I left—what was that restaurant, Syd? Pasta—I saw Gavin Mickey coming out of the Gaansfoot Hotel! He's like the biggest star on HBO right now! Syd, how'd you know he was going to be there?" I open my mouth to correct the restaurant name, his name, and the hotel name and to say how I know him, but I opt for a big glass of wine, walking over to the kitchen bar.

"Must have been in a gossip magazine or *The Post*," I say instead, getting a glass.

"Well, you missed it. Very cool," she says and swirls her wine. "Oh, and I found this amazing seaweed-kale mask at their beautiful spa. (Well, that explains the ultra-green color.) It's the newest thing in skin care. Anny told me I had to have it and bought it for me just before he had to run to his introductory meeting!" Has Andrew seen this on? "It's great, isn't it, Mom?"

"Huh?" Minnie says, trying to wiggle her face in the large mirror. It's not moving.

"So, where are we going to dinner?" Doc says, changing the subject as always, and just in time. He claps both hands together and rubs them back and forth.

"Oh, I made reservations at a new, really popular spot! Does Mediterranean food sound good?" I bubble, taking a sip of wine.

"I hope it's better than this morning," The Sister comments. "And after dinner, Anny's going to introduce me to his friends and colleagues—all doctors. Hope it's okay if I don't go to the bar. We're going to watch fireworks with them." She barely finishes her glass of wine before pouring more.

"That's okay—that sounds fun," I smile. I have a feeling I just dodged a bullet.

"We should get this mask on you right away if we're going to dinner soon," The Sister shouts, as if it's truly urgent. I didn't dodge that bullet.

"Oh, uh, good," I stutter, as she pulls me into my now-spa-inspired bathroom. She's lit candles and has Alexa playing some sort of new age muzak. (Alexa's going to kill me.) The Sister globs the green gunk onto my face. Sister bonding.

Harold looks absolutely terrified peering out of his stiletto as I feed him while resembling the Incredible Hulk. I try to wipe some green off to show him it's me, and The Sister, somehow sensing this, leans into the bedroom sloshing wine.

"Don't touch it!"

Harold disappears again.

While at dinner I begin telling my fabulous news about the bar, but the mention of travel somehow reminds The Sister about her graduation party and the entire conversation gets hijacked. But on a good note, the Pinot Grigio is working. She was very pleased Minnie and I participated in her ritual spa hour, and even though my face feels unusually tight and Minnie looks like she's trying not to scratch, we're having a good time. (Until I order the shishito peppers, which apparently she can't stand.)

I tell Minnie and Doc the fun news while stepping into my cowboys back at the apartment. They're thrilled because they know I love any chance to travel, albeit drunk. (Their words.)

They tell me when I was six, I was adamant about running an elephant rescue with several locations around the world. (Obviously before my "stewardessing" proclamation.) And when asked where we should go on family vacations, I would say places where I wanted my rescues, like Africa (found near Canada), India (found near California), and China (found near India...almost, had I known where India was) along with Sydney (of course), South Dakota, and Disney World. They opted for Disney World and took us to Epcot's World Showcase, where I was next in line to have my photo with Mickey, Minnie, and a real live elephant! That's when The Sister got hungry. Anyway, they said I always had wanderlust, even though it was pretty obvious geography wasn't my strongest subject.

Minnie and Doc were met with clapping and screaming and a big "Hello, Sydney's parents!" as they entered the bar. Minnie even got on the bar to dance with us after we snuck them onto the roof to see the incredible view of the city and some early fireworks. I worried slightly when she started to take off her trendy top (from my closet, a steal from Intermix) while doing the Jitterbug, but she had a tank top hiding underneath featuring the bar logo! She's so cute! The crowd swooned and she became an instant favorite. And with it being a huge holiday weekend, we made so much in tips that I recovered from the still, as of yet, missing cash. Rent will only be a little bit late! (However, I still don't understand how I could have lost it.)

The next morning, I see the family off with encouragement from the parents on my upcoming travel and an eye flutter-roll from The Sister. (The Pinot Grigio wore off.)

And when the apartment is quiet, Harold comes out— and stays out of his stiletto for the first time since the fat comment.

Harold's not fat. He's big-boned.

Chapter 23
GO BIG OR GO HOME

THE SPREAD is like nothing I've seen. I think there's twelve of everything on the menu. Someone taps their glass with a utensil, summoning our attention.

"We're so glad you all could make it in celebration of Claudia and her upcoming nuptials. Welcome to the Food Party!" Claudia's sister, Natalia, says while holding up her glass. "Congratulations, Claudia. We love you and can't wait for your big day. But for now, let's eat! Viva!"

The third and final bachelorette party for Claudia is in full swing. Claudia's family friend, a master chef, has created a feast of Brazilian favorites and American indulgences that has every mouth in the room watering. I don't know if all these parties are a Brazilian tradition or just excuses to celebrate, but the Sirens are all in. The Sirens take bachelorettes, birthdays and any big event very seriously, and a few policies of the night must be followed.

1. Dress according to how the "star" of the night wants her evening to go (in other words, wear whatever she wants you to wear). This could range from LBDs to '80s-themed tutus and fishnets. The only request tonight was to wear flowers in our hair.

2. Bring your best drinking skills. (Do *not* mess around with this one. No Siren shall pass out before the main event and the main event can happen at any time. The main event is the best part of the night and no one knows when that will be served.)

3. Be ready to shake your moneymaker. A given. Obviously.

4. And absolutely, under no circumstances are you allowed to go home until the honorary girl calls it a night. So you can plan on forgetting about any and all activities involving the ability to function the next day.

We eat too much, drink too much, and stay out much too late before dancing (kicks and all) out the doors of an East Village dive bar well after closing time—Gus was finishing a beer. Linked arm in arm and singing incoherently at the top of our lungs, we dance up the block and into cabs.

So I've managed to be running late while feeling completely and profoundly ruined on yet another early morning travel day. The champagne bubbles have gone straight to my head and I feel headachy and more than slightly fuzzy. Why does that always happen with champagne? And why do I continue to drink it?

I ponder this while pouring a tiny bottle of vodka into my Bloody Mary mix. More than one airplane-size vodka now sits empty in front of me and I wonder if I might be overdoing it. But it's working to take the edge off and contain the headache. And I would like to point out that it was Doc who suggested I drink on flights. And not only is he my dad but he's a doctor, so I always listen to his sound medical and fatherly advice.

I take a sip of my medicinal mix.

Smart man.

It's remarkable Mrs. Rich isn't on the flight. It's hard not to look for her since it was such a traumatic experience. (Okay, I looked for her.) The flirty flight attendant takes my empties, pushes my unfinished Bloody Mary into my hand, sweeps my tray into the upright position, and sneaks another vodka into my lucky green leather motor jacket.

"We'll be landing soon and you might need that for later. You're my type of girl." He whispers the last part, then flashes a professional wink and maneuvers up the aisle to make announcements. Lucky, lucky green jacket! I blissfully weave off the plane.

You can almost see the heat pressing on the windows of the terminal, so I remove protective plane layers (in case of emergency landing, prepare for bad weather or the ability to bounce if a crash occurs), adjusting and shoving them into my new and improved roller bag. As a business traveler, I thought it was time for an upgrade. (Also, it looks cool.) I teeter happily toward the exit and taxis wearing a sundress from Lulus and cowboys after buying a huge bottle of water. The taxi driver roars hello, then throws my bag, light to his robust frame, into the trunk.

"Welcome to the Live Music Capital of the World," he booms as I step into the cab. "I'm Randy," he continues and never stops talking. He tells me all about the local hot spots and points out his favorite bars along our way. (I wonder what he'll think of the new bar opening on Thursday night?) He tells me all about the bats that Austin is so famous for and that they are a must-see. Apparently Austin has the largest urban bat colony in North America, and they all fly out from under the Congress Bridge at sundown. He tells me I need to paddleboard on Lady Bird Lake, or as Austinites call it, Town Lake. And tells me the lake was named after First Lady Claudia Alta Johnson, or "Lady Bird," for her efforts to beautify the area. It took me a minute to put together that this was Lyndon B. Johnson's Lady Bird. (Minnie would have known right away. That's one of her memory questions, or her "let's see if you're losing your mind questions" from her psychologist-psychiatrist...whichever. "Name the presidents of the United States and their partners." And partners? Everyone must be losing their minds except for Minnie.)

Randy tells me I need to read up on Lady Bird, that she was quite remarkable, that she bankrolled Johnson's congressional campaign, ran his office, made them millionaires when she purchased an Austin radio station, fought for civil rights, and was a steadfast environmentalist. (I need to get her on my vision board immediately!) And then he mentions that on her first date with Lyndon, Lady Bird recalls having felt "like a moth drawn to a flame."

"Want to know where that first date was?" Randy says, with a glint in his eye.

"Absolutely," I smile.

"The Driskill Hotel," he says, and rolls to a stop. "Welcome to Austin and the Driskill Hotel, Sydney!" I can't help myself; I clap. This guy is an incredible tour guide! I tip out of the cab as Randy grabs my bag.

"You know, Miss Sydney, I would love to set you up with my friend's son, Durward. He's a singer here in Nashville and would be honored to take you for their signature Lady Bird Cocktail here at the Driskill." He scribbles the son's number on a taxi receipt and hands it to me. He did say Austin was the live music capital of the world, with more live music venues per capita than anywhere else. Bring on the musicians! I smile so loudly, he can't help but smile back.

Grandma Shag always says, "Smiles catch faster than shit to shoes and they last longer too." I don't know what shoes *she* was wearing, but I try to throw smiles around as often as possible.

Durward? What a name, I think as I stuff the card into my pink Prada clutch. Who names their son Durward? I can't even say it. I guess *my* parents named me Sydney because The Sister said she wanted a "Syda." But what they didn't know was that she actually just wanted a sister, pronounced "sidda" at age five. Then of course she didn't want me when I arrived. (By then she had probably learned to say "sister" properly and didn't want a "Syda," a nickname Hunter caught on to.) But who knows, with a name like Durward he'll probably be the next big thing.

"Thank you so much, Randy," I say as he rolls me my bag. He sings goodbye and I pad toward the hotel entrance. Everyone must be a singer here. The regal hotel towers above me and I feel a surge of excitement and familiarity as I sidle in.

I step into the grand lobby with its high ceilings and majestic pillars. Apparently everyone plays guitar too. I've seen at least three people just while checking in who are carrying guitar cases. While waiting for the elevator I peer up a set of merging staircases leading to the bar. Remind me to hit that bar for a Lady Bird Cocktail.

I receive a Siren group text:

Abby: Sirens, I'm freaking out. Now Ducky wants to get serious and all I can do is think about Greg! And still no stupid period. They said I'm not prego but now they have to run a bunch of scary tests! I think my hair is falling out I'm so stressed.

Gus: Omigod. Do not lose hair over men. And serious already? What are these guys' problems?!

Bette: I've probably taken all of those scary tests. You're going to be fine.

Me: Abs, you need to talk to Zoey, she'll help you zen out!

Gus: Best idea ever, Syd

Claudia: Abby, you're fine. I know this. So relax. But, I'm not!

I'm going to kill Pax's mom! She's trying to make every decision about OUR wedding. Está loca!

Bette: That little lady? I can take her (cry-laugh face emoji)

By the time I text, talk, and get my things settled in the hotel room, I have to hustle to the new location for training and preparations.

AUSTIN: TODAY, SATURDAY, JULY 15

"Austin, we've heard you know how to drink," I yell from atop the bar. "And I see you have some good-lookin' ladies!" The packed crowd hoots and hollers. Really, they actually hoot here. "Well, ladies, get up here," I shout to more cheers. We pull patrons onto the bar and start slinging drinks. The new girls worked so hard on our prep days that it couldn't be going more smoothly. I wear a cowboy hat almost all night, and clog more here than two nights combined in New York. The weekend flies by because everyone in this town is fun, abnormally talented, and sweet as pie. And boy can they line dance.

AUSTIN: TODAY, SUNDAY, JULY 16

I wake at 6 a.m. for my eight o'clock flight, phone still clutched in my hand after FaceTiming with the Sirens. Quietly moving around the room, I realize I'm almost sad to leave. I didn't even get to enjoy the hotel bar or try a Lady Bird Cocktail. I laugh out loud, breaking the silence at the thought of meeting someone as important as Lady Bird was to President Lyndon B. Johnson here. But there *were* several handsome men at the opening; I toss a handful of business cards into my bag and zip it shut—I don't live here and I'm focusing on my new mantra: *Travel, money, goals. Travel, money, goals.* I still need a catchier mantra. I check my itinerary one more time before saying "bye" to my new favorite city and freeze.

"No, no, I booked Sunday morning at eight," I say into the phone.

"Your itinerary clearly says Monday morning at eight," the nasally voice replies.

"And?" I say, a bit perturbed. It doesn't even make sense to say "and." "And, why am I mad at *her*? She's not the one who booked the flight and is going to miss work in the morning.

"And it says Monday morning at eight," the nose says again.

"Sorry, well, is it possible to get on a flight leaving this morning?" There, that made sense, and I said it with flowers spewing from my mouth, implying "pretty *please*."

"Sorry, ma'am, we're booked all day due to the music festival," the nose nasals. I'm a miss, not a ma'am. Ugh, what is happening? I face-plant on the bed.

After calling to get my fitness classes covered tomorrow, I try to convince myself this isn't going to be so bad. After all, I'm at the Driskill, and in Austin! And I know a really good bar I can go to tonight. Boss, thrilled I have another day, wants me to work on freestyle clogging with some of the new girls. Feeling very Dolly Parton-inspired all of a sudden, maybe because there are pictures of her everywhere (and even more of Willie Nelson) in this town, I make my hair extra done up with long ringlet curls, which of course I pull into a ponytail. I put on a pair of Daisy Dukes with my longhorn belt buckle, cowboys, and a red and white gingham top. I look like a Dollyed up tablecloth. It's perfect!

At the bar the girls are bubbling with stories about how well the opening went and telling them to me—about me, as if I wasn't there.

"You did a stage dive, Syd," a cute brunette says, astonished and excited. I don't often stage dive. The Sirens were howling about that one on FaceTime last night.

"Don't try that at home," I wink.

"She had guys do a pushup contest and made the loser buy all the girls on the bar shots! We've got to do that," a girl with the funniest voice says to the others.

I love listening, and after indulging myself a little longer, we start in on the choreography and freestyle clogging. Then I spend hours going over all their questions.

Ambling through the Driskill lobby with nothing but time, I stop at the desk for a new key card. Because of course I've misplaced mine.

"Why, you must be the head honcho!" the woman behind the front desk says with a huge, endearing smile and a ruffled blouse choking her neck. (Omigod, the ruffles remind me of Marcy Moore, but she's so nice! It's disconcerting.) "I got yer key card right here. I would just like to say that I love yer outfits and I think it's great how y'all really get into it."

Everyone in this *hotel* is so nice! She must have seen me dressed for work and thought I was important to be staying an extra day.

"Oh no. But thank you so much. Have a good day!" I smile and turn to head to my room.

Omigod. We're wearing the same outfit. It's like a nightmare I've had, but this is even more embarrassing than showing up in the same dress at a party.

A three-foot sea of gingham and boots bombards me. They quickly surround me all a-flutter, heading to the front doors in controlled chaos. Little Miss contestants, and I'm an exact replica, only taller. There must be a big group number because I look like the stage-Mom-wan-na-be-from-hell, wearing the same exact outfit as all the little girls. The woman at the front desk thought I was the head honcho of the gingham parade! Though upon further assessment, I definitely need more makeup to hang with these six-, seven-, and eight-year-olds.

I head toward the elevator smiling; they do look awfully cute. I hear little voices murmuring things like, *hello, hi there, is she in the show, is she a judge, I like her boots.*

How cute and sweet are these girls!

Except for one very disgruntled girl. Poor thing, maybe she doesn't want to perform. I immediately feel bad for her. I watch as she points to another girl, this one extra little.

"Marvel is wearing the same ugly boots as last time, Mom," she huffs. Then she points to me. "And that girl needs darker lipstick and more eye shadow. And isn't she too old?" Then she waves at me, smiling sweetly as if I didn't hear.

"Well, your curls are falling," I say—in my head. I just judged a seven-year-old. This can't be good. Then the very little Marvel looks at me and I hold my breath for her judgment.

"Hi," she says, then whispers to the young woman with her, maybe her sister, "Dallas, is she my Barbie?" I gasp. Barbie? She's adorable! I mean, I *am* an adult caught in the same outfit as her so I understand the confusion. I also understand that she's brilliant. I hope she wins!

"Well, hello to you too! You look absolutely fabulous, and I just love your boots," I say loudly, hoping Little Miss Disgruntled hears. I slip into the elevator. Little Marvel smiles from ear to ear at me; so does Dallas. Marvel is going to win. The other one sticks out her tongue at me and, as her Mom turns away, I give it right back. Little Miss Disgruntled's jaw drops and I smile as I watch her tug on her Mom's arm as the elevator closes.

I crowd a group of men all wearing suits in the elevator. I mean, Little Miss Disgruntled will thank me for that someday. Someone ought to call her out; no one called out The Sister and now look.

Staring out my hotel window, I watch as the Lipstick Littles (the name written on their extended minivan) crowd into the back seats. They're adorable but you couldn't have paid me to wear makeup at that age. Although, when I look back at my high school yearbook, I wish I had known half of what those six-, seven-, and eight-year-olds do. I mean, I could definitely have used Makeup 101. (Which I didn't get until college when Tray made me go to the mall with him.)

I always looked really cute in high school, but never sexy. What's even worse, Penny once accused me of being perfect. Perfect? The worst! Did *everyone* think I was perfect? So on photo day instead of looking "perfect," I sabotaged my own photo. The photographer said I should retake it. In fact, she looked downright worried. But I refused. I'll show them I'm not perfect. Who wants to be perfect?

Well, I do, but I didn't realize this until Mr. Moore's yearbook committee started organizing photos and I heard Penny laugh from two doors down. (I was in French watching *Gigi* for the millionth time.)

"Holy cow!" I heard her scream. (Yes, she said "holy cow.") "No way, Sydney. Everyone look at this!"

I had already seen it. It was awful. I didn't care until the moment I remembered it was going to be published for everyone to see. I had a small breakdown. Okay, it was a big one, but Minnie's was bigger. Minnie surmised from that one photo that I would never get a husband, never have kids, and never have a real job. (I suppose she could very well be right.) I tried to tell myself that I didn't care, that, after all, it was just a stupid yearbook photo. I tried to act cool and aloof when Penny asked why I didn't retake it, because I'd made my point. But what I really felt was ridiculous with my half-closed, half-baked-looking eyes. If I were a stoner it would have been ideal. But that wasn't all. I had blackened one of my front teeth with a marker I'd stolen from Marcy Moore. (I always have to go above and beyond.)

Penny felt terrible and tried to sneak in a different photo, but Mr. Moore (Marcy Moore's dad!) caught it. It wasn't fair, he said; no one else got to replace their photos. (We all know why, Mr. Moore. I know, I know, I shouldn't have stolen Marcy's marker, which I totally gave back! Broken.)

I decided then and there to study journalism. Mr. Moore would not have the last say.

When I'm famous for inventing something that will influence millions, like Facebook (why didn't I think of that?) or Instagram (I totally thought of that), that photo will be the one NBC chooses to show their millions of viewers on the *Today* show.

Omigod, the *Today* show! I have to make that photo disappear!

I change, pulling on a pair of jeans and an off-the-shoulder T-shirt and take a peek in the mirror. Little Miss Disgruntled was right; I do need more makeup if I'm going to go out. I have a whole night to myself in Austin! I look at my pink Prada clutch and wonder if I should call

Durward. But first I need a drink. If anything will lead you to the bottle it's being out-Dollyed by a herd of pre-tweens. A drink is in order.

I make my way back through the marble lobby and head up the stairs. From a distance I see that the bar's packed with suits. I'm not sure I'm ready for that crowd, and as I'm contemplating turning around, a charismatic, dirty-blond suit leans out and waves me over. Actually, it's not quite a wave, more of a finger point and wag. On second thought, I feel a free drink coming on from a handsome man.

As I pass tables donned in cowhide and tan leather chairs, I see that the bar is distinctively a Lone Star State space. Of course, I should make him wait a moment. I don't want to seem over-anxious, so I stop at an intense statue in the middle of the lounge with two horses and riders. The plaque reads: "Widow Maker." A man is being dragged by one of the horses, his boot caught in the stirrup. (That happened to me once. Kat tied my shoelace to the stirrup. I never forgot my boots again.) Ms. Ruffles passes me and asks if I need anything, being the bigwig and all. I fudge something about wanting to find a good local restaurant to celebrate and she asks how the Little Miss competition went. "Little Marvel took the whole thing," I say absent-mindedly. Ever the hospitality pro, she begins listing several local restaurants as my eyes wander again to the tall, handsome suit standing at the bar. He's laughing with his friends and then our eyes find each other, and for a brief moment it feels like the heat in the room cranks to high. He smiles.

"...and that one's my favorite," Ms. Ruffles says, breaking our stare and bringing my attention to her as the sounds in the room flood back into my ears.

"What was that?" I ask, but quickly turn back to see him again laughing with his friends. Drawn to his light-hearted demeanor and that smile, like a moth to a flame, I head his way, leaving Ms. Ruffles midsentence.

Flashing my sweetest smile, I walk up to the small, circular bar. We lock eyes, and it's as if it triggers the gun lamps adorning the bar top to shoot rounds into the air, raining sparks onto everyone around us. My body tingles and his smile widens, feeling them stare.

He immediately offers to buy me a drink, which I dutifully accept, while exchanging names with the somehow familiar, strong-jawed man. His name is Tuff. I'm not kidding. His Southern accent is deeply genuine and so thick, I'll only be able to understand half of what he says. Even better.

"What are you all dressed up for?" I wonder at him while batting my eyelashes.

"The guys and I are on our way to a wedding," he says boisterously.

"Need a date?" I say without skipping a beat. I'm so cool! No really, I have no idea how I'm staying so cool with what just came flying out of my mouth.

He looks at me, astonished, and immediately answers a dumbfounded, "Yes."

Omigod, what have I done?

As if on cue, the bartender hands Tuff and me our drinks. (He must detect that I'm in over my head and need a big swig about now.) I take a rather big gulp from the beautifully garnished Lady Bird Cocktail. It's about time I had one of these. I look down at my jeans.

"Why don't I slip into something a little more comfortable?" I croon. Who am I, Jean Harlow in *Hell's Angels*? Did I just say "comfortable"? I meant wedding appropriate! I've been watching way too many old movies.

"May I walk you to your room?" he asks. He wants to walk me to my room? Why, thank you, Miss Harlow.

"Of course," I answer, trying to hide the fact that my temperature just spiked. Are my cheeks red? And why is he so familiar?

He should walk me to my room, right? I should get to know him; he's my date, after all. As we move out of the bar, he introduces me to people along the way and I think this may just be a great idea, albeit impulsive. We walk by the "Widow Maker" and I can feel his friends staring after us, wondering what's going on. Even the huge Longhorn head mount seems to follow us with its eyes. Ms. Ruffles, back in the lobby now, looks a little amused as we head to the elevators.

I think briefly about stab wounds and being thrown from my twelfth floor room by this rather tall, rather muscular Southern man, and I give him an odd look, which, thank goodness, he doesn't notice. We step into the elevator while making effortless small talk and laughing about how shocked all his friends will be when he introduces his date. I feel extremely comfortable around him, but at that very moment a headline flashes in my mind: **Tortured**

Harlow Found in Famous Driskill Hotel Room! Except it says harlot because I'm letting a man I don't know walk me to my room!

Just before the elevator closes, a woman and her dog push in. Tuff leans down and the big fabulous fur ball barrels into his arms. Omigod, he's wearing cowboy boots with his suit. I just swooned. There's something so familiar about those boots. Soft, well worn, and the stitching... there's something about the stitching.

No way is this sweet animal-loving, cowboy-boot-wearing man going to kill me. He can't; he's just my type! Though isn't that how it happens on *Law & Order*? The nice guy usually ends up being the killer even after being "sweet" enough to wrangle a date with one of the prosecutors?

I sip heavily on my Lady Bird Cocktail and almost finish it when I remember to be demure. I pet Einstein the Elevator Dog as Tuff talks to the woman in the bright purple jacket. He seems to know an awful lot about dogs. I wonder about the murder rate in Austin, all the while laughing with them and smiling. I can't stop myself.

The elevator dings, signaling my floor. I swipe my key and, without thinking, I've invited him in. Omigod, haven't I learned anything from all the horror movies I watched growing up? I'm so getting murdered. He notices the worry on my face and laughs. "Miss Sydney, you don't have to worry. Everyone knows I'm up here, including the pastor you met as we were leaving the bar."

Oh good, now the pastor thinks I'm a slut.

I make the broad-shouldered man hold my glass while I get my carry-on. Not because I need him to, but because it will be a good set of prints in case he takes his Maker's on the rocks out of the room while I suffer from head wounds. (I've watched *CSI*, people.) I pull my little black dress from my bag. (Thank you, thank you, LBD and Rule #2! And thank goodness for my new bag, or this dress would be a mess.)

He tells me a bit about himself while I quickly freshen my makeup, trying to remember how the Littles did theirs. I only catch bits and pieces with his deep accent; did he say where he works? I think I heard something about hunting. I picture him with a gun; he probably has a knife in his boot right now. Jack the Ripper pops into my mind.

Focus.

"What's your last name, Tuff? I suppose I should know that if I'm going to be your date," I say flirtatiously. Really I need it so I can text it to a friend. If I'm killed they'll know exactly who did it. Genius.

"Billingsworth. And since you're my date, my whole name is Bubba Dean Billingsworth IV, but no one calls me that," he grins.

Did I just hear wedding bells?

"What?" I tip my head to the side similar to what Einstein did in the elevator. Why does the name Bubba sound familiar? "Why did you tell me your name was Tuff?"

"Well," he says, taking a sip of his Maker's Mark, "when I was little Ma said I never cried when I got hurt, and I was always gettin' hurt because I was into everything. She would tell people over and over again, 'Don't worry, Bubba's tuff.' And when I was in grade school, I was always gettin' in fights and gettin' in trouble and Big Bubba, my Dad, would say, 'Don't worry, Bubba's tuff.' Finally, I guess 'Tuff' just stuck." He leans against the bathroom door, smiling as he watches me put on mascara. Then he asks, "What's yours?"

"Sydney Shag." I smile and wonder if he's going to text a friend too. I laugh to myself, but then he's actually texting someone.

I thicken my eyelashes one last time and then one last time after that. That's better. The more voluminous mascara, the better. (The Lipstick Littles would be proud.) Tuff notices I'm ready to put on my dress and excuses himself.

"I'll wait outside and make this official," he says. "I'll pick you up in two."

"I'll be right on time," I smile. As he steps out, I wriggle into my dress, a sexy number from Big Drop on Spring Street, and spritz myself with my signature scent. (It's Chanel, but I won't tell you which. I have an unparalleled track record with this perfume.) A touch on my neck and, because this is a date, a dab in my cleavage and a little... well, nevermind. Oh, and a touch behind my knees. I read somewhere that this is a hot spot for scent. I smooth on a little more lip gloss and take my hair out of the ponytail, letting it fall sexily past my shoulders, mussing it a bit. I take one more look in the oversized mirror, satisfied.

There's a knock at the door.

And there's a hunk of a Southern man standing outside my hotel room! I do a little twirl in the bathroom mirror, feeling giddy. I rush out, running into the half-open bathroom door. Okay. Reset. I compose myself, close the bathroom door, and open the hotel room door.

"Damn," he says under his breath, rubbing his jawline. He places his arm on the edge of the frame and shakes his dirty blond hair from his eyes as he leans forward. For a moment I think he might kiss me and my stomach flips. *Seriously* flips. "You look beautiful," he says and slowly reaches out his hand. "Sydney Shag, would you like to crash a wedding with me?"

"Why, I would love to," I say in my best Southern accent and take his outstretched hand. We both laugh as if exhaling the sexual tension and head downstairs.

In no time we're walking with his friends to St. Mary's Cathedral just a few blocks from the Driskill. We step inside the opulent house of worship and I stare up at the huge arched ceiling with ornate wood detailing. I take in the masterpieces of stained glass windows and marble statues of Mary and Joseph. While touring Europe, I was told several times that the churches are older than our country, that they are the works of famous masters of art and architecture. Older than our country; isn't that amazing? But this church seems just as breathtaking as their history. I feel as though I could be in a little village in France. I stare up again at the magnificent view and stumble over the threshold to the sanctuary.

Tuff places his hand on the small of my back and steadies me, then guides me to our row. I see a couple of older women check me out and give Tuff quizzical looks. I peek down at my LBD. I bet it's a tad bit short for this exact event, but I don't feel a bit bad about it because Tuff's quite handsome and I'm not going to shy away from revealing a little skin. I cross my legs, making a show of it, and look up at the Southern gentleman, a cowboy, a country boy.

I'm in awe of the detail and regalia on display at this wedding, and I'm no novice, having been in and at ump-teen weddings. Flowers are everywhere, a string quartet is playing softly, and light is streaming in through every window, reflecting gold, blue, and reds all around the large open room of worship. In true Southern form, there are fourteen bridesmaids and thirteen groomsmen dressed to the nines, waiting with the groom as the bride proudly walks down the aisle. Tuff tells me who everyone is one by one and how he knows them. Most are friends from a small town just outside of Austin where they all grew up.

We stare at each other for just a moment when I hear a cell phone. Who has their cell phone on in a church? When it rings yet another embarrassing time, I see Tuff fumble with something in his inside suit pocket. The sound silences but all eyes peel our way. Tuff looks at me and laughs quietly, then whispers in my ear,

"You should've turned your phone off," he teases. I slap him flirtatiously on the knee.

He's totally right, though, all of those eyes are blaming the new girl. He laughs again, this time a little too loud. Then, to make matters worse, I start laughing, which is never quiet, and once I get going it's hard to stop, especially in church. Then our whole row is laughing and whispering. The attractive couple says "I do" and kisses. We clap and whoop loudly, breaking our not-so-silent silence. The celebration has begun.

"Is the reception back at the hotel?" I ask Tuff as we step out of the church pews.

"Wait till you see this," he says with a glint in his eye. I've got to make a plan in case there's assigned seating. It could ruin all of the couple's meticulous arrangements to have a wedding crasher show up with no place card. Clearly, I'll have to steal someone's. Tuff takes my hand, which my stomach duly notes with a tiny flash of butterflies, and pulls me toward a huge bus.

Hold on, a bus? But the hotel's right here. My plotting hits a pause button.

"Tuff?" I look up at him.

"This is how we do it in the South, Sydney. We go big! Wait till you see the open bar and huge buffet at the next spot." He gives my hand a little squeeze.

Open bar?

I pull him onto the bus.

For the record, I never thought I would be boarding a bus and going to an undisclosed location, which is another brilliant way of getting killed. But I always was an overachiever. I'm implementing a new, improved mantra right now and it's right from my vision board. I whisper it to myself: "*Go big or go home. Go big or go home.*"

"Did you say something?" Tuff asks.

"Yep, let's go big!" I say with a twinkle in my eye. Yes, it's true I have no idea where we're headed, but it's also true that this guy is handsome (haaaaand-some) and there's an open bar. I mean, how bad can these people be?

Some guy behind me just got smacked by his girlfriend, the gray haired woman in front of me is tapping a young man's behind and blaming it on her big teal purse, and as we sit down Tuff's friend pulls a flask of Maker's Mark out of his suit pocket.

Totally under control.

But just to be safe, I finally get a chance to text his name to Bette, soon-to-be lawyer; she'll go after him if anything happens. And then to The Sister; she would be the best at identifying my body. She knows every flaw. I know because she's pointed them out for years. Especially ones I didn't know I had. But she says all older sisters do that. Do they?

For the first mile I try to remember the route the bus is taking. I memorize street names and landmarks to tell a car service in case I need rescuing. But soon all the chatter, the laughing, and the swig of Maker's I just took distracts me. *Go big or go home. Go big or go home.* I get lost going for a run covering fewer blocks than this so I will definitely forget that we crossed Lady Bird Lake and are heading down Bee Cave Road. It's useless.

We step off the bus and stare straight into the entrance of the beautiful and pristine Willow Green Golf and Country Club, with its large, magnificent white pillars and perfectly groomed greenery. There's a possibility I've stepped into a Mark Twain novel and Tom Sawyer will run around the corner any minute to trick me into white-washing.

"Well, hell, let's do this!" Tuff says, and leads me into a sprawling entryway where we're greeted by a glorious vase of white magnolia flowers and the bride's family, who point us in the direction of cocktails and food. Tuff and I head straight for cocktails. I may have met my match. I chat with some of the girls and some rather informative mothers who all want to get a word in about the man I have on my arm.

"He was always gettin' in trouble, this one," an older woman says and pinches his arm, "but he was always takin' care of my Mabel. I shore do miss havin' him 'round!" she cackles. Who's Mabel? Her daughter?

"Why, I was like a second mama to 'im, so I'll keep my eye out for you, sweetie," another says, and winks at me and then pinches his cheek. "My Cally misses you. Make shore you're a gentleman, Tuff boy!" Cally? Another daughter? Who am I with?

"I remember you in diapers, so you better behave," the gray-haired woman with the big teal purse hoots. They all take their vodka gimlets and, laughing and clucking to each other, head toward the buffet.

"Now I definitely need a drink," Tuff laughs.

"Me too," I chuckle halfheartedly. Just how well does he know their daughters?

We order a martini and Maker's, respectively, and plate food from the endless array of Southern eats, including all sorts of barbequed items I don't even recognize, candied bacon, okra (what is okra?), black-eyed peas, jalapeno macaroni and cheese (I would eat the whole pan if no one was looking), and many, many more tasty offerings, not to mention the endless amounts of desserts. There are even painstakingly detailed ice sculptures decorating the overflowing buffet. I'm going to need ice sculptures at every event I throw from now on. Birthdays included.

We listen to heartfelt speeches and watch as the bride tears up during the first dance. Afterward, everyone cheers and all the men throw up their cowboy hats. All but one. I notice Tuff doesn't have a hat.

"Yeah, I lost it at a—" He looks at me as if examining my face, then shakes his head just as the band whistles for everyone to join in. He lost it at a what? But before he can finish the sentence, the band rolls right into the biggest hit of the summer, and without hesitation Tuff grabs my hand and pulls me into the middle of the dance floor. I realize immediately I'm dealing with no run-of-the-mill dance partner. In fact, is he related to Patrick Swayze? I swear I recognize those hip thrusts. For a moment I'm lost in thoughts of Kellerman's, the *Dirty Dancing* resort. I picture myself being lifted over

and over again in the water and doing the perfect swan
dive into his arms just like Baby, and I have an overwhelming desire to crawl on the floor while mouthing
the words to "Love Is Strange."

Sylvia?
Yes, Mickey?
How do you call your lover boy?
Baby ooooh my sweet baby, you're the one....

Feeling even more flirtatious now, I twirl to Tuff's lead
and then tug on his tie, pulling him across the dance floor
into my body.

"My God, will you look at that chemistry," the gray-
haired woman with the big teal purse whispers to the other
women. Tuff and I share a laugh as he leads me into the
next song, a Texas two-step. She crosses herself quickly,
then stuffs a handful of delicious cake ball bites into her
purse.

The Texas two-step is big at the bar, and we dance
seamlessly about the floor. He dips me impressively on
the last note and I float off the dance floor, dizzy with a
crush. She's right about that chemistry. Those gun lamps
must have followed us here, because sparks are flying and
I feel as though there's a soft spotlight following us. I'm
feeling sweetly buzzed and want to be sweetly kissed. Tuff,
glistening sexily, leads me by the hand through the double doors and outside for some air. I linger a couple steps

behind, staring dreamily at the band and dancers through the huge picturesque windows, still holding his hand.

I bump into him as he offers me a place to sit on a lone wooden bench guarded by a large weeping willow looming overhead, its branches lazily draping around the seat as if in a hug. We sit to a beautiful view of a talkative little pond, the golf course and the spray of sprinklers misting the grass. Tuff leans into me again, and again my stomach flips. But this time, it's like when you're on a Ferris wheel and the seat rocks just as you hit the top. Then you see the whole beautiful town before you. And just when I think he's going to…an older couple holding hands stops to say hello on their way back inside.

I wonder, as they talk to Tuff, how long they've been together. Forty years, I bet.

"Tuff, the course looks great. I'd love to get out there with you," the gentleman says.

"We'll have to try it out next time you're in town, Mr. Parkes," Tuff smiles.

"Oh, you boys and your golf," the woman sighs. "Tuff, Penelope shore misses your gentle touch. She's seeing someone new now and I'm not sure she likes him. Who is it now, Charles?"

"Dr. Raymond, I believe," Mr. Parkes replies.

"Oh yes, that's right. I don't like him much either." Mrs. Parkes shakes her head and Tuff laughs. Why is he laughing?

"Oh, I'm sure she'll come around," he smiles.

This is *not* funny.

Mabel, Cally, and now Penelope? How many are there? And why are these mothers okay with this? And Mrs. Parkes, your daughter is dating a doctor; why are *you* complaining?

So Tuff's not a killer, but it's pretty clear he's a player! I'm not feeling so romantic anymore. The Parkes walk away saying good night, but not before Mr. Parkes turns around.

"Oh, Tuff, I need you to help Diggs and Ace learn a couple tricks on the hunt. Do tell us when you're coming home for a visit," he smiles.

"Will do, Mr. Parkes," Tuff says and waves.

What? He teaches young men how to snag women as if it's a hunt? And Mrs. Parkes doesn't care? Omigod. I know I didn't hear what he said he did for a living in the hotel room, but...a gigolo?!

I stand haughtily and Tuff takes my hand.

"Where you going?" he asks.

"I think I should leave," I say, trying not to sound too upset. I shouldn't even *be* upset; I barely know this guy!

"Why would you leave? I thought we were having an amazing time!" he says, and stares at me while *acting* confused.

"Mabel, Cally, and Penelope? And you're going to help Diggs and Ace on the hunt?" I actually make quotation marks with my hands on the word *hunt* to let him know I know exactly what's going on.

"What?" he laughs.

"I don't think it's all that funny," I say, crossing my arms. "I'm confused."

"I'm not. It sounds like you get around. I mean, if that's your thing..." I trail off. He can have his *"thing,"* but I don't want anything to do with it.

"Oh, oh, Sydney! Mabel, Cally, and Penelope are cats, and Diggs and Ace are hunting dogs," he says quickly.

What?

"I told you I was a veterinarian," he says, trying to hold back a chuckle. He pulls me gently back onto the bench.

Cats?

Dogs?

Veterinarian?

I let out a weak, embarrassed giggle.

"Oh, I knew that. Cats..."

"You thought...," he starts. I watch as he registers how many "cats" he's been with and this time doesn't try to hold back his laughter.

Not funny.

"A veterinarian? Omigod..." I take a moment. Dirty blond hair. The stitching on his cowboy boots. A missing cowboy hat. Tuff's real name is Bubba...**& Bubba Vet Care Clinic, Goodtown TX**. "You're...Bubba?" I say, stunned.

"Yeah, but everyone..."

"Of Bubba & Bubba Vet Care Clinic in Goodtown, Texas?"

"Yeah, how'd you..." He pauses, then says, more to himself, "It *is* you." He takes out his phone. "I need to check the voicemail I got in the church."

He listens to his voicemail as I realize that this is the man I've been looking for since seeing him outside the bar, since the auto show, since forever. It's just been months and I think I was hoping it was him, but didn't stop to actually put it together. "Like a moth to a flame" comes to mind. He's been on my vision board the whole time. His business card (I guess I *should* have paid more attention to business cards!) and, omigod, his hat. At this point I wonder if I don't have a photo of him tacked to the board because of how unbelievable this is.

"You're SOS?" he says, putting down his phone.

"Sydney Orie Shag," I smile. "Why?"

"Well, holy…" he says, his accent giving way to boisterous laughter. "Syd, you're the girl my sister's been trying to set me up with since New York. I knew you looked familiar, but I thought it was just my overwhelming attract—well, you know," he smiles.

"You're Captain America's brother?" I say, putting it all together. I look at him. "Of course you are." Just look at him. "Omigod, the video," I blush.

"The video is just about the best thing I've ever seen. And it's been incredible for her business. You are, hands down, the hottest girl I've ever seen fall into a garbage can." He flashes a wonderful smile. "After Bitty told me about you and showed me the video, I did everything I could to find you. I went to the bar in New York. I even threw my hat at you at The Hitching Rail. My favorite hat! Hey, where's my hat?" he asks, then squints. "Captain America?"

"I looked for *you* everywhere that night!" I nearly scream, and push him for not being easy to find.

"Ah, it was the worst timing. I got called out on an emergency Caesarean for a first-calf heifer in real distress. I was so mad. There you were, and I had to leave."

He's a hero, I knew it. Disregard everything I said about him being a killer.

"And my hat," he adds. "You had my favorite hat. Golly."

He just said "golly." I giggle to myself.

"I had to leave the bachelor party and go to that farm with no cowboy hat and somebody's drink spilled all down the back of my shirt."

We both laugh in disbelief.

"Your sister looks like Captain America," I say, answering his earlier question. "And that may have been my drink." Oops.

"Oh, yeah, I can see that, to both statements," he laughs. I may have spilled a drink here already. Okay, I did. "She actually was Captain America at least twice for Halloween when we were kids."

"I knew it! I knew you were the same guy. From outside the bar in New York, the flight…omigod, you were on my flight," I say. Omigod, he was sitting by Mrs. Rich! He'll never remember a random conversation with someone on a plane. Right?

"You saw me?" he says. "I knew you saw me outside the bar."

"We made eye contact, and of course I saw you," I say, giving him a once-over as if to say *duh*. "And, you were wearing your hat. I've been looking for you too—I just didn't know I had your business card the whole time."

"She gave you my business card?" He shakes his head. "She's sneaky, that one. Hey, and you didn't call me?" I laugh. "Why didn't you call me? Didn't she tell you how handsome I am?"

"I had just given myself a concussion from falling into a garbage can," I say, making an *are you kidding me* face.

"Good point," he laughs.

"And no, she didn't tell me how handsome you are. I'll have to talk to her about that."

"*I'll* have to talk to her about that." He raises his voice in mock anger.

I feel like my whole body is bubbling, sparkling, or lighting on fire. Tuff or Bubba is a veterinarian currently specializing in large animals here in Austin. He loves his job but aims to get back to his hometown, where he'll work for the family business to which his father has already added his name. He says it includes large animals, family pets, and everything else in between. He says you're always on your toes in a small town; they bring in anything and everything. (I know a little something about that.) I laugh again as I realize we have a lot in common, and that he's not actually a gigolo. Again, I watch too many old movies and possibly too many murder mysteries. I also realize I won't have to explain why I love Harold so much and why our family members include four dogs and a cat.

He tells me that taking over the practice has been a goal of his since he was a kid. Then, in his sexy Southern accent, thick and layered with honesty, Tuff shares more about his life and asks about where I grew up. And for a short while the rest of the party disappears as we exchange colorful small town stories and laugh about childhood pranks. He tells me about his family and how important they are, albeit not perfect, especially him. He describes how bullheaded he is and how he takes after his grandfather, Bub, who was infamous for stubborn behavior and for driving a tractor to work every day. But he was even more well known for his handmade cowboy boots. The stitching! Then Tuff melts me with a mischievous smile. And just as I'm about to take a much-needed breath, he leans in and gently kisses me.

And I swear to God if I didn't see Walt himself (Walt Disney, of course) through the golf course sprinklers winking at me like a rainbow or a fairy godmother. And is that "Someday My Prince Will Come" from *Sleeping Beauty* I hear ever so faintly in my ear?

Chapter 24
PALACE OF SECRETS

AUSTIN / NEW YORK CITY: TODAY, MONDAY, JULY 17

SMILING EAR to ear and around the sun and back, I run toward my gate. I'm always running in the airport; it's a miracle TSA hasn't put me on the terrorist watch list. I barely hear my phone blinging and I quickly dig for it. Would Tuff be calling me already? I peel away from the ticket line and I answer sweetly,

"Hello?"

"You didn't call me back last night!" Minnie yells like we're teenagers.

"Aaaaaah, Minnie!" I pant.

"You always call me back! What were you doing?" she pries. From teenager to Mom in two seconds.

"You'll never believe what happened," I start.

"I thought you were dead. Are you boarding your flight?"

"Yes, don't worry, I just made it. You'll never believe—"

"I mean people go missing all the time." Now I know where I get it. "I would have checked my email for a ransom note, but the computer is broken again."

"Did you turn it on? You're never going to believe what I—"

"You're never on time for flights. I just don't understand. With proper planning and..." She stops midstream to yell at Doc. "They don't go there! Jim! Left, left! I don't know how you make any of your flights, Sydney. *Jim!*"

"Mom, listen, listen to what—"

"Remember when you almost gave your father a heart attack on the way to the airport? *Jim, not there!* Your father never knows where the petunias go."

"I know, now listen—"

"Oh my gosh, that was some trip to the airport. Syd, here's your father—have a good flight!" I hear her hand the phone to Doc while complaining that she doesn't want the petunias near the geraniums, that they've *never* been near the geraniums.

"Hey, Syd, have a good flight! The weather looks great in Austin." He always checks the weather for me when I fly. "It'll be a smooth takeoff for you!"

"Doc, you'll never believe what happened—"

"Let me guess, you almost missed your flight again," he laughs. I hear Minnie in the background still going on and on about petunias, geraniums, and how important placement is.

"Doc—"

"Your mother has me planting and re-planting out here." He lowers his voice. "Truth is, they all look the same to me." Then he mumbles something about the statistics of color blindness in men and the probability of cross-pollination. I try to interrupt,

"Doc, listen—"

"I never know where she wants these things," he continues. "Have a super flight, Spunky, and call us when you get in." I can practically hear his smile through the phone, then he hangs up.

I'll have to tell them when I land. Jeez. Hard to get a word in! I guess they were just happy I made my flight. Gah, speaking of making my flight—I'm the last to board. I flash my phone at the agent and she scans the ticket, smiling and waving me into the jetway. I did almost give Doc a heart attack once with my nonexistent airport strategies. (Though I don't know how Minnie hasn't caused him one in general.)

It was the one time I woke extra early for my flight. It had been an absolutely perfect visit (The Sister wasn't there), and I really wanted to prove to the parents I could be efficient and timely about getting to the airport. So at 6:21 a.m. on the dot, nearly ten minutes early, I was crawling into the three hundred-year-old Aztec.

Oh yes, I said Aztec, the automobile *Time* magazine called, and I quote, "one of the worst cars of all time," and then listed it again as one of the worst inventions of all time. The parents think it's their prize possession. Awkward. Doc even refers to it as "one of a kind." (Yes, because they burned the rest!) To top it off, it smells like wet dog. I absolutely adore our four lovable dogs, but this is an extraordinary accumulation of smells. Minnie and

Doc only use the Mutt Machine with the dogs. And me. Never the high-maintenance, pearl-wearing sister. She only rides in the clean, lemon-fresh Lexus. Interesting, right? I should be in therapy. (No, it's actually because I love being with the dogs as much as possible and wouldn't have it any other way. But an Aztec? I've even suggested my favorite, an old Bronco, perfect for hauling! I mean, something, anything, even a minivan at this point! But Doc is so proud it still drives that he tells everyone how many miles are on it: 216,001. Seriously.)

"Got everything, Spunky?" Doc asked. I think he may have suspected then that something was wrong. I was early.

"Yes, let's hit the road!" I said brazenly, when I was really wondering if I actually *did* have everything. I knew I forgot a lot of cash in my puffy vest (who doesn't wear a puffy vest or jacket in Butter?) and that was too bad, because I was going to use it for the taxi when I arrived at the destination wedding. I figured I could just use my credit card. But after about ten minutes on the road I wondered where the credit card was. After fifteen, I wondered where my license was. After twenty, we had to turn around. But it was like a million miles to the next exit. Missing an exit in the Midwest is like extending a life sentence. It just gets longer and longer and more useless.

Doc clenched his jaw and Minnie started meditative breathing practices in the back seat. Four unsuccessful phone calls to the airport, airline, and two friends to see if they could switch me to a later flight made the parents all the more frantic. The technology of doing such things over the phone put them right over the edge. Internet check-in was closed and there was only one flight to my destination, of course, and if I missed it, there would be one less bridesmaid and no wedding singer. My only chance was to get the license and speed back to the airport before check-in was cutoff.

Doc began grinding his teeth and Minnie fell into an anxiety attack coma in the back seat, not to mention all four dogs were panting. I ran back into the house and grabbed the vest, which, along with the cash, held my credit card, license, and, as a bonus, my favorite lip gloss. Watermelon flavored with a little sparkle, but wears like an adult. It's the best.

We arrived at the airport with three minutes to spare when I realized I had my passport in my bag the whole time. (Rule #3: Always have your passport.) I never told them that, of course; even Minnie may have started looking for adoption papers.

They called me while at the wedding to see if I had recovered from the, in their words, "wild ride." By then Doc was laughing about the near heart attack he had from all the stress and Minnie, I could tell, had slipped a Valium because she was humming "The Itsy Bitsy Spider." It must have something to do with that living on the edge thing they're always talking about because I didn't think it was all that dramatic. I was just glad I had my favorite watermelon lip gloss.

I sit down just as they close the plane doors, buckle my safety belt, and greet the small, balding, jovial thirty-something sitting next to me. I'm bright-eyed, bushy-tailed, and feeling giddy about last night even though I got hardly any sleep at all. Noticing my overly happy demeanor my seatmate says, "You must have had a good night."

His mistake. I can't wait to tell someone, anyone, about crashing a wedding and meeting the man from my vision board. I start right in where the parents cut me off and elaborate on the night, including the drink at the hotel just like Lady Bird, the beautiful church, the outrageous dancing, and dragging Tuff to the bar after the reception. I leave out the dreamy first kiss because sitting on a bench enveloped in a weeping willow with the golf course looking so serene and plush and the constant pitter-patter of the sprinklers as a backdrop is completely too much to tell someone I just met.

I also leave out the bit about seeing Tuff's smokin' body. Chest and abs to die for and very large— "Bloody Mary, yes. May I have the largest Bloody Mary please? Thank you!" It's a mistake to think that women don't want large Bloody Marys. The flight attendant just tried to give me half the can and only one vodka. Appalling.

Where was I? Seeing his body wasn't as sordid as you think. When we hit the dance floor again, he opened his shirt during a rather enthusiastic rendition of the Cupid Shuffle. I was laughing so hard and completely entranced, and so was the gray-haired woman with the teal purse full of cake balls. I watched her choke on a ball when he hit his third button down. I may have choked too if I had had balls in my mouth.

As it turns out, Bubba's Tuff all right. Built like a Ford truck. *Built Ford "Tuff."* (I had to say it.) Okay, I'm not going to lie, and I hate to kiss and tell, but he did wake up with me. But I swear, what you think happened didn't happen. Always follow Rule #5!

And because I followed Rule #5: Never sleep with someone on the first date, I have a voicemail when I land.

Miss Sydney, it's Tuff. Hope you have a great flight. Last night was somethin' else. Call me when you get home. Thank you again for being my date who, by the way, everyone is talking about. Talk to you soon, gorgeous.

Omigod, melt my face off already! Right? I listen to it two more times. Okay, three. Okay, I listen to it five more times but he called me gorgeous in a Southern accent! You totally would too.

NEW YORK CITY: TODAY, THURSDAY, JULY 20

Even Tray wants to hear it as we jump out of the taxi in front of the Carlyle Hotel. We gab at high speed about everything: the bar opening, crashing the wedding, his costumes, his sober streak, and his new healthy lifestyle.

"It was a wake-up call, Syd," he says as we walk to the entrance. He hasn't had a drink since Logan called him out. He pushes me through the revolving doors, still talking even though I'm unable to hear through the glass separating us. I can see his lips moving but I've never been a good lip reader. It's like "I love you" and "olives." I'll always pick the wrong one.

"Aaah, if I have to go alone, I just don't know if I can do it!" he huffs. "So what do you say? You'll come with me? You *have* to."

"Sure," I say. *What did I just agree to?*

"Perfect!" he spits in my eye. I grumble and wipe my eye as he continues, now berating some designer and their awful organza. I swear I need to stand behind a screen when he gets going. And what is organza again?

I spot a Carlyle nametag and ask where we claim our tickets for the New Orleans Jazz Band.

"Right this way," the gentleman responds, and we follow dutifully.

"And then he used tulle. Tulle! Would you look at this place?" Tray continues his stream of consciousness without break. "I should have worn a suit!"

"You look great," I say, though starting to question my own attire as we walk through the luxurious hotel. Tray dives into a description of an "absolutely fabulous" suit he saw the other day and its "rat pooping" expensive price tag.

We take our seats at Café Carlyle, home to jazz, and while Tray orders me a drink, I admire the large murals bordering the walls. According to the bartender, who could have been here when it opened in 1930, they're by Marcel Vertes, and this is the very hotel Marilyn Monroe and John F. Kennedy came to after the infamous Happy Birthday serenade in 1962.

"You're sitting in the "Palace of Secrets," he says. "We're good at keeping them around here." The bartender chuckles and hands me his signature Marilyn Monroe Cocktail and Tray a sparkling water. This is incredible, though Tray doesn't seem to notice anything anymore because a man who *is* wearing a suit takes a stool next to us.

The small, balding, jovial man from the plane, and the man who invited us here tonight, takes the stage in front of us and I watch in amusement as he places his bass just so. And would you know it, another small, balding, and quite famous man takes the stage with him on the clarinet. Turns out, after talking his ear off, my seatmate revealed that he's a fantastic musician with many instruments at his command. And since tonight he was filling in on the bass for a lively night at Café Carlyle, he invited me plus one! And I'm never one to turn down an invitation, so here we are!

I decide Tray and I are both dressed a bit casually for this historic hotel. I mean, I'm wearing a short, flouncy skirt and fabulous heels with my little pink Prada, but it's not quite up to the Chanel-bag-worthy Carlyle. But I *am* wearing my Chanel perfume. If I only had a pair of Christian Louboutins, I would at least have a red sole to flaunt! But I've emptied my Christian fund into my savings account. (That's dedication.)

I swill with excitement, recognizing all the songs from the jazz library in my head. I tap my toe and bob my head along with the great little band. Jovial nods and smiles our way and, as if Frank Sinatra just winked at us, Tray and I beam. I'm smiling so hard my cheeks hurt when they announce a small break. I head to the powder room as Tray flirts relentlessly with the man on the stool next to us, who's clearly with a date, and a female one at that.

I leave him to his devices and, in my own daydream about Tuff, wander to the washroom. (It's classy here so it's a washroom or powder room, not a bathroom.) I make my way through an informal (but totally formal) seating area and notice a familiar face as I drift through the room, thinking about Tuff's hands on my hips. I absentmindedly look at the older woman again. How do I know her? She isn't quite facing me so I can barely see, but I definitely know her. Something nags at me as if she's someone I don't really want to run into. Who wouldn't I want to run into? I must have stared because her two friends of similar age are whispering and pointing at me with their pompous eyes. I pass their table to reach the bathroom (excuse me, washroom), and just as I do, the familiar woman slowly turns to face me.

How is this possible?

The city has over eight million people!

But there she is, her traffic cone orange cheeks ablaze in the soft Carlyle lighting.

Mrs. Rich!

And her rich little friends. She's multiplied. I flinch. Do they all go to the same Bergdorf's makeup counter? And shouldn't this color be discontinued? How is this woman here? And damn, she has money! Her beautiful, huge Chanel bag sits like royalty near her shiny, patent leather, regal but practical Chanel one-inch heels. Practical...I shudder at the thought, but those two inches could send my unborn children to college.

The gazes of all three women are fierce and judgmental as they look me up and down and snicker. What are they, mean girls at age seventy-four? I smile courteously. Mrs. Rich lifts her heavy left hand carrying that unforgettable *blood* diamond and a beam of light stabs me right in the eyeball. I stumble, blinded by the huge sparkler as she twirls her pearl necklace and smirks. (Pearls, I only know one other person who wears pearls: The Sister.) This gives way to more tittering from her cronies.

Regaining my footing, I dart behind the washroom door and hide with all my body weight pushed up against it like the time I broke The Sister's hairbrush. (It was her senior prom and I swear I didn't mean to. Apparently no other brush would do.) What am I doing? I move slowly away from the door, half expecting one of the seventy-four-year-olds to burst in and give me a swirly. (The Sister tried.) Peering into the ornate mirror, I analyze my appearance. What's their problem? I look fabulous.

I make sure to lock the stall door in case Mrs. Rich wants to get me back. Not that it rattles me too much, but I suppose I know what the little bitties are thinking. I don't belong here. I don't have nearly enough money, visible in my clothing, to be visiting the Carlyle, what with my BB Dakota, a bit short (maybe I shouldn't have *everything* shortened) skirt. I do smell lovely, light, and alluring, not that they would be able to tell over their overwhelming floral, powder scent. You know the one.

I hover, then flush the toilet with my foot, as I always do, and step to the sink. (Public toilets. Even the Carlyle's pristine public toilet? Penny and her germaphobia have taken over. Omigod, OCD?) I wash diligently and prepare for my exit. Knowing I'll pass the old bats again, I fuss with my hair, dab some lip gloss from my pink Prada clutch, and turn to check out my backside. (What girl doesn't check out her ass while visiting the powder room?)

To my horror, my lightweight skirt has tucked itself into my Hanky Pankies, and my right butt cheek is out for the world to see. I yank the skirt out and straighten myself. I head for the door, happy to have saved myself from an embarrassing moment; the mean old bats would be appalled and outraged by such a crass show of skin.

With my hand on the door ready to push, it dawns on me. I walk back to the mirror, turn around, and re-tuck my skirt, revealing my right butt cheek once again. I proudly push open the door and walk with, might I say, moxie out of the washroom. With a smirk and a swagger, I pass Mrs. Rich's table. I hear a loud gasp and immediate whispering behind me, then more gasps. A quiet "hmpf" sneaks out of my throat.

Just as delightfully expected, I've mortified them.

Take that, you rich old bats!

Elated, I slip into the café, pulling my skirt out before passing any guests. I rejoin Tray, none the wiser, at the war I have just waged in the other room. (There's another little secret you can keep, Carlyle.)

I *do* feel like a million bucks!

Rule #9
NEVER LET MONEY GET THE BEST OF YOU

This rule is simple but easily forgotten. Never let anyone make you feel unworthy just because you don't have what someone else has. Being happy with what you *do* have is all that matters.

I've forgotten this once or twice.

A year ago I was convinced I had the winning lottery numbers for none other than the famed Mega Millions. And the jackpot was up to $326 million! The night before the drawing I had a premonition and dreamt the perfect alignment of numbers. I knew this was it. I was going to win it all! I purchased a ticket and spent hours planning how I would spend every dollar. Start a business (I didn't know what but, details, details), houses, cars, the elephant rescue (I mean, I had the money now), trips all over the world, ski boots for my winter birthday, everything! I even included a portion to save the children, of course. (Mostly from older siblings.)

Tray came over for the drawing because I convinced him I was going to win. It wasn't hard. He started planning things with my money too. Lots of things. We were going to buy a theater, and apparently a gay dating site so he could find the perfect man. We were dizzy with excitement. While waiting for the announcement, Tray, as usual, dug through my refrigerator and cupboards for food. And, as usual, there was nothing. He went into the bedroom and dove onto the bed, moaning about how hungry he was and how, when I won all the money, he would make sure my fridge was always full. The announcement was near. I yelled for him to hurry back to the living room.

He walked into the room eating out of a box of Lucky Charms. When did I buy Lucky Charms?

I was never allowed to eat sugar cereal growing up, except on my birthday. So I only had sugar cereal once a year, and even then Minnie always "surprised" me with the same kind: Kellogg's Frosted Flakes. The least sweet sugary cereal on the market. She also threatened I might lose all my teeth by nightfall. (Happy Birthday.) The Sirens made fun of me for never having tried the ultimate Leprechaun treat, but I was too busy counting my millions to remember they had brought over a box the night before.

I fell asleep eating marshmallows (just the marshmallows) and playing the kid's games on the back. Tray found them by my bed. And just before the announcement, he also found my winning numbers on the back of the box. The numbers I had written to win a math game called Number Capers—not conjured in a precognitive dream.

My new world of riches shattered around me. I didn't win the Mega Millions and was completely depressed (so was Tray). Until I realized I had let money get the better of me. I *was* rich—rich with friends and family!

So, never let money get the best of you...or for that matter, Lucky Charms. Minnie was right; even though those multi-colored marshmallow bits are magically delicious, they *are* a big fat toothache. I had a cavity by the end of the week. (Those red balloons!)

Chapter 25
MIA

SPRINGING INTO the apartment after amped-up classes at the gym, I take a quick scalding shower (the water in my building is never just a normal temperature), swoop my hair into a Marilyn Monroe towel sweep, and tinker around the apartment in a pair of my very few matchy-matchy undergarments. I call Tray and leave my second annoying message: *Where are you! Call me, call me, call me!*

I putz around some more, noticing Tray's still not home across the street, and decide to call again. I leave yet another message, but this time a singing one: *Trayness, you're a FIREWORK, come on and let your colors burst! TRAY, CALL ME!!!*

Omigod, I really need to stop calling his voicemail. But I can't believe he doesn't want to hear more about Tuff. I promised to fill him in on everything tonight. Everything I didn't already tell him at the Carlyle at the beginning of

the week, which is a lot, since he was busy telling me everything about himself, then everything about the "probably
gay" guy sitting next to us.

I take my clean laundry from the wash and fold into
the bedroom, catching a glimpse in the mirror. I drop the
clothes on the bed and stand back a bit. I model from side
to side, scrutinizing each angle. I move in extremely close
and inspect for wrinkles, crinkle my nose, and scrutinize
some more. Then I make come hither looks and pose sexily but subtly to highlight my best angles. Tuff and I talked
about him coming to visit soon. I mean, he does need to
get his hat, and I don't think we could stand to be apart
much longer. (I know, I know, it's only been a week.) I
push on my bra and try to give myself bigger cleavage.

"Ah hell, maybe I should have stuck to the prayer for
the bigger boobs," I say out loud and laugh to myself. Harold darts into his stiletto. What? (Men never like when
women scrutinize their bodies.) "I get it, Harold, I get it."

I was twelve, sitting on a fluffy pink toilet seat cover
in a pink poodle wallpapered bathroom at Minnie's family
home, twisting my ponytail. Pulling at a string unraveling
on my shorts, I was staring at anything—the shower curtain, the edge of the pink tub, the hair brush, the curling
iron sitting on the pink counter—anything but my cousin,
Eva, floating naked in the bathtub, telling me everything
about kissing boys, having the best time at summer camp,
and whether or not she would join the debate club this
year in high school. On the one hand, she was actually
talking to me, which was so unlike The Sister, who denied

my very existence, so that was nice. On the other hand, um, awkward! I was taking interest in anything I could find (the pink toothbrush, the pink powder puff, the pink...so much pink!) so as not to stare at her naked body. Naked! Who thought it was okay to be naked in front of anyone was a mystery to me. I still dressed hiding behind doors, lockers, cupboards, anything, but she didn't mind in the least. Apparently, this was normal. She was used to being naked in the camp showers gossiping with the girls and in the high school locker room doing the same.

I finally stared down at her as she closed her eyes, dunking under the water. My eyeballs nearly popped out of my head. What the hell was this? I was looking at a lovely pair of breasts. I looked down at my T-shirt with a pug on it. (One of my favorites. Minnie gave it away a month later to a friend-stranger, probably because I wore it too much.) There wasn't so much as a bump. I think Eva thought I was impressed with her ability to hold her breath, so she went under again and I looked at her breasts again, thinking, *I want a pair of those!*

When I got home, I sat in front of my dresser going through my underwear drawer, searching for anything that resembled a bra. There was nothing. I remember very vividly sitting and staring, following the age lines and rivets of the dark wood on my dresser, willing my breasts to grow. I decided in that moment to pray.

Dear Lord, please give me breasts. Please give me womanly breasts. Breasts, Lord, breasts. Thank you, thank you, Amen.

Then I made a grievous mistake. I prayed again.

Dear Lord, I know you're very busy and asking for breasts isn't something that is dire. (Dire: a new vocabulary word. I liked to practice as much as possible.) *I'm sorry for asking for something so superficial. I know there are people who need so much more in this world, like things as basic as food. I'm sorry. I love myself just the way I am. Thank you for giving me all the blessings you have given me. Thank you, thank you, Amen.*

Well, prayers really do come true, people, because I never got boobs. God was busy feeding the hungry with my incredibly unselfish encouragement. Though if you ask me, she should have taken into account I was only twelve and thrown me a bone (or a boob for that matter), especially for being such a humanitarian at quite the young age. I often think back to that day and wonder what would have happened if I hadn't renounced that first prayer.

I cup my handful and shrug; they're perky if not big. And really, I don't want people to starve just so I can have a little more cleavage. "Thanks for making them perky," I say aloud, just in case she's listening. It could be all science and fossils, but you never know.

I straighten the photo of Lucille Ball making a fantastic goofy face on the vision board (always have a sense of humor about yourself) and put on a T-shirt and my college sweatpants.

"Alexa, turn off bedroom," I say sleepily and switch on the swag reading light as I flop into bed.

The chandelier clicks off. I cozy myself in the heavy duvet and extra blankets and, with pillows surrounding me, flip open a lighthearted novel from my reading stack.

But only two pages later, I'm antsy. Tray always calls me back. My phone blings as if hearing my thoughts and I sigh thankfully, knowing who it must be.

"It's about time," I squawk.

"Well, if I had known you were waiting, I would have called earlier," he laughs.

"Oh, Tuff, omigod, sorry, I thought you were Tray. I've been worried about him."

"Can I do anything?" he asks. Of course he can't do anything, but don't you just love that he asked? We continue talking until we both fall asleep.

With the reading light still on and the book stuck between my neck and shoulder (Bette is right about those bookshelves; this seems dangerous), I wake to the faint whimpering of my phone, gripped hard in my hand as if cemented, waiting. This time I check the caller ID. And what time is it? My phone brightly, too brightly, says 2:30 a.m.

"Tray?" I answer.

"Syd, it's really bad. They're after me! Please," he cries.

"What?" I say, wide awake now.

"Syd, please, I'm at my apartment. Help!" he pleads, then hangs up. What is going on? Who's after him? I call back but there's no answer.

I get Logan on the phone and he agrees to meet me at Tray's apartment. If there's someone there, I don't want to be alone for long. I throw on some jeans, because I can't walk across the street in my college sweatpants with this hole in the ass. I knock on Tray's door, then pound, but there's still no answer. By the time Logan arrives, I'm ready to call 911, imagining the worst.

"Tray, we're coming in whether you like it or not," Logan yells, banging on the door. No answer.

"We're staying until you let us in!" I pound again.

"Screw that, I've got a gallery to open," Logan says, almost to himself. Logan is a feminine, quite beautiful man who manages a well-known art gallery in Brooklyn, so I'm more than startled when he thrusts his shoulder into the door, shattering the lock.

We hear a scream. A big gay boy scream.

"Tray," Logan yells.

Tray peers out from behind his Thai changing screen. "I thought you were them," he says, and hurries toward us, noticing our shock. "I look terrible, I know. But I haven't had time to do anything, let alone sleep," he says, pushing us out of the way and searching the hall with his bloodshot eyes. "They've been after me," he hisses.

"Who's 'they'?" Logan asks, clearly upset by his appearance.

"The people after me! I owe them more money," he says, then covers his mouth as if he's told us vital and incriminating information.

"Who are 'they,' Tray? Who's after you?" I ask, baffled. For one brief moment my mind wanders to my missing cash. I push the thought away; that's enough. Why do I keep trying to blame one of my best friends for my own irresponsibility?! He wouldn't. I misplaced it. All of it.

"I'm not sure exactly, but see," he says, looking side to side and then down. "They left this." He points to a piece of paper on the floor, then screams. Logan leans down and picks up the paper. Tray screams again.

"It's a take-out menu, Tray. No one's after you," Logan says and shows him the Mexican restaurant's list of "authentic" cuisine.

"No, no, there are messages in there! See, see..." He points to the taco salad.

"Tray, it's a taco salad. Not even carbs are after you. You need to lie down," I say and lead him to his bed. He checks his back every three steps and lies down as Logan and I exchange concerned glances. I try not to seem as scared outwardly as I feel inside but our friend is in extremely bad shape. He needs help—and more than we can give.

Instead of closing his eyes, Tray rambles incoherently about the people after him, the drugs they "forced" on him, the basement of some building that had several hallways of bad people and other, confusing imaginary details neither Logan nor I can understand. He hasn't been home since we left the Carlyle; he hasn't slept for days. He explains that he needs to change his phone number because "they" will find him if he doesn't. He asks if we can put padlocks on his computer and change all his passwords. My head is spinning and I feel useless. He's making no sense. His paranoia continues like this as we sit with him until the sun comes up.

"Tray, you need help," I say.

"But I have you guys," he says, hopeful.

"This is way over our heads," I respond.

"You need to go where you can get some real help," Logan says, putting his hand on Tray's shoulder.

"I'm never going to do it again, don't worry," he says, putting his face in a pillow knowing what we'll do next. We call his parents. Once they're on the phone I hear him whisper, "Why are you doing this?"

His parents have a rehabilitation center on the ready, aware of his growing issue, but Tray won't agree to go. He absolutely won't. He mumbles that we can help him ourselves. I look at Logan, whose face reads just as distressed as I feel. This is all so overwhelming. I fall into a chair by the bed and look around the loft. Racks are knocked over and fabric is draped haphazardly over every surface.

It's heartbreaking. He's so clearly making the wrong decision. He's convinced it would be detrimental to the new production and his career for him to leave. But it's detrimental to his health if he stays. We have no other choice at the moment but to let it be; you can't force someone into rehab. I look around again at the disarray. I *can* organize and I've helped him with costumes since college. I *do* know how to do that. I stand as Logan pulls the billowy drapes, the color of the windmill blades outside his family home, closed. They curve generously around the windows, making him feel artificially safe.

Chapter 26
LUNCH AND READY TO LAUNCH

NEW YORK CITY: TODAY, WEDNESDAY, AUGUST 2

OLIVIA IS pretending to stretch while talking to me about her next big event. She actually worked really hard during class today but wants nothing to do with cooling down and draining lactic acid. She does, however, want everything to do with telling me all about her huge charity event and wrangling my help.

"Hold on, Olivia, I've got an 'urgent' text," I say, noticing my phone sending emergency blings. "Oh, okay, it's the Sirens." It might not be *that* urgent. (We use urgent texts a bit loosely. But I was worried it was Tray.)

"That's a fabulous idea, darling. Yes, let's get them all to help! It's going to be incredibly fun and we'll make loads of money for the kids," Olivia says, reaching for her toes but really just trying to get a better view of the tight ass outside the classroom.

Gus: Siren lunch, 1:30, Junes - BE THERE! EMERGENCY!
Oh and I just got the best lip gloss ever, it's watermelon fla-
vored with a little sparkle. It's insane! I'm getting one for all
of us.

I told you watermelon flavored is the best. (And wears
like an adult!) Ugh, I can't take more bad news, so this
better be something good. Maybe one of Gus' auditions
went well!

"Of course, sign us up, Olivia! I'll talk to them right
now at lunch. Gotta run." I hug her and grab my things.

"Oh and sexy up the costumes—we're trying to raise
money," she says, then meows.

"You, stretch," I yell as I leave, but she's already heading over to talk to the tight ass. I love Olivia.

We congregate at Junes, where Gus looks distraught
and is wearing the most amazingly tragic-fabulous outfit
I've ever seen. She's in an overly large vest made out of
what looks like lama hair with a red and black lumberjack
flannel underneath, purple shorts, and motor boots. Somehow, on her, it looks wildly cool.

Our regular, prickly waitress moves to our table like
she's walking through molasses. Gus, Bette, and I order
a Ghost of Mary served in a vintage coupe glass, one of
Junes' specialties, as I tighten my ponytail. Abby adds a
spicy margarita to the order, then revises it to a *virgin*
spicy margarita.

Claudia's missing in action because she's left on some
emergency meditative yoga retreat Zoey set up. (I knew

Zoey's powers of zen could help!) Zoey says Claudia's chakra is all out of sorts and that Claudia was about to have a breakdown, mostly due to her soon-to-be mother-in-law. Apparently the mother-in-law is trying to take over the wedding. So Claudia is posted up at some ashram deep in the forests of—New Jersey. She didn't have time with all the planning to go to Costa Rica or even Florida, so Zoey created a zen getaway for her with a family of yogis close by. She's probably knee deep in manure at some organic farm, cursing because they aren't pronouncing her name correctly.

Don't ask me what Claudia's ridiculously expensive wedding planners are doing if she needs to be "realigned spiritually." I'm positive my Ghost of Mary will do the same thing for my chakra. Ommm.

"So I was at this audition with Dee," Gus starts. Dee is her Yorkie mix. Her full name is Dionne, named after Dionne Warwick. "I couldn't leave her at home, you know; she gave me those eyes. And when it was my turn I told some of the girls in the waiting area to watch her. I could already feel I was 'on.' I could really feel it; I was going to be good. I'm always good, obviously, but this was like, everything was buzzing."

Gus looks around for her drink that hasn't arrived. "So, anyway, as soon as I get to the middle of the room, Dee starts barking like a maniac outside the door. I'm almost positive one of the girls got her going because Dee never barks." (Dee always barks.) "So I was like, duh, let her into the room so she won't distract me because I knew I was going to kill it. I let her in and she immediately jumps on the casting director's lap. Amazing, right? So, I'm in mid-mono and the guy starts sneezing, like rapid-fire sneezing, total distraction, but I kept going. Then Dee starts whining, but it was like applauding. She was loving it, but I'm like, fine, it's probably not great for the casting people, so I pick her up and that's when it hits me. I switched my whole audition around and did my mental patient mono-logue, the one where the woman talks to her cat. I used Dee as my cat! Dee looks nothing like a cat, but it was f'ing brilliant. Dee was in awe."

Bette, Abby, and I make eye contact, in search of how to react as Gus continues, undeterred. "Anyway, I can't believe the casting guy sneezed through the whole thing, but I never broke character. I almost told all the other girls to go home when I left. I can't believe they didn't just hand me the part right there."

The table falls silent for a solid minute while we act as if we're looking at the menu.

Gus adds, in case we didn't know, "So, they haven't called yet, which is insane. Oh that reminds me, your insane lip glosses!" She grabs them from her bag and rolls them toward us on the table. We all say thanks and ooh and ah, stalling any reaction to her audition.

"Okay, I can't hold it in." Bette breaks down and cracks up.

"You let Dee in the room?" Abby asks timidly.

"Um, classic," I laugh.

"Yeah, and they haven't called. I can't believe they haven't called," she says, nonchalantly looking at the menu.

"Uh, maybe because Dionne jumped on the casting director's lap who's allergic to dogs," Bette blurts, then tries the lip gloss. "Oh this *is* insane."

"It's my favorite," I add, lathering some onto my lips.

"No, no, he wasn't allergic," Gus broods. "There has to be something else."

"I'm pretty sure he was allergic," I agree with Bette, amused.

"Whatever, they'll call," Gus says with a wave of her hand. "That's not even why I wanted you all here today. We're here because Bette finally went out with Derek and it's like a love match! She needs our advice."

"What-da-you-want?" the waitress interrupts. No smile, no "are you ready to order," and no drinks yet. She hates us and we've never figured out why. We get the same service from her each time we're here: terrible. We continue to come because Bette and Gus insist it's one of their favorite places, but I think we come to aggravate the miserable waitress. At least she's consistent.

I order a beet salad with goat cheese, Bette's going to try a fancy new ricotta appetizer, Abby goes for the shrimp tartine, and Gus orders a couple appetizers for the table and a very interesting sandwich for herself. The waitress leaves without a word. She may or may not put the order in. We'll see.

"Go ahead, Bette," Gus prods.

"Well, you all know I was reluctant at first, but Derek and I are really good together." She emphasizes the word "good," so we all understand the gravity. (It's amazing.)

"He's the sweetest ever! And I know it's like I've disappeared, but it's because…" She pauses for drama. "…we've been spending every second together!" She smiles giddily.

"Bette, this is so great! And you're blushing! You must really like him," Abby melts. Abby can make anybody cry when she starts, and I have a feeling she's about to.

"I do," she says with genuine feeling and unconsciously flips curls off her shoulder. "I didn't think I'd ever feel this way again, but…" She lowers her voice. "…I think I've already fallen for him!"

"Already? You've known him for like ever," Gus interjects.

Bette continues as if she hadn't. "He even sat with me for hours while I studied. And you all know I put everything into that test! He sat with me, just to be near me." Bette takes a deep, dreamy breath.

"This is so exciting," I trill.

"So, here's the thing…he asked me to go away with him for the weekend, to celebrate finally getting together and to celebrate finally taking the bar. Do I?" Bette says, then holds her hand up to pause for our reaction, knowing where we think she's going with this. "That's not the question, because of course I'm totally going, but do I tell the ex? I feel like I should."

We all contemplate this oddly difficult question. Bette and her ex care a lot for one another but just couldn't make it work every day. And they still talk from time to time.

"Hard, right?" she adds. "I just don't think I want him to find out through mutual friends and feel bad that it didn't come from me."

"I already told her what I think. I think it's time to move on and break ties," Gus says, then adds. "It's not your responsibility to take care of his feelings anymore, Bette. Where are our drinks?" She turns to look for the waitress. She's ignoring us. The restaurant is tiny and you'd have to be in the restroom not to see us waiting, but there she is, acting like we don't exist.

"I don't know," Abby says. "If you tell him it might be easier on him. But...I don't know."

"I'm with Gus—move on. Let the ex move on too. Derek's a sweetheart and I think you should focus on him," I say.

"But don't you think he'll feel bad?" Bette asks.

"Sure," I say, "but don't you think Derek will feel bad if you need to consult your ex about going on a weekend getaway?"

"Agreed," Gus says, then utters impatiently, "What is the waitress doing?" The waitress is over her shoulder with our drinks. Of course. Her timing is unbelievable. Gus shoots us a look.

When she leaves, Bette starts back in, "You're right, I need to get over it. It's like I'm still trying to hang on, but I don't know why. I think Derek and I really have something. And you all know I wouldn't say that unless I'm serious. He's just so caring and thoughtful. I never thought I'd feel this way so fast."

Abby, our resident emoter, has a small, glistening tear falling down her cheek. I'm not a pretty crier so I try to avoid it at all cost.

"Then we all agree! Don't tell him and don't feel bad about it," Gus says, then adds, "I better order another drink immediately or I won't see it for a year!" The waitress is over her shoulder with our food. Again, impeccable timing. Gus shoots us another incredulous look.

"Okay, okay, you're all right, I'm moving on. You guys, Derek is unbelievable!" Bette says, smiling from ear to ear. The waitress finishes putting down our plates and looks at Gus deadpan.

"Let me guess, you want another drink," she says, then turns away. It's always someone, and today it's Gus. We discuss more about Derek and the good news, and after much chatter and sharing of food, I decide to tell them mine.

"I think I've met someone too," I start.

"Syd, really?" Abby claps.

"Tell us everything!" Bette leans in and I spill what's left of my drink on the table. Crap, my chakra!

I get nervous just thinking about Tuff!

Bette helps me mop it up while I dish about crashing the wedding, dancing, late night at the bar, and his thick Southern accent. I try to explain how we've been inexplicably connected: his sister, the business card, Bette and Claudia meeting him at the bar, his cowboy boots, and the hat. The scarred hat they all remember.

"Stop, stop, it's kismet, it's too much, *and* you crashed a wedding?" Gus pauses to take a feverish sip of her drink. "F'ing fantastic, Syd!"

Gus is even more excited than normal because it's a Southern man. Gus is from like every state in the U.S. and apparently abroad, at least according to her. Every time we go somewhere she says she's from there. And somehow she always has a compelling story as to why. Most recently, it was Texas while we were at the auto show. Even when we took a girls trip to Cabo San Lucas, Mexico, she was from there. (I'm beginning to suspect she's a fugitive. But she's a Siren, so I'll never tell.) But even though she's from "everywhere," she leans toward the South and can't resist a good Southern man. (Which is why she's still in touch with Ryan, otherwise he would have been long gone.)

"Let me get this straight. You met a small-town country boy who's actually a smart veterinarian-cowboy? Syd, it's your dream man!" Bette claps.

"I know!" I can't even deny it.

"But for the record, I still have a thing for Gavin," she cracks.

"Oh, I know that too," I laugh. "Just wait until you meet Tuff, though."

"Invite him to New York," Abby screams. And quite loud, because I catch the waitress roll her eyes.

"You have to," Gus says in a matter-of-fact tone. "It's your destiny." Now I've triggered Gus' crystal ball. And this is where she'll tell us she's a Gypsy. "I have Gypsy blood and..." Called it! "...I know these things."

"Omigod, we could go on a double date," Bette yelps, excited to include Derek.

"He's already brought it up," I say, just as wound up. "I would love for him to visit."

"Best. Lunch. Ever," Abby gushes.

"Oh, that reminds me, I have something for y'all too!" I say (using y'all with a big smile), and reach into my gym bag. I made a pit stop at my apartment before coming here. "While I was in Austin I got these!" I pull out several pairs of "Cowboys Only" G-string undies. They all go wild.

"Shut up, yes," Gus says, grabbing a pair.

"Derek is going to love them," I crack as Bette takes a pair.

"I don't know how I didn't find these first," Abby giggles, being from Austin and all.

"And I have more news," I say.

"Keep it comin'," Bette says, taking the last bite of her ricotta.

"You know my friend, Olivia? She's throwing a huge bash next weekend on August 12th. It's a children's charity event. No children allowed of course—it's Olivia." Everyone laughs. "And she wants us to help with some of the drinks!"

"I'm in. Her events are unreal," Bette says immediately.

"Done," Gus agrees.

"It's a costume party, so we need to wear something depicting a children's book character. It's all to raise money for low-income schools and reading materials," I explain.

"What day is that? Aren't we working?" Abby thinks out loud and checks her phone calendar. That is our shift, but Bette and I have days off in the books. And, it's for charity...and Olivia!

"Sounds fun! Can we bring dates?" Bette asks.

"Yes, definitely. Bring Derek! And bring a couple new, unused children's books. Olivia doesn't want us buying tickets since we'll be volunteering, and they're something like $275 a pop, but we should definitely take part in the book drive," I say, relaying the information.

"Say no more—I'm in," Gus says.

"Crap, that *is* our shift and I can't take any more days off. But I'll come for a little bit before!" Abby says, never wanting to miss anything. She takes a bobby pin from her hair and puts it in her mouth. "And then at least I'll be dressed up with you when you stop in at the bar after." She places the bobby pin back into her readjusted hair. "Also, I should have all my test results by then and will want to be with you guys."

"Of course! And let's get Beef to come. Then you can leave for the bar together, and he'll love being in costume," I say, teasing about Beef wanting anything to do with dressing up.

"Abs, have you thought about going to see Greg? I know you mentioned it," Bette asks gently.

"We've been talking a lot and he sounds like he wants to really try. He says he was to blame for pushing me away. Always trying to control me." She takes a small sip of her virgin margarita. "But, I don't think I'm ready to make any decisions yet."

"Fair, and you shouldn't have to," Gus adds.

"Can you guys believe I hooked up with Ducky?" She finally says what we've all been thinking. Bette, Gus, and I make whooping noises as she blushes and we all laugh.

We immediately start discussing costume ideas as the waitress clears our table, not holding back a grimace when she sees our new "Cowboys Only" club.

We wrap up our late lunch and I teach my 5 p.m. with a tiny buzz, only a small price to pay for a fab time with the Sirens.

☆ ☆ ☆

I'm waiting for takeout when Tuff calls later that night.

"Syd, what are you doing?" he booms over the phone.

"Organizing next week's schedule." Liar. But I was thinking about organizing my schedule, so Rule #6 applies. What I'm really doing is waiting to shovel a handful of French fries into my mouth. (And whatever else I blindly ordered online.) *So* not telling him that.

"Oh yeah? How's it looking?"

"How's what looking?" I say, distracted.

"Your schedule."

"Oh, good, pretty good!" The door buzzes. I tell him it's the TV. I don't know why, but I don't want him to know I'm eating takeout at 9 p.m. Completely weird, I know.

"So, I've been checking my schedule, and next weekend looks pretty good. Pretty open," he says. I mouth "thank you" to the delivery guy, who's already been paid via my Seamless account, and take my bag of goodness. My mind is on fries.

"Huh?" I ask, not paying attention.

"My weekend looks pretty open," he says again.

"Great." What are we talking about? I take out the (drum roll) French fries and head over to the animal print love seat. I'm about to sit down and enjoy my terrible treat when I hear Tuff talking again.

"So," he pauses, "I was wondering if it would be a good weekend to visit?"

What?!

I miss the love seat by one cheek and slip even more, trying to catch myself. My phone crashes to the floor and my treasured fries tumble out of my hand, scattering into the air.

"Noooooooooo!" I scream, as they land one by one on the hard wood. "Damn!"

"Sydney? Sydney? Syd?" I barely hear his voice coming from the floor. I grab the phone.

"Hello? Tuff? Oops, sorry! Are you there?" I say, hurriedly.

"Yes, I'm here. You don't want me to come next weekend? That was a pretty loud no. And did you say 'damn'? That bad of an idea?" he asks, perplexed.

"Come to New York? Next weekend? Omigod, yes! Of course, yes!"

"Really? Because I'm looking at a ticket online, right now. Should I book it?"

"Do it!" I shout. Then I remember Olivia's event. "Oh jeez, only if you're okay with dressing up like a book character on Saturday night. It's for charity!"

"A book character?" he questions.

"Yes, I swear it'll be fun," I say and explain all the details.

"Let's do it! Let's see," he pauses, "I have a pirate costume from last Halloween. Would that work?"

"We'll make it work. Bring it," I say and we hang up so he can book his flight. This is going to be perfect! I stare at my fries perched on the floor like pick-up sticks. I wasn't terrible at the game, so I salvage a few (oh, you would too) and scrap the rest.

Tuff is coming to New York City next weekend!

Omigod, Tuff is coming to New York City next weekend!!!

Chapter 27
BLUEBERRY PIE

I AM as fabulous as Grandma Shag. I am as fabulous as Grandma Shag. I chant my newest mantra as I set my tiny Manhattan oven to 350 degrees. I love making pies! I mean, I haven't quite done it in real life, but I think I love it.

Somehow I've talked Bubba Dean Billingsworth IV, known to everyone as Tuff, my dream veterinarian-cowboy, into flying in tomorrow from Austin. And what you think happened, that didn't happen, might just happen! (Rule #5 no longer applies!)

I want to give him a great impression of the city, and at the same time I want him to feel at home. And pie is the epitome of country comfort, so I've decided to conquer it with a little help from the Food Network and Grandma Shag's famous blueberry pie recipe, of course. Even though I grew up in the Midwest of the Midwest, Minnie never made pie. Come to think of it, Minnie never made anything. Omigod, what did I eat? (Oh yeah, French fries. And then she didn't want me eating those.)

But Grandma Shag is a natural in the kitchen, so I'm going to get back to my baking roots and be fantastic in the kitchen too! (Even if Grandma Shag usually kicks me out.) Wearing an Anthropologie apron, a gift from Gams when she thought there was hope, I begin rolling the homemade dough on the kitchen bar using a jar. I don't have a rolling pin but I figure Rachael Ray, who's always cutting corners, would use something similar, so it should be fine.

Flour is everywhere and stray blueberries from the Union Square Farmers' Market scatter the countertop, but I find enough room to make a big pie circle. I place the bottom layer into the pie tin, only needing to fix three holes in the dough after placing it! Not too shabby. Excited, I throw the two containers of plump, fresh blueberries into the middle and toss in the strays from the countertop too.

I roll out the second ball of dough, then start cutting strips for the lattice top. It looks startlingly good! But something smells a little funny. I'm not able to put my finger on it. Putting down the knife, I sniff around the small but open kitchen to find the source.

The oven has a cloud of smoke coming from the door. I grab a dishtowel, waft the thunderhead away, and wrench it open. There on the bottom rack are a couple pairs of clean but badly singed socks. I grab the socks with the dish towel and toss them onto the hardwood floor. They're beyond saving, but my favorite pair of underwear is on the top rack! I grab them from the clutches of the little oven and wave them around like a maniac. They're as hot as Hades but salvageable. I open the freezer and toss them inside. They'll be fine after a little cooling off.

I tend to stash things in cupboards, random drawers, or, in this case, the oven, so no one sees a mess if they come over unexpectedly. Yesterday, I washed a few items by hand for Tuff's visit and put them over the oven handle to dry, but Bette stopped over and they ended up *in* the oven. (A favorite hiding spot.)

The truth is, I've never used the oven; in fact, I had One Eye Jo turn the gas off when I moved in. I believe his words were "you'll never get a husband this way," but I was afraid I would light something on fire (eh-hem). So it's been off until two days ago when I had him turn it back on.

"There's hope, bimboshell," he said, then chanted the word "husband" while doing his infamous jig, rattling his keys.

I need to remember that the oven is now a working utility. After throwing the cooled socks in the trash, I wash my hands and turn back to the lattice top. I have the flat screen tuned to some rerun cooking show for inspiration even though some cute guy has surprised a young couple and is teaching them to cook a killer romantic dinner and not making a pie.

I start layering the lattice top, weaving each strip in and out until the whole pie is covered. Finished! And, might I add, it looks pretty darn good. I turn my eyes back to Grandma Shag's recipe because it said something about egg wash or butter on top. I read all the instructions again, realizing I forgot to add the flour, sugar, and cinnamon mix to the blueberries. Are you kidding me? Grrr. I'm going to have to take the perfect lattice top off. Impatience sinks into my chest and I yell a dragged-out "poop," then curse under my breath as my phone blings from the top of a large pile of flour.

I answer with a curt hello.

"Hey you!" Tuff's deep voice bellows.

Immediately changing my tone, I chirp, "Hi, Tuff!"

"Whatcha up to?" he asks.

"Oh, working on a little surprise for you!" I've gone from cursing to grinning ear to ear.

"Oh really. How's that going?" he laughs.

"Absolutely perfect," I lie. "Well, it's going to be perfect by the time you get here." I hope.

"Sounds good, whatever it is then. I was just callin' to let you know I get in around four-thirty tomorrow. Hope that works in your schedule."

"Of course!" I nearly scream in panic and excitement. Not much for phone conversations, he says a couple more things I don't quite catch because of his accent. I think he said something about a vet emergency, then hangs up.

With a renewed sense of enthusiasm I decide redoing the lattice top isn't such a big deal.

I quietly sing the oldie but goodie "Cowboy Take Me Away" by the Dixie Chicks as I finish the proper pie filling and slip it into the oven. Feeling very satisfied by my work, I relax in my favorite leather chair and watch the blond

Australian chef flirt his way through a cooking lesson. He has the wife smitten and the poor husband looking like a hand-me-down while he drizzles a fig leaf concoction over pork chops. Clearly the wife is picturing the Australian in just a fig leaf.

Tray texts that he's getting a haircut so he'll be popping over soon. This was part of our agreement. If he doesn't think he's ready for rehab he has to check in with his friends on a regular basis. I'm elated to show him my state fair-winning pie and do my usual quick clean-up, wiping the countertop of any pie remnants just as he hits the buzzer the usual six times.

He reaches the door just as I'm opening it and I scream. So he screams. Then we both scream like idiots. I have no idea why it was startling, but just ask my favorite UPS guy, Darryl, who's greeted with a scream each time he delivers a package. (Not all of which is from shopping, might I add. Some packages are—omigod, what else would they be? They *are* all from shopping. I make a mental note to address this.)

Tray gives me a big hug, then stares at me with an odd look.

"Sydney Shag, what is on your face?"

"What do you mean, what's on my face?" I ask as he steps inside, still staring.

"You've put too much powder on or you've been, dare I say, baking! Omigod, what are you making? It smells delish!"

"Blueberry pie!" I squeal. Tray pushes me out of the way and peels over to the oven.

"You've actually done it. It looks amazing," he says, and whistles the international chime for "good lookin'." "I'd say about seven more minutes."

Damn if he isn't spot on! Tray is quite remarkable in the kitchen and is always trying to teach me little tricks, which I vow to listen to from now on. As it turns out, I like baking and being in the kitchen while doing something other than drinking. Doc was right—I *can* cook in here. Despite what Grandma Shag says, I could totally be a baker! Tray pads into the bedroom and flops on the bed. I lean on the frame of the French doors and watch him with one eye on the oven timer.

"Did you see my hair? It's too short! If I meet the cast looking like this, I'll die! And my suits are ghastly, just ghastly, not to mention I can barely fit my fat ass into them." He throws his arm over his face in true pantomime fashion.

"Let me see the hair again—I'm sure it's not that bad," I say. I didn't notice his hair because I was wiping a cup of flour off my face. And I'm not even going to address the fat statement.

"No, never. It's shameful! Petra was gone and they had some *novice* do my cut!" he warbles. "But he was totally cute so I agreed and now look, look what he did to me!" I still can't see with him lying on the bed like that. He lifts his head. "Do you think he was jealous and wanted to sabotage my chiseled good looks? And did you see my hips? They're huge! Dear Lord, thank you for my beautiful face, but these hips! Aaah!"

"Your hips are never huge. You're being ridiculous!" I pause, actually noticing his physique. "In fact, I think you've lost weight," I say.

"You think?" he says, excited, and sucks in.

"And you haven't shown me the hair yet. Sit up," I order.

"No, Elizabeth, I won't. I won't do it," he says, channeling Liza Minnelli being asked to remove sequins from her clothing. Tray is huge into birth signs and stars (you have no idea what it's like when Zoey and Tray get started on the stars) and has decided he's Liza Minnelli and I'm Elizabeth Taylor based on our birthdays. And sometimes I think he's right because, boy, is he in a Liza mood.

"Oh come on, why all the self-loathing?" I ask. Not that it doesn't sink its teeth into me sometimes. Like when I hate everything I own because I shop too much and then want to give all my worldly possessions away and become a nun. Okay, maybe not the nun part, especially with the veterinarian-cowboy hunk on the way. On occasion I actually believe The Sister when she tells me I've amounted to nothing, except for a complete mess, and decide I should probably just pour myself over a cliff. I suppose with a sister like mine, who needs self-loathing? I can just give her a call.

Tray stands up and shuffles by me sideways, covering the back of his head with his hands so I don't see the haircut, and in the process, trips on my shiny pig.

"Aaah! Pig!" he wails and pantomimes again, reminding me of Norma Desmond in *Sunset Boulevard*. He hates my pig sculpture for obvious reasons. Cleary distraught, he pulls a bottle of wine down from the iron wine rack, never turning his back to me.

"You know the rules, Tray, no drinking and no drugs. It's the straight and narrow from now on," I say, taking the bottle and placing it back on the rack.

"Straight? Never." He sashays toward the huge mirror and strikes a pose. "Don't worry, I know, I know, I'm just kidding."

I catch a glimpse of the back of his hair while he indulges himself with model-esque poses and pouty lips. A large gasp escapes from my mouth, which he unfortunately isn't absorbed enough to miss.

"Omigod, my hair! It's bad, isn't it?" he shrieks. I gasp again as he turns around.

"The pie!" I yell, trying to disguise my reaction to his hair because the pie really does need to come out. Grabbing the towel that's posing as an oven mitt, I pull down the oven door.

No wonder he's so upset. The novice nearly shaved off the entire back of his faux hawk. I try to figure out how to react to this properly as I pull the perfect blueberry pie out of the tiny oven.

"Ta-da...trumpets and drum roll please...it's our state fair-winning blueberry pie," I say in hopes of changing the subject. I set it on the bar.

"Oh, the pie is perfect! Unlike my hair. Now tell me what you think."

Didn't work.

"I said…" He puts his hand on his hip and taps his foot. "What do you think?"

Oh hell.

"I think it looks like he closed his eyes when he shaved the back of your head," I answer extremely fast, then gasp and throw my hands over my mouth.

"Aaah, it *is* terrible, isn't it?!" he screams, then collapses into the love seat. "It's over, my life is over," he says so dramatically that we both break out into fits of laughter.

Tray helps me clean as he always does and I prep him for his first meeting with the cast of the new production tomorrow. He digs for more details about Tuff and then I kick him out before he can get his paws on my pie. Tuff arrives at four-thirty tomorrow. Four-thirty! Someone should check my vital signs.

Chapter 28
BUBBA DEAN

I'VE RUN around all day for work and, after a long, relaxing shower, I'm doing pretty well staying calm. But now that it's four o'clock and he's in a taxi, I'm panicking. What if he isn't the way I remember him? I mean, it was only one night. But we've spoken on the phone almost every day and I fall for him a little more each time. So it's going to be okay, right? What if he shaved off all his hair and looks like a skinhead? What if he *is* a skinhead? No, he would have told me that or someone at the wedding would have, right? Beef is bald and he looks good. Okay, so he can be bald and I won't care because it's his personality that really gets me. Well, that and his muscled chest and arms.

The door buzzer blares its hello. Omigod! I check myself out in the mirror one last time; casual but tight low-rise jeans, a little blue T-shirt that brings out my eyes (Minnie suggested blue and I listened; I *must* be nervous) and shows a minimal amount of skin above the jeans, wedges, and a ponytail. Nothing that screams I'm trying too hard.

Leaving the door ajar, I walk down the stairs to greet him instead of just buzzing him in. I see him through the iron pattern in the door, catch my breath, and miss the next step. I slip down the last five steps and grab for the wooden banister. I cling to it at the bottom of the stairs so as not to land on my ass. I actually don't fall! But the fancy banister knob breaks off in my hand. Why?! I open the first and second doors, propping them while still holding the knob. I'm not quite sure what to do with it. One Eye Joe is going to kill me.

"Miss Sydney Shag, walk much?" he bellows with laughter as I open the second door. "How the hell are you?"

"Tuff!" I scream, jumping into him. He hugs me into his huge arms. He didn't shave his head and he's as handsome as I remember. I usher him inside and toss the knob under the stairs. One Eye Joe and I will have to deal with that later. (And by that I mean I'm going to have to hide it from him!)

"Syd, are you just going to leave that broken thing under there?" he says, starting up the stairs. "I mean, hell, we can fix that. It'll be easy." Did I mention that I love a fix-it kind of guy with a Southern accent? That accent is enough to send me to the hospital for heart palpitations.

According to WebMD, if palpitations are associated with lightheadedness and shortness of breath (which I'm totally having) I may need medical attention.

"Oh," is all I can say because I've been rendered speechless due to persistent breathing difficulties.

"Oh, you want me to fix it?" he asks.

Sydney, say something!

"Oh, my landlord will have that fixed in no time," I say nonchalantly. I'm not going to tell my landlord, of course. I'm going to duct tape it when Tuff leaves.

"Great! It's so good to be here." He turns and smiles and I get a perfect shot of one of his huge biceps. I swear he just flexed or maybe it's because he's carrying his bag. Either way, I'm definitely going to pass out.

And because I'm behind him, I totally notice his backside in those tight Levi's and cowboy boots. Even better looking than I remember. I slip by him because everyone thinks the fourth floor means fourth, but it really means five flights of stairs. Just as we hit my floor, I push gently on the door.

"Welcome to my little home," I giggle and usher him in. I immediately introduce him to Harold as he sets his bag near the dresser. He thinks Harold is a very good-looking, astonishingly large goldfish. Everyone does. I add the word "muscled" so Harold doesn't feel the need to relive The Sister's "F" word humiliation. Harold's the best and I totally need to get him a new bowl. Maybe a tank. I like the sound of a tank. Tuff says he would love to help me pick something out. Then I let him get comfortable and reveal my masterpiece.

"So, here's my surprise…I baked you a pie!"

"Well, let me at it. I love pie," he laughs. "But first…"

He pulls me into him, and with his hand on the bare of my lower back he bends and kisses me. A tingling washes over my body as our lips touch. I press into him, now on tiptoes, as he gently steadies me while sliding the fingers of his other hand into my hair. We stay locked in the moment for what feels like an extraordinary amount of time and then he meets my eyes. "I've been thinking about doing that since you left." He smiles. "Okay, now, let me at it!"

And that's why I think about this man nearly every moment of the day.

"Hope you like blueberry," I say, in a daze. I step toward the pie, but he grabs my belt loop and pulls me in for one more kiss.

"Even better," he says, and I swear his eyes just twinkled.

It takes everything I have to not crumble on the floor and to summon something, anything to say as I cut into the pie.

"Oh, what was the emergency yesterday? Was everything okay?" I ask, but before he can answer, my phone goes off. I silence it, and ask again, but the phone goes off again, screaming an interruption.

"That might be important," Tuff says. "Go ahead, answer."

"You sure?" I ask.

"'Course. We've got all weekend," he smiles.

"Hello," I say.

"Sydney, it's Holly. Where's Tray? He's a no-show so far." Holly sounds absolutely frazzled. "I've got the whole cast here waiting to try on costumes and discuss how to get in and out of them."

"I don't know," I say, looking across the street at his windows. But all the lights are off.

"Syd, I'm the one that pushed his vision and this direction. He can't leave me hanging like this," she says. I hear the sneeze-snort in the background.

"Ich, I knew this would happen."

I've got to do something. This is his biggest show to date, with his most experimental designs.

"I don't know where he is, but I'm on my way," I say. I don't know what I'm going to do, but I've got to help him. He'd do it for me.

I look at Tuff. "I've got to go to a quick meeting. It's Tray, the one I told you about. He hasn't shown up to the theater and his biggest deal to date could all fall apart."

"Well, let's do this. Where do I take you?" he says. He's incredible. I change quickly into a conservative but chic LBD and heels and we jump into a car Tuff ordered while I dressed. We head toward the theater and I call and call Tray, leaving several messages. I call everyone we know and they keep trying as I walk through the backstage entrance as instructed. He's nowhere to be found.

"Hi, everyone. Sorry I'm late. Tray had a family emergency, but not to worry, I've worked closely with him on this and can't wait to show off his designs," I say calmly while smiling brightly. Holly nearly falls off her chair with joy.

I've worked closely with him on this, only if that means I've held up every costume as he tweaked it and scrutinized it. I've tried on nearly all the female costumes so he could see them on a moving, dancing body. But I've got this. Rule # 1 never fails.

Jumping right in, I help everyone with each gorgeous piece and talk about Tray's vision and why he constructed each this way and that. Tuff sits in the background, smiling and encouraging me the entire time.

When we finish, Holly hugs me so hard I think I might burst. She tells me I've saved the day, and the sourpuss actually says, "Well done." (And, not once have I heard her sneeze-snort since arriving.)

"You're the best! I'm so sorry we had to do this on your time," I say to Tuff as we jump back into a car. I lean over and kiss him and he squeezes my hand, keeping it in his. "I have no idea where Tray is," I say, worry seeping into my voice.

"You were so fun to watch. You're great with people and put everyone at ease. I don't know where your friend is, but that couldn't have gone better for him," he says.

"Omigod, it's nearly seven-thirty—you've waited two hours!" I say, noticing the time while checking for any messages with my free hand as to Tray's whereabouts. I find nothing.

"I think I've earned that pie," Tuff says with a wide grin.

"Yes, you did," I smile. I manage to send Logan a text that the meeting went really well and ask for any update on Tray without terribly interrupting the mini New York City tour I give Tuff on the way back. We pop back into the apartment and I immediately cut him a large piece of pie. "Let's have a drink with this and finally celebrate that you're here."

"I'll pour," he says, remembering he brought me a bottle of Ketel One. This guy is winning points everywhere! I grab him his beer of choice, Miller Light, from the fridge. We laugh, already knowing each other's favorite drinks. A way to a man's heart is through his stomach, via a beer funnel.

"Oh yeah?" Tuff says in a puzzled but flirtatious voice.

"What?" I turn to see him standing at the freezer holding an ice tray with my favorite pair of underwear frozen, stuck, and dangling from it.

My "Cowboy's Only" underwear.

Gah!

Not exactly how I pictured him seeing those.

We laugh and I take a big swig of his beer.

He shakes me a martini, and after a few sips I give him the bedroom and bathroom so he can shower and change. Having him here has heightened every bit of sensuality I possess. My whole body is humming, and it feels to have lifted me ever so slightly off the ground. I can't stop smiling as my phone blings. Tray is still nowhere to be found. I'm pulled firmly back to the floor.

I fix myself up in the living room, spraying my signature perfume on my favorite bits. I've picked out the perfect dress for tonight, and just as I'm pulling the beautiful red Calvin Klein number over my head I see Tuff in the mirror walking up behind me in just his jeans. He flips his wet hair out of his eyes and takes my hips in his strong hands and turns me to face him. My dress has only made it to my waist and I stand in front of him, exposed. He stares at me with such intensity that, once again, I can hardly breathe. He leans in and tastes my lips. Then kisses me slowly, exquisitely, down my body until he's on his knees, where he kisses me there. And stays there until I'm seeing stars. Then he gently slips my dress down, looking up at me.

"I've been waiting a long time to do that," he smiles. I feel like bursting. He kisses me and, in one fell swoop, stands and lifts me into his arms, where I find his lips again. As I run one hand in his wet hair and grab at his jeans with the other, he carries me like a paperweight to the bedroom, where we fall onto the bed in a frenzy of desire. He kisses my neck, collarbone, and shoulders while we both remove his jeans. I reach down to feel him, surprised that he doesn't have on underwear, and let out a small scream of delight.

☆ ☆ ☆

Sitting at the basement-set candlelit restaurant known for its rooftop garden, we order dinner, and with our eyes locked we raise our glasses and toast.

"Sydney Shag, I think I could get used to this," he grins.

"Me too," I say, stupidly. I must have lost brain cells.

"I don't know how much of a gentleman that proved me to be, but I couldn't wait any longer," he smiles. I've already memorized that smile.

"Well, I'm glad you didn't," I smirk, "But, I *was* a little shocked." In more ways than one.

"I figure if we add our first date, the wedding, and all the talking on the phone—because, Syd, I don't know if you've noticed but I'm not usually a phone guy—then we've been dating for quite a while," he laughs. "Well, that and the fact that I feel like I've known you for a very long time." He clinks my martini with his Maker's on the rocks.

"However you add it up, I'm happy either way," I say and take a sip. It's not the alcohol, y'all. I'm falling for this guy and hard.

"Good," he says, and I almost think he heard my thoughts. The waiter comes back to take our order, and by this time we're starving.

This couldn't be going better, except for a minor setback when I flung a piece of bread onto another couple's table while talking with my hands. The tables in the city are always so close, and it nearly landed in the man's drink! But Tuff made us all laugh, recovering for my intrusion.

After dinner, I suggest several fun bars nearby, but we look at each other and head back to the apartment.

NEW YORK CITY: TODAY, SATURDAY, AUGUST 12

The next morning, I feel like I'm in a different world. I met a prince who happens to be a cowboy. I peek at my vision board, still wrapped in his arms, and think about everything that led us here. His business card and cowboy hat both perch on the board as if it were fate. He stirs and kisses me as I wriggle out of his arms. I grab his hat and place it on his head, returning the kiss.

"My hat," he says with his eyes still sleepily closed. "I knew we'd find each other." He blindly fixes it to his favorite fit. "When you're meant to be together, you always find your way back." He looks at me, tips the hat, and grabs my hips, pulling me on top of him.

☆ ☆ ☆

I walk him to Morandi for brunch in a dreamy, happy daze.

"I want you to go to Claudia's wedding with me," I state. Again, I'm shocked at what just came flying out of my mouth.

"I'm in. When and where?" he responds quickly and lightheartedly.

"Really?"

"Hell ya!"

"It's here in the city on October 7th. Do you think you'd be available that weekend?" (And Christmas is seventy-nine days after that; are you free?)

"Count me in," he grins after checking his phone calendar. He types in the date.

We're going to another wedding together! He cuts himself a big bite of the crêpe we ordered to share and I stab it with my fork and shove it into my mouth. "Syd, that was a dangerous move!" he bellows with that huge, now familiar, smile on his face.

I take him to Central Park and we stroll along the lake, passing the Angel of the Water atop Bethesda Fountain, and pick a spot in the grass nearby to people-watch and daydream. The park is busy and I lazily gaze at all the characters moving about their lives amid thoughts of Tuff, and whether or not I remembered to put on matching underwear and bra. (Probably not, but Ivy Andersen would be so proud if I did. She matches everything from head to toe.)

A Jack Russell pulls her human toward a flock of pigeons and then bolts in the direction of an American Staffordshire. Tuff immediately gives a deep, Southern drawl to the pit bull and I dutifully fill in the part of the wild little Jack, and we laugh.

"I might do that on occasion with clients," Tuff chuckles. "Maybe why I do so well as a small town vet."

"And why all those people adore you." I smile, thinking of the wedding and all the "cats" and "dogs on the hunt."

I notice a man in a tan jacket furiously scratching at lottery tickets, one after another, putting each in separate folds of his beat-up leather briefcase. I can almost feel his anticipation, then letdown, as he discovers none of them hold the million-dollar payout. I feel his pain but because of Rule #9, I feel as though I'm holding the winning ticket in my hand. Tuff gives my hand a squeeze and I squeeze back. I put my head on his shoulder and we drift in the afternoon breeze.

I check in with Logan after *still* not hearing from Tray and get a very vague response. But he tells me he's with him and to have a wonderful time with Tuff. It doesn't seem right, though. Why wouldn't Tray text as well, or call? But I decide to listen. I *do* want this weekend to be about Tuff, not Tray. I tell him to let me know if they need anything, and he promises to call after the weekend.

Heading out, we walk through the beautifully manicured, bench-lined walkway of The Mall, then turn into
the Sheep's Meadow, where people are playing Frisbee,
laying out, eating packed lunches, and tossing footballs.

Tuff nabs a throw and tosses the ball with a few guys.
(Smart, athletic, handsome. Check, check, check.) He flips
it to me, which I, to his astonishment, whip back to one of
the guys in a perfect spiral.

"Yeah, I used to play," I say, mimicking every old high
school football player reliving the glory days.

"And to think I had you pegged for a cheerleader," he
says. He grabs me, picks me up under one arm, and runs
with me like a football as I laugh and yell in protest. He
sets me down and kisses my hand.

"Yeah, you better watch it," I giggle. I push him and
run toward the gated exit of the meadow as he tries to
catch up.

We head back to the apartment in a taxi and run up
the stairs, where he continues to chase me. Once inside,
he wrestles me onto the bed, kissing me all over my body.

"We're going to be late," I say, but can't help laughing.

"Are you sure?" he says while kissing my belly button,
then lower and lower.

Well, maybe we have a few minutes.

☆ ☆ ☆

As I shower, I think about my vision board. First travel
and now a cowboy—it's astonishing.

I step into the bedroom with a towel around my body just as Tuff pulls out his meticulously folded pirate's costume.

"What do you think?" he asks, snapping it out of its folds.

"I think you'll make a perfect Captain Hook to my (dramatic pause) Tinker Bell!" I say with a giggle, pulling his hook from the top drawer of my dresser. He laughs. (Harold, though, looks distressed. A hook—I understand and lower it from his view.)

"Won't people stare if we're dressed up in August? It's not Halloween," he points out.

"Nah, everyone's a character in the city. Here's my Tinker outfit!" I say, and proudly show off my wings, Tinker shoes, and sparkling, sequined, green dress.

"What is that, a washcloth?" he laughs.

"I'll have you know Tinker Bell likes her dress short!" (I had it shortened.)

"Who am I to argue with that? Doesn't Captain Hook take Tinker hostage?" He slaps my backside and I lose my towel. "I think I'm going to like being Captain Hook, Halloween or not," he says, raising his eyebrows. I whip him with the towel and run back into the bathroom, screaming with laughter.

Chapter 29
COSTUMES, KISMET, AND A COMMODE

I LOOK at Tuff and think I could really like being around this guy for a long, long time. He wipes his nose on his Captain Hook sleeve. Ugh. Even still, I think I could. I pick up my lucky green leather motor jacket, then remember I have wings! And I don't want to cover my sparkling sequins and toss it back onto the chair. We leave the apartment, but not before I grab my Tinker Bell bottle of pixie dust. Because what's a party without glitter?!

Clifford the Big Red Dog greets us, takes our invites, and ushers us inside the private townhouse in Soho. We make our way through massive cardboard book covers, remarkable costumes, and the silent auction, and soon head up the open staircase toward the second floor bar. We both note the floor to ceiling built-in bookshelves containing no books, but yellow box after yellow box of Veuve

Clicquot Champagne. There must be hundreds. We pass an extensive square section of glass flooring near the DJ, so you can see down to the first floor while showing off your dance moves, and finally reach the bar. I'm astonished by the beautifully lofted space, and we haven't even seen the third floor. Leave it to Olivia to find such a striking location for her event. We step to the bar where Three Little Pigs are doing shots and talking about a bunny and a cat making out on the roof deck. There's a roof deck? And according to what I've just overheard the pigs say, there's a "wicked" spiral staircase that leads you there.

"What should we order?" I say, radiating excitement. Tuff, looking equally as impressed by the space, signals for the bartender, who's dressed as one of the Wild Things from *Where the Wild Things Are*. My phone vibrates.

Bette: Where are you, Derek and I just walked in

Me: Second floor by The Three not so Little Pigs

Bette: OMG I just saw a girl in a big shoe...There was an old woman who lived in a shoe...be there in 2!

"Bette and Derek are here! I can't wait for you to meet them," I say, just as Olivia appears with two bottles of the Veuve Clicquot under her arms. This woman needs a handbag solely for alcohol.

"Oh, you poor unfortunate souls...you don't have any alcohol yet!" Olivia says, quoting some of Ursula's song from *The Little Mermaid*, then yells, "What do you think?" Without waiting for a response, she continues, "I just love being a witch! You must be Tuff, you handsome devil, or should I say, Captain Hook!"

"And you must be Olivia. Thanks for the invite," Tuff replies, helping her set the bottles on the bar.

"Drink up. On me!" she glows, pushing a bottle of Vueve our way. She gives him three air kisses (three!) and hugs him while, behind his back, she feigns grabbing his ass. I laugh.

"Tinker Bell!" Bette yells from across the room. Bette and Derek hurry over, dressed as Raggedy Ann and Andy. "Hi, Olivia," Bette beams.

"Bette!" Olivia glows. "The more the merrier." She pushes the second bottle our way and gives everyone air kisses. "I just love a good costume party. This is one of my best yet!"

Olivia excuses herself to greet other guests and hustles off as the Wild Thing takes care of our pour and we toast to the start of a great night. The guys immediately start talking about what they've heard is on the third floor, which is a game room containing a pool table, shuffle board, and foosball.

"Syd, you did *not* mention the small-town boy was so hot. Def your type, and his accent is sexy," she whispers in my ear. She pinches me and nerves run shotgun through my body. As if an afterthought, she says out loud, "He's so familiar."

"He's cute, right?" I whisper back and look at Tuff. I get another surge of nerves, as if him meeting my friends is making all this real. I down my glass of champagne.

"And you're so cute," I compliment, noting her adorable Raggedy Ann makeup. She has bright pink circles on her cheeks and exaggerated eyelashes drawn in with eyeliner.

"Ooh, thanks," she smiles, pulling one of her yarn braids and posing for a moment. "But he's not cute; he's hot," she says, snapping back to herself. She swirls her champagne, causing more bubbles, and looks at him closely. "And so, so familiar."

"Well, they're getting along," I say, gesturing to Derek and Tuff with my empty glass. They're already deep in conversation.

"That's it," she says, spilling an excited drop of champs. "I don't know why I didn't put it together before. Maybe it was hearing that accent again, but that's the guy, Syd!"

"What?"

"That's the guy who came into the bar. The guy who was asking if you were okay after the skydiving incident!" She smiles, having solved the riddle, which I thought I had already put together for her. Bette is notorious for being the "winner" when it comes to solving problems whether she's actually solved them or not. She adds, "I agree with Gus; it's kismet, Syd. Kismet. And..." She pulls me closer. "...you're right, he rivals Gavin. Now, would you look at Derek? Isn't he sweet? Can you believe he dressed as Raggedy Andy for me?"

"Yes, I can. He's *so* sweet. He's *always* been *so* sweet, speaking of kismet," I say, giving her a look. *It's about time.*

"I know, I know. But this was more like he gently wore me down over time," Bette says, taking a drink of her bubbly. I look into my empty glass. "What's the fancy word for that?"

"Husband," I say, and we both crack up.

"Oh, I almost forgot to sparkle you!" I set my glass on the bar and Bette pours me another as I take out my pixie dust, aka glitter bomb bottle. "Where's Gus?" I ask while dusting her with sparkles.

"I'll text her," she says. Bette types quickly and immediately gets a response. "Gus is on the roof," she reports, "with The Cat in the Hat."

"Oh, did she bring—" I start to ask, then stop short and look at Bette. We share a laugh, knowing she didn't bring a date but found one here.

We gather the champagne and our dates and head up the second set of open stairs to the third floor, then wind up the spiral staircase. There she is, dressed as...well... what is that? A Playboy Bunny? Her legs are draped over The Cat in the Hat and they're...well, they're sucking face on a built-in bench. Oh right, the "bunny and cat making out on the roof deck"—I should have guessed it was Gus. Bette coughs loud enough for them to hear.

"Sirens! You're finally here," she says, pulling her legs off the cat. She barely makes it off the bench as the three of us hug. "Tinker Bell, you're ridiculously hot," she says. "Like, "I die" hot." Another feature of best friends: they may know how to embarrass you or call you out, but they also know how to make you feel crazy good in front of a new guy. "And, hello there, Hook," she says flirtatiously with an extra low rasp. She gives him a welcoming hug and over his shoulder mouths to me, "Omigod, sex-on-a-stick." She hugs Raggedy Ann and Andy. "Bette and Derek, you two look perfect together. Forever. We knew it all along.

"I want you all to meet The Cat in the Hat," she says, pulling him off the bench and we all greet the cat.

"What's his name?" I lean in and whisper to Gus. The guys start introducing themselves and talking.

"I don't know, but he runs his own company and I'm starting to like the money type," she discloses.

"You don't know his name?"

"Syd, may I remind you that you crashed a wedding with a total stranger and went to a golf course with said stranger on a bus full of people you didn't know?"

Gus has a point.

"Well said, Gus," Bette chimes in. "Speaking of money-type, what happened to Ryan?"

"What do you mean, what happened? He lives in Texas, and we're still talking," she says, with "duh" implied. She takes my champagne flute and the bottle I'm holding, pours more into the already half-full glass, tosses back a large gulp, and looks at Tuff. "He's way bigger and way sexier than you let on." She takes another gulp, refills it to the brim, and hands the flute back to me. "Hey, where are my sparkles, Tink?" she says, noticing Bette and I are twinkling underneath the starlight. It's a magical feeling, so I dust Gus everywhere and put a little more on myself. One can never have too many sparkles. A few tickle my nose and I sneeze, upsetting my champagne, which sloshes onto Tuff's back. Oops!

He turns, smiling, and says, "That feels familiar." We laugh and it beads off with one swipe of my hand, which he takes in his, and once again, I can't resist kissing that smile. Derek whistles and we all laugh.

"When are we supposed to help out, Syd?" Bette asks, always keeping us on track. Then, making a funny face at Gus, she says, "What are you anyway, a Playboy Bunny?"

"No," she says, slapping Bette playfully. "Can't you guys tell?" Gus strikes a pose for Bette and me. When we don't respond, she blurts, "I'm the Velveteen Rabbit! I loved that book as a kid."

"Tragic." I shake my head.

"Tinker, I'm not tragic!" Gus says, going for my Tinker bun.

"Oh no, not you—the book! The book," I say, ducking and batting her away. "*The Velveteen Rabbit* is like the saddest book ever. Talk about scarring a kid for life."

"Oh, I know, I loved it," she says, swatting my wings instead. "Well, look again. Can you see it?" Gus poses again but this time from the back, showing off her puffy tail. Um, no, we can't tell at all. We stare some more as she places her "paws" in the universal sign for bunny.

"You're totally a Playboy Bunny and you know it," Bette says, rolling her eyes.

"Bette," Gus yelps, in mock horror as Bette's phone dings to a text as if on cue. I pull Gus' tail to get back at her for the wings and Bette immediately stops her from retaliating. Then she looks at her phone, which reminds me to quickly check on Logan and Tray.

Me: Logan, it's me! How is Tray doing? You guys okay?

Logan: Not great. Syd, he's not himself. This is really bad.

Me: Oh no! What can I do?

Bette bubbles, "Abby and Beef just got here! Let's go back downstairs!" She grabs my hand and starts to pull, yanking me back into the fun as I stuff my phone into my little glittery clutch.

"Tink knows the truth! I'm the Velveteen Rabbit," Gus yells and slaps my ass as Bette pulls me away. "I'm loving this green dress, short and hot, you little huss!"

"Gus!" I shout in protest but laugh as Bette drags me toward the spiral staircase with the guys right behind, chuckling at the hilarity. Gus follows, drinking straight from the Veuve bottle.

"The Velveteen Rabbit. It's obvious," she says in between swigs to no one in particular.

We make our way through the now-packed second floor and spot Abby disguised as Little Red Riding Hood and Beef in full regale. We all stare, shocked that Beef even got into costume, let alone one so impressive. He's immediately forced to explain.

"You girls are always talking about how men should be like knights in shining armor and stuff, and isn't a knight or a prince in like every children's book?" Beef stands in a stately manner, placing his hand on his chest of armor to enhance his costume. "Plus my brother and his buddies were Knights of the Round Table last year for Halloween, so I had the gear," Beef finishes shyly.

I push myself up next to Tuff, immediately associating him with my knight, and give him a squeeze. Careful not to bump my wings, he squeezes me back.

"It's perfect, Beef. Absolutely perfect. And Abby, you look adorable," I twinkle, then shower them both with Tinker Bell sparkles. (Don't worry, Beef is used to being sparkled by now. We sparkle him all the time at the bar.)

"You must be Tuff," Abby says, blushing as she leans in to give him a hug.

"Well, hello," he laughs. "I love how friendly y'all are. I'm so happy to finally meet some of the friends Syd always talks about."

"You mean Sirens." Abby winks and Tuff chuckles.

"It's nice to meet you too," Beef says, and as always at a slow and steady pace. "I'd say you need a beer." He nods toward the sparkles that have gotten all over Tuff and gestures to the bar.

"You'd be right," Tuff laughs again and smacks Beef's back. The guys head to the bar and we follow a few steps behind, giggling and talking about Tuff, Derek, and a Playboy Bunny that may or may not be a Playboy Bunny. At the bar, Abby begins to tell us she has good news, but Olivia interrupts.

"Lovely ladies, it's time! I'm going to give a little speech, then I want you to hand out all the signature shots. Start just after I thank everyone for their donations and books. Oh, and we've named the shots 'Book Ends'— bloody clever, right? When you're done, join me for one! I'll be sure to take care of these boys while you take care of everyone's thirst." She winks and grabs Beef's ass. His rich skin tone hides his blush, but his goofy smile gives him away.

Olivia stands at the DJ booth, commanding attention with the mic, and announces to resounding cheers how much the charity has raised to date. She details what will be done with the wonderful "book booty" and thanks everyone eloquently. We each take a tray of "Book Ends" and start handing them out to thirsty book characters.

I'm instantly bombarded by a couple dressed all in white with green ski hats. They immediately take shots, cheer, and hurry to the dance floor, meeting someone dressed as what looks like a slice of ham. Oh! Dr. Seuss' *Green Eggs and Ham*. Brilliant! Abby and Bette go in one direction and I move away from the bar with Gus and offer my tray of shots to a spider and a very small, tired-looking rat.

"Charlotte, I presume?" I smile heartily.

"Yes! Honey, she knew," she says, punching the rat's arm. "Can you tell he's Templeton? Thank goodness we didn't choose Wilbur; he would look like one of them." She points to The Three Big-Little Pigs. "They're the biggest chauvinists in our office. Kind of ironic they chose to dress as pigs tonight." Out of the corner of my eye, I see Bette swatting at one of the Big-Little Pigs and watch as they each take two shots from her tray. Bette looks our way and rolls her eyes.

"Well, I love *Charlotte's Web*. And you two look great," I say. They each take a shot and Charlotte sips sparingly on hers while Templeton throws his back.

"We're watching our drinking," she smiles, not noticing his gulp.

"Get a load of Robin Hood's, uh, tights," Gus says softly, now standing next to me and holding her tray out for Lucy and Charlie Brown. She eyeballs Robin's package.

"Gus," I say through my teeth while the *Peanuts* characters take their shots.

"I'm just sayin'. I wonder if he has a hedge fund in there?" she adds and smiles broadly. I can't help but snort.

"Oh, I heard that. Just like a Playboy Bunny," Bert says to Ernie. They wander over.

"I'm the Velveteen Rabbit!" Gus protests.

"Yeah, and Bert and I are straight." Ernie, the older of the two, laughs and Bert takes his arm. I snicker at Gus as she shoots me a comical glare. "We know it's a bit of a cliché, Bert and Ernie being gay, but we couldn't resist. It was either that or Winnie the Pooh and Piglet, and that would have put me in a fat suit and—"

"And I would have to be a little pig. And that isn't happening," Bert finishes Ernie's sentence, sucking in his already thin waist.

"I think there's already enough Little Pigs around here," Bette says, passing us while heading to the back of the room with a Big-Little Pig following close behind.

"Here's to the wolf," Bert says as they clink their shots, and we all cheer. They set their empty shot glasses on Gus' tray. "But you know," the very talkative, very attractive Bert continues, "we should have been fairies! Tinker, you have the best wings I've ever seen."

"Ooooh, thank you!" I bubble.

"Ernie, I need a pair of those for Gay Pride next year," he adds.

"There's always something he needs," Ernie says, playfully rolling his eyes.

"I do not! But whatever, I *am* the trophy wife," Bert says, striking a grand pose.

"You two are fabulous and definitely deserve some pixie dust," I giggle and sparkle them both while Gus holds my tray.

"Why thank you, Tink," Bert says with a flourish of his hand. "Seriously, this…" He sweeps his finger up and down in the air, tracing my body. "Love it!"

"You two look even more fabulous now," Gus says, handing me my tray. "But I *am* the Velveteen Rabbit," she adds.

"Sure you are, sweetie," Ernie winks, and grabs Bert's behind, pulling him over to the Mad Hatter as Bert screams in delight.

"How can people not see this?" she says, and in the same breath, "So speaking of *Winnie the Pooh*, Tigger over there looks promising." Gus saunters toward him, her bunny tail wagging, just as more thirsty party-goers step over.

"Hi there, you two. Hope you're having a great time tonight. Would you like a shot?" I ask Harry Potter and Hermione.

"Thanks, we'll take two," Harry responds, then looks at Hermione. "Will you hold them? I'll be right back; I just need to say hi to someone really quick." He walks away before she can respond.

"There he goes and look who he's saying hi to," she says to me. We watch him stride up to Miss Muffet. "Hermione is turning out to be a boring outfit compared to so many of them here." She gives me a once-over as if making her point. "And I really like him. Oh well, I'll hold the shots. Tinker, you're adorable. I love your outfit and sparkles," she says kindly, reaching for the last two shots on my tray. I move it out of her reach.

"Thanks, but one minute," I say and set the tray on the open staircase. "Tinker doesn't go anywhere without her fairy dust and Hermione needs a little tinkering." I take out her ponytail holder and muss her hair before adding some sparkles. I pull out the knot in her schoolgirl tie and unbutton her blouse just enough. Finally, I sprinkle her again and pick up my tray. "Perfect! Now you're Hermione, but from the fourth book. A little older and more grown into herself." I wink.

"You're so sweet," she laughs, and with newfound confidence she picks up the two shots.

"So, that guy over there asked for your number, but I said I thought you were with someone. Let me know," I say, just in time for Harry to eavesdrop.

"Whoa, hello, Hermione," Harry says, walking back over and raising his eyebrows at her new look.

"Everyone has a crush on Hermione," I say to her, then flit off with an empty tray to get more "Book Ends." I think I like this Tinker-tampering thing. Bette and I pick up the last of the shots because Abby and Beef have to leave earlier than expected to help Claudia and the team at the bar. And well, Gus is back in the Cat in the Hat's arms.

"Promise, promise, promise you'll come to the bar," Abby begs.

"Done," Bette agrees. "We'll be there, don't worry."

"See you soon!" I yell as Abby and Beef make their way through the larger-by-the-second crowd to the stairs and first floor.

"Have you talked to the lady dressed as Dory from the movie *Nemo*? She's friggin' funny," Bette says, pointing to her on the dance floor. "She keeps repeating everything she says, and look how she's dancing." We both laugh, watching the woman wiggle like a fish on the dance floor.

"Ladies." Derek sidles up to Bette, looking goofy in his costume. "Just checking in. How are you?"

"We're great! Almost done." Bette kisses him on the cheek.

"Well, you better hurry, because I'll have you know Tuff and I, the two hottest guys in here, are being hit on by a very talkative Daphne and Velma," he says, giving us what he thinks is a suave look. We both laugh.

"I got my eyes on you," Bette jokes, kissing him again. I lean down and take a big swallow from the straw of Derek's Jack and Coke. I peak over at Tuff, who looks to be fending off the clingy *Scooby Doo* characters. I do a little booty shimmy in my revealing Tinker Bell dress to get his attention and he laughs out loud.

"Get back over there and help the man," Bette says, pushing Derek and laughing. She hands me my tray and grabs hers. "Let's get rid of these quick and get back to our men."

"I mean, he's not my man just yet," I say, giddily. We look up and The Three Big-Little Pigs are right on our trays. Bette and I look at each other, then back at them.

"Not by the hair on our chinny, chin, chin," we shout together and roar with laughter. We push around the drunken pigs and finish handing out our shots, then sneak to the bathroom before joining the guys.

"Don't go in there. There's a cricket," a tall, disheveled Pinocchio says as she comes out.

"Just flush it. What's the big deal?" a large Umpa Lumpa says. Just then a very short man dressed as Jiminy Cricket walks out and grins, taking Pinocchio's hand. Bette and I exchange knowing glances.

"How much was each ticket again?" Bette asks.

"Two hundred and seventy-five each or five hundred a couple," I answer.

"I'd say he got his money's worth," she howls, and I crack up. We gather ourselves in the bathroom and gossip more about Tuff and Derek as Bette touches up her doll-like cheeks with bright pink lipstick. "By the way, how's Tray?"

"Oh jeez, I should check again. It's Tuff; I can't think! It doesn't sound great, but he should be fine. He's with Logan," I answer, and look at my phone for an update while we're away from the guys.

Logan: Syd, don't freak out. Tray stormed out. He was mad at me for lecturing him. I know you're busy, but make sure his

*light is on whenever you get home. I told him to leave one on so
we know he's there. Text me he's okay? Sorry xoxo*

Me: Will do, And I'll text him now

Logan: Yes, do. He's not answering any of mine

*Me: Tray, just checking in, did you make it home? Please text
so I know you're okay (blowing a kiss emoji)*

"Bette, don't let me forget to do this." I sigh and hand
Bette my phone so she can read the texts too. Bette's steel
trap of a mind will remind me later, and it's a good thing
too because with Tuff here I'm not sure I can remember
my name.

"Of course," she says after reading the text. "He'll
be fine," she adds, noticing the worry on my face. "Ooh,
what's this!"

"What's what?" I ask. She holds up my phone to a new
text.

Gavin: Miss you. You're all I think about.

I look at Bette with wide eyes. "Omigod, I need a drink.
And don't you say a thing!"

"My lips are sealed," she says zipping her lips, but her
eyebrow says it all.

As we head toward the door, Bette adds, "So you *didn't*
tell Gavin you were seeing someone?"

"Your lips were sealed!" I rezip her lips, adding a lock
for good measure, and toss the invisible key into one of the
toilets. Bette laughs.

I forgot all about that "little" situation. Now it seems like I'm seeing two men at once, but I haven't even talked to Gavin since meeting Tuff!

After rejoining the guys and finding Gus, we have a couple "Book Ends" of our own. Olivia joins us for one of them and whispers in my ear that I'm "arse over tip" and winks. I believe this means I'm head over heels…and I am. I truly am. But I have Bette check my dress to make sure it's still covering my "arse" just in case.

We prance onto the glass floor and drink more champagne, which is definitely helping me forget the poorly timed text from Gavin, while the guys have a hilarious dance-off. Tuff shows off his Swayze hips and Derek imitates Dory's fish moves to a lot of clapping, laughter, and cheers. When we gather by the bar, no surprise, The Three Big-Little Pigs are doing shots of Patron. They pull us in and add enough shot glasses for all of us.

Didn't I have a rule about tequila?

I'm too buzzed to remember. Oh well! Ooooh, I remember another rule though!

Rule #10
WHEN IN DOUBT, DANCE

This has covered me in nearly every situation. When I forgot the words while singing at our state fair, I added a dance break (it was a hit); when I forgot a date's name, I made him dance with me; and when I forgot my senior project at home, I danced. They thought it was a nervous breakdown, calling it an "episode," and I got an extra day to turn it in.

I twirl under Tuff's arm and pick up my shot. "Second star to the right and straight on till morning!" I yell. We all cheer, clinking shots. We drink them and dance out of the party right to the bar.

By the time we arrive it *is* nearly morning at quarter after three. Beef is manning the door as usual and is still in costume.

"Hello again," he booms. "Hey, as it turns out, women really do like a knight in shining armor." He smiles, shaking his head at the drunk Velveteen-Playboy Bunny, the Raggedy Ann missing her cap, and a very flirty, very tipsy Tinker Bell who's been kissing Hook in the taxi. We giggle, whoop, and sidle inside. It feels like the song "Where Everybody Knows Your Name" from *Cheers* should be playing as we are greeted and cheered. But really the jukebox is playing "Honky Tonk Badonkadonk" and we shake our badonkadonks up to the bar. Tuff heads to the bathroom, and when he does, the girls immediately pounce on me.

"Are you going to marry him?" Abby asks, grinning from behind the bar and still rocking the Little Red outfit minus the cape. I think I'm going to pass out. I don't know if it's excitement, nerves, champagne, or that last shot with the pigs.

"She totally is," Gus answers for me, looking a lot like a Gypsy with her leotard sleeves now down over her shoulders.

"I think I, the very manly Raggedy Andy, even has a

man-crush on him," Derek says, making us all laugh again. He orders a round of beers from Claudia and takes them to a booth. In solidarity, Claudia dressed up with us and is sporting blue cat ears after her favorite Brazilian children's book character, which she says in Spanish and I don't understand.

"Quick, before the guys come back, I didn't get to tell you at the party," Abby whispers, waving her hands for us to lean in. "I already told Claudia, but all is well down there." Abby points to her female bits. Bette cheers and Gus exhales a "Thank God." I, however, only smile because all of a sudden I feel really buzzed. "Apparently, stress has caused me to mess up my menstrual cycle, but otherwise, all of the other crazy tests are negative. I'm fine! Still stressed, but working on it. Greg, on the other hand—" She stops mid-sentence and hands everyone a beer, while noticing Tuff rejoining us. Claudia immediately begins chatting him up, and I can only imagine what she's asking him. And I wonder if he said her name right.

"To be continued," Bette says as Abby moves down the bar to serve drinks.

I feel another surge of nervousness. I probably shouldn't have done that last shot with the Big-Little Pigs. I think I've mixed too many drinks. I feel very, very tipsy. Wasn't there a rule about this? A few bar-goers come up to Bette, Gus, and me and ask for a picture before they leave. I pose perfectly for the shot, even remembering to get on my good side and, because I'm Tinker Bell, I also remember to sprinkle some more sparkles around.

"Y'all are some well-known bartenders, huh?" Tuff smiles that adorable smile and laughs at us. I give him a hug because I thing-if I tried-do speak right now I would slurrr. I never slurrr. Omigod, I'm slurring in my head!

Okay, Sydney, focus! I see Gus sitting down with two regulars in trucker hats ready to drink them under the table and make them buy everything. Abby is messing up a dance (good, I can still tell), Claudia is acting busy, and Derek and Tuff are bonding again.

It's just the late night (or early morning) crew left, and when "Redneck Woman" comes on the jukebox Bette and I start singing at the top of our lungs. Oh good, see, I'm fine. "Cuz-Ima-Redneck-Womann-I-aid-no-hi-classsss-broaddd…" I'm in a remarkable mid-slur-sing when tipsy feels a lot like woozy. I dance to the bathroom, which Bette doesn't seem to notice, to assess my state. Once inside, with the door closed and the music softer, I feel sick. Very, very sick.

This isn't good.

This is not good at all.

Claudia steps into the one-stall bathroom right behind me.

"Syd, you okay?" she asks, fixing her ears in the mirror. "Tuff is amazing, and he's the one who came in that day!"

"I keep telling you all that," I try to say, but don't because I burp instead.

Claudia looks back at me. "Uh-oh."

I hug the toilet.

She giggles.

I'm dying.

"Well, welcome to the club! I never thought I'd see the day." She lets out a small chuckle and kneels by me, tucking my fly-away hairs behind my ear.

Why is she laughing? Clearly I've been POISONED! I need to warn the others! I need to tell her what's happened. WHY AM I NOT SAYING ANYTHING?

"Three Big-Little Pigs," I finally muster. "The Pigs. I'm dying," I whisper incoherently with my bottom lip quivering. What I meant to say was, I've been poisoned! I suspect the PIGS! Everyone took that shot— we're all going to DIE!

"You're not dying, silly. Let me get Bette," Claudia smiles. She stands and I look at her, worried because she doesn't seem to understand. At all! "Tink, you're okay. And I'm not leaving. I'll be right outside getting the bar ready for close. Bette will be here in one second."

"Tuff?" I manage to say.

"I'll keep him busy, don't you worry. And Derek's with him. I just saw them getting more beer." She hurries out the door and I hear, "Oh good. Bette, Syd's hugging the toilet saying something about pigs and poison; I'll keep the guys busy."

Oh good, I must have said poison and don't remember. Good, Bette will know what to do. On a bad note, I'm bent over hugging a PUBLIC toilet—on a date!

"Ugh, dying," I say out loud to no one and flush the toilet. Though, I don't know how because I can barely see but, always Minnie's daughter, I try to get sick cleanly. Bette steps in, sits down next to me, and rubs my back.

"Oh, Tinker, how ya feeling?" she says, sweetly.

"Dying," I manage to say, again.

"You're not dyin'. Ya just drank too much," she says, slurring a little herself.

She needs to FOCUS! THIS IS SERIOUS! I hand her my green sparkly heels with clip-on white puffs. "Protect," I say. Oh good, I'm still thinking about shoes. I'm not dead yet—there's time. "Room upside down. Tinker need hospital!" But apparently I'm unable to speak my first language. What if this is how it ends? My grammar goes to hell as I drown in a public toilet. Minnie will be so embarrassed. I can't go out like this! I won't!

"Oh, Tink, ya gonna to be okay," she says and gently takes my shoes, then drops them. "Oops." She hiccups and picks them up. "Ya don't need to go to the hospital. Just get it out." She rubs my back again.

That's it? She's not even considering the fact that I've been poisoned? I put my hand on her shoulder and look at her as intensely as I can in a pair of wings.

"LISTEN HERE, RAGGEDY ANN." I try to find her face with one eye because the two together aren't working. "I'm dying. Do you UNDERSTAND?" There are still three of her so I focus in the middle, which proves to be too much work and I throw up again. I finish and say much more quietly, "I need to go to the bathroom." I feel like death warmed over. Once steadied on the toilet, Bette fixes my falling ponytail, which was once a perfectly high, beautiful Tinker Bell bun.

"Does it look cute now?" I ask, feeling more resigned to my fate. It seems important. If Tinker Bell is going to be taken out by some pigs, she's going to look good doing it.

"Yes, it looks really cute. You're really cute and you're not dying," she says adoringly. That's odd, it looks like she's holding her phone in front of me but the ship keeps rocking and rocking and I can't be sure. My vision has been severely impaired by pigs. It's got to be the pigs.

"I'm not dying?" I ask. "You sure?" I hear a click.

"No, Tinker, you're not dying," she says and giggles, then hiccups.

"Okay. I'll throw up again then," I inform her, while flushing and moving my head into the toilet.

Gus and Abby loudly blunder in.

"Tuff?" I ask, pulling my head out of the toilet briefly, then rest it back inside.

"Hi, little Tink," Abby says in an extremely high-pitched voice (or at least it sounds that way from in here). "Tuff's drinking with Derek. He seems a little mad, though, because we aren't letting him in," she says. I lift my head again and make a face that says: *just look at me—don't you dare let him in!* I don't know how it came out but it must have worked because I hear Gus from inside the toilet.

"Don't worry, Syd, we know. I'll keep 'em busy," she says, and pats my back. Her voice doesn't seem as high. She's definitely a bass, not even a baritone. Definitely a bass.

"Syd, remember the time I was in the bathroom after the Pearl Jam concert? I threw up for a good hour. This is nothin'," Abby says, trying to make me feel better. I can tell she has a bobby pin in her mouth and must be fixing her hair. Somehow it makes me feel better.

"What about the time I threw up all night while I was supposed to be workin'?" Bette offers. "I tried to go shot for a shot with those guys from Louisiana. Remember, Tink? You held my hair." I lift my head out of the toilet and rest it on my arm, letting out a rather low giggle.

"I did?" I don't know why I sound like Dorothy coming out of her dream in *The Wizard of Oz,* but I do. Kind of oddly fitting, actually.

"Yeah. Ya did. And I don't even have to bring up Austin, do I?" she laughs. I don't know why, but she's really got a thick Brooklyn accent right now. I try to laugh and then groan. I'm feeling a little better; maybe I did just drink too much. Can I pass out now? I hear them talking about a taxi while Bette fixes my hair again. Abby leaves, then pops her head back in to tell Bette something.

"Tuff wants to take you home. He's been really worried. Or do ya wanna go home with me and Derek?" Bette asks, brightening my cheeks, which are most likely ghastly pale or the color of my dress at this point, with a little of her pink lipstick. Thank goodness Bette is making me look better. She hiccups again.

"Better go with him and get to my bed," I say, still channeling Judy Garland. *There's no place like home, there's no place like home.* (I think I have a new mantra.)

"Okay," she says and I see her signal for someone to come in. Beef steps around the door in his armor and gently picks me up from the floor. I swear I hear gallant music, and are there little bluebirds flying around his shoulders?

"My knight in shining armor," I whisper as I curl into his arms.

"I gotcha babe," he says and starts to carry me out.

"Wait, wait," I say. I should recognize that anything after a drunk double "wait" would be a bad idea, but I continue. "Sparkles! I need more sparkles!" I look at Bette as if this is urgent.

"Wait, wait," she says, looking for the pixie dust.

Wait—

"That's a great idea, Tink," Bette giggles.

Wait, did she say a double "wait"?

WAIT!!! NO!!!

She sparkles me with the rest of my Tinker pixie dust glitter bottle. The whole bottle. Omigod. I puff a couple out of my mouth as Beef carries me, cradled in his arms, outside where Tuff is waiting in a cab. I crawl into the taxi and Tuff puts his arm around me but says nothing. I'm mortified but tired.

"Sorry," I whisper. Mortified. But too tired. I haven't been this drunk and sick since my twenty-first birthday, and even then I got up again and kept drinking, so this is epic. I'm too weak and too tired to worry about what he's thinking, and when the cab pulls up to the apartment I realize I'm not really awake but my mind is still processing. Is that possible? It feels like I'm watching through one tragic eye. Wait, wait, I might be. I think I'm down to one eye again. I squint, trying to focus my surroundings as he puts me over his shoulder. My favorite guys from the kitchen gather outside, and I hear Jose ask if Tuff needs help.

"Oh no, I got little Tinker Tanked from here. Thanks," he answers.

"*Que lindo trasero*," one of the guys says softly, and all of them smile and one nods at Tuff. (Spanish!) But I recognize *linda* so that's good. It must have really helped when Bette fixed my hair and gave me a little blush. I feel the early morning air on my ass. I try to pull down my dress but I don't know where my dress is, let alone my ass. It's definitely on somewhere, though, because it's choking me. I cough. Wait, wait, that could be Tuff's shoulder cutting off my air supply. My wings are starting to itch and I feel around for those. It's useless. I hang limp as Jose holds the doors.

As we go up the first few steps I see all four of the kitchen guys standing in the doorway still watching and smiling. I lean up onto Tuff's back and give them the Robert Deniro "I'm watching you" hand gesture because I know they saw my ass. But I think it may have looked like a peace sign because they give me the peace sign back and Jose waves. I flop back down onto Tuff's back.

Tuff is so strong and agile that I'm really a fairy flying up the…

NEW YORK CITY: TODAY, SUNDAY, AUGUST 13

I open my good eye. (The other is smashed in a pillow.) Omigod. I slowly roll over and see Tuff fast asleep. My other eye is working! I'm not seeing triple! I sit up slightly and try to think. Think. Details, Sydney, details. I don't have a great concept of how much time passed between when I started throwing up and when I was put in the cab, so I'm not totally clear on how much damage I'm dealing with.

Omigod I was *put* in the cab. As it turns out, champagne bubbles really are my undoing. When will I learn? Well, that and all the shots. Ugh, all the shots. I look at my vision board.

I remember now, Rule #4: Never mix alcohol (especially tequila)...you will DIE!

The Pigs, the Patron, I should have known. I pull the covers over my head to hide. I've always wanted to be like Cinderella and lose a shoe to have a prince traverse the land to find me and fit me with it. I didn't just lose a shoe; I lost two shoes, my dinner, and all the drinks I had...and in the bar's bathroom, no less. And the prince didn't have to *just* traverse the land; he had to manage five flights of stairs with a winged dead weight hanging over his shoulder. Not quite what I had in mind.

I pull the covers just below my eyes and look at pretty Princess Grace. She would never do something like this. Ugh, double ugh.

And I've always wanted to faint into the arms of a steadfast, handsome man just like in all the black and white movies. I was nowhere near the attractive damsel in distress like Elizabeth Taylor fainting in *Giant* or as endearing as the sleepy Audrey Hepburn in *Roman Holiday*. I passed out, and hard, hanging over the handsome man's shoulder. Again, not quite what I had in mind.

I'm never drinking champagne again. Ever! Note, I did not say vodka because clearly this was the champagne's fault. Big mistake, that champagne. Bigger mistake, that tequila shot. Pigs!

I feel like I've been hit by a truck. Maybe I was. Omigod, what if I *was* hit by a truck! It would have been right when they were picking up the city's trash. It makes sense! I'm dreaming all of this and everyone's standing over my bed staring at me because I'm in a coma somewhere! Or what if no one knows and I'm in a coma somewhere and I'm all by myself in a washcloth-sized green dress and wings? The headlines will read: **Tinker Taken Out By Trash!** (It wouldn't be the first time.) **Does Anyone Know Trashed Tinker?**

I look over at Tuff's resting body and calm features sleeping next to me. That's really sweet—I'm thinking about Tuff, the handsome veterinarian-cowboy, in my coma. Though I don't think his mouth would be open like that in a coma dream. My iPhone is on my stack of books by an empty bottle of glitter. It's empty? I briefly pull the covers back over my head. Ugh, double ugh, and triple, quadruple crap and kick my ass. I reach for the phone quietly and text Bette,

Me: SOS! Did I throw up all night? (sick face emoji)

I cross my fingers.

Bette: Hi pretty lady! No, not all night hahaaa

Aaaaaah, it wasn't a dream! I'm not in a coma!

Me: How long was I in the bathroom!!!

Bette: Kind of a long time, Tink. I was drunk so not totally sure. Derek and Tuff drank a lot too, maybe he won't know?? How are you feeling?

Me: Kill!!!!! Feel awwwful...baaaaa!!

Bette: Derek and I are hung-over! He's making Eggs Benedict right now! Isn't he amazing!!

Me: He is!!!

Bette: I know!!! (heart emoji)

Me: Love you! Thanks for keeping me from drowning in the toilet! Baaaaa! (skeleton emoji)

Bette: Baaha!! Love you! Call me later! Oh I have your shoes! (high heel emoji)

Me: Oh good, what about my pride?

Bette: Baahahaa

I peek at Tuff again. He's still sleeping, so I sneak into the bathroom. My tiny green dress is pulled up and bunched around my waist, highlighting my shamrock-covered boy shorts, the only thing I had that would match the dress. (Tragic.) I wonder how long it was like that? In the bar. In the taxi? In front of the kitchen guys? I did see them, right?

I immediately check my reflection in the mirror and let out a small, horrified scream. Squelching it with my sparkling hands, I turn back and look at Tuff; he hasn't moved. I was hit by a truck loaded with sparkles! The motherload. The ultimate glitter bomb. I just had to use the whole container, didn't I? And who put pink stripes on my cheeks? It's like Mrs. Rich but instead of traffic cone orange it's Cadillac pink. "Bette. That little drunk," I whisper into the mirror. Not that I should be throwing stones. My left eye looks like I was punched and is bleeding black eyeliner the size of a small nation onto the side of my face. And what is that? A bug? Omigod. I have a bug on my forehead! I grab a tissue and wipe it off. Gah! I do a tippy-toe, gross-out dance and look at the tissue. Oh, wait; it's a fake eyelash. This must be the side I passed out on because the other eye is oddly perfect. My wings are bent as if Tinker was crushed by a giant fly swatter. Omigod. It looks like I was crushed by a giant fairy swatter!

I close the bathroom door as quietly as I can, sit on the toilet, and cup my head in my hands. I don't remember hearing him laugh in the cab but then again, I don't remember much during the scandal, so I have a feeling this is bad. Is it too late to believe in do-overs? Tuff doesn't leave for the airport until five today. Can I make up for a night of throwing up and looking like Tinker Trashed in six hours? I turn on the shower. I peak out the bathroom door and see he's still asleep. Well, I can at least look sweet when he wakes up. I jump in the shower, scrubbing extra hard because I was on the bar's bathroom floor for God knows how long. I step into my star fruit yellow Lilly Pulitzer sundress, a most innocent looking dress, and sit on the bed. He stirs.

"Morning," I say with my best sorry face. "Sorry about last night."

"Morning, Sydney," he says with a straight face. Not good.

"I'm so embarrassed and sorry. I never ever do that," I say, not counting my twenty-first birthday. No one counts that birthday. Plus I was poisoned then too. Not by pigs, but by Ivy Andersen. I still owe her one.

"Just give me a minute to wake up," he says. Not good at all. He goes into the bathroom and shuts the door. I hear the shower start.

I feed Harold and give him a look that explains how much trouble I'm in. He stares back with his huge eyeballs. They look extra huge and worried.

"Cross your fins," I whisper to him. I slink into the other room and plop into my favorite chair with my phone. I text Bette again.

Me: SOS! He looks upset. Did anything else happen other than me losing five pounds?

Bette: He just looked mad we wouldn't let him help you.

Me: That's it?

Bette: Oh, he might have been mad Beef carried you out.

Me: OMG I forgot Beef carried me out!!! Baaaa

Bette: It was cute; you looked so tiny in his arms with your little bent wings!! (fairy emoji)

Me: Bette not cute! DRUNKEN FAIRY UNABLE TO WALK ON HER OWN!!!

Bette: Baahahaaa

Me: BETTE!!!!!

Bette: Oh come on it's kinda funny! Derek and I are cracking up at the pics! Oh, I should apologize for the blush, I totally thought it looked good when I did it (hands over mouth monkey emoji) I should have blended!

Me: This is a DISASTROPHE!!!!! He's getting out of shower xxx

Bette: Good luck, he's hot xxxxx

Me: Wait what pictures?!!!!!

Tuff gets ready without saying a word and then walks into the living room.

"How are you feeling?" he asks.

"Really good considering. Guess I drank too much, huh?" I say with *please forgive me* written all over my face.

"You think?" he says. There's a giant silence and a giant DRUNK PINK-CHEEKED FAIRY in the room.

"Would you like to get something to eat?" I offer.

"Sure," he shrugs. I can tell he needs food before any talking will begin. We decide on Morandi again, and as we walk the short distance to the restaurant my phone vibrates. While he checks in with the maître d', I look at it.

Oh dear God.

There I sit, on the PUBLIC toilet looking up with huge drunk eyes and wings.

WHY?!!! I try to stifle my panic.

We're seated outside in the gorgeous weather as my phone vibrates again. NO!!! While Tuff orders an omelet I peak at the phone. There I am in Beef's big arms looking like a drunken, sparkled five-year-old with pink striped cheeks, bent wings, and toilet paper dangling from one of my bare feet.

NOOOO!!!!!

Bette: See, ADORABLE!!...Best night ever!!!

This never would have happened had I brought my lucky green jacket.

I order my usual Sunny Side Up Eggs, country toast, and fried tomato with a side of fries. I want to crawl under the table and hide. Forever. (With the fries.)

Chapter 30
A SCANDAL WORTHY OF RED SOLES

ONCE IN the stark white office, I lie down on the rather hard couch and start telling my story of woe. (You'd think the couch would be softer. I mean, this *is* Fifth Avenue after all.) I know it's been a few weeks and I've gone over this several times, but still. I explain how everything was going amazingly well until I started throwing up because of some Big-Little Pigs and was carried out with bent wings by a knight in shining armor and not by Captain Hook. I detail all the events that led up to the scandal and how it was really just a little mishap, how I'm not the type of girl who does this on a regular basis.

"So, what do you think?" I look up at him and ask.

"You really messed that up good," he laughs.

"What?" I exclaim.

He's still laughing.

"That's it? That's all you're going to say? That I messed up? What kind of advice is that?" I wince. This is unbelievable.

And where is Tray?

"Well...," he starts. But then he pauses and is clearly thinking so I wait. This is going to be good. Just then, Tray bounds into the waiting room where I'm situated next to another patient, and screams, then I scream, then he screams again.

"Sorry I'm late! Hi, Syd," he says, flashing me jazz hands, one of the only things I learned in high school that I still use on a regular basis. He checks in with the secretary and sits down at my feet.

"Mr. Friedrich, you can go in now," the secretary instructs. Igor, and I guess his last name is Friedrich, stands up.

"Good luck," he says to me and laughs yet again, which isn't encouraging, and goes into the therapist's office. I could have sworn he was just about to say something helpful. I sit up and adjust my colorful ASOS romper.

But can you really trust a guy with a name like Igor? Childhood must have been rough. I mean, why didn't his parents just name him Quasimodo? No wonder he's in therapy. I grab a magazine. Maybe I should be in therapy.

"Syd, are you telling the Tuff story to all the patients again?" Tray says, too loudly. Embarrassing. He hands me my tall wedges. I may have gotten comfortable.

"Tray, therapy is expensive. One would think you all would be learning something in there to pass on to me. I'm even sitting closer to the relationship specialist's door," I say in hushed tones, while putting on my shoes.

"Gah! Get over it! Move on!" He's extra loud today. "Just look at yourself. You're gorgeous, smart, and, come on, you have your pick of men," he says, boosting my ego. Okay, he can be loud.

"And?" I prod.

"You make everyone smile."

"And?" This is working.

"Oh for God's sake, even my therapist asked about you after the last session."

"And?" Wait, what? "He did?" So unprofessional, but his psychologist-psychiatrist...whichever, *is* kind of cute in that professional way.

"And I'm so lucky you're my friend, and I'm so glad you're here to support me even if I tricked you into it while you were behind the glass of the revolving doors at the Carlyle." (He did.) "Thanks, Galinda," he says, calling me the good witch from *Wizard of Oz* or *Wicked*, which Tray was an assistant costume designer on. At least it's the good witch today. He called me Grimhilde, the seriously evil queen from *Snow White and the Seven Dwarfs*, after the last drug intervention, which happened the same day Tuff left.

I didn't have time to think or sulk about the fact that Tuff didn't speak much that day because Tray was in deep. After I saw him on Thursday, no one heard from him until Saturday, which is when he called Logan for help. He'd been doing drugs for a solid two days, didn't know where he was, and missed one of the most important meetings of his life, which I covered. Logan had to retrieve him from someone's apartment in Brooklyn that Tray didn't even know! Then to top it off, he stormed out of Logan's and tried to do it all over again.

Meth is now his drug of choice, and it's one of the most addictive. That was the sweet smell I didn't recognize the day we met the producers who are giving him his first shot as lead costume designer on a premiere.

That night, we told him he had go to rehab, no questions, no stalling, no bullshit. And that's when he called me Grimhilde. (Can't be too upset about that.)

"No prob, happy to support," I smile, flipping through *Good Housekeeping*. I'm looking for something inspirational, but all I see are pies and it reminds me of Tuff. I'm here for moral support. I agreed to be his "therapy support friend" accidentally while swinging through the revolving doors of the Carlyle Hotel (serves me right to say "sure" when I didn't hear the question), but I may be in desperate need of some support myself. Here I had the perfect guy right in front of me and I blew it. He would barely even talk to me the next day. It looked like he was going to but then I guess he was so upset he couldn't get anything out. I mean, I know I was a disaster but was it unforgivable? He hasn't answered any of my texts or calls. I put the magazine down.

Tray's trying to kick his drug habits in outpatient rehab. (At least we got him to agree to something this time.) And he's trying to kick all of them, of which apparently there are many. It turns out he's been disappearing a lot with no one noticing. He tells one person he's with the other and so on. It's sadly believable with our busy schedules and blended friends.

He stares at his therapist's door looking overwhelmed. Together, they've been trying to pinpoint his reason for using and he's been told he must learn to admit his problem. Confirming this, and taking the proper steps to combat it, will help him focus, which his (cute) therapist says will aid in cutting out the "self-medicating" cycle.

I quietly sing a couple lyrics from "Popular," a show-stopper in *Wicked*, to bring him back to the present, and when I sing, 'I'll teach you the proper poise, when you talk to boys…,' he joins in on his favorite part:

"Little ways to flirt and flounce, ooh!"

I glare at him.

"Drugs, sex, alcohol, STDs, drama," I spit. His eyeballs widen and his face reads panic just as the (cute) therapist steps out and smiles, waving Tray in.

"Good luck," I sing.

"Maybe you should come in with me," Tray says quickly. I went in with him for the first ten minutes last time just to help get him on track, but now that I know his therapist thinks I'm cute, there's no way. But I need to be doing something smart; what am I doing?

"No, I'll wait out here. I need to do some research," I say. Where's *Time* magazine or something like *Men's Health*? I see a handsome man on the cover of one and grab it; I hold it up. "I've got to stay up on current issues," I smile and nod at them in encouragement. Tray and his (cute) therapist give me an odd look just as the door clicks shut. What? I should know what's in the latest *Men's Health*. Maybe they have some interesting workout tips this month. I place the magazine in my lap. Except it's not a *Men's Health* magazine; it's a pamphlet for erectile dysfunction. Oh, for God's sake.

I give up on my "research" and dig through the pile for a gossip magazine. And then I see him. Gavin McKnight, on the front cover. Gossip magazines never get anyone's best angle even when they're being nice, so this is unreal. He looks on fire. His new movie is going to be another blockbuster and he's poised to be sexiest man of the year.

I need air.

I grab my pink Prada clutch and head outside.

Fifth Avenue…the Holy Grail. Why do these appointments have to be on the best shopping street? *I look pretty in the things I have. I look pretty in the things I have.* While chanting my shopping mantra, I stomp by the large, alluring windows trying not to look. However, when I do peek, all I see are western-style yoke, two-patch pocket shirts! Of course they're en vogue now, of course. I turn onto a cross street and dive into a bookstore to hide from everything and nearly take out an elderly gentleman who curses at me. Only in New York does someone as old as that use the "f" word. I text Tray to meet me here after his session; it's my only chance to survive Fifth Avenue without wanting a new wardrobe, and apparently, Tuff. After an hour of wandering the aisles, I'm holding four books that are must-reads.

"Syd! Do you need all of those?" Tray booms. I jump, dropping three.

"Tray," I bleat. But he's right, and that might be natural selection, so I put the three back on the shelf and buy the one that fought to stay in my hands. (But not before walking by the romance section, which I swear has a cowboy on every cover!)

Tray and I have been pointing out each other's faults and fabulousness since high school. It's what we do. He tells me about all my bad habits, like shopping, and I his. Once, I mistakenly pointed out that he hugs me too much and that I thought I was suffocating, to which he responded by making me wear pink in every show we did that year. Never offend your costume designer. This made him best friends with Minnie, who loves seeing me in pink. Now she believes anything he says about me, faults and all. Traitor.

But it finally backfired because now I love pink, and looking back at the pictures, Minnie was right—it works well with my coloring.

"So, I'm officially an addict!" Tray says in a healthy shout as we step back out onto the street, then makes a sour face, adding, "I'm addicted to drugs and sex, I'm not treating my body like the temple that it is, and, oh, I'm also addicted to drama."

"Told you so!" I twinkle, always proud to be right... being a fake doctor and all. Being the daughter of a doctor, some (not Tray, but he should now) believe whatever

medical advice or diagnosis I give. I would make an amazing TV doctor. (Omigod, I should totally be one.)

A window display catches my eye. I probably do need a
new pair of...forget it, this will never work. I hail the first
cab I see and announce we need to go home; otherwise
I'll buy the street. The first step is admitting you have a
problem. (Going with Tray to all these sessions does seem
to be helping.) I pull Tray into the cab.

"We've got to get outta here—I'm an addict," I say.

"Coming with me *has* helped," Tray says proudly.

Tray shakes a cocktail like a pro and like he lives here.
He knows exactly where everything is, even the strainer
I absentmindedly put with the spoons instead of on the
small mirrored tray with the rest of the bar tools. He pours
us a drink and starts into his latest relationship crisis. I
pour his out while he texts and replace it with an O'Doul's
that I now keep at the ready.

"Tray, no alcohol!"

"I was just pouring two for you! Habit, sorry," he says.
"Can you believe this guy?" His fingers move quickly over
his phone. Too quickly. What's he saying?

"Your body is a temple," I remind him.

"He's crazy. Crazy! I've texted him like ten times and
he hasn't texted back. What an asshole," Tray complains.
He takes a swig of the O'Doul's, then adds, "And what's
with the duct tape on the railing knob thingy downstairs?
You should really tell your super."

The duct tape looks fine! (Another constant reminder
of Tuff. Barf.)

"Temple," I remind him again but with less vigor, distracted. I take a sip of my drink and immediately feel it in my knees, always a sign of a good buzz to come, but I realize it's because I haven't eaten much since the whole scandal. I think about my own temple and put down the drink.

"All these texts and he still hasn't texted back. Asshole!" Tray blusters on, rolling his eyes. I consider telling him he might be the crazy one for texting that many times, but I refrain for the time being because I'm proud he took the new drink without complaining. And I'm slightly distracted by the fact that the only thing in the fridge is olives.

Tray wanders into the other room with his non-alcoholic beer to send more disastrous texts. There's a good reason I'm not reaching out to Tuff; I would hate for that to happen. But Tray has always been an overzealous "chaser."

I check the cupboards. My favorite jeans! I really should put these somewhere where I can find them. I pull out some crackers instead.

Tray flits back into the living room, still looking at his phone. Changing the subject, he says, "It's going to rain tomorrow. Your flight to Butter might be delayed." He checks the weather for me just like Doc. I guess I'm known to be a skittish flyer. "You're going to need this for your flight," he says, setting a small pill on the kitchen bar.

"Tray, you're dealing now?" I shove three crackers in my mouth. I need candy; crackers just aren't going to cut it.

"No, no, Syd, these were prescribed to me for all my anxiety and stress. It's just a Xanax. You know, these costumes are going to win awards, big awards! But I swear, I'm losing hair." He fluffs his faux hawk. "Omigod, am I losing hair?" He poses in the long mirror. Satisfied that his hair is fine, he continues, "So anyway, the Xanax is so I won't take drugs."

I raise my eyebrows. Drugs so you don't take drugs?

"I know, I know," he says, as though reading my thoughts. "But it'll help, trust me. You won't get so frantic about flying, especially in the rain." He immediately breaks into song, singing, "Singin' in the Rain" in full-blown Frank Sinatra style (even though Gene Kelly sang it in the movie, and even though he doesn't know all of the words).

I immediately start grinning. He grabs me up and spins me into a dance, singing and twirling, and singing and twirling, and I laugh for what seems like the first time since Tuff left.

"I could totally be a leading man," he says, spinning me softly into my big chair. "Right?" I stare at his beveled leg, and the flames shooting from his hands, and giggle some more. "Oh, shut up," he laughs, throwing crackers at me.

He gets on his phone again, berating the "crazy" boy via text. Tray wonders why he doesn't have a boyfriend. He calls him to no answer. "I'll break him," he says, grabbing his jacket and heading out the door. Sometimes, I wonder why he wonders.

He sings as he heads down the stairs, "I'm laughing at clouds so la la la la. The sun's in my heart and I'm ready for love. I'm dancing and singing in the rain." The acoustics lift his velour-like voice all the way to the top floor.

Thinking about how I really thought I was "ready for love," and after realizing just how much fun I had on the dance floor with Tuff, I try to channel my energy into something positive, like cleaning. Because if I think about it too much, I'll crash into a heap of despair, checking my phone and sending another text that at this point seems useless. Tray gave up on *his* phone too and decided to pay his "love" (this week) a visit, leaving me to stew. But I admire his insistence, and now Alexa is keeping me company with the score to *Singin' in the Rain*. I spray and wipe, spray and wipe, and spray and wipe and clean the fridge.

I sit down when everything looks immaculate and still feel anxious. I look at the pill Tray left me. But I tuck it into my pink Prada clutch and decide, what can a little shopping hurt? *I look pretty in the things I have, I look pretty in the things I have.* I compromise with my goals and decide to go somewhere I know I can't buy. I'll window-shop at the Christian Louboutin boutique on Jane and Greenwich Street. Nothing like a red sole to cheer me up!

I flit back down the stairs, still wearing the romper and wedges with a soft gray fringe leather bag in tow. I pop out the door and relish in the sun streaming down my block. It feels brighter than ever before. I haven't even seen the red soles and I'm already feeling better.

"Hi, sunshine!" One Eye Joe yells from the other side of the street. He crosses toward me.

"Hiya, Jovan," I hoot back. What day is it? Did I pay rent? I scour my memory. Did I pay rent? Yes, I totally did, and early! "Hi there," I say again as he reaches me. (I can be happy to see him now.)

"How's my beautiful lady?" he says. Such a flatterer.

"I'm hangin' in," I laugh. He puts his arm around me and gives me a squeeze.

"Where are you headed looking so adorable?" I just cleaned my apartment; he's really laying on the charm. Do I tell him I'm going to ogle at Christian Louboutins? He could probably buy the store. So, no.

"I'm headed to the bank," I decide to say.

"I'll walk with you. It's so nice out," he smiles. Embarrassing. I'm going to stare at shoes and from the window, no less. It didn't feel like a dumb idea in my apartment. We head down the street.

"So, which bank are we walking to?"

I decide to come clean. "Jovan, I'm really going to look at Christian Louboutins from the store window," I confess.

"Ah, the red soles. I'll take a look too," he says.

I smile. "Jovan, thanks for always giving me some grace time on rent when I need it. I can't believe I misplaced so much money in the last couple months," I say, still perplexed.

"Eh, it was nothin'."

"No really, it meant a lot. Thank you." We cross Bleeker Street.

"Syd, I tell you rent is due on the first. But it's not really due until the seventh." He laughs.

"What?!"

"I figure it's like taking out a beautiful woman. If you tell them to be ready at seven, they won't be ready until nine. And *you* are a beautiful woman."

This man is brilliant. Completely brilliant.

We stroll the short distance to the beautiful little boutique and I stand in front of the windows, pointing out my favorite heels one at a time. All my favorites are, of course, five inches and above. I'm feeling better already.

"Syd, let's go in," he says.

"What?"

Look at that platform pump, look at that platform sandal, look at that—

"Sydney, let's go inside."

"What?" I start to register that One Eye Joe is saying something about inside.

"Let's go," he says and gives me a little nudge toward the entrance.

"No, I shouldn't," I say inaudibly. And before I can tell him that this is a bad idea, he opens the door and gently pushes me inside. I feel lightheaded. I can smell the newness, the rich. And of course I'm positive I can smell the red soles. I hear music.

"Sydney?"

Sweet soft tones ringing in my ears.

"Sydney?"

High notes blossoming into bell tones.

"Sydney?"

"Huh?" I say, but not out loud.

There's no glass between us. The shoes are right...here. I feel dizzy.

"Syd?" One Eye Joe says in mob tones.

"Huh," I say, just barely loud enough for him to hear, and I look at him. "Oh, hi, Jovan. Just look at these shoes!" One Eye Joe pushes me farther into the store. I must have stopped in the entrance because he hasn't even made it inside.

"Why don't you try some on?" he says.

What did he say? Try some on? What? He said that so nonchalantly. No. I couldn't, could I? Where is my credit card? I look in my handbag. Okay, I left it at home. Good idea, Syd. Okay, maybe I could just try on one pair.

One Eye Joe pushes me lightly onto a red velvet settee near the window. I stare at the five rows of red soles perched seductively next to me while a salesman offers us some extra bubbly champagne.

NO CHAMPAGNE!

"No thank you," I say, managing to keep my decorum.

I hear One Eye Joe ask the salesman for some assistance, and before I know it, I've shed my wedges for red soles and I'm prancing in the mirror. They don't fit perfectly but it doesn't dawn on me to ask for a smaller size. I'm wearing red soles; it totally doesn't matter. I'm wearing red soles! I need to sit down. I reach for the velvet settee and take off the heels. I feel my blood pressure return to normal.

"Okay, that was great, we better go," I say, quickly. I might internally combust if I stay and then they'd have to call O'Reilly to get the fire truck and all these perfect shoes would be ruined.

How much money is in my savings account?

Uh-oh.

"We should definitely leave, Jovan," I whisper.

I look at the window for air but I forgot there *is* no air, just shoes, and there she is. A beautiful, black leather, five-inch heel with a distinguished, sophisticated leather bow. An angelic voice sings softly in my ear. They would go with everything I own. Everything. They would make everything I own look gorgeous. One Eye Joe reaches onto the shelf and takes her down.

"It's a stunning shoe, I must admit," he says and hands it to me, "Try it on."

No, I shouldn't.

I slip it on in a trance. It fits perfectly. I float up onto a red-soled cloud. I move my foot from side to side, looking at it from each angle; now that I'm on my cloud I can tell the angelic voice is Pavarotti. The salesman floats toward me with the other heel. Oh look, he's on a cloud too! He slips it onto my foot, and gracefully takes my hand. He helps me to my feet and leads me to the mirror.

"They're a must," he says, with a little gasp as he lets my hand go, putting his to his cheek. I wobble. And wobble again. Then find my footing just as Pavarotti hits the high note in "Nessun Dorma." I see her reflection in the mirror. The bow is divine. Then I see mine. Scratch that, it's not Pavarotti; it's Paul Potts' audition from *Britain's Got Talent* when *he* hit the high note in "Nessun Dorma." Omigod, are those my legs? They look fabulous. Lengthened, lean, and sun kissed. Like Potts, I too just went from being a lump of coal to a diamond! I turn slowly and pose. I take one step back ever so carefully and look again. I look at the salesman, then to One Eye Joe to share this moment and to remember it fully.

"Remember this," I say, with reverence from my cloud. But not really. I really just make a dumb face that prompts One Eye Joe to say, "Those are somethin' else." He's in shock too. I can tell.

"You've been struck by the red soles. A Christian reformed, I can see it in your face," I say, floating.

"Yep, you're right. I'm a big fan," he says and makes a clicking noise with his mouth. I think about my savings account again. The window shoe has a price on the bottom. Do I dare look? I tip my foot carefully to the side and squint at the numbers. The FOUR NUMBERS! I don't even need to see what they are; there are four of them!

I fall, no, plummet from my cloud with a tremendous thud.

"You have to have those," I faintly hear One Eye Joe say from somewhere in the distance. But I'm still in a heap on the floor of my Louboutin dream, so I have no response.

And then something happens. One Eye Joe reaches in his back pocket, pulls out his wallet, and whips out a black card. He hands it to the salesman, who's still floating gracefully on *his* cloud. "We'll take 'em," he booms.

"What? Absolutely not," I say, but ever-ever so softly.

"Good choice—they're unbelievable. I'll be back in a jiffy," the salesman says like an auctioneer. I can't move. No really, I can't move. I might fall over if I try to stop him. I could break a heel. I reach my fingers toward the stealth salesman, whose cloud must be powered by a turbocharged V8, because he's already at the register. I tip-fall toward One Eye Joe. Two more tip-fall steps and I'm next to him.

"Jovan, you're not doing this," I say, finally reaching his shoulder. I sit-fall down by him. I'm going to need to learn to walk again. "What are you doing?"

"You need those shoes. Just look at 'em—they're beautiful!" He cracks a smile and looks at my still-Louboutin-adorned feet. I can't argue there. Look at them.

They *are* GORGEOUS!

I *do* need them!

They would go with *everything* I own!

Sydney, stop!

"Jovan, don't do this. I can get them myself," I say. No, I can't…unless I actually find a pirate's chest full of gold bars, a hoard of gems, and a princess's tiara (because there's always a tiara). And these are a katrillion dollars more than the ones I was aiming for.

"Oh please, I'm loving this, and you should see your face. This is so much fun for me," he says, and twists his gold Cartier pinky ring.

"Jovan," I yelp.

"No, too bad, I'm doin' this. You're the sunshine on our block, in New York City, in the world. You're always smiling. And I'm going to make *you* happy today," One Eye Joe says, and scribbles his signature. The salesman folds the receipt, then removes the shoes from my feet. (On reflex I go to stop him, but luckily I come to and softly pat his hand instead of slapping it away.) He gently boxes them up and places them in a Christian Louboutin signature bag, and before I know it, it's over my shoulder.

"Enjoy. You're going to love them," the salesman whistles.

"Come on, sunshine," One Eye Joe says, holding the door open to the real world.

I have a pair of red soles over my shoulder! Together at last!

Will they disappear when I walk out the door? I hesitate.

"Let's go, I want to walk down Bleeker," One Eye Joe says, still holding the door. I slip my wedges back on and slowly move toward the door.

I close my eyes and step through.

"Those are *some* shoes you got there. You have great style, Syd," I hear One Eye Joe say. Did he say I have shoes? I open my eyes and look over at my shoulder then down. They're still there! Omigod. I own a pair of Louboutins! I start to giggle slightly hysterically as we walk up the block.

"Jovan, you shouldn't have done that," I say, seriously, then giggle some more. He basically paid my rent in shoes.

"Are you kidding? This is worth all the money in the world. Just look at you," he laughs at me.

"You shouldn't have done it, but I love them. Thank you so much," I say, grateful. I do a couple air punches to show just how excited I am.

"My wife wants me to buy another building that she's fallin' in love with. If she'd get one ounce of the joy you got from a pair of shoes, well, I'd buy it for her in a heartbeat."

"Well, they're not just any pair of shoes," I wink.

"Syd, I know you feel bad about that guy." Everyone knows everything on my block. "Let me give you a little advice. I've been around some, and everything seems to work itself out in the end. If he's the one, he'll be back. Especially if he knows how very special you are." He stops me. "You're one-of-a-kind, Syd."

"Jovan, that's so very sweet of you," I say, a bit shocked. I'm touched. One Eye Joe is usually such a hard egg.

"You're the real thing, and a true bim...wait a sec... bombshell," he smiles.

"You said bombshell!" I beam, and startle him with a hug.

"Eh, you know, sometimes I have my moments. And, Syd, if this guy *doesn't* come around—I'll take care of him," he says, a little puffed up. I smile.

Wait, did One Eye Joe just offer to knock Tuff off?

I smile again and he smiles.

No, certainly not.

I smile again and he smiles.

Nah.

"Joe, there's something I have to confess," I say.

"Oh yeah?" he says. "Let me guess, you've been in love with me all along." He does a jig and I punch him jokingly in the arm.

"But seriously, I'm the one who broke the knob on the staircase," I say, making an "omigod" face.

"Oh, I know, Syd. Who else could manage that?" he laughs. "Duct tape?" We both laugh. (I swear the duct tape looks fine!)

I'm still glowing blocks away, proudly clutching my Christian Louboutins and feeling even better after such good advice. I mean, it only seems right owning a pair now. After all, you don't earn your red soles until you've been involved in a scandal.

"Didn't you have a handbag?" One Eye Joe asks.

"Huh?" I can wear my Louboutins with my favorite jeans, my favorite LBD...hell, I'll wear them with...

"A handbag," he says.

A handbag? Yes, I can wear them with a handbag!

I have a pair of red soles!

"A handbag—didn't you have a nice handbag with you earlier?" he says again, and I assess my possessions.

Christian Louboutins.

No handbag.

"Omigod, I left it at the store," I answer. Not that it's very important at this point. I mean, it *is* a nice bag, but what's on my arm costs more than the bag and anything in it combined. I don't need a handbag right now or a Tuff. I'm back on my cloud and it's been turbocharged!

Okay, okay, I'll go get my bag.

Chapter 31
WHAT'S BETTER THAN BUTTER

BUTTER CREEK: TODAY, WEDNESDAY, AUGUST 30

IN TRUE Sydney fashion, I almost miss my flight. The torrential downpour didn't help. I got caught in the rain looking for a cab, and thank goodness my flight was delayed, just like Tray said, or I never would have made it. Tray must have made up with the "crazy" boy because I didn't hear from him the rest of the day. I wanted to show off my red soles, but I'm glad he was in good spirits and not drinking when he left the apartment.

My hair is still wet as I deplane at the only airport near Butter Creek. But on a good note, the flight was great and I was totally fine. I didn't even need to use the Xanax that Tray "prescribed." I'll save that little goodie for more desperate moments...like jumping out of a plane...on national TV...with a boob-flattening jumpsuit on. Marcy Moore will probably make me wear it while waving from a float in the Tractor Days Parade.

Omigod, I never thought of that. She probably will.

The Butter Creek Tractor Days Parade and Celebration. Only the biggest parade of the year. And it kicks off tomorrow! Just in time for me to get out of the city and get over my self-loathing and ongoing pity party. I haven't so much as heard a peep from Tuff and it's all I can think about.

I step out of the terminal (the only terminal) and outside to the hugs of both the parents and enthusiastic barks from all of our rescue dogs. A sensitive Rottweiler named Thor, a klutzy Newfoundland named George, a smart Pug named Maz, and a beautiful-faced, naughty mutt named Mustard.

"Oh, Syd, is it that bad? Oh, Jim, I told you," Minnie says, and hugs me again so hard you'd think she weighed more than a buck.

"Huh?" I say, confused.

"What did that jerk do to you? Jim, I told you," she says.

"You okay, Syd?" Doc says. "You look a little..." He trails off.

"What are you guys talking about? I'm fine," I say as I see my reflection in the car window and gasp. Mustard sees me too and starts howling. I mean, really howling. (We've always thought there was some Basset Hound in his mutt roots.) Everyone in the parking lot looks at us.

Well, that explains all the sweet-talking flight attendants and free drinks. My hair isn't the only thing that got wet. My favorite mascara is bleeding down my face and it looks like I've been crying. Hard.

"Oh, for cripe sake," I say, and grab a towel from the Mutt Machine to wipe my face. "It was rain, just rain."

"Oh, Syd, I wouldn't use that," Minnie says, but it's too late. "Nevermind, no big deal. Let's go, shall we?" She climbs into the Mutt Machine, moving Maz and Mustard, who's still howling, from her seat. Maz crawls right back onto her lap and, in true Pug form, starts reverse sneezing.

"Your mother used that towel to clean drool from the seats for you," Doc says, loading my carry-on and laughing. I look in the side mirror. Yep.

Welcome home.

I sit between Thor and George and pet their heads as we get on our way to Butter Creek, just shy of an hour away. Minnie begins her national news update. Even if I *had* been crying about a boy it wouldn't stop the national news update.

"Did you hear about the woman who was texting while driving?... You should never do that, Syd.... She drove another car off an overpass...it turned out to be her own husband! Isn't that just terrible? Those cell phones are dangerous, Syd.... You have to be careful...right, Jim? Oh my goodness...did you hear about the man who was gored to death by a goat right in his own barn?... Where was that, Jim? And to think, I've always wanted a goat. Was it a goat? It could have been a bull..."

She pauses for dramatic effect—or maybe just thinking about the goat she always wanted—before barreling on with her updates.

"Oh, and there was another awful tragedy...this was at that park.... Jim, what's the name of that park?" She digs in the glovebox and hands me a Kleenex. "I don't know all the details yet, but a biker disappeared and they suspect a mountain lion...they found his bloody shoe...only one!"

I can't resist. "Where's the other shoe?"

"I don't know," Minnie screams. "It's too horrible to think about." Almost in the same breath, she adds, "So, what would you like for lunch?"

As if I could eat now—people are texting and driving, a man has been murdered by his goat, and there's a savage mountain lion on the loose somewhere in the world with a biker's foot in its mouth.

Ah, home.

The fields are bright green and laden with row after row of rich, sun-speckled sweet corn, the sky is so blue it looks like a blueberry snow cone from the county fair, and the air smells incredibly fresh...well, except for that pig farm we just passed.

I wouldn't miss Tractor Days Parade and Celebration for the world. (Except if Marcy Moore gets wind of that jumpsuit.) It's standing tradition for Penny, Kat, and I to watch the parade together and there couldn't be a better time for a happy distraction. I temporarily stop petting George, the Newfy, to ask what time the parade starts, and he leans his big head into my leg and prods me to continue. And I do.

"Oh, I don't know, Jim, when does it start?" Minnie asks.

"Nine sharp," he says, navigating rush hour. There are at least three other cars on the road.

We roll down the long, winding drive and pull up to our flower-adorned home. The dogs jump out and I follow suit. I drop my suitcase on the open porch and run out into the yard, throwing a tennis ball for Thor as George bounds around him and the little dogs wrestle in the well-trimmed grass. Minnie's obsessed with the riding lawn mower; there hasn't been a blade of grass out of place on the expansive property since they purchased it. And she always wears the same thing. The tinted, gargantuan goggles and yellow construction vest. A bumblebee. Minnie looks like a busybody bumblebee when she mows.

Doc walks by carrying a couple two-by-fours to the work shed, mumbling something about the projects we have to do while I'm home. I think he said something about finishing a bridge over the little creek on the back property and putting up a couple birdhouses near the pond. It's like Fern Gully out here, I swear. And I love it.

The home phone rings and Minnie yells from the porch that Penny's on the horn, just like when I was a teenager. I knew she got my text. I run into the house.

"I want to know everything you're planning," Minnie says, holding the phone away from me. I laugh and fight for the receiver. As if she won't try to listen in, one of her favorite pastimes while we were growing up.

"Penn, I made it! What are we doing?" I boom.

"Everything," Minnie mouths and I swat her away. Busybody bumblebee.

"I'm so happy, happy, happy you're home!" Penny screams. "Here's the story, morning glory, you're going to meet Kat and me just before the parade to help with all the kids! Just the thought of candy and they're already bouncing off the walls. And they can't wait to see you!" She positively shines through the phone.

"Sounds perfect!"

"Yay! So, get to Kat's house at eight in the morning and I'll meet you guys at the corner store," she says, while simultaneously telling her kids to stop squirting glue on the wall.

"Okay! Omigod, do you remember Kat and I used to ride bareback in the parade dressed as Sioux Indians?" I giggle and think about how many times we've all been in our small town parade. And how many times I've been bucked off of those horses! (Omigod, and how inappropriate it was that I was dressed as a Native American! Kat's family has rich ancestry, her great grandmother being Sincangu Lakota, but still.)

"Oh jeez, I know. I showed Sally (her three-year-old daughter) pictures of us at the parade when we were her age. She's just over the moon that we're keeping up the tradition. Do you know what she said?" I can tell she's smiling at Sally.

"What did she say?"

"She said, 'It's nice Sydney's here so we don't have to fly all the way to York City.' Can you believe that?"

"Adorable! York City? That's too cute."

"See you soon, OKAY!" She screams that last part, but means to scream at her kids who have now, it seems, glittered the dog. I have a momentary relapse thinking about all the glitter that was stuck to even Tuff's face that morning and cringe. I don't know how Penny does it. She's active on nearly every community board, is a dental hygienist (not the obvious choice for a germaphobe), and has two wild kids with one on the way. She's nearly seven and a half months pregnant and planning our day at Tractor Days. She's amazing.

I stroll back outside and lay down in the grass. All four dogs crowd around me, George at my feet, the small dogs begging for attention, and Thor lying as near to my body as possible. I lift my head and put it on Thor's muscled, Rottweiler shoulder and gaze at the white cotton candy clouds as they move slowly along in the blueberry snow cone sky.

Except for that one damn cotton candy cloud that looks like a cowboy hat.

Chapter 32
TRACTOR DAYS

BUTTER CREEK: TODAY, THURSDAY, AUGUST 31

SOFT BEAMS of light stream into my log cabin-like room, and I peer out the window from my bed to watch as the morning crests with a beautiful pinkish glow over the trees. Meow, my ultra-skittish cat who may very well be twenty years old, sneaks out of the room as I slide out of bed and head toward the shower.

Drinking from the orange juice carton, I notice the photo of Grandma Shag on the fridge. She's on the deck of the cruise ship in her signature large-brimmed sun hat holding a frozen cocktail with a pink umbrella and beautiful fruit garnish. Grandpa Shag, not the highlight of the photo, is sweating in the background with uneven sunscreen visible on nearly his entire body. Gams has always had a flare for the dramatic and I'm sure she's keeping Grandpa on his toes. (Again, definitely where I got it.) Whipping out my phone, I text her on a whim about the whole situation (not even Minnie and Doc know how to text) and she responds almost instantly with this:

Grandma Shag: Dear, never let a man tell you that you've had one too many. Tell him to put on your heels while you have another. We'll see who's on their face first.

Then I text her the infamous photo:

Grandma Shag: You are sparkling dear, just sparkling. (Really you're actually sparkling, how did you manage that?)

"Sydney!" Minnie yells, and I jump. I put the empty carton back in the fridge and run outside as Minnie shakes her head and laughs. After petting all the dogs, I jump into the truck and drive the backroads, rolling by my old brick house middle school that is no longer in use, feeling every bit of nostalgia for whispering in the old stairwells, concerts on the rickety but majestic stage, flirting on the lawn, and hot lunches. (Totally kidding about the hot lunches. Blagh!) I love this town and the memories it keeps. I pull through the high school parking lot, a shortcut to Kat's, and even more memorable moments flood my mind. I curb check (oops) as I make the left to her house. I quietly park in her drive, but it doesn't work because two little towheads have heard me and push their way through the screen door and run into my arms as I close the truck door. Brick, her little boy and, youngest, immediately gets shy after the first hug and, as usual, runs back to the door as Kat steps outside giggling. Kat is always giggling. She has the most extraordinary laugh—one that is completely contagious. I immediately start giggling with her while Caley, her little girl, takes my hand and doesn't let go.

"Well, look who it is," Kat says with a bright smile.

"Throwing me on Silver when you knew he would buck!" I bellow.

"Canoe on the pond when you knew it would sink!" she shoots back.

"Taking the ladder away from the hay loft!" I trill, holding back laughter.

"Taking the ladder away from the treehouse!" she hollers and I let out a large belly laugh. We break out again into uproarious giggles. This is our ritual greeting; we go back and forth with old stories about getting each other into trouble. (I didn't actually know the canoe would sink, but I take credit for it now.) Kat's eyes fill with laughter tears as she hugs me. Kat always gets tears in her eyes when she laughs, another of my favorite things about her. She wipes them from her clean skin and tucks her natural, never-been-colored, sun-kissed hair behind her ear. Then, looking me up and down, she flashes a teasing grin.

"Well, let me get my *fancy* flip-flops and we'll go," she smirks. Kat always thinks I'm fancy even when I'm wearing jean shorts and wedges. She steps back into the house barefoot with Brick in tow while I talk to Caley about the importance of a good pair of wedges. She returns with her "fancy" flip-flops and we all pile into her Suburban. Caley slips into her car seat as Kat wrestles Brick into his. Brick will be taller than Kat by the time he's ten and by then she'll

really have her hands full. As kids we used to measure ourselves constantly back-to-back. I finally surpassed her, but
not until college, where I grew a couple winning inches.
Kat and I were in the same kindergarten class together
and laughed until tears nearly every day. And nearly every
day we had to put our heads down on our desks for causing
trouble. We were never put in the same class again...one of
the pitfalls of a small town. Every teacher knows that you
were troublemakers in kindergarten even when you get to
high school.

Or even when you're at the Kum & Go in your twenties.
While looking at which brand of water might be good for
kids (why are there so many brands of water?), Principal
Matthews says hello and reminds us how naughty we were
in Mrs. Samson's kindergarten class years and years ago.

"Told ya, troublemakers," Penny shouts, while racing
after her kids who are barreling through the store. To this
day, Penny says she tried to warn us about being bad in
class.

"Morning, Penn," I say, crossing my eyes and making a
funny face like we're six years old just as Sally jumps into
my free arm with Caley, again, holding the other. I give
Sally a big hug, lifting her up. Penny's son, Aiden, gives
me an uninterested smile. He doesn't care for anyone but
his mom and dad right now. I wave back, willing him to
like me.

"You look great! And glowing, of course," I beam,
referencing her baby belly that may just be the size of a
basketball.

"Oh my gosh, I'm ready to pop! I'm so happy, happy, happy to see you, Syd," she says again, trying to hug me around all the kids and her growing belly. She manages, as always, to give the best hug and smashes my face into the extremely tight, coffee-colored curls framing her face. (It's a perm, but don't tell. I didn't even know perms still existed. I picture her getting it done by Truvy from *Steal Magnolias*.) Her one darling cheek dimple radiates cheer as she yells "Kat!" and hugs her too.

"Morning, Penn. We're going to have our hands full. Syd always gets them all riled up," Kat giggles, setting several water bottles onto the counter. I move slowly to the register holding Caley's hand, with Sally in my arms and Brick hugging my leg.

"Caley, grab some Swedish fish. We might need some if they don't throw enough candy," I say, nudging her toward the candy aisle. Swedish fish—still a favorite.

"Hello there, ladies." A gravelly, subterranean voice crashes our party. And then, somehow deeper and even more menacingly, says, "Sydney."

I turn slowly.

"Oh, hi, Officer Lorell," I smile and giggle nervously as he towers over me. Officer Lorell has always reminded me of Lurch from the *Addams Family* and today is no exception. I watch as Caley grabs five packages of Swedish Fish. Omigod. Stay away, Caley, stay away. Penny and Kat greet him with a warm hello, but say "Sheriff." I don't know why because he's just an officer.

"Have a great time at the parade today, girls. It's rumored to have more tractors this year than ever before," he says, pouring coffee into a hunter green thermal mug. I see Caley out of the corner of my eye; she's headed right for me with *so* many fish. Officer Lurch looks me square in the eye with his deep-set gray stare and says, "Stay out of trouble," just as Caley shoves all the Swedish Fish into my hand. I try to bat them away. "And make sure you pay for those fish this time," he says. Barf.

He ducks his huge frame through the door and it jingles as he leaves with free coffee. (Free for police officers, firemen, EMT, and veterans—oh and military. So, almost the whole town.) I look out the window following him. He looks back just as I'm popping several, as of yet unpaid-for Swedish Fish into my mouth. Poorly timed on my part. Panic eating.

About that other little incident...

I shove more fish into my mouth.

We move out onto the community-lined street and choose a spot along the curb where the kids will be able to gather the most candy. I say hi to everyone nearby, including two of my favorite coaches and three teachers. We situate our lawn chairs, picnic blankets, kids, water bottles, and Penny's numerous anti-bacterial hand sanitizers in anticipation of the triumphant start, signifying the beginning of Tractor Days Parade and Celebration. Sheriff Smitty is always the grand marshal of the parade and leads from the front in his patrol car. I look for him down the street.

Officer (omigod!) Lurch presides over the parade, leading in a patrol car that reads "Sheriff of Butter Creek!" My face must display horror because Kat laughs.

"Yeah, *Sheriff* Lorell. Sheriff Smitty retired. Try to stay out of jail, Syd," she giggles.

Why did Sheriff Smitty retire? He's only ninety-two! Lurch doesn't even fit in a patrol car. Officer-Sheriff-Lurch-Lorell slightly slouched and, with his head still skimming the roof of the car, gives us a peace sign and I feel myself calm down. But then I'm nearly positive he makes the number five with his hand, or is he just waving at me? Right at me. A peace sign and a wave? Or a *two* and a *five*?

Here it goes...

About that other little incident...

Officer Lurch suspects I had something to do with the Speed Limit 25 sign that went missing on Birch Street years ago. He could never prove it, but he had his Lurch eyeballs on Hunter Boone and me for years. Sheriff Smitty, who always loved me (square dancing prodigy and all), finally made him drop it for lack of evidence. (Because the evidence is well hidden, buried in the backyard. HE'LL NEVER TAKE ME ALIVE!)

Is there a time limit on the prosecution for traffic signage theft?

I need to check the backyard.

Uncountable numbers of tractors—shiny, rusted, vintage, brand new, red, blue, green—fill the street. Three proud homemade floats (one of which Marcy Moore is riding—Secretary of Butter Creek waving at her constituents with extra ruffles decorating her always-buttoned top button blouse) amble down the road alongside local vintage cars (many of which Penny's dad has worked on), the Rotary Club motorcycles, the town fire truck, the recently purchased ambulance, the Shriners in their mini cars (retired Magistrate John Baard, is always driving his drunk), numerous dogs dressed in costume, impeccably groomed horses, and the high school marching band proudly playing "Hey Baby! (If You'll Be My Girl)" a little out of tune and with one rogue tuba player, smaller than his instrument, falling behind. And they each get more shouts, cheering, and flag waving than the last. Candy fills the air, and we wave hello and yell thank you to all the people we know in the parade.

I slip off my wedges and run around with the kids barefoot, gathering all my (I mean their) favorite sweets. Caley challenges me to a bubblegum blowing competition with our newest loot, and I immediately accept. Sally's telling everyone that "Sydney is home from York City," while Aiden is trying to steal candy from all the kids around him against Penny's wishes. Brick, being the youngest, is overwhelmed but knows the name and make of every tractor that's rolled by. Kat lifts him up and he high fives his grandpa on one of the big green, vintage John Deeres while Caley and I show off our bubbles. Grandpa, knowing us all too well, tells us to stay out of trouble as we all laugh and holler. (It seems everyone says that to us.) But suddenly amidst the laughter the memory of Tuff describing how his grandpa taught him to drive a tractor while we sat touching hands under the willow tree washes over me, forming a lump in my throat.

"Syd, another, another," Caley yells, pulling my arm, oblivious to my impending meltdown. Her face scrunches into concentration as she forms a bubble, encouraging me to do the same. Her resemblance to Kat is uncanny, and I can't help but smile doing as she commands.

Kat puts Brick down and picks up my wedges. "Syd, how do you walk in these things?" she says, slipping off her flip-flops and putting them on. "My gosh, what are they, three inches?" I look at her over my Hubba Bubba bubble and watch as she giggles, trying to keep her balance.

"I wobble and waddle enough as it is," Penny laughs. "But I think I need a pair of those to pick the kids up from swim lessons." She whistles at Kat, who has stopped to pose. Caley pops my winning bubble with a giggle.

"Ha ha, you guys." I say sarcastically and laugh. The lump in my throat disappears as I'm pulled swiftly back into the present. And my wedges are four inches, but I'm not going to tell them that. Nor am I going to tell them that they're my practical sandals. We all know wedges are perfect with summer shorts, and are easy-peasy to walk in. Kat falls back onto the curb laughing. Maybe not.

After hitching a ride with one of the numerous tractors giving hay rides down to the fairgrounds and our first run at the go-karts, I plant myself on top of one of the picnic tables just outside the mini tilt-a-whirl. The kids have no problem with this beastly ride. I would surely throw up, and it's the kid version!

Which reminds me, I threw up when Tuff came to visit. I told Tuff all about this parade, and I wish he were here...or at the very least talking to me. I stuff a caramel from Penny's kids' candy into my mouth, feeling a surge of depression, and watch them go 'round and 'round and 'round. Yep, I would totally vomit; I feel nauseous just watching.

Penny only allows her kids three pieces of candy each, so as far as depressed sugar-stuffing goes, I'm in luck. During Halloween her kids have to leave most of their Trick-or-Treating goodies for the Candy Witch—one of the pitfalls of having a dental hygienist for a mom. Last Halloween I graciously volunteered to be the witch. Now they just hand it over and imagine my teeth falling out. Kat's kids don't have the same candy rule and love eating sweet treats with me. After Halloween, Brick asked when I was coming home again to go "candy-huntin," and here I am! I'm starting to think I plan visits around sugar.

I dig around in the paper bag for more goodies and find Lemon Heads. I haven't had these in ages. I shove six of the sour drops in my mouth. You have to cram as many as you can into your mouth to get the worst pucker face ever and best taste. Kat, Penny, and I used to do this all the time. My cheeks are full and I'm starting to get the desired effect when I see my high school sweetheart. He walks over just as my face screws into a pinched pucker.

"Sydney! How are you? You look amazing as always," he says. I look amazingly like a chipmunk storing Lemon Heads. I try to fix my unattractive pucker but the sour is so strong I have to squint one eye or I'll cry. Now I look like a one-eyed pirate chipmunk. Ugh.

My cheeks are so full I'm unable to respond as he hugs me. I panic and spit the whole wad into my hand while in his arms.

"Hi, Blake! So happy to see you. You look great too," I finally respond and with way too much enthusiasm. He totally does too. He's still just as handsome as ever, even with a little extra weight. (Omigod, now I'm just being mean.)

"Well, I've got a little weight to lose, unlike you."

Omigod, he read my mean mind. And did he just check me out?

"How are you?" I say, as if I don't know what else to say.

"I'm pretty good. What are you doing in town?" he beams. His smile still gives me butterflies. Isn't that stupid?

"Just visiting the fam and hanging out with the girls," because I played with too much pixie dust and sparkled myself right into the Tinker tank, embarrassing myself yet again, with yet another failed relationship. "You know, just visiting." (Otherwise known as hiding out!)

I don't know why I didn't marry Blake. Everyone else married their high school sweethearts. I'm an official idiot. Maybe he's divorced; please tell me he's divorced!

Dear Lord, please give me the man I was supposed to marry. I think I messed up!

"Hi, Sydney. How are you?" his wife chimes, popping around the pie stand.

Lord, why? Why did you have to marry off my high school sweetheart...and take my boobs? Couldn't you have been happy with just feeding the hungry?

It's possible I'm just panicking. But if I married Blake, I wouldn't have taken those shots with the Big-Little Pigs and tinkered myself into trashed.

I realize I haven't greeted his wife, Misty, in return, and I stick out my hand for a shake. Six gooey Lemon Heads plunge from my hand and drop squarely onto her foot.

"Gah, I'm so sorry. Jeez," I wince. I offer her napkins from the picnic table, but because she's wearing practical Keds lace-ups (Keds? Are you kidding me?), she just kicks the goo off and tells me not to worry.

Practical. I was never meant to be practical. I'm not even able to walk in my new Christian Louboutins, and if that's wrong, I don't want to be right. I wipe my hand off and offer it again. "Hi, Misty. Great to see you." Not. Gag.

"It's good to see you too. We saw your YouTube video. We both thought it was so funny," she laughs. "It was just like at our wedding. You know, when you fell on the folding chair after catching the bouquet."

Ha ha. Yes, I remember. I was trying to get away from one of your hairy family members who was trying to feel me up! Misty isn't hairy. It must just be the men in the family. Misty is actually glowing. Barf.

"Oh, Syd, Marcy Baard is trying to find you, speaking of that video," Blake says. "You better hide." He smiles.

"Marcy Baard?" I ask.

"You know, Marcy Moore. She got married," he says.

Of course she married the magistrate's son! (He's a drunk, too.)

"Shi…" I think better of using profanity in front of Misty, Laura Ingalls incarnate. "…oot!" I manage. Blake laughs, knowing what I wanted to say and knowing that I've been hiding from Marcy Moore-Baard for years for various reasons that are getting too many to count. I look around but don't see any stifling ruffles.

"So, about the bouquet? You're the next to get married! Anyone special in your life?" Misty is trying to kill me. And is it just me or does she have a glint in her eye?

"Hey, Blake! I got you a beer. Come on over!" Speaking of the magistrate's son. He's leaning out of the beer barn double-fisting Pabst.

Blake waves. "We're on our way! I don't want that to get warm, Misty. We'll see you later, Syd." He gently takes Misty's hand as I say goodbye and they head to the barn.

I can't believe it. Saved by Pabst!

Plopping back onto the picnic table, I hope Misty's just getting fat and the extra weight isn't the secret trimester. Glowing. Gross.

I should just drink myself into oblivion and drown my sorrows with the local toothless crew at Whiskey River. I feel another toilet bowl-hugging situation coming on. I mean, who wears Keds and a French braid these days except for in Utah? And what's with the knee-length mom shorts? Omigod, she *is* pregnant. Is she pregnant?

Just as I'm about to strangle myself with licorice rope, Caley jumps on me, begging for a piggyback ride to the snow cone stand.

"Was that Blake?" Penny asks.

"Yes," I answer coolly. They're all back, and just in the knick of time! I shove the licorice rope back into the bag.

"Oh nice—you look hot! I bet he was dying," Kat says, helping Caley onto my back.

"I looked like a pirate chipmunk and hurtled gooey Lemon Heads at Misty. I don't want to talk about it," I say, pained.

"What!" Penny screams. Sometimes Penny just screams, usually in the street after one drink. "You're ridiculous," she laughs.

"He still loves you," Kat giggles.

"Kat, he's married," I gasp. But I secretly hope he does.

"So what? We need some good gossip around here," Penny says facetiously.

"Sydney and Blake, sittin' in a tree," Kat starts.

"K.I.S.S.I.N.G!" they finish together, like in fourth grade. There was a good month in the fourth grade that we sang that song every day about every boy.

"You two," I growl, but we all laugh. We never grow old of making fun of each other. The kids continue the teasing and taunt me for being a scaredy-cat about the mini tilt-a-whirl as we kick up dust to the snow cone stand. I'm not above bribing my way out of the scaredy-cat nickname, so it's my treat. As soon as I hand them their cherry, cherry-orange, blueberry, and cherry-blueberry ices (after Penny sanitizes everyone's hands, of course), I'm the "Snow Cone Princess." And even though I don't feel like a princess right now, I am in their eyes.

With syrup running down our cones and stained tongues, I snap a selfie with the kids in front of a vintage tractor on display and send it to the Siren group text.

Me: Tractor Days!

Abby: Eeeeeh you guys are soooo cute!

Bette: OMG I swear you're on a Hollywood "small town" set. Those kids are adorbs and you look REALLY happy!

Gus: Adorable!!! Gimme a snow cone right nowww!

Gus: BTW I swear I saw Tray walk by the bar well after midnight last night.

Me: What?

Gus: Sorry, thought I should mention?? Could be nothing, but it was so late and I know you're trying to help him stay out of trouble.

Me: Ugh, yes, thanks for telling me. I'll text Logan.

Claudia: Love you, Syd!!! Miss you! Get back right now! (heart-eyes emoji) Also, why is your snow cone brown?

Me: Oh! It's a Suicide! All the flavors in one cone (grinning emoji) I can never decide which flavor I want, it's been my favorite since I was their age.

Bette: That explains a lot (hands over mouth monkey emoji)

Me: Ha ha, very funny

Gus: That was before, Bette! She did choose this time! She chose Tuff and he's being an idiot. Has he called yet, Syd?

Me: No (puke face emoji)

The puke face emoji couldn't be more appropriate on so many levels. Ugh. But what a significant observation. I *did* choose. Indecision wasn't a problem. I chose Tuff. It just didn't work out.

Double ugh.

I manage to send a few more texts to both Tray and Logan before the kids pull me to the bumper cars. Letting Caley drive my car cheers me up significantly.

After more rides, carnival games (my favorite), more reminiscing, and seeing just about the whole town, we trek to the cars and Penny waves goodbye. They're meeting her husband for dinner, and the kids are excited to see their dad.

"Enjoy the crickets!" Kat and I yell, snickering even though we've said it a hundred times.

"You guys," Penny laughs and jumps in the car after strapping the kids in. Penny's husband, Jason Taylor, ate a cricket on a dare in the lunchroom when we were eight and we won't let her forget it. Kat straps Briggs into the Suburban and Caley piles in on her own.

"Sydney? Sydney!" I hear a voice from several cars down but I don't spot the owner.

"Caley, red alert, puke noises, now," Kat says, quietly.

"Sydney!" the voice says again.

"Whoorl-hauh-hauh-whoorl!" Caley, with her head all but in her bag of candy, impersonates puking like a pro, and before I know what's going on, Marcy Moore (now Baard) is asking Kat if Caley is okay.

"Too much candy, great parade, but we've got to get home STAT," Kat replies.

"Oh, of course, feel better, Caley," Marcy Moore-Baard says, fussing with her ruffles as if puke somehow sprayed on them. "But, Sydney, you know, we can't wait to talk to you about that little video and—"

"Whoorl!" Caley is really good at this.

"Gotta go," Kat says, pushing me into the Suburban.

"I'll be in touch," I say, leaning out the window, politely lying, as Kat locks the doors and rolls up the windows, nearly crushing my head. Of course I won't. Marcy will have me posed like Oscar the Grouch for the *Butter Creek Chronicle*!

"Good night, Marcy," Kat says, waving and hitting the gas at the same time just as the windows snap shut. A short half block away, she high fives Caley in the back seat and looks at me. "How do you think I get out of PTA?"

"It's the the Batmobile!" I laugh.

"We prefer the…" the kids join her, "Kat Mobile." Kat giggles her perfectly perfect giggle.

Kat drives me out to her parents' farm and we give snacks to the horses and say hi to her husband, Pete, the quietest boy in our class. He waves shyly, even though we both know it only takes two beers and he'll be rattling off all his best big fish stories. I sing Disney songs with the kids (because I know them all) and we explore the farm. We take the golf cart and ATV for a spin, then jump back in the Suburban and drive ten minutes to Cedar Pond.

We run barefoot on the banks of the almost lake that I always thought looked like a grizzly bear's head and where I used to run with our cross country team. We splash in the water with Caley and Brick before hitting the swing set. I fall flat on my face trying to give an underdog and the kids giggle while I try to redeem myself.

The laughter seems to lift away my heartache. Maybe I don't have to feel bad anymore when I check my phone and see Tuff still hasn't called. And maybe it's because I should be focusing on that big career I always thought I would have. Kat always knew she was going to marry Pete and have kids and here she is, living her dream. I know what I have to do.

The sun sets as we roll into her driveway and I wonder how I ever left this small town to travel and live in the big city. Everything's right here, I think, as I hug her tired little kids. Then I hug Kat and crawl into the truck.

I blare the radio and sing at the top of my lungs while rolling along the roads I know so well. I know where the deepest pothole is and swerve around it. I know where the Jeffreys' dog may dart out and I look out for him. I know where the hill is that will make your stomach jump if you hit it at just the right speed, and I know where my turns are, even in pitch black and in between fields. I scream-sing the last chorus of an old song that played at almost all of our high school dances while pulling in front of the house.

✩ ✩ ✩

I blow in the front door expecting to see Minnie and Doc sitting in the open kitchen. All the dogs greet me, nearly knocking me down, but the parents are nowhere to be seen.

"Minnie! Doc! Where are you?" I yell. Leaning down to pet the dogs, I fill them in on my plan. "I need their help with my resume, don't I guys?!" I hear a high-pitched hoot from the back porch. Was that Minnie? Then I hear Doc.

"We're back here, Spunky," he shouts. I scurry to the back of the house and open the sliding screen door off the sun porch, leaving it ajar.

"Oh, Sydney," Minnie emotes. She stands up, knocking over her chair, and hugs me. Who gave Minnie a drink?

And then a shudder runs through my body. I spot two wine glasses on the table. I look around the deck, then run to the railing and look into the backyard. No one's there. Relief slips out in the form of a deep exhale and I turn around.

GASP!

Fear seeps into my pores.

"Dad, Syd didn't put the truck in gear and it rolled into the drainpipe off the garage." Eye flutter-roll. "Way to go, Syd. Surprise, I'm home."

The Sister.

"Oh jeez, Syd," Doc says, leaning his head back.

My shoulders sink. "Sorry. I really didn't put it in gear?" Not that it's altogether astonishing. I've been known to do that.

"I was in the front yard, taking Ruby out to go pid-dle, and I watched it roll while you ran inside," she says, then mumbles something (nothing good) under her breath and reaches for her wine. Just then Ruby, her Chihuahua, comes running onto the porch, barking and nipping at my heels.

"Well, did you park it, Krissy?" Doc asks.

"I had Ruby," she says, taking a sip of her wine.

"Jeez, you guys," he says, heading out to the front.

I try to smile at The Sister. "I didn't know you were coming this weekend."

"Yep," she says and looks me up and down. "What are you wearing?" She flares her nostrils and smirks. What? I look at my cute wedges, short-shorts, and V-neck T-shirt. What? What are *you* wearing? She must have been at the same moms-only summer sale on knee-length shorts with Misty. They're not even moms! (Ugh, Misty probably is.) But instead of saying anything, I smile. Like an idiot.

"Oh noooo!" Minnie says in a much-delayed reaction to the truck. She's clearly had two or three sips of wine. "What's wrong with the truck drain?"

Minnie, what's a truck drain?

Minnie picks up Maz, who's having another reverse sneezing fit. I'm not sure pugs were built for breathing, but snuggling, yes.

"Don't worry, Mom. Dad's taking care of it. Sydney..." Eye flutter-roll. "...took the drainpipe to the garage off with the truck." She sits down by Minnie and does noth-ing about Ruby, who's still yipping at me.

"It took off the whole thing?" I say, rather to myself, and head back inside. Ruby chases me off the porch, then quiets down, jumping into The Sister's lap. I walk out front to see the damage with three dogs in tow. Doc has re-parked the truck and is futzing with the pipe.

"Sorry," I say. Thor, George, and Mustard circle around me, asking for attention. "Is it bad? Can I help?" I ask. I kneel and pet them all one by one.

"Truth is, Syd," he starts, and I brace myself for the worst, "it's not that bad, and..." He looks over at me. "...I did the same thing last week. So I don't know if you did this or me." He chuckles.

"You did?" I laugh.

"But, gad, don't tell Minnie, she'll kill me," he adds. He works the bent end of the drainpipe into the remaining piece on the garage, still laughing and shaking his head. Even when I was in high school, Doc and I would run into the same spot on the garage door. Minnie never knew who to go after. Like father like daughter. "Grab me some duct tape, Syd. It's on the workbench in the garage."

After mending the drainpipe, we go back inside and Ruby leaps off The Sister's lap, staying airborne for an unusual amount of time, then hits the floor running. She comes right for me, yapping again, then squeals and makes a wide turn, slipping on the hardwood floors.

"Not so tough when it's three against one, are you, Rubes?" I giggle. Ruby runs for the safety of The Sister's lap again with the three bigger dogs right behind her. I swear The Sister took a piece of my clothing and taught her to attack.

"So, Mom told me you screwed up yet another relationship," The Sister says with a well-placed snort-laugh even before I step back onto the porch.

Thanks, Minnie.

"It wasn't like we were *together* together," I say, sounding less than intelligent and trying to make the "scandal" less agonizing. Thor and George perch on either side of me as if knowing I need backup. I pat their heads.

"She said you messed it up good," The Sister continues. Again, thank you, Minnie. Glad to know what you really think since you were on my side about it yesterday. "So how did you manage it this time?" She swirls, then sips her wine.

"Oh, I never know what to say with you girls," Minnie warbles. Again a little delayed and alcoholically over-emotional. "I just love you both so much!" Three sips, that's all it takes. Suddenly, The Sister trills with excitement and Ruby bark-wines, apparently excited too.

"You found it," her voice climbs three octaves. "Eeeeeh!" She jumps out of her chair and takes the Pinot Grigio from Andrew's hand, holding Ruby nearly upside down in the other. Mustard starts howling in the excitement. Really howling.

"Oh, hi, Andrew! I didn't know you were here too. Good to see you," I beam. Andrew looks slightly sweaty and disheveled. Where did he get this wine? I just adore him and his fearful little Chihuahua, Milly, who's cowering in his arm. Yes, they both have Chihuahuas, separate Louis Vuitton carriers, matching doggy wear, and rhinestone collars. I don't know how to feel about this. But Milly is a little spoonful of pure sugar and looks like a cross between a hamster and a bunny.

Ruby, on the other hand, looks like a rat.

"Oh, hi there, Sydney," Andrew says, quietly but cheerfully. He tries to straighten his hair. I pet Milly, who trembles and then licks me hello. "Krissy, there aren't any liquor stores in this town. I actually found that at the grocery store after driving around for an hour," he smiles. Really, he smiled. An hour? Then he must have driven around town at least a dozen times. Nope, you can probably do that in half an hour. He must have taken a wrong turn at Coach Beckford's house and hit gravel.

"You haven't been driving around for an hour," she counters and pops open the bottle. If he took that turn, he's probably been driving around for two (lost on country roads). And we do have a liquor store; it's just in Kat's dad's man cave. Few know about it.

"Oh no, you're having more wine?" Minnie says, a crease appearing between her eyebrows. She thinks The Sister gets looped after three sips, like she does.

"I've barely had any," The Sister says, filling her glass. That sounds familiar. Though I remember it as, "I barely touched her," after she punched or pushed me growing up. I think I'll have a glass too.

"Would you like me to get you a glass, Andrew?" I ask. The big dogs lie down, sensing some calm. Mustard, however, is lifting his leg on Andrew's pleated pants and no one seems to notice. I grab him up and head inside. But Mustard's put on weight and it's not going as effortlessly as planned. His long body dangles from my arms as he tries to lick me.

"No thanks, I'm on call tonight," Andrew says, raising his voice so I can hear as I struggle toward the kitchen. Andrew's a dermatologist. Do you have to be sober for that? Mustard's still trying to lick me, unaware that his life hangs in the balance…what are they feeding him? I set him down and come back with a glass.

"Have you had any calls tonight?" I ask, trying to be cordial and start conversation. I reach over The Sister and pour some wine. Ruby growls as my arm moves over her little body. Thor's head pops up in case I need help.

"He's had some doozies. I cannot believe how much can happen when we leave town," The Sister answers for him. They've driven in from Minneapolis, of course. "Some woman's eczema flared up and desperately needed Andrew's advice, and another needed an emergency prescription of clindamycin," she all but shouts. Is that an emergency? Clindamycin is a zit cream.

"How's school?" I ask The Sister.

"It's so hard. I've been studying twenty-four-seven these last couple months."

"Wow, great, almost there!" I cheer.

"You have no idea what the real world is like, Syd. It's *so* hard," she clinks my glass. The Sister doesn't consider anything I do "real."

"So I've gotten out the croquet set," Doc says, stepping onto the porch and, as always, interrupting just in time. "We're playing early in the morning. So you all better get some good sleep," he says and claps his hands, rubbing them together in excitement. "Nothing like a little gentlemanly competition with the Shags!" He slaps Andrew healthily on the back, and Andrew falls forward slightly.

"Good idea. We've traveled a lot today and I'm so tired from studying." The Sister pours more wine into her glass, then picks up the bottle and stands as Ruby slides precariously off her lap. She signals to Andrew to follow. "Night, you guys, see you in the morning." They head inside and upstairs but not before Ruby looks back and growls at me one more time.

As soon as they're out of earshot, Minnie looks at me. "Do you think she's..." She pauses and looks around. For those of you who don't know Minnie, she's looking for any possible neighbors who might be listening (they live acres away). "...a wino?" Maz snorts loudly as if on cue.

"No, Minnie, goodness no," I say. She totally is, and it's my favorite thing about her. I don't want Minnie going and ruining that. Doc laughs and takes Minnie's unfinished glass and swigs. I drink my glass of wine with them, giving The Sister and Andrew ample time to get ready for bed, then head upstairs. But I run into The Sister as she's coming out of the bathroom.

"Oh, good night, nice to see you," I smile, warming up to her.

"Night, and if you want Andrew to look at that zit on your chin, let me know," she smiles.

What? Ruby bark-growls at me, then prances after The Sister, into her bedroom. What zit? I don't have a zit. I walk into the bathroom and stare into the mirror. I get really, really close and still don't see anything. I don't have a zit! My skin is absolutely clear!

I take out my toothbrush. Something feels oddly warm on my bare foot. I look down. I'm standing on a wee-wee pad that Ruby just finished peeing on. Aargh.

I curl into my bed with a smirk cresting on my face. I know I just stepped in pee (who puts a wee-wee pad in the *middle* of a bathroom?) but I've taken care of that. I got ready for bed and just before leaving the bathroom, I lifted the toilet seat as if Andrew left it up. Collateral damage, Andrew. Collateral damage. Sometimes you have to sacrifice the weak—Doc taught us that. I feel a giggle rise in my chest. The Sister always uses the bathroom in the middle of the night. Revenge is mine!

☆ ☆ ☆

BUTTER CREEK: TODAY, FRIDAY, SEPTEMBER 1

I wake up in the morning with a zit. The Sister may be a witch. I'm not kidding. I mean, I've been convinced for years. Or she could just have a voodoo doll in her bag.

I wouldn't blame her for using it because I heard the shrillest, most piercing scream in the middle of the night. I haven't heard her scream like that since she was in fifth grade and her trendy haircut went terribly, terribly wrong.

(I dare say she sported a mullet for quite some time.) I woke, instantly knowing what had happened. I had to muffle my laughter in a pillow. She fell into the toilet as I had so deviously planned.

I cover up my tiny imperfection, a small price to pay for such a wonderful turnout with the toilet, put my hair in a ponytail, and spring down the stairs. No one's up yet but Doc. He's always up. I grab an apple (Claudia is starting to rub off) and find him working on something in the yard. I pop outside and sit in the grass, where he's mumbling and working with a bunch of two-by-fours.

"Morning, Doc," I say cheerfully.

Mumble, mumble.

"What are you working on?" I stare at the miscellaneous pieces he's brooding over. Thor bounds over and tries to lie in my lap but only a third of his body actually fits. Doc mumbles again as George steps clumsily onto his apparently well-laid design.

"George! Syd, it's just a couple more slats and the bridge will be done. Come on," he says, and motions for me to carry the wood, just so, to the self-designed construction out back. By the time we finish putting on the last couple slats, everybody's awake.

We head inside to quite the commotion. The Sister is laughing. Laughing?

"Andrew fell in the toilet last night," she says, cracking up. "I don't know how you didn't wake up, Syd. He screamed so loud!"

"What? Oh, I didn't hear anything." I feign laughter. That was Andrew?

"Yeah, apparently he was so tired that he went to sit and fell right in," she says, still laughing.

"I must have left the seat up," Andrew says, blushing to crimson.

"Poor Anny, someone should make him eggs," she says, using baby talk vocals while stroking Ruby's balding head. That someone will be me. "Did you two set up croquet?" She looks at Doc and me as Ruby jumps from her arms.

I can't believe she didn't fall in the toilet. And I can't believe Andrew screams like a fifth grade girl. (Or can I?) Foiled again and with a zit to show for it. I can't seem to get anything right. Ruby screeches around Andrew's pleated pants and latches onto my sneaker with surprisingly sharp, Piranha-like little teeth.

Chapter 33
COUNTING YOUR COWS

KAT, HAVING the day off from work, is taking the kids to the Science Center in the "big city," and on the way, they're dropping me off at the airport. We all sing with the radio and then I take requests from Caley for Disney tunes. After the third time through the abridged version of "Let It Go" (as it turns out we only know the chorus) from *Frozen* and the whole glorious "Part of your World" (I know every word) from *The Little Mermaid*, the kids start counting cows.

I'm lucky to have unbelievably wonderful friends in Butter Creek and in the city, and I realize there's just no reason to get all worked up over a guy. Right? I mean, I still need a little convincing, but I'm way better than I was. In fact, Kat and Penny laughed out loud when I told them the Tinker Tanked story (and I only winced two times).

Twenty-one cows and we haven't even gone a mile. (Really, it's twenty-two; they missed one.)

The Shags played more than a few rousing rounds of gentlemanly croquet. I'm joking about the gentlemanly part, of course. The Shags have never played a gentlemanly round of anything. It's always cutthroat. Doc won every round while acting more and more nonchalant each time. Infuriating. The Sister and I even teamed up to try and beat him and we thought we had him. But he knew exactly what was going on and calculated every move, brushing it off as if it were luck. Doc wouldn't dream of losing; even when we were little, he never threw a game to let his kids feel the pleasure of winning. He made sure we knew exactly how bad it felt to be a loser. Character building.

The Sister had a severe blood pressure spike when Andrew beat her, and that round was quickly called into review. I fought Ruby, who clung to my shoe relentlessly, while trying in vain to win. Minnie missed almost every turn, wandering around the yard checking on her flowers, but still managed to beat both her daughters in a round. That was demoralizing; Minnie didn't even know we were competing; she thought we were stomping out weeds with bocce balls. Bocce balls!

Thirty-seven cows. I didn't even know they could count that high. I've lost track but I'm almost sure thirty-seven wasn't a cow.

Speaking of being sure, I made *sure* The Sister's wine glass was full the rest of the weekend, and it actually worked because we got along surprisingly well. We even had a big night out together at Whiskey River. I felt bad about Andrew falling into the toilet, so I helped him with all the bogus errands The Sister kept sending him on. But Mustard, looking quite proud, finally managed to pee on his pleated pants (not the same pair, of course; he must own dozens). Doc gave him another treat anyway.

Distracted by pigs, the kids miss a gold mine of seven good cows.

The pigs remind me to text Tray again, who I haven't heard from. Logan said he spoke with him and that he seemed fine on the phone. Then why isn't he getting back to me? Something just feels off.

"Syd, are you counting?" Caley asks, quick to notice me on my phone.

"Yes, what number were we on? I was just checking for messages," I smile.

And I did check on my incriminating evidence in the backyard, but didn't get a chance to dig. Twenty paces from the treehouse, two jumps to the left of "snake," a fallen tree that looks like, well, a snake, and under the rock marked with an "x." (Maybe we shouldn't have marked it with an "x.") But, I didn't have time to get in the dirt because Minnie, always buzzing about, was getting suspicious and because she was wearing her goggles and a yellow construction vest, she was drawing too much attention to the treasure.

We all hold our breath as we pass a skunk. (Roadkill, unfortunately.) Kat and I make it a game and see who can hold theirs the longest.

After four days in the country I feel rested and renewed and like I can conquer the world. And on the subject of conquering the world, Doc and I worked on my resume.

After Minnie reviewed it, pointing out several stretches of the truth (that Doc and I ignored), I sent it to a few marketing firms! (After having a drink.)

"Oh, I almost forgot, guess what Caley asked me last night?" Kat says, with a glint in her eye. I see Caley perk up in the side mirror. Kids always listen when adults lower their voices.

"What?" I smile.

"She was watching *Tangled*, you know." She looks at me for recognition.

"Um, of course," I glow. Exclamation point, exclamation point! I love *Tangled*.

"Well, she was gettin' all excited for her favorite part, but right in the middle of it she got up from the couch and walked over to me. She stood at the kitchen counter and asked, very seriously, 'Mom, is Sydney Rapunzel?' with these huge doe eyes." Kat giggles.

I gasp loudly.

"How did she know?" I whisper and look in the side mirror to see Caley's jaw drop. Kat and I giggle. I need to hang out with these kids more often. I could get used to this princess identity. (I mean, I did put it on my vision board, after all.)

I hug the kids at least three times each and squeeze Kat, then run into the airport. I throw my bag onto the conveyor belt to be x-rayed and step through the metal detector. A TSA officer picks up my bag,

"We've gotta check this one here. It'll take just a minute; follow me," he says. You'd think I was Gus. I follow him just a few steps down the line. This will definitely take more than a minute because he's on country pace and I've just switched to New York pace. My flight leaves in twenty minutes and I really have to use the restroom. "We've got an object we need to check; it looks a little dubious (he pronounces the *dub* like *tub*). Also, I think you've got some liquid issues. I'm sure we can figure it all out," he smiles.

I rack my brain. I've never had trouble at any of the New York airports nor at any other. Uh-oh, I probably have a lot of liquids and I know what the sharp object is.

"I think you're looking for my longhorn belt buckle," I smile, unlike a terrorist.

"Oh, that sounds 'bout right. Let me just git a good look here," he says, while unzipping my bag. My underwear and jeans fall out. I've got to stop overstuffing my fancy roller bag.

"Kinda full," I say, and laugh half-heartedly.

"Oh," he manages, and tries not to look. He uncomfortably sets my "Cowboys Only" underwear aside. Why did I even bring those? What are they doing in there? I grab them and stuff them into the top pocket of my lucky green jacket. "Yep, it was the belt buckle all right," he laughs, holding it up. "And a cool one at that. You know, my cousin has a buckle a little like this. I'm takin' my kids to see him and the Butter Cow at the state fair next week."

"I love our state fair!" I can't stop myself. "We just went to Tractor Days—did you happen to go to that?"

"Yeah, we did. My wife's parents live not far from the fairgrounds. The Jeffreys."

"No kidding, the Jeffreys? They have a great big coon hound!"

"That's the ones. Small little town, huh?"

"You must be married to Tessa's oldest sister, then." I smile.

"That's right." He looks pleased I put it all together. "Tessa's getting married next weekend, in fact. Is she younger than you?" Yes, okay, back to the bag, mister. "So anyway, this here's okay, just a buckle, now let me git a look at the liquids." I have to go to the bathroom and he's talking slower than an ice wagon, but he's so nice and I know the Jeffrey family, so I can't help but tell him how lovely they are. (I leave out the part about Tessa being a slut.) This could go on for hours.

He tells me all the rules and regulations on liquids that New York obviously doesn't care about. (Not feeling so safe about *those* airports now.) He sighs loudly and holds up my body wash and sunscreen. I'm going to pee my pants. "I'm so sorry to have to do this. Now, I'm going to give you a Ziploc for your smaller thangs but you're gonna have to throw these."

But he whispers that because I know the Jeffreys, I can keep one. He must be a fan of Rule #8.

Oh, and for the record, he's going to tell his wife, and his wife is going to tell her sister, Tessa, and Tessa's going to tell her mom, and her mom's going to tell Minnie that I have a pair of "Cowboys Only" G-string underwear. It'll be the talk of Tessa's wedding. That and the fact that she slept with the groom's best man in high school.

Chapter 34
LIZA'S LIES

BACK AT my apartment, I immediately greet Harold, who's doing a show-off lap around his stiletto and looking quite healthy. (For the record, Bette took care of him this time. And he looked happy in every picture she texted me, and in each shot she included the current day's paper!) I check my voicemail while feeding him some fish flakes.

Syd, it's Logan, there was another incident, call me.

Hi there Sydney, it's Evenlyn, Tray's Mom, I'm really worried. Call me, please. Thanks bunches.

Sydney, it's Gavin McKnight. I'm going to be in town this weekend, let's get together. Give me a buzz!

I call Logan immediately. He informs me that things are worse than we imagined; Tray's been lying to us. We didn't think he was using anymore. He is, and to top it off, he lied about how much he was using in the first place. He told us he dabbled once every couple of months and that it would be a snap to quit. As it turns out he's been using almost every day. My heart sinks. Logan puts Tray on the phone so he can run to the gallery.

"So you heard?" Tray says.

"Hey there, mister. How are you?" I say, feeling defeated.

"Not good, Sydney girl, not good. I think I need to go away," he says, sullenly.

"You're right and a rehab facility will be really good for you, Tray. I'm so glad to hear you say that," I encourage.

"I think I need to stay with you and Logan until I leave. I know I'll go out and find trouble if I don't."

"Sure, no prob. I just got home."

"I'm going to stay with Logan tonight, but I need to stay with you tomorrow," he says quietly, sounding beaten.

"Okay. Should we plan with your parents?"

"Yes, go ahead. Aaah. This is horrible!" he says, dramatically. That sounds a lot more like his old self.

"No, this is good. You're going to come back stronger and ready to dress all of Broadway. Come on, you can do this! You're Liza, for crying in the mud!" But as I play cheerleader, truly scary thoughts swirl in my head. He is going to get through this, isn't he?

"You're right, Elizabeth, I can do this," he says and sings, not a Broadway show tune, but Britney Spears' "Stronger." Well said. He *is* going to get through this. I join in. And then we're scream-singing and laughing.

I settle in at the apartment, changing into my comfy dragon kimono (sans the tail), and wrap my hair into my thinking cap-turban. I add to my vision board and study it, focus on my intention, and plan for the week ahead. I still feel positive about the board, even after removing the business card for **Bubba & Bubba Vet Care Clinic, Goodtown, TX**. After all, so many amazing things have come true. I mean, just look at the pair of Christian Louboutins I put on the board that are now in my closet. (They're totally not in the closet. I'm displaying them on one of the windowsills in the bedroom! Obv.) So, career woman, here I come! My LinkedIn page is up, resumes have gone out, and I even printed one just to tack on the board. (When people come over, though, I'll turn it over. I pasted Audrey Hepburn's famous *Breakfast at Tiffany's* photo to the back. I don't need everyone reading my reso. Gah.)

"Hi, Syd, how's Tray?" Logan asks, calling early the next morning and while I'm setting up for a fitness class.

"Well, he seemed okay yesterday but really down. How is he right now?" I ask, getting my music ready.

"What do you mean right now? Wouldn't you know that?" he responds quickly.

"He's at your place, so, no," I say, confused.

"He said he was staying with you," he blurts.

"He said he was staying with you," I yell.

"Son of a bitch."

I drop my phone.

I pick it up and throw it into my gym bag.

"Olivia, can you help?" I plead, hurrying over to the corner of the room where she's rolling out her designer mat. I hand her my iPad full of playlists and give her a look that she reads immediately.

"Of course, honey, go," she says, and I run out of the room. I know she'll jump into action and get the class covered. She knows exactly how to handle emergencies even when she doesn't know what they are.

Logan and I meet in front of Tray's apartment building again. We bang on his door until we hear him moving around. There's another menu outside his door and I crumple it and hide it in my hand so he doesn't have another episode with "menu messages." Logan pounds louder and threatens to break the lock again.

"Okay, okay, just give me a minute," he yells. A few moments later he opens the door. "Why are you two here?"

"Because you're killing yourself," Logan screams and pushes into the apartment.

"I'm fine. I'm fine! Leave me alone," Tray says, following. Then he steps in front of us so we don't move behind the Thai changing screen.

"Tray, you're not fine," I say, staring at a friend I hardly recognize. He has lost weight and not in a good way. He steps backward as we move closer, inching him toward the bed, where we see what we thought we'd find. Drugs and paraphernalia on the bedside table.

"You need help," Logan says, aghast.

"*You* need help," Tray spits back at him.

"Tray, you can't do this anymore," Logan yells.

My head is spinning. I've never seen Tray so spiteful, and I can't wrap my mind around why, when everything is going right for him, he seems to be deteriorating and throwing it all away. "You really need help, Tray," I repeat softly, trying to calm both of them.

"I don't need help!" he screams and pushes me. I stumble backward and Logan catches me.

"This is ridiculous," Logan says, in shock.

"It *is* ridiculous. And you're both ridiculous for coming here. Just leave! And leave me alone!" he yells. I've reached my limit. I regain my balance and throw the crumpled menu at him, hitting him square between the eyes. Stunned, he stumbles backward onto the bed.

"You need help, Tray. You're destroying yourself, your talent, and your life," I say, somberly and sternly.

"I'm calling," Logan says, taking his phone out of his back pocket. He dials Tray's parents.

"I won't go," he screams, over and over again as I try to calm him. Logan moves into the kitchen, leaning on the beautiful island that's covered in alcohol bottles and trash.

When Tray takes a breath I say, "Yes, you will. You'll go."

"I won't! You two are terrible!" he blasts, nearly frothing at the mouth.

"Tray, you have to go," I say again. He starts crying and knocks everything off of his bedside table.

"I took all of your money!" he screams, and falls into a ball on the floor.

"What are you talking about?" I ask, trying to console him. *Trying* to make sense of what's happening.

"I took it all!" he yells. Snot bubbles from his nose as tears pour from his blood-shot eyes.

"It's okay, Tray. It's okay. It's going to be okay."

Within minutes, his parents have a sponsor at the door to pick him up. Tray isn't in the proper state of mind for goodbyes. He's angry about leaving and yet, somehow, in the end, willing to go. Somewhere far back in the recesses of his mind, he must know he's killing himself.

Two months without Tray singing me show tunes, eating all of my olives, and always making me feel beautiful even when I'm a disaster is going to be hard. I hate him for doing drugs. I hate the drugs for making him dependent, and I hate that he was going through the pain of addiction without talking to me about it. A feeling that I can only describe as homesickness climbs into my heart as his car drives away.

My phone blings as I walk back to my apartment. I don't even look at it. I'm not feeling up to talking to anyone.

Chapter 35
MARRY THAT GIRL

ONLY A few days later, I hear from Gavin McKnight. I vaguely remember hearing his voicemail when I got back from Butter. But so much has happened that I haven't caught up on voicemails and I totally forgot to call him.

Putting my resume on the board worked! Although I was still feeling terrible about Tray's situation, I got an extremely exciting email from the firm Stage Presence, known for marketing the biggest shows on Broadway and beyond. They want me to work with them! It's bittersweet not having Tray here to celebrate but he was there in spirit. Apparently Holly and Jan, her partner (you know, the sourpuss) gave a glowing review of my "talents" and frankly, wouldn't work with the firm if I wasn't on the team. They said I knew the cast intimately (working with them to fit the costumes was a big deal for the two) and knew the costumes in and out (I've literally been in and out of them), and they want someone on the firm's team that has their back. (Something tells me Holly has more up her sleeve, what with her being my "representative" and all.) The production is going to be one of the firm's biggest accounts to date and, without even knowing, I helped get them the client! They're a multimedia-based team and I'm pumped. I start next week!

Gavin is in town and wants me to a join him at a party at the Standard. I gingerly agree to go because why not celebrate? Tray's safe now, I'm feeling great about working with a marketing team, and I always laugh with Gavin. I could use a good laugh. I put on a sleek pair of tight black Rag & Bone jeans that almost pass as leather and zip at the ankle, highlighting my Christian Louboutins, and a silk spaghetti strap top. And grab my glitzy Lulu Guinness lips clutch for sparkle. Casual but cool. I hail a cab and gracefully step in with my red soles. We're meeting at a little restaurant around the corner before hitting the Standard, and I give the driver the address.

"Do you know how close you are?" the driver asks. "And it's actually closer if you walk because I have to go around the block," she says, turning and looking at me.

"Of course, but did you see my...Louboutins," I wink, leaning back and lifting my heel into view. (Thank you, yoga.)

"Those are some good-lookin' heels," she says, giving me a thumbs-up.

"Right? Now, we all know these aren't for walking, so away we go!" I laugh. Heels happy, here I go. Back out there. She steps on the gas and zips forward across Seventh Avenue and turns right twice and squeals to a halt in front of Waverly Inn. It really is disgustingly close to my apartment. My Butter girlfriends are going to crack up and, of course, make fun of me when I tell them I took a cab a couple blocks because of heels. (The Sirens will totally understand.)

Gavin is, as always, witty and charming and his friends are amusing to be around. And they all seem to be "somebody." When Gavin announces I've landed a gig marketing the newest Broadway show, they all go nuts. I tell them all about the unbelievable costumes that are going to be the talk of the town, not to mention the writing and actors, and suddenly I'm bombarded with people who want tickets. They all want to be the first to see it. Being first, it seems, is a prerequisite for this crowd. I need to get in front of the team and enlist all these "somebodys" for the premiere! (Let's make some buzz!) Gavin winks at me. He knew this would happen and he's just helped my career tremendously.

He leans over. "Now will you let me into the bar?" he asks. And I laugh out loud. I wouldn't let him come to the bar while bartending, but now he's got a personal invite. I'll probably have to start doing marketing for the bar too when he shows up! (Wait, that's not such a bad idea.)

When we arrive at the party at The Top of the Standard it's lively and happening with a three-piece band decorating the top of the circular bar. We move between tables and secret rooms with ease, and for a moment I feel "back at home" in the crowd. Peering behind the band reveals a bartender with a handlebar mustache and big grin. Pete sends Gavin and me a free drink.

"You know everybody," Gavin smiles and leans in to kiss me. Just for a second, as our lips touch, guilt sweeps into my stomach and a deep unsettling feeling of loneliness gushes over me. I smile and play it off as the band starts another rousing song.

Realizing my carriage is about to turn into a pumpkin in front of everyone when we rejoin the group, I excuse myself to the restroom and sneak out, utilizing the Irish goodbye. I just don't know how I feel.

I buzz Elan because I have no idea where my keys are. I could swear I put them in my lip-shaped clutch. Wait, maybe they didn't fit. Elan, a genius with a stratospheric IQ score and a dry sense of humor, buzzes me in and opens his door, wide awake and with vigor before I even have a chance to knock. Odd.

"Sydney, where have you been? I knocked on your door at eleven— that was hours ago. I called, left voicemails, and sent texts. I wanted to go for a drink! I need some advice," he says hurriedly, his eyeballs nearly popping out of his head and touching the rim of his overly large spectacles. He pulls me into the apartment. Elan is really awake, overly anxious, and drinking a beer. Elan never drinks beer.

"Oh, I haven't checked my voicemail in forever and I didn't see the texts. Sorry," I say, half yawning. I walk by him and head sleepily toward his kitchen drawer, pull out a knife, and head toward the window in his bedroom.

I feel him following at my heels. "Elan, it's two in the morning—what are you doing up and with a beer?" I ask without turning around. I get my body halfway out the large window and he pulls me back in.

"Syd, wait." He nudges me into the living room and sits me on his stiff couch. "Have a beer!" He runs to the fridge and comes back with a high-end beer that I don't recognize. He fiddles with a fancy bottle opener, hopelessly unfamiliar with it. "I think I love Lydia," he says wildly, flinging the beer cap off across the room. Is it just me or is he a little manic right now?

I recognize the symptoms because Minnie has them often. WebMD describes them as euphoria, excessive talking, racing thoughts, unusual energy, less need for sleep, and impulsiveness. I describe them as charming, delightful, and the most interesting mom in town. It seems Elan is less neurologist and more Barnum and Bailey right now, which is actually an improvement on his usual buttoned-up self.

"And?" I prod.

"And what if I marry her?" he says, handing me the beer and throwing back a swig of his own. I set my clutch and the knife on a stack of indecipherable papers lying on the couch, which is as hard as a table. This could take a minute.

"Well, she's certainly cute, and very forgiving after I swung a knife at her. I like her. Why wouldn't you marry her?" I say, and take a sip of the mystery beer.

Barf.

The beer. Not the possible proposal. But how many weddings do I have to deal with while my love life flails about?

Omigod, it's just my love life. Not my life in general! I'm starting a career next week. I take another swig, feeling better. I'm starting a career!

I make a face; this beer tastes like moths. Doesn't he have a PBR or something normal? He downs the rest of his beer and goes to get another one.

"She's Muslim and I'm Jewish," he yells with his head in the fridge.

"And?"

"And my parents don't love the idea for obvious reasons," he says, bounding back into the room and struggling again with the opener. I set my drink down on the coffee table, also covered in indecipherable papers. I take the beer from his hand, open it on the button of my jeans, and hand it back. "How did you do that? I want to learn how to do that! Should I marry her?" he says, standing above me as I pick up my beer.

"Do you love her?"

"Yes!" His eyes look even wilder. I take another sip of the malty moth and cringe. (From the aftertaste, not the marriage—jeez, I'm not that bad off.) I look up at him.

"Will you promise to comfort, honor, and keep her for better or worse?" I ask, taking a long sip.

"Yes," he says, and begins to pace. Maybe it isn't so bad. The beer.

"For richer or for poor?" I raise an eyebrow.

"Yes," he says quickly.

"Well, that doesn't count. You're going to be a richy-rich neurosurgeon doctor-man." I take a gulp...what the hell, maybe it's not so mothy after all. "So, in sickness and in health? And forsaking all others and be faithful only to her? Forever?" I stare at him, seriously.

"Yes, oh yes, I love her," he says, raising his arms in excitement. He spills beer all down his button-down and pressed pants. I don't think Elan owns casual wear.

"Then marry that girl!" I raise my beer.

"I should, shouldn't I?" he says, grinning from ear to ear.

"Yep."

"Did you just say marriage vows by heart, Syd?"

"Yep." One million weddings and counting.

"And I said yes!"

"Yep."

"But what about my parents?" he asks, a worried look replacing his grin.

"Elan, you're in your early thirties, right?"

"Thirty-three."

"And you went to the same college as you mother and father?"

"Harvard."

"And you became a neurologist because your father is one?"

"Dr. Ismere. He's had his own practice for thirty-nine years."

"And you live in New York City, because they do?"

"Yes, though I would quite like Wyoming."

"What? Wyoming? Nevermind, the point is, if you're always trying to make them happy, what will ever make *you* happy?"

"Lydia."

"Marry her."

"Holy shit, you're right," he yells. Holy...Elan just swore. I sip the mothy beer. "You're a genius!" He hugs me with his long, lanky arms and beer-soaked shirt, pulling me off the couch. He jumps around. I can't help but laugh. I'm happy for Elan and Lydia, though I may need to wave a knife again if he tells his parents I had something to do with the engagement. I grab my clutch and the knife and once again head to the window in his bedroom.

"Syd, you're the freest spirit I've ever met. You always do just what you want," he says, leaning his head out the window. I turn back to him and clink his beer with mine.

"A free spirit who may actually have her life on the right path for once." I smile. I actually might. "Good night, Elan." I tip down the fire escape in my heels.

"Good night, Syd. Syd?" he says, again.

"Yes?" I look up.

"I've always been told where my life is going. This will be the first big decision I've ever made for myself," he says. He looks serene.

"Then it's the right one," I smile, and nearly trip on the next step because I'm wearing my uber-high Louboutins, and looking up at Elan and not at the stupid fire escape. I spill a big gulp of beer.

"Thanks, Syd. You're amazing!" he shouts and pulls himself inside, smacking the back of his head on the frame. I don't think he even felt it. I flash a huge smile that warms my whole face.

Elan thinks I'm amazing.

I *am* amazing!

"You're an idiot!" a woman yells up at me. Well, that didn't last long. I look down and realize my beer spilled right on her white jacket.

"Oops, sorry!" I shout and flop into my gaping window. Oh yeah, I left that open. I feel bad about the jacket, but she didn't need to call me an idiot. She's not supposed to wear white after Labor Day anyway.

I lie in bed on top of the covers, place my red soles on the stack of novels, and think about Elan and Lydia and how delicate relationships are. You can lose love over religion, where you live, what you do, money, and something as basic as timing. Timing seems to hold a very fragile key. (Well, that and tequila.)

I go over all the men I have ever fallen for, the embarrassing moments (of which there are many), and all the wonderful moments (of which there are even more but I didn't pay enough attention to at the time). And then I go over how I screwed up all those moments…or didn't. It doesn't matter because I feel lost. Somehow I have my life in better shape than I ever have before, and yet I also feel more scared than I've ever felt before. I feel lost, or scared, or both. I don't know how I feel. Tears begin slowly rolling down my cheeks, and I give in to a heart-wrenching cry that I haven't let out in years.

I shift off the bed, tears now streaming down my face in an unstoppable flood, and move into the bathroom, stepping into the empty tub, still in my clothes, and curl into it. And cry. Quietly. To myself.

I make it back to my bed after what seems like an hour in the protected space of the bathroom and the comfort of the cold porcelain.

NEW YORK CITY: TODAY, SATURDAY, SEPTEMBER 9

I wake up in a mess of covers and pillows and wearing my Christian Louboutins. One Eye Joe was right; all I had to do was put them back on and...happy. Well, that and falling asleep to *Some Like It Hot* starring Marilyn Monroe, Tony Curtis, and Jack Lemmon. My phone is blinking with voicemails and text messages. I look at the last call at 3:14 a.m. Gavin. Probably trying to figure out where I went. And I'm pretty sure that's a booty call.

Syd, you little minx, I'll figure you out yet! (Omigod, he's oozing charm right through the phone!) *I'm boarding my flight in two hours, then I'll be back on set. Try to reach me soon, okay, babe?*

I panic and hit delete, which accidently wipes out all the other calls. Aargh! How? I just erased a week's worth of voicemails! The phone blings and, just as panicked, I hit "Talk." Without saying hello, I hear, "What's wrong with you?"

The Sister.

"Um, I don't know?" Does she know I had a meltdown last night?

"Well, I woke up thinking about you."

What? And just when I think The Sister doesn't care, she calls because she must know I had a rough night. I always knew we were connected. I'm sure she wants to give me a pep talk.

"So, I was thinking about my graduation party." Nevermind. "Remember, you're throwing it!" she says, and she begins itemizing the long list of details, getting more and more elated and specific as she goes.

Maybe originally it was because she wanted to remind me to throw her a graduation party, but she did say I was really good at throwing parties, which is totally true and a compliment, so, a pep talk all the same!

"Have a good day, Syd. And try not to think about how you're not graduating from medical school or engaged like me. It's okay. Bye!" She clicks off the line.

Almost.

I jump out of bed and feed Harold, who seems relieved I gave up blubbering, and stare at my vision board. I'm traveling again, I'm starting a new career, and I even tried to skydive with plans to try and check that off again soon. And I've started saving money! I have so much to feel good about. So what if I'm not married, or even close. I never really felt that much pressure to get married until I put it on myself, and what does an eleven-year-old kid know anyway? (Well, she did know how to save money.)

I can't wait to tell the Sirens all the good news! I look in the mirror at my swollen eyes and decide to refresh myself with a shower and ice cubes for the puffiness. No sense letting on that I had a breakdown about my life last night. And I certainly can't bartend looking like this!

Putting goals and dreams on a vision board really does work. Out of the shower and already feeling better, I tack a picture of the Butter crew at the Tractor Days Parade on the board to remind me of who I am and who I've always been.

Chapter 36
WEDDING BELLS

"SYD, YOU'VE got *The New York Times* on line three and I've had more calls for tickets today than ever!" a coworker says, tossing me a pen. I can never find a pen. Everyone in the lofted, open office space of Stage Presence cheers. The show officially opens one month from today and pre-sales have skyrocketed! It didn't hurt that Gavin helped me get all those big names for the premiere, *and* I proposed a social strategy that took off. (Of course I did. I've got moxie!)

Gavin won't actually be able to make it, though, because he's doing some sort of "helicopter" scene that week. He'll probably be dangling from it, or so Bette says. She's been keeping up with all the internet spoilers. But I'm almost a little relieved he's not coming. I still don't know how I feel about all that stuff. Better I just stick to work. And Holly and Jan couldn't be happier with my focus the past four weeks and that we're all working together. Even Jan, the sourpuss, is wearing a smile. And I couldn't be happier that

Tray will make it to the premiere! His costumes are a big reason the show is getting so much press, and I know he'll be thrilled. Though I haven't heard from him, his mom says his release date coincides with the opening, and we're saving him a seat!

My schedule is more than busy but my "secret" savings account is really benefitting. Between working for the firm during the week, teaching a few of my favorite fitness classes in the mornings, and bartending on the weekends, I'm paying rent in advance. (A little thank you to One Eye Joe for making me feel so wonderful when I was low.) Happiness is a pay-it-forward feeling. Pass it on! Remember those who brighten your day, like my favorite, skinny, graying homeless man, and brighten theirs and others. (PS, I bought him a ticket!)

Bette should be here any minute for wine and gossip and, in her words, "some big news." I wonder if she got her exam results early? It's been an unbelievable week and it's only Thursday. We still have Claudia's wedding this weekend!

Bette bounds into the apartment in a maxi dress that's hugging every curve and squeezes me hard. I mean, really hard. I pour two glasses of Pinot Grigio (the only bottle left from The Sister defense system) while she settles across from me at the kitchen bar on a Toledo stool setting her "Neverfull" Louis on the floor. I hand her a glass and pull a stool around for myself as she wrangles her reddish-brown curls into her emergency hair clip that's perpetually attached to the bag's handle.

"Syd, I want you to sing," she says, a bit giddy.

"What? Okay," I say hesitantly. "What do you want me to sing?" I crinkle my nose. It's not such an odd request— we sing all the time—but it's just usually at a Japanese karaoke bar. And I thought she said she had big news; what are we doing singing?

"Something for a wedding," she says, and looks at me expectantly.

"Like the song for Claudia's wedding this weekend?" I ask.

"I was thinking something a little more my style," she says and lifts her glass, putting a very shiny diamond in my face.

"What!" I scream.

"I'm engaged! Derek asked after our shift on Saturday," she blasts. "He tried to wait until after Claudia's wedding, but when I came home from the bar he was wide awake, overly anxious, and drinking!" Uh, did Derek and Elan talk? "And then, well, he just spit it out! Everything he's… we've been feeling and asked!"

"What? This is insane! I'm so excited for you," I scream, again. And I really, really am. One million and two weddings and all.

"Me too! I know it seems quick but Derek and I just know. It just feels…" She looks at the ceiling searching for the right word.

"Like home," I say, quietly but sure.

"Yes. That's the perfect description," she says, and I smile knowingly. "I want you to help me with everything."

"Of course!" We jump out of our stools and dance around the room, hugging and screaming.

"We're going to be engaged for at least a year because this is all so sudden. And Derek knows I have to pass the bar before I go down the aisle."

"Omigod, that's what I thought the big news was, your exam results!" I laugh. "But anyway, you've already passed," I say, encouragingly. She tells me the results won't be released until November typically, but I know she aced it. No one studied more than Bette. I don't think it would be physically possible to study more than she did!

"Thanks, Syd. Omigod, this is it!" she squeals and sends a quick text while I bask in her happiness. "So we tried to wait and tell everyone until after Claudia's wedding, but—" My door buzzer shrills and I look at Bette; she lifts her Rock eyebrow and I run to the intercom.

"Who is it?" I ask.

"Buzz me in, bitches!" Gus wails into the speaker.

"Gus pried it out of me," Bette screams. "She's been waiting downstairs so I could tell you!"

Gus swoops in with an overly large, dramatic scarf and puts Dionne down to run amok in my apartment. As usual, Dee goes straight into the bedroom, jumps on the bed, looks right at Harold, and starts barking her head off as we all scream. Gus puts a bottle of red onto the counter and squeezes us both. "Isn't this amazing?" Gus starts crying. "I am so happy! Dee, shut up!"

"I knew they'd be perfect together!" I yell.

"Me too!" Gus screams.

"Me too!" Bette shouts.

"No," Gus says, shaking her head.

"No," I say, shaking mine.

"No, you didn't. We did," Gus says and Bette cracks up. Dionne barks wildly out of control while we scream and cry. I suspect Harold's hiding in his stiletto imagining Armageddon.

We pour a glass of red for Gus and spend the next hour planning a destination wedding. Discussing the dress, the colors, music, and anything three Sirens can think of. Gus and I make jokes that we'll be going to a second Siren wedding before we even have boyfriends.

"Speaking of boyfriends, though, I met this guy," Gus says casually. She moves the scarf a bit and pulls down the neck of her shirt, revealing a patch. A nicotine patch.

"Spill it," I urge.

"He's so talented. He's kind of ugly in a really hot way and plays guitar. And he's encouraging me to quit smoking." She gestures back to the patch, and Bette and I look at each other. We've been encouraging her forever. "And he's an actor! So he totally pushes me to go to auditions. He actually got me a really big one tomorrow and he's going to watch Dee," she explains, while refilling our glasses.

"Is this the guy from acting class? Jeff or Jack or something like that?" Bette asks.

"Yeah, Jason. How'd you know?" Gus replies.

"Because you started dropping his name two weeks ago, and I remembered it was a "J" name. Did you already sleep with him?" Bette says, as if Gus is in an interrogation room.

"Yes, but…" Gus starts.

"Gus!" Bette and I shout.

"He's the most caring man ever! I even let him stay the whole night."

"Gus!" we shout again.

"What, you guys? I had to—he played guitar for me. It was so hot. But," she smugly sips her wine, "I used protection." I drop my head to the countertop.

"You're always supposed to use protection! He's a new partner," Bette groans.

"No, not always. Not when I know the guy," Gus says. "But now, I'm going to use it either way. I went to Abby's gyno, who is super fabulous by the way, and she says I should always use protection. No matter what."

"*I've* always said that!" Bette cries.

Gus glosses right over her declaration and says, "I need to be careful about getting pregnant. The whole thing with Abby scared the bajeezus out of me."

"What about STDs?" Bette yells, finally throwing up her arms.

"Oh, I've only been with like a few guys since my last ex and, duh, I knew them all," Gus smiles, grossly under-exaggerating. "Plus the gyno says I'm fine."

"Only you, Gus, only you." Bette flares her nostrils and takes a drink. "The one time I didn't use protection, well, we all know what happened." We do. Bette was so pissed she wouldn't serve men at the bar for a week. Dionne starts barking again, and I take it as an opportunity to check on

Harold and bring Dee into the living room for some much needed attention.

"Oh, I should have brought a wee-wee pad," Gus says, following me and noticing piddle near the French doors, near the bed, and near the toilet. "Let's just put down paper towels or something." Dee has a tendency to pee when excited and well, we *were* jumping around. Gus comes back and grabs the whole roll of paper towels to do a quick clean-up.

"Unbelivable," Bette whispers to me while she's in the other room. "How did she miss Sex Ed!" We start laughing.

"I hear you guys!" Gus yells. "I missed Sex Ed because I was making out under the bleachers. Baahaa!" Bette's about to have a heart attack. "I promise to use protection from here on out. Not just because I can get pregnant but also because I need to protect myself. Is that better, you crazies?" She walks back into the room crossing her heart.

"Your body is a temple," I say majestically. I remember saying that to Tray after therapy. I should have noticed he was losing weight. I should have noticed he was doing drugs. I try to wipe those thoughts from my mind. We did notice and got him to a great rehab clinic. It's just I feel guilty I didn't catch it sooner.

We cheer to this and gossip more about the ugly-hot guy and her audition. Bette, needing to check off some boxes on the spreadsheet in her head, asks about Ryan from the auto show, and Gus divulges that she still texts him late at night. And he's still in the running if ugly-hot doesn't work out. Then they very carefully bring up the subject of Tuff.

"Syd, I don't know how these things happen to you." Bette shakes her head. "I can't believe you end up in the toilet on the one night you're out with your perfect man."

"And while in costume, don't forget." I shake my head. Somehow, even after all this time, it *still* feels a bit raw. Bette snorts and Gus holds back laughter.

"Come on, it *is* kind of funny, you have to admit," Bette says. I fight back a small smile.

"What's the big deal anyway? I don't get it. You're hot. So what? You threw up," Gus says, and it totally makes sense for about two seconds. You've got to love your best friends.

"He probably thinks I'm a raging lunatic drunk that crashes weddings and gets carried (or dragged!) out of bars all the time," I laugh. Ugh, he probably does. My stomach lurches at the thought.

"Well, it didn't help that we had Beef carry you out," Bette adds.

"And cheers to that. Imagine if he saw me hugging the toilet bowl in fairy wings—kill!" I hold up my glass, Bette clinks it with hers, and I sip.

"Oh, I have a pic of that too!" Bette smiles. I spit out my drink.

Omigod.

"That's nothing'. He should see you stage dive," Gus laughs.

"Gus. You're not making me sound any better," I whimper. That makes 'lunatic drunk' sound like it could be true. (But I do that sober!)

"Whatever, you're fabulous. His loss. Speaking of fabulous; how's Gavin?" Bette asks.

"What?" I respond, my mind on tinker tampering and toilet bowls.

"I can't believe he happened to text that night. And if I remember correctly, it was pretty heavy."

I shoot my eyes to Bette. "I completely forgot! You don't think Tuff saw that, do you?"

"Uh-oh," Bette mutters, quietly.

"Uh-oh," I repeat just as quietly. My thoughts swirl, but he couldn't have seen that. Could he? And anyway, it's too late. It's just too late.

"I think we need martinis!" Gus opens the freezer. "Heavy on the vodka…"

"And a little bit dirty!" Bette and I finish.

Bette gushes more about dreamy wedding ideas and Gus follows Dee around, cleaning up pee as I bubble about work.

Then I remember. "Omigod, Gus. Bette, I almost forgot to tell her," I say, and dive into the details of the fear-conquering TV spot taking place after Claudia's wedding.

Chapter 37
COWBOYS ONLY

CLAUDIA'S WEDDING is just hours away! Well, six hours to be exact, but it feels like two as I run last-minute errands. My handpicked dress is hanging on the French doors between my bedroom and living room with my Christian Louboutins perched below, ready to go. In true Siren form, we told Claudia we'd wear whatever she wanted. After all, it's her big day. Claudia chose each dress with care, and they're perfectly fit to our personalities. (She chose mine from Alice and Olivia and I couldn't love it more!)

Jose is cleaning the sidewalk and I yell hello to him and wave to the guys in the kitchen.

"Morning, *linda*," he says and puts his broom down. "UPS left a package with us for you."

"A package?" I swear I didn't order anything.

The kitchen guys wave at me again as he grabs the package. They were always sweet to me before the Tinker

Bell incident but now they're absolutely syrupy, which just confirms my suspicions. They so saw my ass!

I take the package. "Thanks, Jose. See you later," I say with a smile.

Bloomingdale's? I swear I didn't order anything. I tiptoe through the suds to my door as well as I can in my cowboys, an LBD by Free People, and a bright comfy scarf to welcome in fall while carrying a few items for the wedding. (I was out of mascara!) I realize I haven't checked my mail in weeks and decide it is time to face the music. I open the age-old mailbox and three junk mail magazines fall into my hand. It's stuffed like a gourd. I fight to pull out each envelope. Bill, bill, coupon, baby announcement from Penny! She said she was sending me one—so cute! Bill, savings account update, and omigod, a letter from Tray!

I grab the remaining junk mail and run upstairs. I set the package down on the entryway table, throw all the bills on my big chair, and put Penny's adorable baby boy on the fridge. Then I run into the bedroom, flop down on the bed, and rip open Tray's letter.

Dearest Sydney, CHECK YOUR MAIL!((((((((((((((((((
(Cleary, he loves exclamation points as much as I do. And he's right, I should have checked my mail sooner!)

Hi!!!!! How's my Sydney! Okay, well, I wasn't doing so great, but now I'm doing really good! I tried to call but it's hard because we only have access to ONE phone and only ONCE in a blue moon. It's RIDICULUS! (Omigod, his spelling.) They'll read this before it goes out...I need a phone! RIDICULUS! (I'm going to have to spell check.) I wanted to tell you on the phone how sorry I am for pushing you. I feel so terrible. Please, please, Syd, accept my apology! And answer the phone! I know you're not answering because it's coming from a "PRIVATE" caller. But it's me! ANSWER!!!

I've been in therapy and taking classes. And it's been really wonderful but really hard. Okay, sob story, blah, blah, enough...I promise I'm getting better! And I can admit now, sober, that I stole from you. you didn't misplase any money. I took it all. (It *was* him.) I cannot believe I did that! (I can't either!) I'm truly sorry and I wasn't in my right mind. I knew you would be okay. you were okay. Right? (No.) But, you weren't. I'm sorry. ANSWER THE PHONE!

I'm so proud of everything you've done. Mom has kept me updated on the costumes and all the press and I can't thank you enough. (I'm crying now!) The premiere is going to be amazing. I can't wait to go to with you! I'm so nervous!

Okay, but Syd, on another note (I just made a joke because I'm going to talk about Broadway songs!), I've had to sing my favorite Broadway show tunes from memory because they don't have internat (rat pooping Stone Age over here!) or sheet music! Aaah! And you know how bad I am with the words to songs. Aaah and SPELLING!!! Do

NOT spell check me, Syd! (Oops) So, all I can remember from CHICAGO is:

Come on babe, why don't we run the town

AND ALL THAT JAZZ!

I'm going to rouge my lips and pull my stockings down (that doesn't sound right does it? Too slutty?)

AND ALL THAT JAZZ!!

Something - something, I know a woopy spot (speaking of, there are a few cute boys here)

where the Gin is cold (I'll probably get in trouble for writing that...but I'm here for DRUG ADDICTION, people! NOT ALCOHOLISM! They say they're related.)

But the pianos hot!

It's just an all-boys hall (I know that's not right but it sounds too good!)

where there's a nightly call? brawl?

AND ALL THAT JAZZ! (I'm really good at that part! well, you know.)

So some of that doesn't seem right. Does it? well, you make up words to songs too...don't lie! (we all remember HAIR our sophomore year!) withdrawl from show tunes has been harder than withdrawl from drugs. Please have tons of songs ready when I get back and we'll sing, sing, SING!

Sydney, I promise to be a better caretaker for Harry (It's HAROLD!) from now on. I've also vowed to get a fish when I get back and learn to love and care for it. They think it's a good idea to be responsible for another living being. And Syd, you know how I feel about dogs, so a fish is perfect. Remember my ep had a dog. I wanted to murder him in his sleep, then get rid of that dog! That poodle was always trying to destroy my costumes, the little monster! And remember the fluff ball always woke me up at 5 in the morning? Until I started feeding him chocolate. I can't believe I had to spend that much money on a dog. Who knew dogs were allergic to chocolate? Anyway, a fish is perfect!

Anyhooooo, I miss you!!! I promise to pay you back! Please forgive me. Please?! I'll dieeeeee. I'll pay you back! Anyway, I'm so epcited to come home and show you all my progress! I'm so thankful to have you as my a friend and to have all your support. (If you forgive me for pushing you and stealing! Omigod!)

LOVE you!!!!!
Tray

This is all such good news! And of course I forgive him. I would have given him the money if he'd just asked, even with the extra work. Then at least I wouldn't have felt like I was losing my mind or so irresponsible. This is a huge relief! And he really is terrible at spelling. Thank goodness he's a costume designer.

"Harold! Tray's doing well and wants to get a fish when he gets back," I yell. Harold darts into his stiletto. "Yeah, maybe you're right, probably not the best idea. Okay, but we have to be encouraging," I say and float fish flakes on the top of his water. He slowly comes out. I hear my phone chime and check the text. It's from Gus.

Gus: Siren Alert!!! I have been cast as the "lady" in a National Commercial! It isn't official so don't tell anyone, but my new man (the one who got me the audition, ugly-hot), knows the casting director and says it's already been decided!!! See you all tonight! AAAAH!!!

Siren replies:

Me: CONGRATULATIONS!!! This is insane-fabulous!!!

Zoey: Oh beeeeeautiful news!! (Just landed!)

Bette: Friggin' Fantastic!!! LOVE YOU! And love the ugly-hot guy for getting you the audition!

Abby: You are the BEST actress EVER!!!

Claudia: WTF I didn't know anything about this audition... AMAZING!!! More to celebrate tonight! (PS getting my hair done now! And I want you all in the pictures, so don't be LATE!! Besos, besos, besos!) Claudia attaches a picture of her crunching into an apple with huge Velcro rollers perched all over her head.

This day just keeps getting better!

I jump off the bed and return with the package marked Bloomingdale's. I open timidly. There's no way I bought anything. I put a stop to my "enthusiastic" online ordering, but this is clearly something.

A typed letter sits on top of the tissue. Attached is a 20% off coupon.

Dear Sydney Shag,

We received your concerned email and agree, no one should ever have a *Little Brown Bag* pop in their face. Please accept this letter with our sincere apologies. We look forward to your continued patronage as a valued customer.

Sincerely,

The Bloomingdale's Team

Then in a handwritten note below,

PS, We're glad you didn't find any gray hairs! We've included some shampoo and conditioner samples to keep it healthy and a sample of our favorite wrinkle cream (just in case). And we're giving your "Little" Brown Bag an upgrade.

Don't worry, Cinderella's prince didn't recognize her right away either. (smiley face)

Good Luck!

Elle & "The Bloomies"

(The Girls in the Bloomingdale's Breakroom)

First of all, what the *hell* did I say in that email? (Some serious TMI, obviously.) Then I remember I was drinking vodka (a third of a bottle), so that explains that. And, second, this is insane. Insanely awesome! I rip through the tissue to find a *Medium Brown Bag*, PVC (for durability!) tote printed in their signature block lettering. It's fabulous.

And inside I find a stash of even more fabulous samples of Bloomingdale's products.

The Bloomies are totally Siren worthy! I make a note to remove Bloomingdale's from all my banned shopping lists.

"This day just keeps getting better!" I hang my new tote by my dress for the wedding so I can admire it. Then I admire my dress again. "I'm going to wear this hot little number and have fun stag tonight, Harold!" I smile. But, all of a sudden, the memory of inviting Tuff to Claudia's wedding rushes back. I cringe.

I need to get some air.

"Want to go for a walk, Harold?" He wiggles his tail fin. That's a yes. I dig in my closet and find that old Louis Vuitton. Oh, what the hell. It's emptied of all the cash, invested now, and Harold's been with me longer than any boyfriend has; he deserves a Louis. I grab the scissors. (Before you go worrying about the state of my mental health, remember the Louis was a present from an ex and I've always known it was a knockoff. That's why it sits in the back of the closet.) I cut a large lookout hole in the side of the vinyl and place Harold in his new carrier.

I head downstairs slowly and steadily in my cowboys, my lucky green jacket, and bright comfy scarf because it's getting chilly. Harold needs a bigger tank, and we're going to go get one, right now. The Frou-Frou Pet Shop, only a few blocks away, will know exactly what he needs when they see him.

I've seen plenty of people out walking their dogs *and* cats. I've even seen parrots riding on shoulders, a lizard on an arm, and surprisingly a potbelly pig out for a stroll here in the city. But I've never seen a fish, so this may be a first. (Though it's New York City. I doubt it.)

Harold and I step out the door and take in the refreshing breeze of a perfect fall afternoon. Claudia's lucky to have such a beautiful day for her wedding. The leaves are starting to change and a few have fallen and are skipping down the block as we follow along.

My phone jingles several blings and I reach in my lucky green jacket's inside pocket and press "Talk."

"Hello," I say, rather chipper.

"Hello there, Miss Sydney." I freeze. Even though I've tried to wipe that accent from my memory, I know who it is.

"Tuff?" I barely say into the phone.

"Miss Sydney, I made a mistake."

"A mistake?" I say, breathlessly.

"Well, yes, didn't you get my voicemails? I've been stubborn not allowing you to explain, and I think I jumped to the wrong conclusion."

"What voicemails? And you did?"

"Sydney, we've all had a rough night now and again, right? And it's not like we ever said we were exclusive. I just thought… Well, it doesn't matter because I really care about you. I think that's why I've been afraid to, well, I told you this on the voicemails. I'm sure you've been upset with me too."

"Yes," I say, absentmindedly trying to remember any voicemails. What voicemails? Oh crap, I erased a whole bunch of voicemails after the epic cry. Crap. Double crap!

"You *are* upset with me, then?" he asks, his voice drops.

"What?" Upset with him? "Oh no, no, I'm not upset with you. Of course not. I was upset with myself. And what do you mean, exclusive?"

"I was pretty jealous after seeing the text message from that guy. I told you, I can be bullheaded sometimes. Stubborn to a fault. I think I mentioned that."

"What guy? Logan? Tray?" I laugh, then gulp as it hits me. "Wait, you mean Gavin?" Omigod, he *did* see that text.

"When I got you home, you somehow remembered to text Logan about Tray's light, which wasn't on, then you handed me your phone and passed out. I shouldn't have looked. I don't even know why I did. I'm sorry about that."

"This whole time, I didn't understand. I thought what I did was at the very least forgivable even if you never wanted to see me again." Stunned, I begin walking again as if in a trance.

I must have been silent for a while because he asks, "What are you doing?" My mind is all over the place. I look down at Harold. Omigod, how do I explain this one?

"Um, I'm walking Harold," I say, a bit muffled. Now I'm the trashed Tinker Bell who walks her fish. Great.

"Miss Sydney, did you say you're walking a fish?" he clarifies.

"Uh, yes. I mean, I'm on my way to get him that new fish tank we talked about." I continue to walk, only now wondering how foolish I look with a fish in a knockoff Louis Vuitton.

"Just where are you?" he asks. I've wandered down to Waverly near Morandi.

"Rounding the corner to Morandi. You know, the restaurant where we had—"

"Yeah, I know the one." And Bubba Dean Billingsworth IV puts his phone down on the outside table and stands in front of me with those familiar rugged good looks and cowboy hat.

My knees nearly buckle.

"But, I thought..." I start.

"You must have thought I was a jerk," he says. "I never even gave you a chance. As soon as I realized—well, it was really my sister. She told me I was an idiot, but I tried to call. I called a lot, Syd. You never answered, and I thought that was it. I gave up. Until I got the reminder I set about Claud..." He corrects the pronunciation. "...Claudia's wedding."

"You were so—"

"Syd, I believe when you're meant to be together you always find a way back. I had to give it one last shot," he says, taking off his hat.

I stare at him.

"I was wondering if I might get a second chance," he says, and pauses. "That is if you're not seeing someone, him, already."

I stare at him.

Omigod, don't just stand there, Sydney! Say something!

"Claudia's wedding is today, right?" he asks.

"Tonight," I say quietly, finding my voice but just barely. Thank God. But I'm so stunned. So shocked. The butterflies in my stomach may as well be kamikazes; I might puke. *Dear Lord, do NOT let me puke again!*

"Need a date?" he says with that dazzling smile.

"Yes." Yes!

"Sydney Shag, would you like to crash a wedding with me?" he asks, putting out his hand.

"Why, I would love to," I say in my best Southern accent and take his outstretched hand. Well, the best since the day he stood in front of me at my hotel door at the Driskill Hotel. Tuff pulls me in, gently wraps his muscular arm around my waist, and leans down and kisses me so breathtakingly well that all the customers sitting outside at Morandi whistle and clap. He pulls away and we lock eyes.

"I found my way back," he says, places his cowboy hat on my head, and kisses me again.

Fireworks. A whole slew of fireworks.

I'm so happy I could burst. I swear, I'm in a movie. I remember, just in time, to lift my leg ever so slightly before Tuff pulls away and smiles. (Really, I need to stop watching so many old movies.)

Omigod, my lucky green leather motor jacket is so lucky!!!

☆ ☆ ☆

"Miss Sydney," Tuff laughs and takes Harold carefully from my hand.

"Don't even say it," I interrupt.

"You are the most ridiculous girl I have ever met." He said it.

"I told you not to say it!" I laugh.

"And I told you we'd get Harold a new tank, so let's go." He smiles and holds out his arm. "Oh, I almost forgot," he turns and grabs his phone and a bouquet of flowers sitting on the outside table near us. "For you," he says and hands me a beautiful array of wildflowers. I beam. (Remember, you can buy flowers on like every corner in Manhattan; if you don't bring flowers, you're an idiot.)

A table of gay men claps. (I don't know if it's for the flowers or just Tuff in general.)

I link my arm in his and stare up at him, feeling weightless. It seems I've floated up onto another cloud.

We head to the pet store, both wearing cowboys and with me digging about what he said in all these voicemails. I bubble about the wedding and then see One Eye Joe standing on the steps of what must be his new building across the street, his hair a little more silver than usual, but looking pristine. I wave and he smiles, holding up a new set of keys. I point toward Tuff and he nods his head in acknowledgement. When Tuff smiles at him, One Eye Joe points his Cartier adorned pinky finger at him with a straight face, then he breaks into a smile. A little intimidation never hurt.

"One Eye Joe?" Tuff whispers.

"The one and only," I laugh.

We make our way by the picturesque shops, and as we walk by a high-end vintage clothing shop, I greet the friendly owner standing outside, who I see nearly every day.

"Good afternoon!" I say, overly cheerful because I'm on Tuff's arm.

"Hello, Sydney, and..." The owner holds out his hand and Tuff shakes it with gusto.

"It's Tuff. Nice to meet you."

"Syd, you're finally using that vintage Louis Vuitton Speedy from our shop. That's a rich piece of Louis vintage you're holding there, Tuff. Cost a mint," he says proudly, then whistles. I can feel the blood rush to my head. Tuff lifts the *authentic* Louis Vuitton and turns Harold toward the owner of the *high-end vintage* shop.

I think I feel...

"You mean this old thing with the hole in it?" Tuff says with a chuckle.

...faint.

Lastly...
THE POSTSCRIPT

SO, I fainted. Shocker. (You would too if you cut a hole in a vintage Louis Vuitton worth thousands! Barf.) But Tuff says I fell quite attractively (thank goodness) and he caught me, of course. My prince, my knight in shining armor, but in real life, just my veterinarian-cowboy and not-so-perfect Captain Hook. And Harold got his new tank, a zero-edge aquarium—Tuff went all out.

"Are you ready?" Tuff asks. He takes my hand and we step out of the elevator into a beautiful lofted space surrounded by a sweeping view of the city.

Impressive and awe-inspiring, it's everything Claudia and Pax have been dreaming of since she popped the question. We file into a row of seats with all my favorite people. Gus immediately notices Tuff's cowboy boots and fans herself with the program. Cowboy boots and a suit, is there anything sexier? With flowers cascading around them, Claudia and Pax say "I do" and the celebration begins. They're glowing, happy, and lit. I, on the other hand, have decided to watch my drinks just a little more closely. (NO champagne! And absolutely NO tequila!) Tuff is the perfect date, charming everyone just as he charmed me that fateful night when we crashed our first wedding together. He witnesses us flashing Claudia after chant-singing the Siren Wedding Rite on the rooftop. Though I'll never be sure how much he actually saw, he's learning what a rowdy, late-night group of wildcats we are, and I think he'll fit right in.

We toast to Claudia's marriage, Bette's engagement, Zoey making it to the wedding all the way from Australia (with bright pink hair and a new girlfriend who loves yoga and reality TV as much as she does), Gus booking a national commercial, my new job, and as Gus puts it, "Tuff coming to his senses." Abby announces she'll be going home for the holidays this year and staying because she has to "see about a boy," and we all cheer. It's hard to accept that she's moving away, but it's exciting to know she's doing what her heart tells her.

Then we all dance! We do one of our choreographed numbers from the bar to huge applause, and Tuff and Derek even show us up on some line dances. And then I dance with Tuff like no one else is in the room. That's when he leans in, his lips brushing my cheek softly, and tells me he feels "pretty damn lucky" in the sexiest Southern accent I've ever heard.

I sing Claudia and Pascal's love song with the band (yes, they have a DJ and a band), then as a surprise they give everyone Brazilian carnival headdresses! And with feathers decorating our heads, Claudia has the DJ mix "Girls Just Want to Have Fun." (A Siren favorite!) We go nuts and together we sing the chorus at the top of our lungs, and on the last note I twirl into Tuff's arms. Arms that feel like home.

Then this...
THE POSTSCRIPT
(AFTER THE POSTSCRIPT)

TUFF DUCKS into the taxi as I wave from the doorway. Even though we hate to part, we'll be together again soon. After all, I'll be jumping out of a plane with his sister, and there's a premiere to go to! I run up the stairs to my apartment, passing the banister knob that Tuff fixed. He insisted this time. (The duct tape looked fine!) I close the door to my apartment and take a deep breath. I cannot believe everything that's happened. I grab my phone—yes, I know, I'm already checking to see if he's called. I have a voicemail! He did! Although the number is reading as a "PRIVATE" caller. Oh, Tray?!

Syd, I'm coming to the premiere. I can't stop thinking about you. (Omigod, his voice is throbbing right through the phone!) *I'll see you soon.*

Gavin McKnight.

Shi…

Rules to Live By

1: DON'T JUST STAND THERE

2: BYLBD

3: ALWAYS HAVE YOUR PASSPORT

4: NEVER MIX ALCOHOL (ESPECIALLY TEQUILA)...
YOU WILL DIE!

5: NEVER SLEEP WITH SOMEONE ON THE FIRST DATE

6: NEVER LIE (WHEN YOU CAN TELL SOME OF THE TRUTH)

7: NEVER SHOW PANIC (IT'S A SIGN OF WEAKNESS)

8: ALWAYS WEAR SUNSCREEN

9: NEVER LET MONEY GET THE BEST OF YOU

10: WHEN IN DOUBT, DANCE

"We are all of us stars,
        and we deserve to twinkle."

-MARILYN MONROE

OU'VE FINISHED!

)N'T WORRY,
ORE FROM
IIS AUTHOR IS
)MING SOON!

ALL THE LATEST AND THEN SOME AT:
WWW.CYNDIGRYTE.COM

@CYNDIGRYTE

WATCH FOR THE SIRENS COCKTAIL BOOK

Cheers!

☆ ☆ ☆

THANK YOU FOR READING!

&

THANK YOU

TO ALL THOSE WHO HELPED MAKE THIS HAPPEN!

40416229R00295

Made in the USA
Middletown, DE
26 March 2019